TOUGH CHOICES

A DYLAN O'CONNOR MYSTERY

A Novel

by

Cliff Bonner

Tough Choices is a work of fiction. Names, characters, places, and incidents are either the product of the author's imagination or are used fictitiously. Any resemblance to actual persons, living or dead, events, or locales, is entirely coincidental.

Other books by Cliff Bonner:

RIDE THE WIND   A western novel about an incredible horse
                named Wind, and a young man discovering his
                true strengths. Available on Amazon.

TOUGHER CHOICES: The sequel to TOUCH CHOICES, coming
                   soon to amazon.com

DEDICATION

To Mother Nature, who first inspired the idea for this book.

And to my parents, Cliff and Joyce, who are fantastic thorns, meaning protectors.

PROLOGUE

"BUFFALO SHIT," Merle informed his cousin Wayne, via his cell phone. "I think that's what you are full of. You're too old and you should admit it to yourself instead of lying to me like that."

"No, cousin," Wayne replied into his own cell phone. "This time I'm not full of no kind of shit. This time I really had my shit together. I'm in my car right now, driving home, and when I get there I'll show you the check. Then you'll believe me."

It was true that Wayne was a damn good Native American dancer, but like cousin Merle said, he was getting old. And it seems that the prize money for dancing and singing competitions grew larger every year, causing the number of good dancers to grow with it. Seems they got younger every year too, which gave them an edge.

But it also seems Wayne wasn't ready to go to the happy hunting ground yet, he still loved to dance too much. So he decided to use his years of experience to perfect his technical performance, in hopes it would make up for a lack of stamina or energetic expression. And at the big Pow Wow in Arlee, Montana the strategy paid off and he took first place. Seems that now Wayne liked how much the pow wow prize money was growing.

"You really won? You won the big one? In Arlee?" cousin Merle asked skeptically.

"Yeah, I really won this time," Wayne repeated.

"How soon will you be home?" Merle asked. "I can't wait to see that check." Meaning he would be surprised if Wayne arrived at the expected time and with the entire amount of the check still in his possession.

He never heard Wayne's answer. At the very moment Merle Yellowkidney asked his cousin Wayne Lefthand his question, a woman leapt off the curb into the path of Wayne's car. Wayne heard the loud bang of his car striking the woman at the same moment he slammed on the brakes. He dropped his phone and grabbed the steering wheel when he braked. Cousin Merle also heard the bang of the impact, and then only the ensuing silence of the lost connection.

Wayne's car stopped mere inches from the woman's body, now lying in the road where his car had propelled it. He stared at it with the fixed glare of a person in shock. If he had been going any faster, or reacted any slower, he would have run over her again. The realization of that fact caused him to shudder.

He was still staring at the woman's body when a tap on his window frightened him, making him jump. He looked at the window and saw a Highway Patrolman. Because he had never heard of a law enforcement agent in

Montana responding instantly to a scene, he thought, correctly it would turn out, that maybe he'd been unconscious for a period, probably from shock. He rolled his window down to talk to the Trooper.

"You OK?" the officer asked.

"I'm not hurt," Wayne answered. "How about the woman?" He nodded toward the body in the street, terrified and concerned that she might need immediate attention.

The trooper glanced briefly at the woman lying in the street, then turned back to the driver, realizing he hadn't seen him check the victim's pulse, verifying her demise. Now probably still was not a good time to break the news to him. He changed the subject smoothly, explaining to the driver that he had been driving right behind him and had seen what happened, thus explaining the quick response. He also told the driver that the woman had leapt off the curb and into the path of his car so suddenly that he would never have had a chance to avoid hitting her.

Wayne, recalling his cell phone call to his cousin, reached down to pick the phone up off the floorboards. He panicked at the thought that the Patrolman might have seen him talking on the cell at the time of the accident. There was no law against using a cell phone while driving in Montana, yet, but he was an Indian, and as such he knew from the long history of Native Americans that he could be punished, even if he was innocent of an actual crime. But crime or not he wished he hadn't been on his cell phone when the accident occurred. It only served to increase his already overwhelming guilt.

"Don't worry," the highway patrolman said, as if reading Wayne's thoughts, "I won't put it in the report that you were using a cell phone."

"Thanks," Wayne said, frowning. His fear of punishment was abated by the officer's offer, but he wondered why he wasn't rushing to help the poor woman lying in the street.

The trooper nodded a final time and Wayne watched as he walked to the woman's body, which was still lying, unmoving, in the road. He prayed she was still alive. The Patrolman leaned over the body and gently touched her cheek. Wayne barely heard him whisper one word, "Jesse".

OOO

The Montana Highway Patrolman, Tommy Sanderson, finished writing his report of the accident and clicked on the print button, sending it to the laser-jet printer to be spit out as a hard doc. The report concluded that the woman, by the name of Jessica 'Jesse' O'Connor, was killed by the impact of a moving vehicle after she had leapt off the curb into its path, and that the driver of the vehicle had no chance to stop. Purely an accident, the report stated, though he knew better. Oh yeah, he knew. But there was no way he was putting that in the report.

He still worried about what the driver, Wayne Lefthand, had seen. Tommy had given him enough time to tell him, but the man said nothing. Tommy hoped he'd been distracted enough by his cell phone call that he didn't see what Tommy had seen. He couldn't be sure of the fact, but questioning Wayne about it might have tipped him off that something about the accident was not kosher.

He walked the hard copy of the report across the room to the sergeants desk, where he laid it in the in-basket. He returned to his own desk and picked up his cup of coffee. He sat pensively for a while, remembering how his day had started.

The day had started the same as it usually did, with Tommy gulping down steaming hot coffee, and then swearing because it burned his mouth. After the swearing, he ran out the door and drove to the station.

The cause of his ritual morning rush was a not very delicate obsession. It was, of course, an obsession with a woman. But in his case the obsession was slightly different than those of most men, he had never actually met the woman he was obsessed with. Yet they both knew of each others existence. He knew a lot more about hers than she knew about his. But that was another story, from another city, and in another time. Back then her name wasn't Jesse O'Connor.

"Saw your report," Sergeant Ingram said evenly. Tommy hadn't seen him approach and the sound of his voice pulled him out of his mental meanderings.

"What's that?" Tommy asked him.

"Your report," he repeated. "I read it. Must have been a shock, seeing it happen like that. You OK?"

"Yeah, sure," Tommy murmured.

"You don't look so hot," the Sergeant said. "Why don't you go home. Take the day off." Understandably, he had concluded that Tommy's foul mood was the result of witnessing the death of a fellow human being, an experience that could traumatize any individual.

"I'll be OK. I've seen worse before," Tommy told him, going along with his misdiagnosis.

The Sarge, still firm in his diagnosis of Tommy, was sure that he had seen worse. He was a veteran cop. From Las Vegas. Probably saw a lot of heavy shit in his time. And that was what worried him. He couldn't figure out why seeing a woman hit by a car would effect him so seriously. Admittedly it was not a pretty sight no matter how many gruesome things a person had seen in their life, but Tommy seemed to have been rattled beyond what the Sargent thought would be normal for someone as seasoned as him.

"Just take the day off," the Sarge told him. It was more of an order than a suggestion, and Tommy knew he was done for the day. No sense arguing with the Sarge.

During his drive home Tommy wondered what he would do now that Jesse was dead. She had been his reason for being in Montana. His reason for being a highway patrolman. His reason for living. She'd been his obsession, and now she was gone. The irony didn't escape him. He'd been planning for this moment for a couple of years, and yet, now that the moment had finally arrived, he felt lost.

Maybe he would call in another favor from his friends in high places, he thought. Like he'd done to get himself assigned to the Highway Patrol in Flatrock Montana, where Jesse lived. He might ask them to help him get a cushy assignment somewhere nice, like Florida. Or Hawaii. He could work part time and then spend the rest of his day on the beach working on his tan and drinking cold beer.

Nah, he told himself, its too late for that. He'd already made up his mind what he was going to do. He wished he hadn't. Wished he could just change his mind and forget what he was thinking of doing but he knew he couldn't. What he was about to do would most likely end his life as he knew it. Maybe end it for good. But it didn't matter, he would do it anyway. He would do it because his plan was more important than his immediate survival.

Tommy arrived home and called his girlfriend, Helen, in Las Vegas. She answered on the first ring, like she had been waiting for his call with her hand hovering over the phone. And maybe she was. He told her the news about Jesse.

"I'm coming there," she said after a few seconds of silence.

"Not a good idea," Tommy told her.

"I don't care," she said, "I should be there, with you."

"It's too risky," he warned. "Might raise too many suspicions. People might start asking questions we don't want them to ask."

"I'm coming," she said and hung up.

"Damn it!" Tommy swore.

Helen arrived that evening, and as they sat in his apartment and talked about the days events he admitted to himself that it felt good having her there, in spite of the risks.

CHAPTER ONE

A FEW DAYS LATER, Jesse O'Connor's son, Dylan, was experiencing a dream so terrifying, so vividly real that he might as well have been awake.

In the dream he was driving a car that acted like it was possessed. He could not turn it, or stop it, or speed it up. He tried all of those things but the car did not respond. It went wherever it wanted and at whatever speed it wanted to get there.

In the beginning of the dream the car moved too slowly, which made Dylan self conscious, worried it would attract the attention of a cop. But stepping on the gas pedal didn't cause it to speed up.

He resigned himself to the fact that the car was not in his control, and at that moment he somehow arrived in the passenger seat, without really moving. You can do that in a dream, since dreams, being what they are, do not follow the same rules that we are required to follow when awake.

There was no one in the driver seat, yet somehow, except for going very slowly, the car was doing a fine job of driving itself. He wasn't a passenger for very long, however, before reappearing as the driver, at which point the car quickly accelerated, although he did nothing to cause its acceleration. The car approached dangerous speeds, but pushing on the brake pedal did nothing to slow it down.

Then, without warning, in the dream, his own mother jumped off the curb into the path of the possessed car. It hit her hard, then it kept speeding away. Dylan panicked, opened the door of the car and jumped out, expecting to hit the pavement. However, instead of hitting the pavement, an inexplicable force, found only in dreams, pulled him into the air.

He wanted desperately to go to his mother to see if he could help her, but the inexplicable force pulled him higher and higher into the sky. As he rose he heard the loud bang of the cars impact with his mothers body, over and over again. Bang! Bang! Bang! It was the last thing he heard before all went black.

CHAPTER TWO

BANG! BANG! BANG! Dylan, startled out of his deep sleep, came to life painfully, slowly, not fully aware of himself yet. As he emerged from his nightmare he recoiled at another round of head splitting noises. BANG! BANG! BANG! The horrible noise itself was unmistakable, but its source was not so easy to locate. For a moment he wondered if it was coming from his head, which was most certainly pounding.

He hadn't opened his eyes yet. At least not long enough to see more than the brief burst of light that caused him to shut them again instantly. That brief moment hadn't allowed him to see where he was, but he assumed he was at home, in his bed.

His mouth was dry and rotten tasting, so he opened his eyes again, hoping to see a bottle of water nearby so he could get a drink. This time his eyes stayed open for more than an instant, in spite of the daggers of light that were penetrating them, but he didn't see any water nearby. He didn't see his bedroom either, and the shock of that made him disoriented. He panicked, and was rewarded with an overwhelming rush of adrenaline.

More banging noises invaded the room, and this time he knew that the sound was not inside his head. Sounded more like the front door. Like cops trying to bang their way in, and maybe it was. Since he couldn't remember anything about the previous night, he couldn't rule out the possibility that he did something illegal. Like a hit and run. He thought about that for a second and then thought about getting up and walking to the door, but he wasn't sure he could move. Then he heard the pounding again, just as loud and just as irritating. BANG! BANG! BANG!

"Damn it, stop that," he yelled and regretted it at once. The effort and the loudness of his shout made his head pound. It didn't take much genius to figure out that he was badly hungover. Very badly. And to make things worse he was still sweating and shaking from the terror of the dream he had before he was so thankfully awakened. He recalled very little of the dream, and he thought that, if he was lucky, it would stay that way.

He needed water and tried to formulate a plan for getting some, forgetting about the banging on his door. Under normal conditions a person would not need to make any sort of conscious plans to get a drink of water. They would simply get up, go the sink and get a drink, probably without thinking at all. But so serious were the symptoms of his hangover that he doubted his ability to carry out the simple task.

His head pounded heavily and he felt himself being sucked into an intense confusion, causing him to worry about his sanity. Only the knowledge that he had drunk too much alcohol kept him from slipping over the edge into a whirlpool of madness.

He made a pact with God. If God would help him get out of this mess that he had drunk himself into, and restore him to some semblance of mental stability, he would promise to never take alcohol to excess again.

Thankfully he did not hear an answer from God. Voices in his head would surely cut the fragile thread by which his sanity now hung. But he did hear more banging, and feared for a moment that the horrible dream had returned to claim him. Another series of bangs caused him to look in the direction of his front door and he recalled, vaguely, that he once wondered if it was the cops. He recalled thinking that, but had lost track of time so didn't know how long ago it had happened.

"Come in," Dylan hollered, causing his head to pound even more.

Dylan had been right when he suspected that the cops were pounding on his door. He watched as officer Brent Butler entered his living room. Brent was a local Flatrock, Montana policeman. He was also Dylan's best friend.

When Brent saw Dylan sitting on the couch, still wearing the previous nights clothes, his first reaction was a feeling of pity. No decent human would feel any differently after witnessing someone in his condition. He had obviously slept in his clothes, even his shoes. In fact he was dressed exactly the same as he was when Brent dropped him off at home the night before. When he looked more closely at him he noticed that Dylan's skin was pale and waxy looking and he looked toward Brent with a bloodshot steady gaze that made Brent's heart skip a couple of beats, worried that he was dead. He was relieved when Dylan spoke.

"Why the hell are you pounding on my door like a cop?" Dylan asked in a much lower voice. In spite of the low volume of his voice it was still painful to do so much speaking all at once and he groaned when he finished.

Brent ignored the obvious answer that he was a cop and said," I thought you were dead. I've been knocking on your door for ten minutes. Two more seconds and I would have been breaking the door down. You would have really loved the sound of that." He said it sarcastically, but he had a worried look on his face that betrayed the sympathy he actually felt.

Brent was not in uniform, a fact that Dylan was in no shape to notice. He was dressed casually in jeans, light hiking boots, flannel shirt and fleece jacket, the standard uniform of an ordinary Montana male rather than an ordinary cop. And no matter which uniform he wore, he always had a magnetic effect on women. A fact that always annoyed Dylan.

But to be honest, being a cop probably did increase the magnetism, indirectly when he wasn't in uniform, and directly when he was. The job

11

required him to be in top physical condition, so he engaged in a regular workout program which kept the fat off and kept him in shape for his duties as a cop. He wasn't short, but calling him tall might be pushing it. He was just under six feet. He had dark, jet black hair which he kept cut short. Maybe those things helped too. You'd have to ask a woman.

"Well, that would have been really stupid since it was open and you just now walked right in," Dylan said. "And now that I mentioned it, why didn't you just walk in instead of doing all that pounding?"

"I am a cop don't forget," Brent explained.

Yeah, like that makes a whole lot of sense, Dylan thought. Maybe it referred to the fact that he had to follow one of the constitutional amendments or something.

"What exactly happened last night?" Dylan asked, changing the subject in order to avoid a constitutional debate with Brent.

"Wow," Brent said. "Musta been worse than I thought. What's the last thing you remember?"

Dylan thought about it for a while, and then said, "I don't recall".

"What do you mean you don't recall? That makes no sense. You sure you're alright?"

"Of course I am not alright. Do I look alright? Do I sound alright? I feel like shit and I can't even remember what it is I don't remember." That was more talking than he should have done all at once, making his head hurt worse than before, which he did not think was possible.

Brent didn't respond, instead he stared at Dylan intently with a worried scowl on his face.

"I think you need a hair of the dog," he said. He went to the fridge to get a beer but it was empty. Not just empty of beer but empty empty. Brent could only imagine how Dylan had been eating.

He came back into the living room and said, "You're out of beer, I'll be right back."

OOOO

Brent had been so preoccupied with getting into Dylan's house that he didn't notice the car parked across the street, nor the black haired woman inside it. She had been parked there, watching Dylan's house for some time. She'd been watching when police officer Brent Butler arrived, and had felt a moment of panic, afraid he might spot her. She almost drove away but worried that the noise of the car would attract his attention.

Panic was not an unusual condition for her recently. Nor was the feeling of dread and constant fear she'd been living with since learning of Jesse's death. They said Jesse was hit by a car, but she knew better. She knew Jesse would never be as incapable as that, allowing herself to be hit by a car. Accidents happen, sure. But not like that. Not to Jesse anyway. And what if Dylan was next? Or her? Or her own daughter?

Her anxiety rose another notch when Dylan didn't respond to Brent's furious knocking on his door. When she saw Brent enter the house she relaxed slightly, but only until she realized that Brent had let himself in. She hadn't seen Dylan.

A few minutes later she saw the door open again and Brent walked out. Again, no sight of Dylan. And again, she felt the slight panic at the prospect of being discovered, but Brent walked intently to his car and drove off without looking at her. She had been lucky, again.

After Jesse's death she knew that her own existence could be in peril. Being somewhat fond of her existence, such as it was, she concluded that she better do whatever it took to maintain it. So, not knowing who to trust, she did the only logical thing. She gave up trusting a single soul. And until she knew exactly what had happened to Jesse she intended for it to stay that way.

CHAPTER THREE

AFTER BRENT LEFT, Dylan looked down at himself and saw that he was still wearing the same clothes he had been wearing the night before, even the shoes. And the fact that he was on the couch in the living room meant that he had never made it to the bedroom. It had been a long time since he had drunk this much.

"Mother taught me better than this," he said out loud but quietly.

"Shit," he whispered as he recalled the funeral. More accurately he recalled that there had been a funeral, even if he could not recall the details of it. Tears began streaming out of his eyes, as if they possessed a will of their own and were not in any way connected to him. Impossibly, his head hurt even worse, and his mouth felt like he'd just eaten a gallon of chokecherries.

He sat like a pathetic wooden statue, trying to muster up the courage to go get a drink of water. But his mind wandered, the lack of concentration caused by an overdose of distilled ingredients. Instead of making a plan for procuring a drink of water he found himself wishing he could talk to his mom. And see her, and touch her.

"Ahhh shit, mom. I miss you so much," he whispered, and this time the tears were all his. He hadn't been crying long when he realized that he wouldn't be able to prevent the bile from coming back up from his gut.

Apparently he was wrong when he thought that he was unable to move, because, by some miracle, he made it to the toilet before he puked. But at a cost. The room was in a spin not previously achieved by any amusement park ride in history. If there was any silver lining to that cloud it was that he quit crying.

When he finished throwing up he stuck his head under the faucet, splashed water on his face and finally got the drink of water he needed so badly. He looked up from the faucet he saw himself in the bathroom mirror. It was not a pretty sight. His face was so pale that the usual splash of freckles was barely visible on his cheeks. In fact it was so pale that he questioned his vital existence. He closed his eyes, preferring the darkness to the truth, but still found himself wondering if he was dead.

If he was dead, how did it come about? Did he die from alcohol poisoning last night at his mom's wake? He didn't think so, he'd survived greater amounts of alcohol before. Maybe he had died and gone to hell for his sins, and was being made to suffer. He was unaware of any sins he had committed that warranted such extreme punishment, but then he was so hungover that he was unaware of just about anything. Thus, he really could have committed a righteously punishable sin. Aware of his sins or not he was suffering, so he must have done something sinful. Right?

He opened his eyes, curious to see what a ghost in hell looked like. Lifeless black rimmed, bloodshot eyes, clammy skin and dried up crusty drool on his chin. His clothes were wrinkled, shirt half unbuttoned and pants unzipped. Is this what Brent saw when he came into the house? Brent was here?

Wishing to escape the mirror and its attendant horrors, he crawled back onto the couch, without doing a single thing to improve his appearance. He felt a sudden shiver of cold and instinctively thrust his hands into his pockets in an attempt to get warm. His right hand encountered something hard and round in his pocket, the ring that his mother had given, reminding him once again of her recent death.

It was a strange irony that he was unable to recall the events of the previous night, yet the memories attached to that ring were still as clear as anything in his mind had ever been. He fell asleep in the comfort of the mental picture of the day he had been given it.

When he opened his eyes again, Brent was standing there looking at him.

"Don't look at me like that," Dylan said accusingly.

"How else am I supposed to look at you? I thought you were a corpse. And I've seen a few. A couple of them looked better than you do now, by the way."

Dylan wished Brent would not have likened him to a corpse when he had such a fragile grip on being the opposite.

"I bet they felt better too," he replied.

"That bad eh?" Brent chuckled.

"Yeah, now shut up and give me a beer before I become one of your good looking corpses."

CHAPTER FOUR

BRENT OPENED A COUPLE of beers and handed one to Dylan, who looked at it as if it was a lethal snake. He hesitated to drink it but finally took a tentative sip, after which he grimaced.

Brent, on the other hand, had not drunk an overdose of fermented substances the previous night, and so had no reservations whatsoever about drinking his beer. He sat down and took a long draw from the bottle. Neither of them spoke, seemingly more interested in their own thoughts at the moment.

Appropriately, following a funeral, Brent was thinking about Dylan's mom, Jesse, which unavoidably led to thinking about Dylan as well. He and Dylan had been friends for most of their lives, starting when they were six years old.

They grew closer than most friends because of a sort of eerie psychic connection that grew between them. They sometimes didn't have to speak, but could look at each other and know what they wanted to say, or what the other was feeling.

When he was young Brent had noticed a similar connection with Dylan's mom, Jesse.

And speaking of Jesse, Brent realized that he had always been curious about her. There was something mysterious about her. Something he felt like he should have known about her but could never quite put his finger on it.

One time, he recalled, he was subconsciously staring at her while trying to figure out just what it was about her that made him so darned curious. She had turned suddenly and looked right into his eyes and he realized he had been caught staring at her; a thing which his mother had always told him was not polite. For a split second, while looking into her eyes, he thought he heard her say something to him. For the rest of that day he tried to remember if she had actually spoken to him out loud or not. He never did figure out for sure whether she did or not, but what he heard her 'say' that day stuck with him his whole life.

She had said, "Try all you want to Brent, you'll never get inside my head." Those words, and the uncertainty of whether they were spoken out loud or not, caused such a giant mystery for him that he had never stopped wondering about it.

Another thing about Jesse, she had immense patience. But at the same time her will could be unbending and irresistible. Brent recalled feeling comfortable around her. Now, he wondered if it wasn't her comforting presence that drew him into Dylan's world as much as it was Dylan himself.

He allowed that he was really going to miss her. No macho denial- I'm a man I don't cry - bullshit this time. It was a plain fact of life that he missed her a lot. But he would never forget her. She was the kind of woman that it was just not possible to forget. He couldn't point out a single trait about her that caused her to lodge forever in one's memory, because it isn't just one thing, or two, or three, it's everything about her in one composite result.

Her physical appearance was an important part of that composite. She had an elegant face that was fine lined and smooth skinned. Her eyes were hazel and hair dark brown and long. She was thin without being skinny. She stood at five feet seven inches and had perfect posture. When she moved it was always with determination but appeared to be utterly without thought or effort. No motion was ever without purpose. Her voice was always clear and easy to hear and understand without being loud or assertive. When she spoke to you it was like you were the entire center of her attention and, for that moment, you were the only important thing in the world. Her dress was usually casual and simple, but well thought out and always clean and neat.

"Hey, Brent," Dylan said softly, breaking the silent reverie. "Thanks for the beer," he said, though he had barely touched it, "and thanks for being here."

"No problem, man."

"How come you're not at work?" Dylan asked.

"I took sick leave," Brent answered easily.

"You sick?"

"No, you are."

"That's putting it mildly," he responded. "You took sick leave because I'm sick?"

"Yep." Brent wasn't surprised that Dylan had not figured that out already. After all, Dylan had not yet fully returned from his little excursion outside reality.

"Thanks," Dylan said. Then he asked, "So what exactly did happen last night?"

Brent raised his eyebrows and had the distant look that people get when they don't really know how to answer a question. If he wanted to be brutally honest he could have said "You got shitfaced and made a total ass of yourself." But he didn't say that because society allows for a certain amount of insanity during funerals and wakes. And besides, Dylan probably already knew he was thinking it.

"Nothing really unusual at first," he said. "At least not unusual for a funeral." He hesitated, recalling the events of the previous night.

He recalled that there were few people present for either the funeral or the wake, something he wondered about. Brent and Dylan were there of course, and Dylan's girlfriend Joan. Charlie, the police chief, was there, along with a couple of local cops who knew Dylan and Jesse. Besides the preacher, that was

17

the entire crowd of attendees. It seemed to him that a lady as grand as Jesse had been might have had more people that cared for her enough to show up at her funeral. Or maybe if they were the partying kinds of friends they would at least show up for the wake to drink their fill of booze.

The funeral service had been typical. It was led by a preacher who read from the bible while the few onlookers stood silently. Joan cried and wiped tears from her eyes and Dylan just stood there with a blank stare into the unknown. When the preacher finished reading from the bible he asked the few persons in attendance if anyone would like to say words over the departed. No one volunteered and the service ended.

Unobserved, there was one other person present. It was a dark haired woman, taking shelter some distance away, hiding behind some trees. She wept shamelessly, wracked by grief.

After the funeral the group went to Dylan's mom's house for the wake. As it turned out Dylan was the person who showed up at the wake to drink his fill of booze. He started drinking and didn't let up until Brent found him a couple of hours later, passed out on the couch. Brent told Joan that he would take him home. Joan drove herself home, sad and confused.

During the drive home Dylan muttered, "It's not right. It's not right," over and over again.

"What's not right?" Brent had asked him,

"The accident," Dylan slurred. "It's just not right." He repeated it a dozen times before passing out again.

There was something about the way he said it, and the way he repeated it that made Brent think that it had some unique meaning to Dylan. If he'd been capable of giving him a comprehensible answer at the time, Brent might have asked about it.

He finished his answer to Dylan, "But then you started drinking at the house and never stopped until you passed out, and then I brought you home. That's it."

Dylan was quiet for a moment and then said, "I embarrassed myself didn't I?"

"Yep," Brent confirmed.

"What did I do?"

"I think it was just the drinking. People were worried about you," Brent said.

"Joan?" Dylan asked, remembering her at the funeral now, and feeling a mere iota more mentally stable because of it.

"Yes."

"You?"

"Yes. Sort of. It was the drinking binge. It was like you were on some sort of mission or something. It wasn't like you."

"Yeah, and it's not really like me to not have a mom any more either," he snapped, instantly regretting it.

"Sorry."

"Forget it," Dylan said, mad at himself for reacting the way he did. Brent was only trying to help him, he didn't deserve to be treated rudely.

Both men, regretful of what they had said, fell into a rueful silence.

CHAPTER FIVE

"DON'T HATE THE THORNS," Jesse said. OK, maybe she didn't say it, she was dead after all. But Dylan heard it nonetheless, clear as day. After the previous night's overdose of alcohol, and the subsequent nightmare, it was almost miraculous that the sound of his dead mother's voice didn't send Dylan right over the edge of sanity into the abyss of madness. She often spoke in code, some deeper meaning underlying her words. This was likely just another instance of that.

Whatever the deeper meaning of 'don't hate the thorns' may be, he knew he was in no condition to go wandering through the recesses of his mind in search of it. The little reminder of his mental condition brought on more unwelcome doubts about his sanity and he felt his pulse quicken.

Meanwhile, Brent, whose untroubled mind had been engaged in pondering ways to help his friend Dylan, also heard the unexpected voice of Dylan's mom in his head. It said, "Don't even try for the hard ones."

The unexpected appearance of voices inside his head – loud and clear voices, not just thoughts – made Brent wonder if he had drunk too much. But he had only had one and a half beers. Not enough alcohol to cause the onset of hallucinations. Maybe he was reading Dylan's mind again, who had definitely drunk enough the night before to cause him to hear voices.

In case his hallucinations were caused by a lack of alcohol rather than an abundance of it, Brent took a long drink of his beer. Then he considered who's voice it was and knew at once that the words he heard Jesse say would have a special meaning. Her words always did. And he knew that he would figure out their meaning eventually. Maybe.

Neither Dylan nor Brent mentioned to each other that they had heard Jesse's voice. Instead, they continued their mutual silence, and eventually fell asleep.

Two hours later they awoke at the same moment. Both had heard Jesse's voice again while they were asleep. Dylan heard the rustle of clothes against couch leather and looked over to see Brent looking at him.

"You heard something didn't you?" Dylan said.

"Yeah," Brent replied, "you too?"

Dylan sat silent for a minute, deciding whether he should say anything or not. Or maybe how to say it.

"I heard my mom's voice," he finally blurted. "What about you?" Brent's brow furrowed.

"I heard your mom's voice," he said. The first time he heard her voice he could almost believe it was some kind of fluke, but now that he had heard it again, and so soon after the first time, it wasn't so easy to dismiss.

"What did she say?" Dylan asked.

"She said, 'Don't even try for the hard ones'," Brent told him. "What did she say to you?"

Instead of answering, Dylan asked, "Do you think she was really talking to us? Was it really her talking? You know, like from the beyond or something?" The idea of it began another tide of mental overwhelm and he felt cold sweat forming on his skin.

Brent said, "I don't know what to think, but I know one thing. I don't see her standing here in the room right now, talking to us. Do you?"

"No," Dylan said, slightly relieved.

"That's good to hear. Now tell me what you heard."

"I heard her say, 'Don't hate the thorns'."

"Does that mean anything to you?" Brent asked.

Again, there was a faint summons from a small, remote piece of Dylan's brain, which promised the possibility of an answer to Brent's question. And again Dylan was not prepared to go there.

"I'm not sure," he said, not really lying, yet not really telling the whole truth either. "It seems to ring a bell, like she might have said that to me once. You know how she was. How 'bout you? Did what you heard mean anything to you?"

"Nothing at all. But I have that same feeling that you do, that it probably has a special meaning."

Dylan nodded, concluding that he was in no condition for shit this deep.

"How much sick leave did you take?" Dylan asked, changing subjects.

"Two days. How 'bout you?" Brent asked, referring to how much grieving time Dylan's employers had given him.

"They told me to take whatever I needed but I have a feeling there is a limit."

"There's always a limit. How long do you think you'll actually get?"

"A few days maybe, but it probably won't matter. I'm thinking about not going back at all." Brent raised his eyebrows at this admission

"Really?"

"Yeah, really. It seems like life is throwing me a curve right now and maybe it's telling me something. Maybe it's telling me to follow the curve and go in another direction."

Dylan, who never never made it all the way through college, was not the sort of person who was interested in what some would call a real job. His present job was no exception, it was a dead end kind of job. Something to pay the rent and the bills. Brent wondered what sort of new direction life might send him this time, and what Joan would think of the change.

Dylan's occupation was a sore spot between him and Joan. She wanted him to move up in the world and make something of himself. Brent had seen her nag Dylan about doing something that would make him more money. It was a difference between them that made Brent wonder what kept them together. He guessed it was the sex. She was a great looking girl with a sexy body. And Dylan was a guy.

"What does Joan think?" Brent asked.

"About what?"

"How much time off did you tell her you had?"

"She thinks I have three days off."

"You didn't tell her your plans?"

"I haven't had a chance to make any solid plans yet, but no, I didn't tell her what I just told you. You know how she is. She would just have a shit fit and I'm not ready to deal with that."

"Yeah, I know how she is," Brent said sympathetically. Then he asked, "You think it will last?"

"What, the hangover?"

"No."

"The job?"

"No, with Joan," he said.

"Who the hell knows? Sometimes I doubt it." He made the response without thinking, but as soon as he had spoken it he felt a twinge in his heart. It was a twinge that bespoke a painful loneliness he was apt to feel if Joan were to leave him.

Brent had always doubted their relationship would last too. Until now. His connection with Dylan made him aware of the pain that Dylan had felt at the prospect of losing her, and it gave him pause. Perhaps he had been wrong about Joan.

"What do you want to do for the next two days?" Dylan asked.

"I don't know," Brent answered, happy for the change of subject. "What about Joan? What's she going to do?" he asked without thinking and cursed himself for it. So much for the change of subject.

"Work, I imagine," Dylan answered. "She hasn't mentioned any plans to me." Or had she, he wondered. In his present condition would he even remember it if she had? He started back down that slippery slope of mental instability and began to imagine what other memories might be buried in his blackout? Like running her over with his car. Maybe his killing spree included more that just his mom. Maybe he ran down all the women he knew.

Brent noticed the change overcome Dylan, a look of desperation, and wished he knew how to help him. "Maybe she will take off work and come see you," he suggested.

"Yeah, right," Dylan said with a shaky voice.

"So what do we do now?" Brent asked. Call the loony bin and ask them to send over a straight jacket, he wondered.

"Let's order pizza, I'm starving," Dylan answered. The idea of pizza had the magical effect of helping him climb back up the slippery slope into relative sanity.

OK, skip the straight jacket, Brent thought, cravings for pizza is a sure sign of a sane person.

CHAPTER SIX

BRENT PAID THE PIZZA delivery man and dropped the boxes on the coffee table. He and Dylan grabbed up slices, not bothering with plates or napkins. They ate out of their hands and when their hands got dirty they wiped them on their pants. Just like the good old days.

When they were stuffed with pizza and beer they sat back on the couch and groaned in that satisfied way people groan after overeating food they really liked. Then they fell asleep.

OOOO

The car was out of control, its accelerator pushed all the way to the floor and the engine was whining from the high RPM as it gained frightening speed. Dylan panicked and let his foot off the gas but the car didn't slow down. He stomped his foot on the brake but the car kept on speeding down the road like a runaway train. If he didn't stop the car soon he was bound to have a horrific accident of some sort. Maybe. Or maybe not. Maybe the car knew what it was doing and would avoid an accident. Or better yet, it may decide to slow down, or even stop.

Unwilling to pin his hopes on mere luck he considered bailing out of the car. If he jumped out of the car now, before the car gained even more speed, he would probably suffer injuries. Or he could stay in the car and hope that it would gain control of itself. It was a tough choice to make and for a moment he was incapable of deciding.

He looked at the door handle, wishing he had the nerve to open it, when BAM!, a thunderous, metal crunching bang came from the front of the car. The sound startled Dylan and he flinched, then jerked his head up to look out the windshield, seeing nothing.

Then he heard the sounds again, the banging, over and over. BAM! BAM! BAM! The noise drove him mad but no amount of will power made it stop. He shut his eyes, hoping that if he couldn't see it, it would go away.

When he opened his eyes again he was out of the car, which had mysteriously stopped, and was standing on the asphalt. The banging in his head had stopped as well, and he was relieved by both facts. He had no idea how he got out of the car, or when, he was just glad he did. But where was he? He looked around to see if he could get his bearings and found himself in the middle of the road. He decided that he better get out of the road or risk being run over. He saw a sidewalk several feet away, and when he took a step toward it he tripped on something.

He looked down to see what it was he tripped on. It was his mother. She was lying on the pavement, unmoving. Was something wrong with her? BAM! BAM! He heard the noise again. PLEASE STOP. He looked at his mom on the ground again. A Montana Trooper was feeling her neck for a pulse. Dylan wondered why he would do that.

He leaned down and reached out to touch his mom. When he touched her she reached out with her hand and took hold of his arm. She used it to leverage herself up off the ground, and then stood facing Dylan.

"Answer the door," She told him.

OOOO

Dylan was awakened for the second time in the same day by a pounding on the door. This time he was not as hung over, but still shaken by the dream he had just experienced.

BAM, BAM, BAM! the door said.

He heard someone on the other side of the door shout, "Open the door."

"It's open!" he hollered. He wished people would quit pounding on his door, and just let themselves in.

The pounding on the door had woken Brent as well, and they were both staring at it when Joan walked in. Dylan couldn't help thinking that she, of all people, should know that he never locked his door, so why all the knocking?

She took a couple of steps into the house and stopped. She made a quick survey of the room and the two men in it, coming up with what seemed like a logical conclusion. She didn't comment on what she saw, but she did stare at the two men with patent fury. They stared back at her.

Joan's beauty was usually sufficient to cause any normal man to stare at her, but in this instance her anger put a bit of a damper on the two mens' desire to leer at her finer traits. Instead, they could only wonder what had gotten her so riled up.

They stopped wondering when she said, "You assholes. You're drunk. I can't believe it. What are you sons of bitches thinking? Didn't you learn your lesson last night, Dylan? And a lot of help you are, Brent. What a couple of losers. Screw you! Just screw you." She turned, red face and all, and stormed out the door, slamming it shut behind her.

25

Brent and Dylan, somewhat stunned, stared at the door for a few seconds after it slammed shut. Then they looked at each other for a couple of more seconds before looking around the room, seeing what Joan had seen.

The table was covered with half empty pizza boxes and empty beer bottles. The two them, sloven, red-eyed and half asleep. They made the connection. It didn't look good. But they didn't have the chance to tell her that it wasn't how it looked. Or maybe it was. Either way there wasn't much that could be said now. Joan would have to be dealt with later, and it was entirely up to Dylan to deal with her.

Outside Dylan's house, the dark haired lady watching from her car lost her breath at the appearance of Joan at Dylan's door. She drove away quickly right after Joan entered the house, glad she hadn't been seen. She never had the chance to see Joan's hasty retreat from the house. If she had, she would have wondered what could have made Joan so furious in such a short amount of time.

Back inside Dylan's house, he asked Brent, "What do you want to do now?"

Brent shrugged. "Up to you," he said. "What do you feel like doing?" He figured it should be Dylan's choice, since he was the one who just buried his mom.

"Let's go out," Dylan quickly replied. He needed to get out, get some fresh air and take a little more time to recover

"Good idea. Where to?" Brent said.

"Where else?" Dylan said knowingly.

"The Outlaw," Brent concurred.

"You got it," Dylan confirmed.

The Outlaw was more than just a bar, it was *their* bar. It had been their go-to place for all occasions since they were almost old enough to drink. It had nursed them through the bad times, like heartbreaks and lost football games, and it had celebrated all of their triumphs. It was probably the most therapeutic place for them to be at the moment, except for one minor drawback.

"You plan on another hangover tomorrow?" Brent asked him.

"Good point," Dylan said. He was sure that another night of drinking would push him into taking that last step across the border of Sanity City into Loonyville.

"How 'bout we eat dinner there? Maybe have a couple of beers and come home early."

"Ok, except I'm driving, so I'll only have one beer," Brent responded. "And we leave when I say leave."

"Fine with me," Dylan said.

"You better shower and put on some clothes that aren't covered in puke and pizza," Brent reminded Dylan, who somehow overlooked his appearances in favor of rushing off to his favorite watering hole.

"Good idea," Dylan said, rushing into the bathroom.

Brent had brought an overnight bag with him, containing clean clothes and his toilet bag, just in case, and when they were both ready to go they got into Brent's jeep and started down the road.

They had barely driven a single block when Dylan said, "It would have been a lot more fun if you brought the cruiser." Meaning Brent's police car.

"Why?," Brent asked him. "So we can abuse official police property by unnecessarily turning on the lights and siren and scaring the shit out of unsuspecting innocent people, and running red lights on a code three, and generally breaking all kinds of other laws?"

"Exactly."

Brent thought about that for a minute, then said, "Ok, let's go get it."

"You serious?" Dylan asked, unbelieving.

"As a heart attack." Brent knew that it would lift Dylan's spirit, making it worth the risk.

"Yeeeeehaaaaah!" Dylan whooped, vindicating Brent's intentions.

CHAPTER SEVEN

BRENT WORKED FOR the police department of the, by Montana standards, medium sized town of Flatrock. The town name was derived from the obvious landmark of a flat rock. However, there were so many flat rocks in the area that an ongoing debate had been raging, almost since the town's establishment, about precisely which flat rock took the honors. To date, the list had been reduced to three agreed upon, bona fide candidates. Brent thought that they should just rename the town Flat Rocks and end the whole argument forever.

In spite of the feud over its mascot, Brent liked the town and he liked being on the force. The town was big enough to generate enough crime to keep him interested and busy, and had enough recreational activities to keep him occupied when off duty. Like all Montana towns it was surrounded by an infinity of excellent outdoor activities year round. Oh, and it was large enough to have plenty of women.

During the five mile drive to the police station Brent employed a great deal of his imagination and creativity coming up with a way to borrow [steal] the police cruiser without, firstly, getting caught, and second, in case plan A failed, not getting fired. The result of his fired up imagination was to park his jeep a few blocks from the station in a tiny strip mall parking lot, which was hard to see from the main road.

His plan B, in case he got caught, was to straight up lie. He would say his personal vehicle broke down and he needed some wheels, and then hope like hell that no one found his jeep strip mall.

They walked the couple of blocks from the strip mall to the station, where they picked up a set of keys and drove off in the police black and white. They were barely out of sight of the station when Dylan started in on Brent.

"Let's pull someone over and make them bribe us to get off," he said. "Then we'll have some money for The Outlaw." He said it like he was serious but Brent knew he wasn't.

"Hell no," he said.

"What good is it to take the patrol car if we can't have some fun with it?" Dylan demanded. "Can we at least turn on the flashing lights and watch people freak out a little bit? Maybe blow through a red light?"

There were only six real, lighted traffic signals in the town of Flatrock and Brent considered which ones were the safest to run on a code three – illegally of course – for the sake of the needy [Dylan]. He settled on the traffic signal with the least traffic; Spring St. and Reserve.

"I guess that's why we got the car," he agreed. "Ok let's do it." He flipped some switches and the flashing lights came on. People in both directions started pulling over to the shoulder of the road.

Dylan looked into the car windows as they passed, noticing the people's faces. Some of them looked bored, some looked nervous. He looked ahead at a lighted intersection noticing that the light was red. Brent wasn't slowing down enough to stop and Dylan realized he was going to blow through it.

Brent ensured that any cars approaching the intersection had seen his flashing lights, and had stopped to allow him passage, then stepped on the gas and sped on through.

"Yeah, yeah. Go, go!" Dylan whooped.

Seconds after clearing the intersection the police radio squawked.

"Brent, you in the patrol car?" Brent recognized the Chief's voice. He shut off the siren and lights and slowed down.

"Shit!" he said. "Don't make a sound," he ordered Dylan, certain that the Chief or another cop had just witnessed his joy ride.

"Yeah, I'm here," he said into the hand mic, prepared to launch plan B.

"Where are you?" the Chief asked him.

He put plan B on hold. "I'm at Reserve and Spring Creek."

"You need to come to the station right away. It's urgent. It's about Jesse."

The Chief knew about Brent and Dylan's relationship so Brent figured, correctly it would turn out, that it had something to do with his request.

Whatever this was about, Brent knew it couldn't be good. No kind of logic would lead to any other conclusion. Brent also knew that if Dylan was involved he had to tell the Chief that he was in the car with him, even if it got him in more trouble. He put the handset to his mouth and said, "Uh, sir, Dylan's with me in the patrol car."

There was a moment of silence on the radio. Brent figured that the Chief must be thinking that one over. He was right about that assumption, and if he had been in the station at that moment he would have heard the Chief swear.

"OK, take him home and drop him off," the radio squawked again. "Then get in here. I'll be waiting. Over and out," he finished, with more than a little irritation in his voice.

"Shit," Brent said again. Things were going downhill in a hurry, and just when he thought everything was getting better. Thanks a lot Murphy.

Brent didn't even want to look at Dylan, much less talk to him. But he knew he would have to do both eventually so he reckoned it might as well be now. When he glanced over, Dylan was already staring at him with a look of disbelief, the anxiety showing on his face.

"What the hell is going on, Brent?" he asked. He was beginning to sweat a little, in spite of the cool temperature in the car, and an inner confusion was approaching, all too familiar in the past couple of days.

"No idea," Brent said. And it was true. Well, almost true. Actually it wasn't true at all. Brent had all kinds of ideas. But none of them were good, and none of them were ones that he relished revealing to Dylan.

What Brent did say was, "I got orders and I'm following them. I'll be real lucky if I don't get busted for this. I'm taking you home. Sorry."

The mood in the car during the trip back to Dylan's house was quiet and anxious. When they finally arrived and Dylan got out of the car, Brent said, "I'm coming back as soon as I'm done at the station. Save me some pizza."

Dylan stood in the street without moving and stared after Brent's car as it disappeared. He felt a familiar feeling coming over him, the mental confusion and loss of control worming their way back into his head. An intense anxiety that he could feel in his stomach threatened to engulf him.

Instinctively, and out of desperation, he knew that he had to direct his attention outward and stop the unbridled introversion. He began looking at things – objects – around him. He intentionally focused his attention on items around him in an attempt to take attention away from the runaway flood of thoughts inside his skull. It was a drastic attempt to save his sanity, and it seemed to be working so he kept doing it.

Soon the stomach sensations subsided, and soon after that he thought he might actually survive physically intact. He wasn't sure about mentally. As if waking from a dream he realized that he was still standing in the middle of the street, and went inside.

The dark haired woman witnessed the entire event from inside her car. The lost and desperate look on Dylan's face saddened the woman so much that she wept. She wanted to go to him, to hug him, to comfort him. Perhaps to share his sorrow. But she was too scared. When Dylan went inside she drove off, still weeping, headed for Joan's house.

Dylan flopped down on the same couch he had occupied most the day. He was damned tired and knew he needed rest badly, but he was afraid to sleep. Afraid of another bad dream.

Welcoming its distraction, he turned on the TV and watched an old western movie.

CHAPTER EIGHT

JOAN DROVE STRAIGHT HOME after stomping out of Dylan's house. She remained furious during the drive, attempting to create in her mind the necessary justifications for why she'd reacted the way she had. She predicted that the reasons for her behavior would be useful, in the near future, when she would have to explain herself. The trouble was, she was having difficulty coming up with the precise reasons, which was puzzling to her.

She recalled reading an article in a woman's magazine that explained a persons inability to think logically when they were feeling intense emotion. Especially anger, the article had emphasized. It advised not making any important decisions while in an upset mood. She followed the advice and took a deep breath, trying to calm herself.

By the time she got home she felt a little better. After a meal and a glass of wine she was close to normal again, but still hadn't come up with a precise motive for getting angry with Dylan and Brent. She began to consider the possibility that she had done so irrationally. If so, she worried that it may have caused her to lose Dylan, and felt a dreadful emptiness at the idea.

She had never understood the forces of nature that drew her to Dylan, but nevertheless they cast their spell on her the first moment she met him. She felt safe with him. She was comfortable around him. She felt loved by him, unconditionally. She needed him. Her need was as inexplicable as it was powerful and she found it impossible to deny.

While Joan contemplated her need for Dylan, a dark haired woman was parked outside her house, in a rented car, struggling with her own undeniable need. Joan was unaware of her presence. Unaware of her disheveled appearance and eyes reddened from lack of sleep and from crying. She never heard the moaning sigh of the dark haired woman as she reclined her seat and attempted to sleep. A sleep which, when it finally came, transported her from an unbearable real world to a world of unbearable dreams.

CHAPTER NINE

BRENT WAS NERVOUS, worried about what kind of trouble he might be in for taking his little joy ride in the cruiser. As much as that worried him, he dreaded what the Chief had to say about Dylan's mom.

The Chief was so anxious to see Brent that he was waiting for him at the reception counter, just inside the stations main entrance. "Look, about the patrol car", Brent started. Before he could finish, the Chief interrupted him.

"I don't care about that," he said. "But next time clear it through me, ok? That way your ass is a bit more covered if anything happens. Let's go to my office." He turned and started walking down the hall to his office. Brent followed him in and sat in the chair across the desk from the Chief, who was staring across the desk at him silently, as if considering how to say something that may be difficult to say.

The Chief was not a Flatrock native like Brent and Dylan were. He wasn't even a Montana native. A fact that none of the natives seemed to ever hold against him, like they sometimes do with newcomers. In the Chief's case they perceived something in him that told them he was different, and they took to him quickly.

His history probably sheds some light on what they saw in him. Chief Charlie Armstrong was a military veteran - retired. He had served twenty years in the Marine Corps and retired with the rank of Master Sergeant. He had no blemishes on his military record and had even acquired a few honors. A large part of his time in the military was spent in Military law enforcement.

In civilian life he operated, on all levels, with the ordered and structured habits resulting from his military career. He was even-minded in almost all situations and could evaluate the appropriate responses required with a cool detachment. And yet he was not in any way without emotion. There was passion in everything he did. And what was most endearing about him, to Montana natives, was that he wore all of his attributes on his sleeve. What you saw is what you got, and what you saw was honest, sincere and courageous.

Courage figured prominently in what a Montanan looked for in a person. To them, courage was defined as being able to face adversity, and persist through it until it was overcome, and that translated into a person that they could count on to help them when needed. This type of mind-set came from Montana's general history and its environmental challenges, requiring such a virtue in order to survive. As a Marine, it was second nature to Charlie to watch his comrade's back.

It was exactly this natural instinct in Charlie that compelled him to commit an act that would eventually land him the Chiefs job. A job he had not been searching for.

It was in his first six months of retirement – which were also his first six months of residency in Montana – that he had risked his own life to save the life of his neighbors' wife.

Charlie's closest neighbor was almost a half mile away. He had never met them but he knew their last name was Severud. He saw it on their mailbox every time he drove past it. He could see their house from his kitchen window. And so it was that one morning, just like most mornings, while drinking his coffee he noticed his neighbors' wife get in her car and drive away.

From experience he knew that she would return at four p.m.. Since he had never met or talked to his new neighbors, he had to assume that she must have a job that kept her on such a schedule.

Later that same morning the sky turned black with clouds and it began to snow. The snow grew heavier and the wind began to blow out of the north. By afternoon it was a full blown blizzard, and by evening time it was an especially heavy blizzard. Visibility was very close to zero and the fading sunlight made it even worse. Soon he could see nothing beyond his window glass. That's when the thought struck him. He had not seen Mrs. Severud come home.

It could have been any number of reasons that he did not see her return. Maybe she stayed with a friend instead of driving in the storm. Maybe she worked late. Maybe she actually did come home but he had somehow missed seeing her. Maybe a dozen different maybes, but only one maybe meant anything to Charlie – maybe she was in trouble.

What he did next was not a matter of decision; it was a matter of his natural instinct. He put on his winter jacket, boots and gloves and got into his jeep. The jeep made its way very slowly down the drive towards the road. Several times he had to stop, get out of the jeep and look closely around him using the cars headlights, to make sure he was still on the path. He made it to the main road and turned toward the Severud's driveway.

He saw the faint outline of nearly-filled-in tire tracks in the snow, which indicated that someone had driven on the road fairly recently. He followed them to his neighbor's driveway but there were no tracks leading up the drive. Something in his gut told him to turn around and follow the tire tracks back down the main road.

After following the tracks for a few hundred yards he came upon Mrs. Severud's car. It was stuck in the heavy snow, but Mrs. Severud was not in it, and she was nowhere in sight. He drove past her car and continued on down the road until he saw an unnatural looking lump leaning against the fence that ran along the road. He stopped and got out of the car. The lump turned out to be the neighbors' wife. She was huddled against the fence with her coat wrapped around her and she was unconscious. Barely alive – but alive.

Charlie carried her to his jeep and got her home against many odds. Her husband was astounded. It turned out that when she had not come home he assumed that she had stayed in town with a friend rather than try to drive home. The high winds had blown down the phone lines and he didn't have a cell phone. He has one now.

As in all small towns the story of what Charlie had done got around quickly. Overnight he had become best friends with the entire population of Flatrock. Shortly after that the chief of Police announced his retirement and Charlie became the favorite replacement candidate.

And now, ten years later, here he was sitting across from Brent, who had been with him for a few years and was the best cop he had since becoming chief. He knew he favored the boy some, and occasionally let him slide on things he might otherwise be disciplined for, but he couldn't help it. There was a paternal instinct he felt for Brent that he could not prevent. Something about him convinced him that he could have been the son he never had.

As for tonight's little illegal excursion in the cruiser, he felt that he could adequately justify letting him off the hook. What he was about to tell him about Dylan's mom far outweighed his minor infraction with the police cruiser.

Brent felt awkward watching the Chief, who sat there staring at him for some minutes, lost in thought and looking troubled. He was uncertain what the Chief's problem was and less sure what he should do about it.

"What's up, Chief?" Brent finally asked him.

To Brent's relief, the Chief finally spoke.

"We just got a call from the U.S. Marshal's office," he said. "It seems they got a hit on the National Crime Information Center computer when Jessica O'Connor's death certificate was filed. Apparently Jesse was part of a witness security and relocation program. Maybe her death makes them suspicious, I'm not sure. But a couple of Deputies will be here in the morning to check it out. No one in this department is supposed to know anything about it except for me and you. Me because I'm Chief, and you because of your relationship with Dylan." He gave Brent a minute to consider what he had said and then continued, "You guys have been close for most of your lives, right?"

"Yeah," Brent said quietly, stunned by what he had just heard.

"You ever hear anything about this?"

"No," Brent answered. "And it's the last thing I would ever have suspected about her."

"You think Dylan knew?" the Chief asked.

Brent knew for a fact that Dylan didn't suspect it any more than Brent did. He knew it the same way that he knew everything about Dylan, their strange mental connection. But there was no way he could say that to the Chief.

"I doubt it," Brent said.

"He never mentioned it to you?"

"No," Brent said, still reeling from the news.

"Would he, if he knew?"

"I'm not sure," Brent said. But what he really wanted to say and couldn't, was that a secret of that magnitude could never go undetected by Brent. Which begged the question why it *had* gone undetected. Undetected by both Dylan and Brent, and apparently everyone else in Flatrock.

The Chief was not chief because he was an idiot. He'd been around the block and he could see that Brent wasn't saying something.

"You know him pretty well don't you?" the Chief probed.

"As well as someone can know another, I guess."

"Don't BS me. You know what I'm asking. You know him, right?"

"Yeah, I know him," Brent admitted.

"What's your take on him?"

Without hesitation he said, "He doesn't know. If he did, I would know about it, even if he didn't tell me." He stopped talking, but it was too late. He had already mentioned the very subject he was trying to avoid. All he could do now was hope that the Chief didn't notice.

"What do you mean?" the Chief asked. "How would you know such a thing?"

Shit, the Chief noticed. "This may sound weird," he started, "but we've always been able to know what the other was thinking, ever since we were kids. We don't know why, and we don't experience the same thing with other people. Not much, anyway," he amended after recalling hearing Jesse's voice that morning.

The Chief said, "That's good enough for me, but it will be different when the Deputy Marshals show up. You might not want to mention that story to them." He had no idea how wrong he was about that. "Go rest up and get ready for tomorrow. Be here at eight."

Brent, relieved by the Chief's almost indifferent acceptance of his answer, got up from the chair, ready to leave.

"By the way," the Chief said, stopping Brent. "I saw your car parked behind the strip mall. Next time pick a better hiding place." The Chief smiled at him. Brent nodded, then turned toward the door and and left the station.

CHAPTER TEN

BRENT LEFT THE STATION wondering how to break the news to Dylan. He walked to the strip mall to get his jeep, stopping at the convenience store on the way to buy some beer. By the time he arrived at Dylan's house he'd still not come up with an easy way to tell him what he'd just learned about his mom. He was sitting in the parked car thinking about it when Dylan came outside and hollered at him.

"What are you doing out there?" he yelled. "Come inside."

Brent carried the beer into the house, opened two cans and gave one to Dylan. Dylan took it without question.

"What's up?" he asked, suspecting he wasn't going to like whatever it was Brent had to say to him.

Dylan looked Brent right in the eyes, making their special connection, and making it easier for Brent to say what he had to say.

"Sit down," he said. Dylan sat down, looking even more worried because of the request.

There was nothing for it so Brent began the tale without any further hesitation. "Your mom was in a witness security and relocation program. WITSEC for short. The filing of her death certificate triggered a response from the U.S. Marshals. A couple of Deputies are coming to the station tomorrow morning to check things out."

Dylan's response was, "This is a joke, right? You're getting even with me for something, right?" He hoped he was right, but inside he knew he wasn't.

"No joke, man. Sorry."

Dylan was as bewildered by the news as Brent had been. "This is insane. Totally insane. Makes no sense at all," he said.

"So you had no clue?" Brent knew the answer but he had to ask.

"No, no clue." In hind sight Dylan was already seeing some things that this might explain. But until now he had no idea whatsoever. "Do the Deputies think she was murdered?" he asked. The thought of it was so unthinkable that he was surprised to hear himself ask the question. But why else would the U.S. Marshals be here?

"I don't know anything more than what I just told you," Brent answered. "The Chief said they were suspicious. That's all he said and that's all I know. What I think is that it's standard procedure. They probably investigate the death of every witness because of the nature of the program.

The implications of the news regarding Jesse was maddening, but if she really was murdered it would explain why they had been having a hard time believing that she would do something as dumb as walking out in front of a moving vehicle. It would not explain, however, the witnesses stating that that was exactly what she did. And what the coroner said she did. And the highway patrolman who investigated the incident.

Brent looked up at Dylan, who looked as though he was about to go mad.

"Listen, don't get too wrapped up in this thing right now," he advised. "Just put it on hold until we talk to the Marshals tomorrow, ok? Maybe we will be able to understand it better after we talk to them."

"Yeah, right," Dylan said, meaning just the opposite.

"Yeah, well, I'm worried about you," Brent said.

"Yeah, well I'm worried about me too, but I imagine that somehow I will pull through."

Brent had no reply to this so they looked at each other for a moment and all was said.

"I saved you some pizza, you want some?" Dylan asked.

"Yeah, thanks, I'm starving." They both ate some pizza and drank beer until they were full. Then Dylan asked, "You staying over tonight?"

"If it's ok."

"I'd like it if you did. I'll take the couch. I'm starting to grow fond of it."

"Thanks, but I've got to get up early to meet the Deputy Marshals at the station. It would be easier for me if I was on the couch. If you don't mind."

Dylan did not want to be alone in a room for the night, in case he had another bad dream. "Let's both sleep out here," he said. "I'll take the big chair, you take the couch."

"Fine with me," Brent said. "Now let's get some sleep."

CHAPTER ELEVEN

SOMETIME DURING THE NIGHT, Dylan heard his mom's voice again. "It's not like baseball," it said. "You don't always keep your eye on the berries. You keep a watch in every direction. Watch the ground. Watch the sky. Watch all the other bushes and check your back. But mostly watch the ground closely. Watch it for signs and clues." The words did not wake him, and he slept peacefully for the remainder of the night.

When he awoke he was vaguely aware that something had happened in his sleep. Something nagged on the tip of his brain, but it wasn't coming to him. From recent experience he reckoned it had something to do with his mom, and the thought of her triggered his memory, the sound of her voice rushing back to him.

He understood the words themselves and their individual meanings, but he hoped that there would be a deeper meaning to them. Something that would help him understand why his mom had been in WITSEC.

Failing to make find any underlying meaning, he wondered if it was possible that the words he'd heard were memories, and not messages from the heavens or some such. He made an effort to recall various childhood incidents which involved his mom, hoping to find a connection there, and came up with a memory of a time when he and his mom had gone off into the woods to pick wild blackberries. He remembered her saying the same things he had been hearing her 'voice' say to him in his sleep. It didn't explain why she was in the witness security program, but at least he knew that she wasn't talking to him from beyond the grave, the words were just his own memories.

Brent, who had also heard from Jesse, eyed Dylan after he woke up.

"What did you hear this time?" he asked, yanking Dylan's attention to the present world.

Dylan repeated the words he heard and added, "I know where those words came from. I remember them. She said them once when we went into the woods to pick wild berries. She must have once said, 'Don't hate the thorns' too. I think these voices are just memories, not voices from the grave.

What did you hear?" he asked Brent.

Brent was waiting for that question. "They're not worth it," he said. "You understand that?"

"Yeah, I do. It's a completion of the sentence that was started the first time I heard her voice. 'Don't even try for the hard ones, they're not worth it'." He thought for a minute and then continued. "I think you're right, I remember her saying that when we were picking berries. It was the only time I ever went picking with you guys."

He also remembered, but didn't say so, that he thought Jesse was full of shit when she said the hard ones weren't worth it. The hardest berries to get your hands on are always the biggest, fattest and juiciest berries and Brent thought they were definitely worth it. He understood her logic though. You can pick five decent ones in the same amount of time you spend on the one big one. But he didn't care, he still thought they were worth it. If you like them enough, and want them enough, the hardest ones are always worth it.

Instead of saying he thought his mom was full of shit, he asked Dylan, "Do you remember that time?"

Dylan said, "Yeah, I do. I remember that you stepped on a nest of ground hornets. The mean, black ones. You were wearing those flip flop things and the hornets started stinging the shit out of your feet. You threw your berries in the air and screamed and started running for the car, getting chased and stung by the hornets the whole way. We lost a gallon of berries that day because no one wanted to go back near that hornets nest to pick up the ones you threw."

"Yeah," Brent said, "and you laughed at me the whole time and said 'Always wear shoes and protective clothing, and always watch the ground and the other bushes and the sky'. And I never went picking berries with you again."

Dylan realized something. "Starting to sound familiar isn't it?" he said. "Us hearing these words about the times we picked berries with mom. By the way, sorry I gave you shit back then, when you were getting stung."

"Water under the bridge. It's time for me to get going to the station. I don't want to be late. What are you going to do today?"

"Wait for you to call me and tell what the fuck is going on."

"Right. I'll call as soon as I find out."

CHAPTER TWELVE

BRENT ARRIVED AT THE STATION a few minutes before eight, entering through the reception area to a small room at the back of the station that they referred to as the conference room. It was a small, drab room with dull linoleum floors. It had a small, cheap table in it, with a few cheap metal chairs around it, making it nothing like most real conference rooms.

The Chief and the two Deputy Marshals were there waiting for him, occupying three of the cheap metal chairs and drinking coffee. Brent noticed a carafe of coffee on the table, probably supplied by the Chief. It bore the logo of the place in the strip mall where he tried to hide his car the night before, an aggravating reminder of his mistake. He grabbed one of the white Styrofoam cups and poured himself a cup of coffee.

The Chief made the introductions. Their names were Connor McDermott and Jake Tillman, sent out from the Denver office of the U.S. Marshals on loan to the Montana U.S. Marshal. Connor was the lead man of the duo and looked close to retirement. Jake was younger, probably a rookie, or was not long ago.

They were not wearing the usual Men In Black uniform. They were dressed casually, like they were trying to blend in with the Montana lifestyle. It worked, if only because there is no common style of dress in Montana. The only constant in clothing in Montana is that you almost never see anyone wear a suit and tie, unless it's a lawyer.

After introductions they sat around the conference table engaging in a casual social conversation. The Deputies were considerate of the local PD and thanked Brent and the Chief for helping them out. They had an easygoing manner, without an attitude of superiority. Smooth operators. Brent liked them.

It was no accident that the Deputies were doing their jobs to Brent's satisfaction. There were several things about them, and their histories, that set them apart from the average Deputy. The more subtle of which Brent would come to know well over the next few days. The more factual reasons included their history as Deputies together, Connor's extensive experience and the fact that he had been to Montana before. Jake had never been to Montana, but due to other virtues Connor had selected him specifically for this assignment.

Connor was pushing sixty years old and looked it. Not that he looked badly, he just looked his proper age. He still had all his hair and it was mostly black but starting to gray. He had all the physical attributes of what are called the 'Black Irish'. At present his expression appeared troubled, but the lines on his face indicated that he was usually happier and normally smiled a lot. Something uncommon in a federal employee. He was a bit taller than an average man – about six feet even. Not a bad looking fellow either, but he wasn't wearing a ring.

Jake was a direct contrast to Connor and conveyed everything there was about 'young'. He was baby-faced, he was full of vitality, his eyes were bright, and he still had an enthusiastic interest and curiosity about life. He was about the same height as Connor but his hair was brown and thick and he wore it just a tad longer than regulation length, the minor rebellion against the dress code marking his youth.

There was one thing special about him. Something that he had in common with Brent, and Brent recognized it right away where others might not. He was enjoying his bachelorhood. Brent definitely liked him.

But they had to get around to business sometime so the Chief led into it by asking, "How can we help you guys?"

CHAPTER THIRTEEN

AFTER BRENT LEFT, Dylan eased onto his new friend, the couch, and reflected on how suddenly and drastically his life had changed. Random and mysterious force were jerking him willy nilly through the sands of time, and he felt the loss of control keenly. Desperate for a bit of mental stability, he searched for something, anything that he had any measure of control over. Inevitably, that search led him on an examination of a long list of things he was absolutely not in control of. Items including, but not limited to, uninvited memories about picking berries with his mother. Wait! Hold the presses!

If it had been only him experiencing the uninvited memories, or 'words', he would never consider it as anything other than more of his mental unhinging. But what about Brent? Brent was definitely not unhinged, nor hung over. He was of sound mind and body. Did that fact establish a degree of control over the uninvited memories? Hell no. It provided something better, a bit of certainty that gave him direction. Gave him a plan. Gave him some control. He was now certain that his mother was trying to tell him something important.

CHAPTER FOURTEEN

AT THE STATION, the two Deputies briefed Brent and the Chief, starting with Jesse's real name, which was Brenda Nightingale. Brent liked the name, and wondered what she would have been like, before something happened to her that made her have to change her name, not to mention her entire life.

"I came in on Brenda's case over twenty years ago," Connor continued. "That was when she approached the Vegas Metro PD to offer testimony against a notorious drug ring that the cops referred to as the Zorros. The foxes, in Spanish, because they were so sly, and were difficult to bust.

"I stayed with her twenty four hours a day, seven days a week, while she was doing her courtroom duties, and giving statements and sworn testimony. When she was finished testifying I brought her to Montana, relocating her and replacing her past identity with a new one. When that was done I left here and moved on to my next case."

Brent noticed that Jake had not said a word, making him wonder what his role was. Wait and see, he told himself. Meanwhile he had some questions for Connor.

"What motivated her?" he asked.

"You really want the whole story?" Connor asked him. Brent frowned.

"Why wouldn't I?" he asked. Connor stared at him, assessing him, as if trying to understand something. Then he recalled Brent's relationship with Dylan.

"I forgot, you were close to her, weren't you?" he asked Brent.

"Yes," he said. "Dylan and Jesse were like a second family to me."

"Yeah, well, it all started when Brenda married James Nightingale," Connor explained. "He was a no good, but she fell for him, blinded by her infatuation. I guess that happens when you are young.

"They married in Las Vegas, where she had been living since she was old enough to leave home. Her concerned parents were still living where she left them, in Columbine, Colorado," Connor told them. Brent detected something in the way Connor spoke about Jesse's parents.

"Was there trouble in her home growing up?" he asked. Connor shrugged.

"She never complained to me about her parents or her home life, but she told me that she didn't like the town. She said that drugs were becoming prevalent there and taking hold of the community." Something about that didn't make sense to Brent.

"Weird. If she'd been that aware of drug use in the area, you'd think she would have noticed James condition."

"I see your point," Connor agreed, "but you've assumed James was taking drugs. Truth is, he never took drugs. Brenda told me that. She said that he sold them for money, but never took them. And another thing, the drugs in Columbine were not illegal ones. The ones Brenda complained about were prescription drugs. The kind that were intended to control depression and other mental issues. She said that they made people act crazier than ever and she couldn't wait to get away from there."

"I read something about that when the school shootings took place. But that must have been after she left." Brent said.

"Yes, she'd been gone a while by then. Anyway, her new husband, James, was involved in narcotics without Brenda knowing. Unfortunately, the Zorros were a tough gang and he got pretty well trapped in it. You guys know what happens once you are in a gang, getting out alive can be difficult." Brent and the Chief both nodded their understanding of how gang life works.

"Eventually the marriage began to flounder," Connor continued. "The infatuations had lost their original excitement and James was acting in a way that made her suspicious that he was dealing drugs. She was pregnant by then, which motivated her to do something about her suspicions. She hadn't told James she was pregnant, and didn't want him to find out, so she had to act fast."

It was a fantastic story. One that neither Brent nor the Chief would ever had guessed and both were spellbound by it..

"So what happened?" the Chief asked. "Did they all go to prison?"

"Yes they did," Connor told them. "Most of them are still there."

"Most?" Brent asked.

"Her husband James got out five years ago." Brent glanced at the Chief to see if he'd reacted to this statement the same way he had.

"I know what you're thinking," Connor said, reading the suspicious look in Brent's face. "We watched him, and Brenda, closely after he was released, but he never left Vegas, and he never tried to contact Brenda. He's been well behaved." Brent nodded acknowledgment.

Connor had covered the basic history of Jesse's life, but had omitted a great many of the details, ones that he himself didn't know. Details he wished he did know, because they would have answered some of his own long unanswered questions. Like how she had learned so much about the drug gang's operations, and the details of some of the transactions. He had been under the impression that she was only the wife of a minor employee of the dealers and that she'd even been unaware of his true occupation for most of the time that they were together.

"What about connections outside prison," the Chief asked Connor. "Wouldn't they have outside connections who are free to do as they please?" Connor knew what the Chief was asking.

"We kept an eye on the ones we knew about, but there could have been some we didn't know about. Unfortunately it's hard to cover every possibility. That's why we set her up with a new life here in Montana, a remote area, outside of a great deal of American society."

Connor hesitated a moment, as if he was weighing whether or not to mention the leader of the Zorros, Bennett Alivio. The one who should have gotten the longest sentence, maybe life, but by some strange twist of irony had gotten one of the shortest sentences, serving only two years. Jefe del Zorros was a sly one.

Connor did his best to keep track of Bennett after his release, but it had not been easy to know where he was, and what he was doing at all times. He was pretty sure Bennett was still in Las Vegas, and even more sure he'd never been to Montana. But he was not one hundred percent sure that he couldn't have been involved, somehow, in Jesse's death.

In spite of the logical conclusion that Bennett should be the number one suspect of Jesse's demise, Connor doubted that Bennett had anything to do with Jesse's killing. Still, he wasn't ready to rule him out entirely. For now he decided not to mention Bennett to the cops in Flatrock.

Brent could see that Connor was burdened by Jesse's death. There was obviously a personal connection there. Probably created by the period of time they were required to spend in tight proximity. It's hard not to get attached to someone under those circumstances. And it was impossible for anyone to be around Jesse for long without liking her.

CHAPTER FIFTEEN

WHERE DO WE TAKE IT from here, gentlemen?" the Chief asked, looking at Connor.

"For now," Connor answered, " we want to review whatever information has been gathered here locally as a result of the accident. That would include the reports from the investigating officer, witness reports, forensic reports, etc. Was there an autopsy?"

"No, it was declared accidental death, so no autopsy," the Chief answered. "We did send the body to the state crime lab in Helena but the state Medical Examiner, but he said the injuries were consistent with the collision and didn't see anything that would cast suspicion otherwise.

"So we start with the incident report. Who filed it?" Connor asked.

"State trooper Tommy Sanderson," the Chief told them. "Apparently he witnessed the accident," the Chief added. Jake and Connor glanced at each other in response to that bit of information. Brent could see that it made them suspicious.

"You think that's a problem?" the Chief asked Connor.

"Hard to say," Connor answered. "It is unusual though. It's not often that one hears about a cop actually witnessing an accident. And since Jesse was one of our witnesses, yeah, I find it a little odd. Tell me about this trooper, Sanderson."

"He's new here," the Chief told him. "Been here a couple of years. But he's not a rookie. He was a Vegas cop before he came here. He seems competent enough."

Connor nodded, but gave Jake another questioning glance. He didn't like the coincidence of Tommy being from Vegas.

"You have the files here?" Connor asked.

"Yes sir, I brought the file with me." Charlie slid a manila folder across the table to Connor. "The report is in there. So is the coroner's report and all other documents pertaining."

While leafing through the file, Connor asked, "Were there other witnesses, besides the trooper?"

"Yes, their interviews are in the file."

"Ok, we'll study the file," Connor said as he slid the folder across the table to Jake. Then he said, "We know she didn't have a job at the time of death so we can't do place of employment and co-workers. But we will need to talk to Dylan." That was a given. They didn't know it, yet, but he would turn out to be the most key person in their investigation.

46

"I'm sorry, officer Butler," Connor added, "but you were very close to Dylan and his mom, so we may have to ask you some questions too."

"I will help in any way I can, and please call me Brent."

"Ok, Brent, it seems that the obvious place to start is with Dylan. As soon as we review the file we will want to see him. Do you mind arranging it?"

"Sure," Brent said. He wondered if he should warn them about Dylan's fragile condition, but decided against it when he couldn't come up with a way to explain it that wouldn't create a horrible first impression with the Deputies.

"Thanks. We'll call you when we are done reviewing the file," Connor said, dismissing Brent and the Chief.

"What now, boss?" Brent asked the Chief after entering his office.

The Chief said, "Go keep an eye on Dylan until I call you to set up the meeting."

"Yes, sir."

CHAPTER SIXTEEN

THE FIRST TIME DYLAN remembered picking berries with his mom was when he was about eight years old. He remembered her giving him various instructions, like telling him to put his shoes on.

He remembered that instruction because it was summertime and he liked to go barefoot during the summer. He'd argued with her about the shoes but she'd said that no matter how tough his feet were he would be glad he wore shoes. And she was right. The woods are rough on bare skin.

Dressed to her satisfaction they drove into the woods with their buckets and started picking. He wasn't keen on the idea of picking to start with, and after he'd done it for a few minutes his lack of enthusiasm was vindicated. Berry plants have thorns and are usually located amongst other less than friendly plants on steep hillsides in the heart of bug and bear country. Nevertheless he stuck his hand back into the midst of the thorns and kept grabbing.

In a short time his fingers were purple from berry juice, and most of what he put in his bucket was already mush from having to squeeze them hard enough to keep hold of them without the thorns grabbing them and pulling them back out of his hand.

His hands and arms became scratched up by the thorns, and occasionally he would look at his mom pleadingly with the hope that she would take pity on him and take him home. What he got in return for his pitiful countenance was an angelic smile as if she was enjoying his discomfort. That didn't help his enthusiasm at all. No sirree, not at all.

Eventually she bestowed a little pity on him. She approached him and quietly said, "Let me show you." She gently picked up a branch of the berry plant, pointed to the thorns and said, "See how the thorns are curved inward towards the center of the plant?"

"Yeah," Dylan answered.

"If you have to reach in to grab a berry, the thorns let you in. But when you withdraw with the berry, the thorns grab you, or the berry," she explained.

"Yeah, I noticed that," Dylan said, looking down at his bloody forearms and hands. "That's why I try to pick the ones on the outside of the plant."

"You're learning, and that's a smart way to do it. But the best berries are not on the outside because those get too much sun and shrivel up. At some point you will have to reach in."

He already knew that but he didn't care, he just wanted to avoid the thorns.

"Aren't the shriveled ones still good?" he asked her.

"Yes, if they are not too dried up they are still good," she explained patiently. "The thorns are protecting the good ones in the middle. They are like the plant's children and she wants them to survive, so she uses the curved thorns. Don't hate the thorns. They are only doing their job to guard the children."

There it was. The first time he heard those words "Don't hate the thorns."

CHAPTER SEVENTEEN

DYLAN HEARD THE CRUISER pull up outside and was surprised that Brent had returned from the station so quickly. When he heard Brent's footsteps reach the front door he hollered, "Come on in."

Brent walked in, beer in hand as ordered, shut the door behind him and walked across the room, plopping down in the big chair. He set the beer on the coffee table, let out a sigh and said, "You're not going to believe it." As an after thought he said, "I don't believe it."

Dylan said, "I'm ready, lay it on me."

"Well, to start with, her real name is not Jessica O'Connor, it's Brenda Nightingale. That is her married name, her maiden name was Macintosh."

Dylan took the news without distress. Brent wasn't sure if that was a good sign or a bad one. "It's a pretty name," Dylan said.

"Yeah, it is," Brent said.

"What's my real name?" Dylan asked him.

"They didn't say, but I'll see what I can find out," Brent said. Then after a short silence he added, "It won't matter you know."

"What won't?"

"Your real name. What's it matter? You've been Dylan O'Connor your whole life and you'll be Dylan O'Connor the rest of your life. No matter what."

"I guess you're right, but I still want to know. I …… just want to know."

Brent understood. He would want to know too. He filled him in on the rest of what the Marshals told him and waited for his response, not getting the one he expected.

"I remembered when she said 'don't hate the thorns,'" Dylan said. "I was eight and it was the first time I could recall that we went out in the woods to pick berries." Brent wondered if Dylan had finally gone over the edge of reason.

"So what's that got to do with anything?" he asked him, as if to test Dylan's sanity.

"I'm not sure how yet, but I know it's important somehow," he answered. "I think these 'berry picking words' from my mom are a message, something she wants me to know. If I was the only one to hear them, I wouldn't have suspected a hidden message. I would have suspected that I was hallucinating. But you heard them too, every time I did. That convinced me that it must be a message."

Brent could accept that, even if he couldn't completely understand it. He could accept it not only because his friend needed him to accept it, but because he agreed with the logic. Both of them hearing similar words from Jesse at the same time seemed like more than a coincidence. Especially knowing Jesse.

"The Deputies want to interview you," Brent said, changing the subject. "They are going to call soon. You ready for that?"

"I guess, but do we have to go to the station?" he asked.

"I don't know, why?" Brent asked.

"I'd rather do it here. I'd feel more comfortable."

"I'll see if I can make it happen."

"Thanks."

The Deputies must have been reading their minds because at that moment Brent's cell phone rang. It was the Chief.

"Dylan is a bit fragile," Brent explained to the chief. "He's not too keen on going to the station. You think the Deputies would be willing to come here?" He knew they would interpret the word 'fragile' as 'grieving', saving him the trouble of explaining what it really meant. Hungover. Insane. Grieving.

The Chief said, "Hang on a minute." He must have had a conversation with the Deputies and when he came back on the phone he said, "No problem, we're on our way."

"They're coming," Brent told Dylan after he hung up.

"Ok, what should I expect?" he asked, looking a little pale again.

"Probably just the routine questions. Just tell them the truth to the best of your ability and when they are done it will all be over," he said, wishing it was true.

Dylan had no trouble seeing through Brent's amateurish attempt at public relations and stared at him like he had just transformed from Brent Butler into a werewolf.

"Are you on drugs?" he asked Brent.

Brent shrugged and looked helpless, which had the effect of making him look like the real Brent again.

"Can we drink some of that beer before they get here?" Dylan asked.

"I wouldn't recommend it," Brent said, but was thinking it may be just the thing they needed.

"Yeah, I guess not," Dylan reluctantly agreed. "I'll put it in the fridge."

When he returned from the kitchen he asked Brent, "What are these guys like?"

Brent told Dylan about the Deputies and gave his positive opinions about them, hoping it would make him more relaxed about talking to them.

CHAPTER EIGHTEEN

THE DEPUTIES ARRIVED with the Chief and were introduced. When they were settled into various chairs around the living room, Deputy McDermott started the conversation by giving their condolences for Jesse's death. Dylan noticed a heartfelt sorrow in Connor and agreed with Brent's opinion that he must have gotten close to his mom.

Jake was young, Dylan's age he guessed, and didn't talk much, but seemed sincere. Dylan felt easy around him, which was a good sign.

During introductions Dylan had noticed a coincidence in Connor's and his mom's name, and he mentioned the fact to Connor.

Connor responded with, "Its no coincidence, son. We needed a new name for her and I guess we weren't feeling very imaginative at the time so we stole one of my names and used it."

"Just curious," Dylan said. He didn't bother to mention his slight annoyance with Connor's use of the word 'son'.

The interview began with the most obvious question and got the obvious answer, which was that Dylan never had a clue that his mom was in the witness protection program. A fact that bothered Dylan more than just about any other fact.

They asked him about the people in her life. Who did she know? Who did she hang out with? Did she have any close friends? Did she have any new friends or contacts in the past five years? Any unusual or strange visitors? Where did she shop? Was it the same places every time? Did she ever contact her parents, or allow them to visit?

The question about her parents unsettled Dylan. The simple answer to it was no. But the implications sent him into a new level of curiosity. When he'd become old enough to be aware of such things as grandparents, his mother had told him that they were dead. He had asked her what they were like and she talked about them for an hour or so, always in the past tense.

Since then, he barely gave their existence a second thought. Now that Connor had told him in so many words that they still lived, he began to feel a certain amount of guilt that his mom had cut them out of their lives.

The questioning ended but he got the idea that he had not contributed anything very helpful, and that bothered him. What he couldn't know yet was how much it bothered Connor.

The more Dylan considered the questions that had been put to him, and their possible answers, the more he wondered how he had missed the fact that his mom had a previous, unannounced, life.

Until now Dylan thought of his mom as an outgoing person, not in any way reclusive. But in hindsight, he realized that she didn't have all that many friends. She had a few mere acquaintances, but no one that she 'hung out' with, and her contact with others was really quite meager.

And now there was the news that she had parents. A mother, a father. And she had lived her life without them, pretending they were dead. How sad, and lonely. How incredibly brave.

What he also found incredible was that he'd never noticed her reclusiveness, nor suspected her role in WITSEC. He had the ability, the gift. Just look at how he and Bent interacted. And he had always thought he had the same gift with his mom. So what happened? Why didn't it work when it came to her past?

While Dylan was pondering these imponderables, Connor came up with another question for him.

"Can you think of anyone who might have wanted to harm her for any reason?" he asked. It sounded routine but that didn't make him feel much better about its implication.

"No," Dylan said. "You guys should know more about that than me. You tell me who would want to hurt her." He said it without holding back his resentment.

"Fair enough," Connor said patiently. "We already told you about her husband, James, but we are pretty sure he's been a good boy. The people who are still in prison have associates on the outside. Some we know about, and we can check them out. But there are, undoubtedly, some that we don't know about." Connor considered mentioning Bennett Alivio, but, once again, decided not to. "But that is what we know. You could know something we don't, that's why we asked you if you knew of someone."

"Well, I don't," Dylan said.

"Ok," Connor said. "But it might not matter. We still haven't established that her accident was anything but just that, an accident. Unless we find something here to indicate otherwise, we'll let it stand as an accident. People have accidents all the time, even federally protected witnesses."

Dylan detected something a little fishy about Connor's reply and asked, "Do you think it was only an accident?"

Connor hesitated and in that moment Dylan knew the real answer to his question. It wouldn't matter what Connor said.

"No," Connor answered honestly. Dylan's heart sped up. It confirmed a suspicion he'd harbored since Brent first told him that his mom had been in the witness security program. His suspicion had suddenly become a fact; there was trouble in Flatrock, Montana. There was murder.

"Why not?" he asked.

"You might think this sounds funny," Connor began. Then he sighed and said, "No, I don't think you will. There is no forensic evidence to support my opinion, yet, but I just won't accept that your mom would walk out in front of a moving vehicle." He looked sad, mad and determined, all at the same time.

Dylan said, "You're right, it doesn't sound funny to me at all. It's quite unlike her, to say the least." Things had gotten to a point where Dylan really wanted one of those beers they had put off drinking before the Deputies arrived.

"Anyone want a beer, I do?" he asked.

Connor asked, "Is that a Montana custom?"

Dylan knew that Connor didn't care whether it was a local custom or not, he was just looking for someone to give him a good justification for having a beer, like a good Irishman.

"Absolutely," Dylan obliged. He glanced at Brent, who was a bit wide eyed at Dylan's temerity. "It's time," he said.

Brent got up and went to the fridge, returning with the twelve pack he had bought earlier. He handed beers around, surprised that the Chief took one, but he supposed he wanted to keep in step with the Deputies. Brent was the only person not to have one.

Connor didn't miss the 'It's time' that Dylan had said to Brent. He asked Dylan, "Time for what?"

"Oh that. It's an inside joke with me and Brent. It means it's time for beer."

Connor chuckled like he knew more than he was letting on.

After they all had a couple of sips of beer Dylan asked, "What's next?"

Connor asked Dylan, "Would you mind taking me to her house?"

He didn't mind Connor being in his mom's house, but he was a little bit hesitant about going in there himself, it being the scene of his drinking crime at the wake the other night, among other reasons. "No, I guess not," he said.

"You want to stay here and let me take them?" Brent asked Dylan.

"No, I'll go too, thanks. I need to get out."

Brent understood Dylan's motive and said, "Sure thing, a little fresh air eh?" But he knew that the actual problem was that if Dylan was left to sit alone in his house he might go into a spin, or have another bad dream.

"Yeah," Dylan said.

"We'll drive," Connor offered, "You mind riding with us?"

He looked like he had a reason for wanting Dylan to ride with him so he agreed. He glanced at Brent and shrugged. Like always with them, it was all it took for Brent to understand and he smiled back at Dylan.

CHAPTER NINETEEN

TO SAY THAT THE dark haired woman had been distressed since Jesse's death would be an understatement. But something she'd just seen had elevated her distress to a new high.

She had returned to Dylan's neighborhood that morning and parked her rental a short distance from his house. She had seen Brent leave, and then return some time later. During that time there had been no sign of Dylan.

Then, shortly after Brent's return, another car arrived. Three men got out of it. She recognized two of them, the Chief and Connor. The third man was obviously another Deputy, but one she'd never seen before. The appearance of any U.S. Marshal's Deputies would have rattled her, but seeing Connor terrified her.

She was petrified that he would notice her, but she remained parked where she was. She had to know.

They entered the house and she waited. A short while later they exited the house, Dylan included, and drove off in two separate cars. She followed them in her rental car.

CHAPTER TWENTY

JAKE DROVE THE RENTAL to Dylan's mom's house, following the directions supplied by a computerized GPS system built into the car, while Brent and the Chief followed.

"I'm glad you rode with us," Connor told Dylan shortly after getting underway, "I wanted to talk to you alone."

"Jake is here," Dylan pointed out, unable to resist pointing out the obvious.

Connor smiled and said, "We wanted to talk to you alone."

"What's on your mind?" Dylan asked, smiling back at Connor.

"First I want to clear something up that you might be wondering about. You know, now, that your mom had another name. But your name has never changed. Before you were born she asked me to arrange to have your name registered as Dylan O'Connor on your birth certificate. She was worried that if there was any record of a connection between you and her original identity it could be traced, increasing the risk to you. So you were born with your current name.

"Everything she did with us was because of you, son. She would never have come to us if she wasn't pregnant with you. You, without knowing it, of course, were her inspiration to do the right thing."

"Let's get something straight," Dylan responded. "I am not your son. I resent the use of that word when you address me. It's demeaning," he said flatly.

"You're right, of course, and I apologize," Connor said with some embarrassment. "I meant no harm by it, it is just an unfortunate figure of speech that I have gotten into the habit of using. But I can see how inappropriate it is and I promise to curb my usage of it."

"Thanks for telling me about my name," Dylan said as a way of accepting the apology. "I was curious about it. But there's something else on your mind."

Connor brightened and said, "Exactly. The fact that you know that, that you could sense that, is one of the things I wanted to talk to you about.

"Your mom had that gift, the ability to read people. I had never experienced anything like before I met her." Dylan interrupted him to ask something he had been wondering about for a while.

"How close, were you two in love? Were you lovers?" Dylan thought Connor might be uncomfortable with this subject but he was wrong. Connor seemed proud of his answer and more than willing to talk about it.

"I loved her, I know that much," he said. "And I think she loved me as well, but we didn't talk about it openly, or act on it, for all the obvious reasons. Your mom was a special and unique person though, and as you know, verbal communication was not always necessary.

"Before I met her," he explained, "I was a typical Deputy, in the sense that I depended only on physical evidence. That was how I was trained to think, and psychic mind reading and all that hogwash was just that, hogwash. But the time I spent with your mom changed my mind. I think you know what I mean."

"Yes," Dylan agreed.

"I thought so, and that's why I wanted to talk to you away from the others. They are cops, so they might not be open to non traditional approaches to a case. I, on the other hand, think it would be wise for us to use any means available to figure out what really happened to your mom. So far, traditional methods and physical evidence haven't been much help to us. In fact all the evidence I've seen seems to support the theory that she died in a mere accident.

"If it wasn't just an accident, we need to know. I *have* to know. And it's possible that the only way we are going to get a lead of any kind is going to be with your 'special' help. If there was foul play and if you can help us get a start on a trail of any kind, no matter how faint, then maybe we can solve it. Otherwise........ ." Dylan knew it was rude to do so but he couldn't help himself, he laughed out loud.

"What the hell is so funny about that?" Connor asked indignantly.

"I'm really sorry, sir. I'm not laughing at you, or what you said. It's just that the situation strikes me as so ironic that I can't help but laugh. You see, Brent and I are old friends and we have both been..... uh, 'spiritually talented' for our whole lives. We were recently warned by the Chief not to talk to you about it, in case you weren't 'open to non traditional approaches'. And now here you are asking me to be a 'psychic detective' for you." Dylan laughed again at the thought.

"OK, I see your point. It is all a bit unusual isn't it?" Connor replied. "So what do you think, really?"

Dylan didn't answer right away. He knew what Connor wanted from him. He wanted answers. He wanted the kind of answers that he thought only Dylan would be able to give him. And he understood why Connor thought that, but he was wrong.

Dylan didn't have answers. All he had was a long list of unanswered questions, starting with the cause of his mom's death, which was hard to accept and raised a lot of suspicion. And now this news about witness protection and U.S. Marshals, and finding out that her parents were alive. His grandparents. It raised oh so many questions. But there was one question he asked himself over and over. The one question that, if answered, might open the answer floodgates and explain many things: How could he have missed this?

How could he have not known something so important about his mom's, and his own, life? How could he miss something like that? It all kept coming back to that question. He always thought that he could tell what she was thinking or feeling. So what had happened that caused him to be so blind to this? If he could miss something so blatant, for so long, then what made him think he had any talent for finding mysterious answers now?

He wanted to be able to help Connor, but he wasn't sure that he could. He wondered if it would be mean to reverse the situation, and ask Connor the questions. Mean or not, someone's questions had to start being answered soon. Might as well be his.

He told Connor, "It sounds like you are assuming some things. You're assuming that it wasn't an accident, and that I know something about what really did happen, or that if I don't already know, I can somehow find out. But I'm not certain about either one of those things. Maybe we suspect it wasn't an accident, but we don't know it."

"Wait a minute," Connor objected. "We both know that it was not an accident. Didn't we just establish that? You changing your mind on me?"

"No, I'm not. Yes we 'know' it was not an accident. But what I am talking about is evidence. You and I both know that we need real evidence. Something a bit more substantial than 'me and Dylan agree, she was murdered'. It might partially satisfy us to know for ourselves what really happened, but I am assuming you want to do more that just know about it. I certainly do. I want to be able to prove it, and to be able to bring someone to justice for it. So, unless there is something you know about it that you haven't told me, we are still at square one.

"And I don't know why you think I know more than you do about what happened, because I don't. So far you have been the one telling me everything that, until now, I had no clue about. Maybe you think I am all psychic and shit, but if that's true then tell me why I had no idea that my mom was in the witness protection program. And that she had a previous life, lived by another name. Or that my father was still alive? And my grandparents weren't dead? How did I miss it all?"

"I can't answer that for you," Connor admitted. "But you are right about needing real evidence."

Dylan sighed and sat back in his seat, looking at the car's headliner, thinking. He knew that Connor wanted him to tell him he would commit himself to trying to prove his mom had been murdered. And that he wanted him to use his special talents to do it. He would tell Connor what he wanted to hear, but first he wanted to know how Jake fit in to all this.

He asked Connor, "Who assigned Jake to this case?" Dylan thought he already knew the answer, but needed to hear it from Connor.

Connor quickly answered, "I requested him." It was the answer Dylan expected to hear.

"Why?" Dylan asked.

"Because I knew he'd be on board with this."

"How?"

"The same way you 'know' things."

"Ok," he said, satisfied by the answer. "I'm on board too. Now let's prove that it was no accident that killed my mom. And let's get the bastard who's responsible. And when we find them, I won't be responsible for what I do to them. OK?"

Connor let out a brief laugh and said, "More than OK. But I might get to the bastard first, and if I do I won't be responsible for what happens to him either."

"Agreed," Dylan said. "So what do you want me to do?"

Connor sighed with relief, then snorted a quick, semi embarrassed laugh and said, "To tell you the truth, I don't know where to start, or what it is, exactly, you can do. I think we are going to have to figure this out together."

"Alright," Dylan said. "We agree that there is something about the accident that doesn't sit right with us, so let's start by finding out what that is."

As soon as he said that, a memory flashed into his mind. He recalled that, before the funeral, he kept thinking that it was not right. The accident was not right. In fact, now that he was thinking about it, something had felt wrong about it from the first moment he was told about it.

CHAPTER TWENTY ONE

THEY ARRIVED AT JESSE'S house and waited by the front door for Brent and the Chief. Brent climbed the two steps to the front door and Dylan handed him the door keys. He opened the door and let the others in. Dylan stayed outside.

Connor didn't miss the fact that Dylan had stayed on the front porch and he asked Brent if Dylan was ok.

"He's nursing a bit of a hangover," Brent told him. Of course there was a lot more to it than that but Brent did not feel that it was his place to say so.

Connor knitted his brow, not fully comprehending Brent's answer, but he didn't ask for clarification, for which Brent was grateful.

Dylan sat in a chair on the porch and looked out at the mountains. It was the first time he had done so alone. Once, when he was young, he sat on this same porch, looking at the same mountains with his mom sitting next to him. She had told him that she picked out this house because of the view of them. He marveled again now at the view.

Later in life Dylan figured there must have been other reasons for her to buy this house, because, by then, he had realized that almost every place in Montana has good views, especially of mountains.

Now, after hearing about her real past, he wondered if his mom ever picked this house out at all. Maybe the U.S. Marshals had picked it out for her. Probably Connor found it and set it up long before she ever saw it.

He wondered, too, how his mom paid for the house. In fact, now that he thought about it, he wasn't sure how she'd paid for anything, she rarely worked.

Brent came out to the porch and interrupted Dylan's thoughts. "You coming in?" he asked.

"Yeah," Dylan said. He followed Brent into the house, where he found Connor, Jake and the Chief in the living room looking somewhat lost and frustrated.

Connor said, "I need to ask you about a few things, do you mind?"

"No, go ahead."

"Did you go through your mom's house after she died?" he asked.

"Yes, but it was before I knew the truth about her past and I wasn't specifically looking for anything. I was just reminiscing I guess." Connor nodded his understanding.

"Thinking back on it now, was there anything unusual or out of place, or something that catches your attention now?" He asked it in a funny way, as if he either knew that something was out of place and wanted Dylan to confirm it, or that there was something wrong and he wanted to be sure Dylan hadn't noticed it.

"Maybe I should look around the house again. See if something comes to mind," Dylan said.

"Thanks, I'd appreciate it," Connor said.

Dylan walked around the house, not looking for anything specific, but just looking at things in general. His eyes were looking at what was there, but what he saw was all the reminders of his past. Of the years of his life when he lived here with his mom.

The house hadn't changed much except in one major way, no Jesse. Everywhere he went in the house, everything he looked at shouted her lack of presence, and yet every place he looked he saw her there, from the past. Her absence created a vacuum in his world that was a deafening silence and he started to lose control of his water works again. He made a beeline for the exit, running past the other men without looking at them.

He sat on the porch chair and took a few deep breaths, looking at the mountains and thinking about nothing in particular. He heard his mom's voice again.

"Don't keep your eye on the ball," she said. "Look all around, especially at the ground. Watch it for signs and clues."

He had some intuitive idea that the words were important. Something on the tip of his brain. And, like before, he wished he knew how.

Frustrated, he said out loud, "Why can't a damn omen just say whatever the hell it has to say and be done with it?" In the very second that he asked himself that question he recalled asking his mom what she meant by those same words, when she first said them to him as a child.

"What clues and signs am I supposed to see?" He had asked her.

"Some day you will know", she had answered. "You will know what signs to look for."

That had made no sense to him at the time, but he was used to his mom saying weird things like that so he hadn't pushed it. But now he suspected that there was some greater significance to what she said. That the 'some day' was at hand and that he should know what signs he should be looking for. But he still had no idea what they were.

"You ok?" he heard Brent asking. He looked up at Brent who looked like he may have been standing there for a while.

"Yeah, I'm good. I didn't see you come out. How long you been here?"

"Not long. We thought we should give you a few minutes alone after seeing you walk out. What happened anyway, did you see a ghost or something?"

"Something like that. What's up?" he asked.

"Just wondering if you're ready to come back in."

"Sure." He felt anything but sure, but was too spent to resist Connor's desires. And, what the hell, you seen one ghost, you seen em all.

When they walked back in the house Jake surprised Dylan by saying, "I lost my mom not too long ago. It wasn't easy. If you need to talk, I'm here." Jake didn't talk too often, but when he did, he meant it.

"Thanks, I appreciate it," Dylan said. "I think I'm better now."

Jake said, " That's good, I'm glad. But the offer stands. Any time."

Dylan nodded his thanks, then gave Connor, a questioning look.

"Jake, let's go back to the station," Connor said unexpectedly. Then to Brent he said, "Can you take Dylan home? We don't need to finish this now, we can come back later, when he's more ready for this. Besides, Jake and I need to get started on some data verification and check up on some reports. It takes time to run the info through the data centers, so the sooner we start the better. The Chief can ride back to the station with us." He was in a sort of rush that bordered on frantic.

"No problem," Brent said, frowning.

"Thanks," Connor said. "Can we meet again tomorrow?" he asked while running for the door. Jake was on his heels, hoping his boss hadn't just lost all his marbles. The Chief was close behind, wondering if he had the local spin bin phone number on his cell phone's contacts list.

Dylan and Brent agreed to meet him in the morning, as requested. Seconds later they were alone in the house and staring at the door. When the wonder wore off, they made their way to Brent's car.

On the ride to Dylan's house Brent finally found his tongue and asked, "What happened in there?"

"You mean with me or with Connor?" Either episode would warrant the question.

"Both I guess, but I was referring to you."

"Everything I looked at in the house reminded me so much of my mom that I couldn't see straight, or think straight. I had to get out," Dylan said. Then suddenly, "Wait, let's go back. I just thought of something I need to check."

Brent made a U-turn. "What is it?" he asked.

"Do you recall seeing any photographs around mom's house? Like family pictures of me, or us?" Dylan asked. He wanted to see if he was right about his suspicion – if maybe Brent had noticed the same thing he had.

Brent tried to recall seeing photos in Jesse's house. He could recall seeing the type of photos Dylan was asking about in other people's houses. Proud photos of some relative or another, grand kids on the walls, spouses on night stands or desks, etc. But not in Jesse's house. He only recalled seeing one picture in her house. It was a picture of Jesse and Dylan when Dylan was an infant. It had been on the mantel forever.

"Just the one on the mantelpiece, of you and your mom when you were a baby."

"Yes, the one that's been there forever. I think it's gone but I can't be sure. I was kind of distracted by my emotions when I was looking around in there. I want to go back and check to see if it is still there or not. Do you recall seeing it?"

"No, I don't," Brent replied. "But I never looked for it specifically either, so I could not tell you for sure if it is there or not." They continued on to the house.

The picture was gone.

CHAPTER TWENTY TWO

AS SOON AS THEY ENTERED THE POLICE STATION, Connor began barking orders at Jake. He told him to get the NCIC to run background checks on the owner of the car that hit Jesse. And on its driver, in the event that they were two different people. In addition he wanted the car impounded again and to have a full forensics redone on it. He wanted background checks on Tommy Sanderson and any witnesses named in his report. He wanted to put in a request to the judge to exhume Jesse's body for an autopsy. He told Jake to contact all the witnesses and schedule them for new interviews. In short he was going the extra mile, leaving no stone unturned.

"One more thing," Connor said after a brief hesitation, "get me everything the Vegas Marshal's office has on Bennett Alivio."

"Who?" Jake asked. He had never heard the name before.

"He was the leader of the Zorros drug ring," Connor answered. "He's been out of prison for years now." He gave Jake a meaningful look, conveying the significance of the statement.

"Got it," Jake said with a frown. He carried out his instructions, but he worried about the direction Connor's orders were taking, namely conducting a full investigation.

Connor had no authority to be undertaking an investigation into Jesse's death. In fact he would be in some trouble if the Marshal found out about it. Jake knew this, but since he had a special affinity with Connor he decided to support him for a while, see how far Connor was going to go with it.

Connor noticed Jake's discomfort and he understood what caused it. He was a WITSEC expert, not an investigator. The Marshal only let him take the assignment in Flatrock because he had already decided that it was just an accident, and therefore there was nothing for Connor to screw up. He knew even further that if he found evidence proving that it was not an accident, or found out anything else to indicate an investigation was warranted, he was obliged to inform his seniors who would certainly take over for him at that point.

He knew all these things but he ignored them and forged ahead on his own anyway, not caring about the consequences. All he cared about was finding out what really happened to Jesse. He had his reasons, undisclosed of course, for not agreeing with his bosses assessment of the accident, and those reasons were driving him, passionately compelling him, to find the truth.

It was a tough choice but he decided to keep his own counsel for now, and not speak up. For better or worse he decided not to tell Jake that he might have discovered the first piece of real hard evidence indicating that there was foul play afoot.

CHAPTER TWENTY THREE

A THOUSAND MILES AWAY from Montana, in Las Vegas, Nevada, James Nightingale was putting gas in his car at the same Rebel gas station where he almost always put gas in his car. While he was waiting for the pump to finish filling his tank he went inside to get a giant fountain soda.

While waiting for the fountain pump to finish filling up his giant cup, a man approached him. He seemed somehow familiar, he'd seen him somewhere before, but he could not place it. The man spoke to him.

"You don't have to worry about your canary bitch ever singing again," he said, handing him a photograph. James took the picture and looked at it closely. His heart leaped in panic. He looked up to ask the man where he had gotten the photo, but the man was no longer there. He looked out the window of the store, but he had disappeared. Leaving his soda under the machine, he hurried out to his car. He stopped the gas pump, got in his car and drove off.

When he got home he made one phone call, to the U.S. Marshal's office.

He finished his call and leaned back on his couch. It wasn't until that moment that he allowed himself to face the unwelcome conclusions the photograph ignited in his mind. He felt the emotional reactions welling up from deep inside, and knowing that he would be unable to stop them he didn't try. He screamed once in frustration, then laid over on the couch, put his face in his hands and sobbed.

CHAPTER TWENTY FOUR

CONNOR WAS WAITING for responses to his various inquiries when he got the call. It wasn't one of the calls he was expecting though. In fact he would never have expected a call like this one at all.

His supervisor, Dennis Wheeler, calling from the Denver office, told him that James Nightingale had contacted the Marshal's office in Las Vegas, notifying them that he had vital information regarding Brenda. He said that James wouldn't give up the information over the phone until the Marshal answered some of his questions. Dennis wanted to check in with Connor before making a decision about what to do with James.

"Send him out here to Flatrock as soon as possible," Connor instructed. Too late he realized his mistake. Not only was there a desperate tone in his voice, but requesting that a potential witness be sent to Flatrock could imply that Connor was up to something more than he was authorized to do.

There was a long silence on the other end of the phone and Connor knew he was in trouble. He tried to come up with a cover story that he hoped would cover his ass, but he guessed it might be too little too late.

"What the hell is going on there, Connor?" the supervisor asked. Unable to come up with a decent explanation Connor threw up a hail Mary.

"You don't happen to owe me any favors do you, Dennis?" Connor asked. He heard an 'oh no' sigh on the phone, and then another short silence.

"No, Connor," Dennis finally answered. "I can't think of any reason I would owe you. So just tell me what the hell is going on."

Connor explained the situation to him, throwing in as much pleading for sympathy as he could muster.

"You're whining," Dennis complained.

"I know," Connor admitted with not a bit of shame. "Come on, Dennis, I'm desperate. I gotta do this. I promise I won't get in too deep without letting you know. If it gets hairy I will back off and call you in." Dennis sighed again.

"Let me think about it," he said. "I'll call you back in a few days and let you know. Meantime I'm sending James to Flatrock." There was another silence, during which Connor held his tongue and his breath, knowing he may be getting a break he didn't deserve.

When Dennis spoke again he said, "Don't you fuck me on this, Connor." The phone went dead and Connor took a deep breath and blew it out. He'd gotten a break, but if he screwed up he would go down. All the way down. And he might be taking a few Deputies with him.

CHAPTER TWENTY FIVE

"THERE WAS ALWAYS SOMETHING funny about that picture," Dylan told Brent. "It looked like another person had been cut out of it. I used to wonder if it was my dad, but my mother told me he had left us before I was born. I wish I had asked her about it." Brent watched him contemplate the matter for a minute, then Dylan snapped his fingers, indicating a realization. His face transformed, becoming red and twitching like a meth addict, his eyes glazed over.

"I know who it was," Dylan spit out, "and why my mom never told me. That person can only be one man. Connor. He came to see her. That son of a bitch."

Brent said, "Hold on, don't jump to any conclusions. You don't know any of that. Connor cared a lot about her safety." Dylan gave Brent a hard look, eye to eye, and Brent gave up on his skepticism.

Brent said, "OK, so he came here. So what? How can you know that his visit harmed her when we don't even know yet if what happened to her was an accident or not?" Dylan gave him another hard look. The look was mean, almost evil, and out of character for the normally mild mannered Dylan, even scaring Brent for a moment.

The hard looks were interrupted by Brent's phone ringing. It was Connor asking if them to meet him at the station.

"Good, let's go," Dylan said, his mind writhing with the imagined evils he intended to bestow on Connor.

Brent read Dylan's attitude and said, "If you are planning on doing anything stupid I'll leave you here."

"You can leave me here if you want, but I have my own car don't forget."

"You better go with me then, so I can keep an eye on you." He said it menacingly, but Dylan just smiled at him. It was not the kind of smile borne of fondness.

They pulled into the police parking space, and before Brent had come to a complete stop Dylan was out of the car, marching toward the station. Brent stopped the car and ran to catch up with him, determined not to let Dylan out of his reach, in case he became truly stupid. As bad luck would have it, the first person to come into Dylan's view was Connor.

"You son of a bitch," Dylan snarled at the startled Deputy. "You came back didn't you? And I bet you took that picture out of my mom's house so I wouldn't find out."

Brent, fearing that Dylan was going to take a swing at Connor, stepped between them.

Connor didn't try to defend himself, looking instead at the floor and shaking his head, the tough choice of when to confess having just been made for him.

He said quietly, "Yes, now you know. I came here twenty years ago to see her new baby, you. And now I have to know if my visit contributed to her death. I loved her more than I ever loved anyone, and if I did something to cause her death I couldn't live with myself. I'm sorry, Dylan. But I didn't take the picture from the house.

"We had that picture developed the same day we took it," he explained, "we cropped me out of it, framed it and set it on the mantel. Jesse said that she was going to leave it there forever, as a reminder, so she would always remember me. Today, when I noticed that it wasn't there any more, I wasn't sure what happened to it. I have not been in her house for a long time, so I had no idea how long it had been missing. I wanted to ask you about it but I couldn't bear it. And now that you say it has gone missing recently, I fear my worst nightmare may be coming true."

Connor's sad confession, and obvious discomfort, had a slight sobering effect on Dylan. He backed off a little, uncertain whether to hate Connor or feel sorry for him.

"You're coming with us, Connor," Dylan said. "Come on, let's go, Brent."

"Go?" Brent asked. "Go where?" Maybe Dylan wasn't lost in the depths of despair any more, but he was certainly caught up in a whirlwind of anger. Brent wasn't sure it was any better, and was certain that a police station was about the best place Dylan could be right now.

"The outlaw," Dylan informed them.

"You sure?" Brent tried not to imagine what it would be like with Dylan in The Outlaw in his present state of mind.

"Absolutely. Connor interrupted our last trip to the place so now he's going with us." Brent wondered about that kind of logic.

"We're going to some place called The Outlaw?" Connor asked in wonder. "What is that?" A place in Montana called The Outlaw didn't sound overly inviting to him. Especially given Dylan's present attitude.

On the other hand Jake was smiling excitedly, like he was embarking on a wonderful new adventure. He must have guessed that The Outlaw was a bar, and any bar with a name like that was a bar he wanted to visit.

"You'll see," Dylan answered Connor. "Let's all go in the cruiser."

It was either out of a sense of guilt, or due to the inability to resist the tide of Dylan's emotional intensity, but for whatever reason they all followed Dylan out of the building and into the nearest police car, with Brent driving. Luckily for Dylan the Chief was out of the station at the moment, or his plan may have never gotten off the ground.

The drive to the bar was openly silent. When they arrived Brent parked the cruiser and the group went inside.

Jake fell in love with the place immediately, smiling broadly, like he had just returned home after a long absence. Dylan, noticing Jake's infatuation, wondered if they were going to have a hard time getting him to leave. Brent was sure of the fact.

Connor may have been to Montana before but he had never been in a Montana bar. It was a new experience for him and he took his time looking the place over, taking it all in. If he was expecting to see room full of outlaws, he was disappointed. The place was near a university and was popular among the students, although, typical for Montana, you could find people of all ages there.

Brent had been in the place a million times, but never in uniform. He wondered how well that would go over. He found out when the normal roar of the crowd dwindled down to a pregnant silence.

The bartender, who looked more like a college professor than an outlaw, stared at them, appearing more ready to answer questions than to serve them drinks. Dylan surprised him when he walked up to the bar and ordered a pitcher of beer and four glasses. The bartender poured the beer, but his suspicious eyes never left Brent.

They found a table and the bartender brought the pitcher and glasses to them. Dylan poured all the glasses and said, "Cheers."

Except for Brent, they all lifted their glasses and took a drink. Brent thought it was bad enough that he'd arrived in a police car, wearing a police uniform. He didn't want to push it by drinking. Connor took a long drink of his beer and relaxed a little.

"Ok, what are we doing here?" he finally asked.

"A few things," Dylan answered. "First we are completing a mission. Brent and I were on our way here in a police car when the Chief called off our mission because of your pending arrival. Second we are blowing off some steam. Or at least I am. Up to you if you want to or need to. Next, I am trying to decide what to do with you." Brent was somewhat relieved that Dylan was not still in a full blown rage, but it was obvious that he was on some kind of a roll.

The last item shocked Connor a little bit. "*You* are trying to figure out what to do with *me*?" Apparently he wasn't used to the tail wagging the dog.

"Yes," Dylan told him almost proudly. "I'm conflicted. I don't know whether I should be really pissed and hate you or be an understanding soul and help you get out of the trap you fell into. So we're going to sit here and share grog and break bread together for a while and see where we end up, which will depend a great deal on how you handle this." He knew he had just thrown proper protocol out the window, but he figured Connor started it by neglecting protocol when he came back to Montana for his little visit.

"Ok, I guess I'm on probation here. I understand and I deserve it. What do I need to do to get your trust back?" Connor petitioned.

"If I knew I would tell you," Dylan said. "There's a lot of shit going on right now that I don't know shit about. So you figure it out. If I like it, then we're golden." He experienced a little pleasure from torturing Connor, and he wondered if he ought to feel shame over it. He considered that for a moment longer, then decided he should feel precisely the way he already felt about it – splendid.

"Fine," Connor responded, "the rules are set and I'm ready to play." Then the son of a bitch got himself out of the hole with one damn sentence. "What time is it?" he asked.

Dylan was stunned, but only for a split second before he burst out laughing. 'What time is it?' was an old line they used when referring to the fact that it was time to drink beer. A kind of variation of Miller Time.

When the laughter had died down, the charged atmosphere had calmed and all was right with the world. Brent poured more beers and said to Connor, "That was perfect, how did you figure it out?"

Connor said, "You guys aren't the first ones to use that line. I've heard it before, and when Dylan told you 'it was time' back at his house, I put two and two together."

Dylan was wiping laughing tears from his eyes when he lifted his glass to a toast. Touching glasses he said, "Here's to chronometry."

That got another laugh, but the levity was about to end. If Connor wanted to stay in good standing with the fold, he knew that he couldn't hold back vital information.

He said to Dylan, "I hate to spoil the mood but you need to know something. Your dad, James Nightingale, contacted us. He said he had information about your mom. He's on his way here to Montana." He let that settle in for a moment.

When Dylan heard the words 'your dad', the fuses in his brain blew, and for a few seconds after that his mind was blank. "What did you say?" he had to ask to be sure he heard right. Connor repeated himself, more slowly and deliberately this time.

"Why?" came out of Dylan's mouth of its own volition.

"Why what?"

"Why is he coming here?" Dylan asked. There were a million other whys rattling around in his head. And just as many whats and whos and hows. But for now the one why was enough.

"I requested it."

"Why?" he asked again.

"He said he had important information about your mom, so I him brought here to see what he knows. We need all the leads we can get."

He said it matter of factly, as if Dylan were stupid for not already knowing it. He regretted the attitude instantly, but he could think of no way to reverse

71

the damage. Fortunately Dylan was too preoccupied to notice. "Wow," he said, then got lost somewhere way back inside his head.

He wondered what it would be like to see his father for the first time in his life. He also wondered if he might have a connection with him, similar to what he has with Brent. If he did, he wondered if he might get some greater understanding of recent events, understanding of what happened to his mom.

When Connor saw Dylan disappear into himself, he thought he may have underestimated the effect of the news about his father would have on him.

"I know you never knew him," Connor said. "You ok with this? You don't have to meet him or even see him if you don't want to." Dylan said nothing, which worried Connor. He was relieved when Dylan finally came out of his shell and looked over at him.

"When is he arriving?" Dylan asked.

"In a couple of hours," Connor told him

"I want to be there when he arrives. I need to meet him," Dylan said, settling the matter.

CHAPTER TWENTY SIX

BRENT HAD BEEN RIGHT. Jake loved The Outlaw so much that he was determined to stay until closing time. His plan was preempted when, long before closing time, Connor ordered him to go to the airport and pick up Dylan's father, James. Quite reluctantly Jake walked out to the rental car and left for the airport. The others returned to the station, where the Chief was waiting there for them in the conference room.

"I got a call from The Outlaw," The Chief said to Brent when they entered. "It was a complaint about a uniformed officer who arrived in a cruiser and drank beer with three other guys. I told them it was official business and not to worry." Meaning he was covering for the department but it still wasn't ok for Brent to do it.

The Chief shook his head, which Connor mis-translated as an expression of his disgust for what Brent had done. The real meaning was that the Chief couldn't believe he was covering for Brent again because of his personal feelings about the boy. Connor tried to cover for Brent by saying it was his idea and that he insisted Brent be there.

The Chief said, "Yeah right, but thanks for trying." Connor looked at Brent and shrugged the 'Hey, I tried' shrug.

Brent said, "I wasn't drinking, boss, but I was there." He hated having to give excuses. Those times that he did do something wrong he was willing to accept the consequences. But he loathed taking the rap for something he didn't do.

The Chief said, "Forget it." He believed Brent, but not at face value. He had checked his breath when he got to the station and didn't smell any beer like he did on the others. "Come with me," he said.

Brent followed the Chief into his office, wondering what he was planning. It had to be something he wanted kept private, or he would have stayed in the conference room with the others. The Chief shut the door behind them and indicated a seat for Brent.

"I was gone," the Chief started, "when you guys left the station. But one of our cops, who was here in the station at the time, told me that things looked heated between Dylan and Connor just before everyone left. You mind telling me what I missed?" he asked.

So, Brent thought, now I know why the privacy. "Yeah, it was tense for a minute. I thought Dylan was going to take a swing at him at one point. It's why we went to The Outlaw, to cool things down."

Brent explained the missing photograph, and how Dylan figured out that Connor had come back to visit Jesse and baby Dylan. He told him that Connor admitted to it and that it was why he was obsessed with finding out what happened to Jesse.

"Christ," the Chief said. "I guess that explains Connor's real reason for being here, instead of letting the usual guys deal with it. I have the feeling this thing is going to be pretty tough on him."

"I have a feeling it might be tough for us all," Brent replied.

"You're probably right," the Chief agreed. He thought for a moment then added, "You think we should report this, to Connor's boss or something? I mean just in case our asses get busted along with his if the shit hits the fan?"

"I'd rather not," Brent answered with a pained look. The Chief saw the look and frowned.

"You look like there is something more to this than I know," he said. Brent knew what he meant by that, and he was right, but he waited before replying so that he could come up with the words to explain it to him.

"It's like this," Brent told him. "I am worried about Dylan. I think he needs to resolve his mom's death more than Connor does, for different reasons of course. His life has just been turned upside down, and in spite of that, or because of it, I have begun to see some changes in him. Some good changes, like the fact that he is so committed to something, namely Connor's mission. He's not the sort of person who normally shows so much interest in aspects of his life, if you know what I mean."

"Yeah, I know what you mean," the Chief said. "And I see what you are talking about. I've noticed how different he is lately." He thought for another second then said, "I'm going along with you on this, I'm not reporting Connor. But I want you to know why." He fell silent, trying to gather his words, trying to broach a subject with Brent that he'd tried to speak about many times, but had never been brave enough to get the words out. Brent waited patiently, noticing the Chief's discomfort.

"Look," the Chief said after deciding, once again, that the subject could wait, "it's just that there is a personal reason I am going along with you on this, so make sure nothing goes wrong that gets us in trouble, OK?"

"I'll do what I can, but if the shit really hits the fan I don't think anyone but Connor is going to take a hit. It's his ball game, not ours," Brent assured him.

"Yeah, you're probably right."

CHAPTER TWENTY SEVEN

THE REGIONAL JET landed at the smallest international airport that Deputy U.S. Marshal Ted Stanley had ever seen. At his side was the reason he made the flight, a witness named James Nightingale, who evidently required some form of either protection or custody.

As the two men deplaned they were met by Jake Tillman, Deputy U.S. Marshal, who displayed a badge proving the fact. Whereupon, Deputy Stanley remanded custody of James Nightingale to Deputy Tillman, who took over the responsibility of babysitting James. Jake drove his new consignment to the Flatrock police station, where he was introduced to Connor.

James had never asked to be flown to Montana under U.S Marshal escort, but somehow that was the deal and now here he was.. He was not sure how that became the deal, since his only demand was that he be told what happened to Jesse before he told of his experience of being handed the picture in the gas station in Vegas. But if the U.S. Marshals wanted to pay his way to Montana before talking, that was fine with him.

Connor and Jake escorted James to a small room inside the police station, which looked a lot like an interrogation room to James. He was introduced to the local police chief, Charlie Armstrong, who offered him a cup of coffee, which James accepted. He was then asked to wait, which, not having much choice, he did.

———

The dark haired woman watched the police station from inside her rented car, parked in a store parking lot across the street. She had been debating what to do since the arrival of the Deputies but could not decide on a course of action. It seemed that every option she weighed carried too much danger with it. It was the worst dilemma she had ever experienced, right up to the point that she saw the young Deputy escort James into the station, creating an all new worst dilemma.

One thing was certain, she was going to have to decide soon to either run for her life or walk through the station doors and ask for mercy.

Charlie joined the others in his office, where they watched James on the monitor. James did nothing but sit there, and it didn't take long for them to realize they wouldn't learn anything by staring at a closed circuit feed of a sitting man. Connor asked Charlie to give them a few minutes to gather in the conference room and then bring James in for the interview.

James was brought into the conference room, where the Chief introduced him to Connor, Brent and Dylan. As previously agreed upon, Dylan had been introduced simply as 'Dylan', no mention of his relation to James.

James took a seat and Connor started the conversation by saying, "I hear that you have information about Brenda, but that you won't share it until we give you some information you want. Is that true?"

"Yes."

"What kind of information do you want from us?"

"I want to know if anything happened to her." He was holding back his emotions only with extreme willpower.

"It isn't going to happen that way," Connor told him. "We are not at liberty to give out any information about her at this point. You tell us whatever it is you've got to say first, and then, if we want to, we will tell you what we can. It seems to me that you are here out of concern for Brenda," Connor said, using her former name in case James wasn't aware of her new name of Jessica. "So if you really care about her, you will tell us what you need to, if for her benefit only."

Dylan watched as James was being questioned, trying to see if they resembled each other. He looked to see what his mom might have seen in him, and to see if he had a 'connection' with him. And basically looking at a dad he had never seen before. He observed his face closely and could see that there were some similarities in their traits. The hair color was the same – dirty blond. They were about the same height. Overall Dylan could concede that they were related.

James was the right age to be his father but he looked a bit younger than his forty years. Dylan knew he had been a drug dealer, so he had assumed he was also a user of drugs. Now he wondered how a drug user could look youthful. All of the druggies he had ever seen were aged well beyond their actual years, and were usually very thin. James did have that in common with druggies though, he was thin.

He was dressed in well worn jeans, a polo shirt that was too large for his skinny frame and Nike tennis shoes. All of which was not exactly dirty, but appeared to be on the verge of it. His skin and his hair was the same way –

almost dirty looking. On close inspection though, it was clear that he was very clean and well groomed. He was one of those people who have that natural, but unfounded, appearance of being a slob.

What few people knew, was that James had never taken drugs. Like every person his age he had encountered the temptations of drugs; 'friends' who wanted to share them with him, girls who wanted to get high and have sex with him, joints passed around to him at parties and concerts, and once, right after his release from prison, he even had a state psychiatrist recommend pot and other controlled substances as a way to smooth his transition back into society. He left that appointment with a prescription for anti-depressants that he would never fill. But none of the temptations or advices were ever more powerful than his reasons for not taking drugs of any kind.

Few people in the world who knew Jame's reasons for not taking drugs, Bennett Alivio was one of them. Desperate for a job to support his new bride, a friend had referred him to an interview with Bennett. James explained his reasons for avoiding drugs and Bennett, knowing the hazards of hiring users all too well, hired him immediately.

By the time James got out of prison he'd learned enough to know he wasn't going back to selling drugs. But his life had never prepared him for another type of career so he had to work at unskilled labor jobs. He paid his bills and behaved himself. He dreamed of Brenda every day and held her memory in his heart as his only true regret in life. It was that passion for her that was the reason he was here in Montana. He was scared for her.

"I'm sorry," James told Connor. "You're right, I am here because I'm worried. I'm not trying to play games with you. It doesn't matter anyway because I've already figured it out. If everything was ok you wouldn't be here, you for sure wouldn't bring me here, and no one in the Marshal's office would even acknowledge that they've ever heard of Brenda. So I'll tell you what I've got and maybe it will help you. I hope it does."

He shoved an envelope across the table to Connor who opened it and looked at a photograph. He was visibly shaken by what he saw. It was the missing photo from Jesse's house. But if seeing the photo shook him up, what he was about to hear would rattle him to the core.

James spoke evenly and factually when he said, "A man approached me at a gas station in Vegas and told me I didn't have to worry about my canary bitch singing any more, and then he handed me that photo and walked away. Who is the baby in that photo?"

Connor merely put the picture back down on the table in front of James, then got up from his chair without saying anything. On his way to the exit he said softly, "That's your son, Dylan." Then he walked out and shut the door behind him.

James and Dylan stared at each other and there was a connection there. They both noticed it. It was an awkward moment to say the least. What do you say to a father you never met? What do you say to a son you never met, or never even knew existed? They said nothing for a while, and then James said the only logical thing.

"I don't know what to say."

"Me neither. Do we have to say anything right now?"

"No, I guess not," James said, relieved.

"Can I see that picture?" Dylan asked.

James slid the photo over to him. It was the missing photo from Jesse's house. Jake looked over Dylan's shoulder, wanting to see what had caused such a serious reaction in Connor.

Unsure when Connor would return, Jake took over his role and asked James, "Did you recognize the man who contacted you and gave you the photo?" It was obvious now that whoever gave James the photo had been in Jesse's house. Or he, at least, had connections to the person who had been, and they needed to find that person.

"Yeah, but I don't know where. I mean he looks familiar, I know I've seen him somewhere but shit, I can't figure out where. I have been trying hard to remember but no luck yet. Can someone tell me what's happening now?" James asked.

In light of what James had just told them, Jake figured there was no reason not to let him in on what was going on, so he told James about the accident.

James didn't get up and leave like Connor did. Instead he stayed in his chair and nodded his head up and down, like he was nodding 'yes', only when people do that it is not because they are saying yes. They do it after hearing bad news because.... well, who the hell knows why they do that. For whatever reason, James was doing it. When he stopped doing it, he looked at Dylan and said, "I'm really sorry."

It was only his masculine sense of pride that prevented James from breaking down at that moment, like he had at home. His one true love, his sole regret in life, his motivation towards decency and his inspiration for efforts to rise to higher levels of human greatness, his beacon, dead and gone. It was more than an ordinary man should be required to handle, and he was no ordinary man. The speaker of the words he heard next would become the only life ring capable of bringing him his life back. His son. His and Brenda's.

"Yeah, me too," Dylan said. He had watched James' reaction to the news of his mom's death, and although he tried, there was no way James could disguise the pain. It was as if a light in James soul had been suddenly extinguished. So palpable was the sudden darkening that, for a moment, Dylan's own world had dimmed. The same experience he had suffered when he had first heard the news of his mom's death. James and Dylan's worlds had collided and would continue to merge for some time. Ironic and sad that it was precipitated by Jesse's death.

Dylan returned to examining the photograph, thinking he might see something in it that he hadn't noticed during all those years it had hung in his house. But there was nothing new.

Jake spoke up and told James, "We would like you to stay and see if we can't get an identity on the guy who gave you the picture. Can you do that?"

James cleared his throat. "No problem," he said

"Have you arranged for a place to stay?"

"No."

"We'll get you a room at the same motel we are in."

"Thanks."

CHAPTER TWENTY EIGHT

AFTER LEAVING THE conference room, Connor walked to the bathroom, where he washed his face with cold water in hopes that it would stop the sweating and hide the tears. The guilt he felt was crushing. The information James brought with him was bad. Worse than bad. The implications were almost more than he could contemplate.

He stood over the sink, supporting himself with one hand on each side of it, looking down into the bowl like someone who was getting ready to throw up in it. But he wasn't going to throw up, he was just standing there, looking.

Dylan walked into the bathroom and saw Connor standing at the sink. Assuming, incorrectly, that he was finishing washing up, he waited a moment. After several minutes Connor still hadn't moved. He didn't use the sink, he didn't look up, and he didn't speak. Connor's true condition was much worse than anything he'd expected. Dylan felt compelled to say something, anything. "The other guys are waiting for you in the conference room. They're not sure what to do next," he said.

Connor didn't move or speak.

Dylan said, "Wait here, I'll be right back." Although it seemed unlikely Connor would go anywhere.

Dylan returned to the bathroom a moment later. Connor hadn't moved a fraction of an inch. "I told Jake to take James to the motel and drop him off for the night and come back here," he said. "Is that ok?" He was hoping for a response but it didn't. The statue that was Connor remained rock solid.

Dylan knew Connor was feeling the added guilt that James' report and the photograph brought along with it. He understood that. But he didn't understand the total meltdown. Connor should be stronger, he was a seasoned U.S. Deputy Marshal for heavens' sake. When Dylan's mom died he didn't melt down this badly, and she was his mom, not a short term love affair. He said exactly that to Connor and got a response.

"You didn't kill her, I did," Connor said without moving.

"You don't know that," Dylan said.

"You're the one who practically accused me of killing her, and that was before we knew what James told us," Connor replied.

"Yeah, I was mad, but that was because you broke the rules when you came here, which might have given us away. And if I find out she died because of that.., I don't know what I'll do but we don't know that your visit had any influence on it. That is part of what I had to figure out at The Outlaw. You came here twenty years ago and anything could have happened in that amount of time. And I realized that there could be a hundred other explanations and since we don't know what happened yet, I couldn't rightfully blame you, and neither can you. In spite of what James told us, we still don't know. So cowboy up."

"Cowboy up? Where did that come from?"

"It's a saying in Montana that means to get tough, stop whining, man up, don't be a baby, get over it, be a ....."

Connor interrupted him, "Yeah, I know what it means. I just didn't expect you to say it."

"Why, don't I look like a cowboy to you?" Dylan was relieved to be having an almost normal conversation with Connor.

"No, not really. Are you?"

"No, not really."

"So there you go."

"Where?"

"Where what?"

"Where am I going?"

"This is getting crazy," Connor said, sounding almost normal again. Then he asked, "What time is it?"

"The Outlaw?" Dylan replied.

"Why not. We need to make some plans and I can't think of a better place to do it. After all, we are probably headed down the outlaw trail ourselves in some ways."

"I'm sold," Dylan said. "Let's go strip the blue off Brent and go."

Brent and the Chief were waiting for Dylan and Conner when they returned to the conference room.

Dylan asked the Chief, "Can Brent come out and play now?"

"What's up?" the Chief wanted to know.

"War council."

"Where?"

"The Outlaw." The Chief's face fell.

"Great."

Connor said, "It was my idea, Charlie. I'd like to make some plans and it seemed like a good place. You coming?"

The Chief considered it for a moment and said, "What the hell. But no uniforms and no department vehicles. Brent can go change and come back to pick us up in his personal car."

"Great," Connor said. "Where's Jake?"

"He's taking James home," the Chief said.

"Ok, I will call Jake and tell him to meet us there," Connor said.

"Tell him to bring James along too," Dylan requested. He had a feeling that James may have something to contribute to the war council.

"You got it," Connor said.

CHAPTER TWENTY NINE

THE 'WAR COUNCIL' at The Outlaw consisted of Connor, Jake, the Chief, Brent, Dylan and James. Connor was elected as leader by unanimous nomination. James was on probation but no one mentioned that in front of him. The gathering took place around a pitcher of beer and this time Brent could hoist a pint.

The easiest part of the agenda was taken care of first. Jake was to oversee the review of the original reports of the accident. He would be using the NCIC and other agencies to gain as much information as possible on the car, the driver, the witnesses and any other known facts or pieces of evidence so far.

His first priority would be to help James track down the identity of the man who gave him the photo at the gas station in Las Vegas. Whoever the man was, he was a connection to the most damning piece of evidence they had. In fact it was their only real evidence, and was their sole excuse for believing that their protected witness, Jesse, turned out to be not so well protected after all.

The Chief volunteered as Jake's liaison, to work with him on the local level, as well as helping the rest of the team with their local needs.

Connor considered including Bennett as a prime suspect, in need of investigation, but decided, once again, against mentioning him. Jake, who was aware of Bennett's role as a person of interest, thought about him as well but assumed there was a reason for Connor not bringing up his name.

Connor did have such a reason, but it wasn't easy to explain. He only knew that he felt a strong sense that he should hold off. He was mystified by the feeling and the decision, but it seemed inexplicably vital not to expose Bennett at this time.

The hardest part of their planning turned out to be determining exactly what Dylan and Brent would be doing. Their job description was a little bit nebulous. It's kind of hard to lay out a precise procedure for something that you don't know how to control, such as random voices from the dead, chance clairvoyant moments, mental or spiritual 'connections', forgotten memories, strokes of luck and generally, things that you can't take hold of with your own two hands. In his younger years Connor would have called it 'things that go bump in the night'.

As a solution to the difficulties of making plans for Dylan and Brent, the supreme and fearless war council leader, Connor, tackled the subject head on.

"Anyone got any ideas about how to do this?" he asked.

Dylan thought it might come to this. Not because he picked it up out of 'thin air', but just by using pure logic. No one can plan these sorts of things.

"There can be no master plan other than this," Dylan said. "We go wherever our 'hunches' take us."

The word hunches seemed to be more acceptable and better understood by people in law enforcement, and those at the table nodded their heads in vague agreement with the plan, while secretly thinking that the less they had to know about it the better.

But Dylan had a different idea about that. He felt they should have a more complete understanding. and he felt it was his duty to impart that understanding.

"I've already started following a line of hunches," he explained, "and I think it would be best for me to continue in the direction they are leading me. Brent is also on a line of hunches of his own and they overlap with mine, so we should work together on that. By the way, there is something I should ask all of you. Have any of you heard any 'voices' or 'words' from my mom?"

Connor hesitated for a moment, wondering how Dylan knew that he had been hearing Jesse's voice recently. He thought he had hidden it pretty well.

"Yes, as a matter of fact, I have," Connor said. "How did you know that?"

"I didn't know for sure, but I thought it was a pretty good guess that you did, since you were close to her." Then he told Connor about himself and Brent hearing her words.

"As a matter of fact," Dylan explained further, "those words are the hunches that Brent and I are following. And now I am even more certain that they are the hunches we should be following. What were the words you heard?"

"She said, 'I wish that someday you could pick berries with Dylan'," Connor told him.

"When did you hear it?"

"Two days ago, and then again last night"

"Did it mean anything to you?"

"Yes, it's one of the things she said to me when I came back for my visit, just after you were born. We were out in the woods picking berries at the time. I had a hard time imagining why she would say something like that. You were such a wee thing then that I couldn't picture you picking berries. I guess you could say I was much more short sighted than she was." His eyes began to well up and he was struggling for control. Most people are a lot more short sighted than my mom, Dylan thought.

"What else did she say to you on that visit, besides the normal conversation stuff?" Dylan asked.

The question reminded Connor of something he had spent nearly twenty years trying not to think about. His heart broke each and every time he recalled being with her. It was true that, on one hand, he felt wonderful being with Jesse. Together they were 'comfortable' and while with her he felt as if he was whole.

On the other hand, there had been a rather unfortunate reality to consider. In truth there were several points of reality which he chose to ignore because they were too disenchanting. One of them was the fact that he had to lie continuously to his supervisor in order to keep up the charade that he was somewhere completely different than where he actually was. He had to lie to him because he knew being with Jesse in Montana was wrong. It went against every aspect of his duty as a Deputy Marshal. He was supposed to be keeping witnesses out of danger and protecting their location and identity, not making social calls to them.

And then there was the real fact that he could never stay there with her, as he most fervently desired. The knowledge that he would have to leave her again soon, and probably forever, was the worst aspect of the whole trip. Then there was the other torturous factor, the sleeping arrangements.

Knowing that it would make their imminent separation more unbearable if they 'consummated' his visit, they agreed not to sleep together. They never had, never could, and never would sleep together. During his visit he slept on the couch, or rather he lay awake on the couch at night, thinking about Jesse in her bed, in the next room. So close, and yet impossibly distant. And it wasn't even that he wanted sex that badly, which he definitely did. He would have settled for, and been blissful just lying next to her and holding her. It was as if they were two magnets, held apart, straining with the natural law of attraction towards each other. The infinite urge to do the impossible was a nefarious and finely honed torture.

He answered Dylan's question, "She once said, 'Dylan has a gift. Remember that when you guys become friends'. I didn't think much of it at the time, again because you were so young, and I thought that all new moms thought their kids were gifted."

Dylan said, "If you think of anything else, let me know." Then on another guess he asked James, "How about you James, you hear anything?"

"Sure I did. I heard her say, 'Be a good thorn'. Damned if I know what the hell that means, but it don't sound good to me." James didn't know what it meant, but Dylan had a good idea.

"When?"

"The other day."

The Chief seemed a little exasperated when he asked, "What the hell is going on here? This shit you guys are talking about is not just hunches. Will someone please explain this to me?"

Brent stepped up to the plate and said, "Sorry boss. I should have told you earlier, but it's not something that is easy to explain. You remember yesterday when you said, 'You know Dylan'?"

"Yes."

"Well, think about what you meant by that question. You were aware that we had a special connection, right?"

"Yeah, I guess that's right," he said reluctantly.

"Ok, it seems Jesse had a connection something like that with all of us, except maybe you, because you didn't really even know her. And, apparently, all of us have been getting her voice in our heads lately. Or hearing words from her, or remembering words she said to us at one time. We don't really know. That's the part that is hard to explain. But somehow it seems to us that her words might provide a key to solving things. Don't ask me how. So we're calling it a hunch, of sorts, I guess."

The Chief still looked a bit disconcerted when he asked Connor, "What do you think of all this?"

"I'm with them. I knew Jesse too well I guess." He seemed to think that that would explain everything. The Chief shook his head in disbelief.

"Christ," he said. But Connor wasn't through.

"There's more, Charlie," he said. "I'm convinced that we need more than just routine police work to solve Jesse's death and that's why I wanted this meeting. We need whatever 'gift' Dylan, or his mom, or anyone else has. You don't have to buy into it if you don't want to. We still need to do the routine police work and you are a huge asset to us there."

The Chief had one more question, "Do you guys believe that Jesse is talking to you from the great beyond?"

In unison they answered, "NO." And hoped it was true.

The mood grew tense while they watched the Chief digest what he'd just been told about the 'hunches'. Several minutes went by and he sighed, some of the tension leaving him. "What time is it?" he asked.

No one laughed, or started pouring beer. Instead they looked at each other hoping one of them would know what the Chief meant by the question. Did he just want to know the time or was he talking about another beer? The Chief saw the uncertainty in their eyes

"You're not the only assholes to use that line," he said. "I've been using it since before you were born. So someone pour us another round, I think I need one."

They relaxed and let out a laugh while Jake poured the next round. Now they could get down to business. But before they got serious again, Dylan couldn't resist asking the Chief, "So, Chief, did you hear my mom's voice?"

And, in turn, the Chief couldn't resist saying, "Hell yes, she said her son was a gifted asshole," causing more laughter.

When the laughing subsided the Chief turned serious and said, "I've been sitting here listening to what you have been saying. I don't know what I believe or don't believe about all the psychic shit. Or maybe I should say I don't know what I'm willing to admit that I believe. But I do know this. You're mom was one hell of a woman, and just hearing about the things she did and said is enough to convince me that she knew things that most people don't. She had an uncanny foresight for sure. And I've also figured out that she had a hell of a lot of courage. She deserves the same courage from us, and our total commitment to resolving what happened to her. I'll go along with anything you guys say." He also thought, but didn't say of course, that he was starting to understand Connor's dire need to find out what really happened to Jesse.

"Here's to Jesse," Brent said as he raised his glass. They clanked their glasses together and drank to Jesse's memory.

"Ok, so now what?" Connor asked after a brief silence. Dylan had already figured that out.

"Tonight we drink beer, eat pub grub and hang out for a while. Tomorrow Jake and James get to work and you guys leave the 'psychic shit' to me and Brent. We meet here at the end of every day to brief each other and compare notes. OK?" They agreed and a good time was had by all at The Outlaw. Once again, when it was time to leave they had a hard time convincing Jake.

"It's not even two o'clock yet," he protested. "We got a few more hours."

Connor had to intervene again and told Jake that he needed to drive him and James to the motel. Now, not later. Jake relented and they got in the rental car. He took them back to the motel while Brent taxied Dylan and the Chief. He dropped the Chief at the station and then took Dylan home. This time Dylan didn't mention anything to Brent about staying overnight and Brent agreed to pick up Dylan in the morning. Brent took that as a sign that Dylan was recovering, and although that was true, it was not the real reason Dylan didn't mention it.

As soon as Brent drove away Dylan got in his own car and drove to James' motel. He'd been ignoring the situation between them all day. It was time to deal with it. He had to do it for his sake, for James sake, and most of all for his mom's sake.

CHAPTER THIRTY

AFTER ARRIVING BACK in his motel room, James couldn't help thinking about Dylan. He decided that it would be a good idea to face up to him and try to work something out. He didn't know how, but he had to try.

Not having Dylan's contact information, James walked down the motel hallway to Jake's room and asked for help. Jake used his cell phone to call Dylan, but there was no answer.

"Sorry," he told James. "If he calls back, I'll come get you."

"Ok, thanks," James said.

As he approached the door to his room he saw Dylan standing in front of it.

"Hi, I just asked Jake to call you but you weren't home," James said to him.

"Imagine that," Dylan said good naturedly.

"Yeah, come on in," James said.

They sat silently in the room and looking at each other, neither knowing how to break the ice.

"Sorry about not saying much to you today," James finally said. "I wasn't trying to ignore you. It was just sort of awkward and I didn't really know how to handle it."

"Yeah, I know what you mean, I felt the same way." After another moment of silence Dylan said, "I guess I'm still not sure what to do. I mean what do you say to a father you never met?"

"Shit, man, how do you think I feel?" James asked awkwardly. "At least you knew you had a dad, somewhere anyway. You got a little head start on me. Hell, I had no idea you even existed until today." When he finished speaking he instantly regretted everything he had said.

"Well, you're right about that I suppose," Dylan responded. "But what if you had known I existed all this time. How would you like it if you spent over twenty years wondering about me, not knowing who I was, or where, and wondering how and why did I disappear in the first place, and did I hate you or still love you, would you ever see me again, or would I just be a word – son – that you heard once? Yeah, I got a big head start on you for that shit, because you're right – I knew I had a dad, somewhere."

Dylan never anticipated getting this upset, it just flooded out of him on its own. Feeling guilty about the outburst, he froze up, unable to speak.

Shit, shit, shit, James mentally scolded himself, I fucked up, I fucked up, I fucked up. Damn it, I should have kept my mouth shut. I knew I should have kept my damn mouth shut. Idiot, idiot, idiot. I ain't saying another word man, not another word. He was so frenzied that he was rocking his upper body back and forth like some kind of blithering idiot in an institution.

They stared at each other, feeling their own unique shock, and both wanting to bolt from the room, but unable to move. When Dylan thought he couldn't take it anymore he stood up.

"I gotta use the head," Dylan mumbled. Locked safely away in the bathroom he stood over the sink with his hands on each side of it supporting himself and looked into the mirror. He laughed spontaneously at the image. Anyone watching him would have thought he belonged in a straight jacket. But he hadn't laughed as a maniac might have, he had laughed because when he saw himself in the mirror he also saw Connor in the station bathroom posing in just the same way that he was now. He sighed with some relief and returned to the room with James.

The look of suffering on James face saddened Dylan. "Maybe we better start over and start slower," he said.

"Yeah, ok," James said tentatively. He was heartened a tiny bit by Dylan's improved mood, but still pretty sure that if he opened his mouth again he would screw things up.

"Maybe we should just start with simple questions like, where do you work?" Dylan asked him.

"I work in a casino in Vegas doing maintenance," James answered carefully. "It's a dead end, just pay the bills job. What job do you have?"

"I think I might be out of a job right now, or at least soon will be."

"Oh yeah? What were you doing?"

"Same thing, dead end, just pay the bills job. I worked for a national chain store called World Imports."

James reacted to that with a slight frown, which Dylan did not fail to notice, recalling, from his earlier drug days, that the World Imports chain was owned by some mafia business men and was used to hide a few of their less than legal activities. He didn't mention this to Dylan, figuring that World Imports was a big chain with a lot of stores and a lot of employees, and that Dylan was probably just another employee. "Your mom did the right thing you know," James said, changing the subject.

"When?"

"When she turned me in."

"How do you figure?" Not that he disagreed, but he was surprised that James would think so.

"It probably saved our lives," he said, then realized his mistake. "I mean at the time," he added.

"Don't worry, I know what you mean," Dylan said.

"I never held it against her," James continued. "I was young and stupid, and in love when we met. I never stopped loving her though, and that's why I never wanted to find her when I got out of prison. I mean I wanted to see her and be with her again, but I loved her enough to respect what she did and stay away from her. And now I really feel guilty. She might be alive today if we had never hooked up. I'm a little bit pissed, though, that she never told me she was pregnant. I would have liked to have known you all along. It seems that you turned out real well."

"You mean except for the years when you were in prison?"

"Yeah, I guess," James said, looking chagrined. "I really fucked up."

That reminded Dylan of something he wanted to ask James. "Don't take this the wrong way; I know you were a drug dealer, but did you take drugs too? It's not a big deal if you don't want to talk about it. I mean I don't want to pry into private things and all."

"Nah, that's ok. I guess you are the only family I got now, so you have the right to know." He hesitated a moment while trying to get his thoughts together. It had never been an easy explanation, and it was no easier this time.

"There is this thing I got," he started uncertainly. "It's an emotional problem I guess. I have had it forever I think. Whatever it is, it freaks me out. Sometimes I feel like I'm hallucinating, sort of, I guess. I don't know man, it's really hard to describe, but I feel like I can see myself. It doesn't happen often, and it happened a lot more when I was a kid."

Dylan interrupted him, "You can see yourself? How do you mean?"

"Good question. I'm not sure how to say it. It's sort of like I am in the air and looking down at myself. At my body. Like one time when I was just a kid I was asleep and I was watching myself in bed sleeping. I was trying and trying to get up, but I couldn't. I started to panic and then suddenly I was awake, in my bed and gasping for air. I was shaking and sweating and my heart was racing. I mean I was scared shitless, man. I was so young then. It really terrified me."

His description made Dylan think back on the dream he had the other night. Different dream, same physical reaction.

But Dylan still hadn't made the connection between the incident James just described and his reason for not taking drugs.

"Were you on drugs at the time or something?" He asked.

"No man, you're not listening. I was too young to take drugs when that happened, and I have never taken a drug in my life. And almost no alcohol either."

"Wow, that's impressive. I didn't know that," Dylan said, surprised.

"I know, I already said you weren't listening," he replied indignantly.

"Sorry!" Dylan quipped. "Please continue."

"Yeah, ok. So no, I wasn't on drugs when it happened. But a few years later we were watching those drug education films in school and the people in the movie who took drugs were hallucinating and they were looking at themselves, just like I did that time when I was young. Those people in the film ended up in the loony bin. That scared me because it was very much how I felt when it happened to me and I hadn't even taken a drug. So I guess the short answer is that I'm just too chicken to take anything." He looked at Dylan sheepishly.

Dylan thought about his recent close encounters with insanity and how frightening that was.

"Don't worry, I know exactly how it feels."

"Really?" James asked with happy surprise.

"Yeah, really," Dylan said reassuringly.

James thought of something else he wanted to say to Dylan. "Your mom was the first person I ever told about my drug fears. Her reaction to the story was one of the main things that made me love her so much. Actually she didn't react at all, she just accepted it without judgment of any kind. She accepted me completely and loved me the same in spite of it. It was like, with her, I could just be. She could just let me be me, and it was ok." He reflected on something for a moment and then said, "Hell of a woman." There was sadness in his voice, and tears welled in his eyes.

"Yeah, that's no lie," Dylan agreed. "So why did she leave you?" he asked. "I mean it sounds like she must have loved you and all."

"I thought about that for a long time. I never got a chance to ask her but I think I figured it out eventually. She didn't leave *me,* she left the drug ring. She knew I couldn't get out, but she was unwilling to be in it. Can't blame her for that."

"No, I guess not," Dylan agreed again.

"Still, I wish I never hooked up with her. I would give up all of our happy and loving time together if I knew it would prevent her death. I feel so guilty it's killing me." Dylan knew that James was looking at Jesse's death from the same fantasy world of hind sight that Connor was.

"You're not the only person feeling responsible for her death," Dylan said. "But beating yourself up about it won't bring her back. You didn't kill her, I didn't kill her, and none of us killed her. Only the killer killed her, and the only thing we can do for her now is to find out who is really responsible and exact revenge on them, with extreme prejudice."

"You wouldn't turn them over to your cop friends?" James asked with surprise in his voice.

"Only if they were inclined to follow my mode of justice."

James let out a brief laugh and said, "Now you're starting to sound like your old man."

The ice might not have been broken yet, but it was getting thinner, so Dylan asked, "Really? You'd take out the perp?"

"I would consider it the greatest accomplishment of my life. It might even come close to some sort of redemption."

They were silent for a couple of minutes, after which Dylan said, "We need to concentrate on finding who really killed my mom, and I need your help. Did you plan to stay the course, or were you just going to make your report, find out what happened and go home?"

"You're a Montana boy, have you ever heard the saying, 'I ride for the brand'?"

"Yes, but how have you heard of it?" Dylan wondered. The saying was usually known as a cowboy idiom, and James seemed more like a city boy.

"I read Louis L'Amour western novels."

"Yeah," Dylan said. "So what's your answer?"

"I'm riding for the brand."

"Good, I'm glad you will help. But what about your job?"

"It's a dead end, remember?"

"Yeah, right." Something else they had in common, he said to himself.

Dylan wondered how long the U.S. Marshal would foot the bill for James' room. If they stopped paying for him it might make it hard for him to stay on and help.

"Why don't you stay at my place?" Dylan asked, explaining his reasons.

"If you don't mind I'd really like that," James answered.

"I only have one bedroom so you would have to sleep on the couch or maybe we could set up a bed in the living room. Would that be alright?"

"Sure."

"Ok, you're probably paid up for tonight so I'll pick you up in the morning."

CHAPTER THIRTY ONE

THAT NIGHT JOAN felt as lonely as she had ever felt. And as guilty. She missed Dylan, and because she hadn't heard from him since she left his house in a huff, she feared the worst, that she'd lost him.

Several times she picked up the phone to call him, but put it back down before making the call. Maybe she was too afraid of what he would say when he answered. Or maybe she was more afraid that he wouldn't answer at all.

Always before, when she was upset, she went to her mom for comfort and reassurance. But she couldn't even do that now. Her mom had moved out of town to Las Vegas and she had tried to call her but there was no answer.

She laid on her bed, silent tears wetting her pillow, until she finally slept.

———————————

The dark haired woman, parked in front of Joan's house, spilled quiet tears on the sweatshirt she was using as a pillow. It killed her to ignore Joan's call on her cell phone, but she was too scared to answer it. She was exhausted but it was a long time before sleep found her.

CHAPTER THIRTY TWO

THE NEXT MORNING James sat in the motel lobby nursing a cup of coffee while waiting for Dylan to pick him up. His packed suitcase sat on the floor next to him Jake noticed him, and the packed bag, on his way out to the car. Last he heard, James had agreed to stay on and help ID the mysterious photo messenger. He wondered if there was a problem.

"Where are you going?" he asked.

"To Dylan's. He's letting me stay at his house." Jake nodded, seeming pleased by the idea.

"Sounds good," he said. "Are you still coming to the station this morning?"

"Yep, I'll be there," James confirmed.

Dylan drove up, James threw his bags in the back seat of the car, got into the front seat, and they drove off. Jake walked to his rental car and drove it up to the motel room door, where Connor got in and they drove off. The work day had begun.

When Dylan arrived at his house with James, Brent was there waiting for them. They dropped Jame's bags in the house and rode with Brent to the station. James was met by Jake and the two got to work searching for a photo of James mystery man. They were using Jake's fancy new computer. Supposedly it was bigger in some way that geeks understand, which made it better. Jake said it would perform searches quickly and had the capacity to analyze millions of mug shots, all of which failed miserably to thrill James.

Connor gathered up Dylan and Brent, leading them into the conference room. "Ok, gentlemen," he said. "What should we do first?"

Dylan raised his eyebrows and said, "This is a joke right? You guys are kidding." He had his hands raised, palms up, waiting for an explanation.

Connor frowned and gave Brent a questioning look, hoping he could explain. Brent was as clueless as Connor and they both looked back at Dylan hoping he would clarify his remark. Dylan clarified exactly jack, forcing Brent to ask him.

"I don't follow you, Dylan. Are we doing something you didn't expect here?"

"You can't possibly expect me to start my first day of police work without coffee and donuts can you?" Dylan demanded.

Brent and Connor were surprised by his question, and yet a bit relieved that he hadn't completely lost his mind overnight.

"We don't usually start our days like that, Dylan," Brent lectured him. "That is just TV bullshit. So can we get started here?"

"Hell no," Dylan said belligerently. "I'm not doing a thing until I get coffee, and especially donuts." He crossed his arms across his chest to prove his resolve on the issue. Connor was nonplussed.

This is a joke right? You're kidding aren't you?"

"No, I am not joking. I mean it, no donuts, no work. I'll even go buy them if you pay. Honestly I was expecting them to be here already, waiting for us when we arrived."

At that moment the Chief walked in. Before he could speak, Dylan looked up at him and said, "What kind of a rinky dink operation are you guys running here, Chief?"

The Chief looked over at Connor. "Is there some kind of problem here, guys?" he asked.

Instead of answering the Chief, Brent said, "For Christ sake, Dylan, come on. I mean, I know you are going through a rough time and all, but jeez, give us a break. It isn't the Chief's job to supply the department with donuts. OK?"

"Gotta be someone's job, and if they aren't doing it, it's the Chief's responsibility to make sure they do. Just give me the money, I already said I would do it," Dylan responded.

"Am I hearing this right?" the Chief asked. "Is there some kind of problem with donuts?"

A bit shamefaced Brent told the Chief, "Dylan won't start working until he's had some coffee and donuts." Brent expected an unpleasant reaction to this by the Chief, who, unexpectedly, burst out laughing.

"Well," he said. "What are you waiting for, Officer Butler? Go get us all some donuts and coffee. I like the kind with sprinkles on them." He turned around and walked back out the door, still laughing.

"I'll be right back," Brent said. "Don't start without me," he said facetiously. He obviously didn't take Dylan's demands as humorously as the Chief.

With no concern for Brent's ire, Dylan said, "We won't, but hurry up and get back, we got a lot of work to do here." A slight smirk betrayed that he was enjoying Brent's annoyance a little too much.

"Don't push it, O'Connor," Brent threatened as he left the office.

"You were already pushing it, Dylan," Connor said after Brent left the room. "And you were enjoying it as well." Dylan considered the statement to be a little bit like a spanking – if he had been a young boy.

"Brent is a big boy, Connor," Dylan said easily. "He can take care of himself. Besides, we grew up together. We do this shit all the time. If I quit doing it he would think I didn't love him any more."

Connor laughed and said, "Point taken. Are you really going to wait for donuts or do you want to get some work done while we are waiting for Brent to get back?"

"You don't really think I would waste a bunch of time doing nothing just because of a lousy donut while my mother's killer is still walking the streets do you?" Dylan asked him.

This was too much for Connor. He opened his mouth like he was going to speak but no sounds came out. Instead, all he could do was shake his head with his eyes closed tightly.

Dylan took pity on him and said, "I have been working all night, and all morning and ever since I got here. I was never waiting for donuts. It's just that this is the first time I ever did work in a police station and I thought it would be really cool to have some donuts. And I really could use some coffee."

"Yeah, ok, I sort of see that. If you have been working all this time, what have you been doing? Exactly? Besides irritating all of us."

"I've been thinking," Dylan told him.

"Good for you," Connor said. "I've been thinking too, but I'm not calling it work. So tell me what your thinking has accomplished."

"Well, not much now that you put like that. But like we said yesterday, we need to figure out what it is I can do that will help us. So I have been thinking about what I can do, exactly," Dylan told him. Connor said nothing, waiting for Dylan to relate the results of his thinking. But Dylan didn't say a thing.

"And?" Connor asked, hoping to encourage a more fulfilling description of Dylan's conclusions.

"Ok, here it is," Dylan stated, as if he was building up to breaking some bad news to Connor. "Basically, there are so many loose ends that I don't know where to start. I need to pick one of the loose ends and pull on it until things start to unravel. Only trouble is I have no idea which thread is the right one to grab hold of."

"That's not very encouraging," Connor told him. "Sounds like we are still right where we started if you ask me."

"Yeah," Dylan said. "Does to me too. So I came up with a plan."

"Oh good, a plan," Connor announced sarcastically. "Am I going to get to hear about this plan or is it top secret?"

"I will tell you the plan," Dylan said. "But don't expect too much. I'm afraid it's not exactly an eye popping sort of thing. I think we should consolidate all the things that we have all been experiencing lately. Like all the words or voices, all the 'feelings', and whatever else. I think that once we have them all written down we can analyze it and see if it helps me pick out a thread. Maybe we'll see some common denominators or something. I don't know. What do you think?"

"Actually I think it's a great idea," Connor replied. "You're right that it's not eye popping, but given the situation we need a place to start and I think it will help us find one. Good work."

"Thanks," Dylan said, taking silent notice of Connor's use of the word work.

"You're welcome," Connor replied. "So where do we start?"

"First we make a list of everything we've been hearing my mom say; they seem to be related mostly to berry picking. That's another thing I have been working on recently, recalling the various words and memories about berry picking, trying to consolidate them.

"Second, we list all of our hunches, or whatever you want to call them." He didn't mention dreams, he was not ready to deal with that yet, but he wondered if anyone else was having them.

"You been having any weird dreams about her?" Dylan asked, curious if Connor had been having nightmares like he had.

"No, not really. I've had a couple of the same kind of dreams I've always had about her. Wouldn't call them weird or unusual." Dylan didn't want to imagine what kind of dreams they were.

"Ok, for now we'll skip that, unless Brent or James comes up with something. And speaking of James, we better get him to add his stuff to the list too."

"Yes, you're right."

"Him right, not likely," Brent announced as he walked through the door with a box of donuts and a carafe of coffee.

"Hey, that was fast," Dylan noted. "You didn't have to run you know. We could have waited." He smirked again.

"I'm going to get you, sucker," Brent threatened.

"Yeah, I've heard that before," Dylan said.

"I mean it this time."

"Sure you do."

Connor decided he better end their little game or it might go on forever. "Give us some damn donuts and I'll get some cups for the coffee. Then can we get to work?"

"No problem," Brent and Dylan said in unison.

Connor got some cups, poured some coffee and ate a donut, while Dylan filled Brent in on the same plan he had just explained to Connor. They recalled all the 'words' anyone had heard from Jesse and wrote them down on a pad. Then they wrote down the things they 'knew'. Things like not believing that Jesse would walk out in front of a car. Brent brought James in long enough to add his items to the list.

When they were done they read through the list, trying to glean some insight from it. Nothing was said for several minutes, until Connor finally spoke up.

"I don't see the next step yet, do you?" he asked.

"No, I don't see the next step either," Dylan admitted. "But there is something missing from our list."

"Oh yeah, what?" Brent asked.

"The photograph. We've been looking at it as hard evidence, but it also has a special significance that fits into the criteria for our list. Special because it's the only photo mom kept around the house. And special again because it was taken out of the house by someone, then ended up in James' hands in Las Vegas, only to find its way back home. Kinda freaky I'd say." Brent and Connor could hardly disagree.

"Exactly where and when was that photo taken?" Dylan asked Connor.

"It was taken six months after you were born, in the park near Jesse's house," Connor replied, mildly curious about where Dylan was going to go with this.

"Ok, now try to recall all the details you can from the time when the photo was taken, and write those down on the pad," Dylan requested.

"Ok, I'll try," Connor said. As he scribbled notations of whatever came to his memory, he wondered what good it would do them. It was so long ago that he doubted there was anything from that time that could have any bearing on what happened to Jesse recently. He finished writing and handed his notes to Dylan.

Dylan didn't see anything in the notes that appeared useful. It read like a sloppy narrative of a couple taking a stroll through a park on a spring day. Better suited for a dime romance novel, but still it couldn't be omitted from their collection.

"Ok," he said, "add it to our list. Now let's go to the park where the picture was taken."

Brent asked, "What are we going to be looking for at the park?"

"I don't know exactly. Nothing, everything, and anything. I just think it might help to jog some sort of memory, or more voices or something."

CHAPTER THIRTY THREE

JAMES HAD WADED THROUGH THOUSANDS of photographs, hoping to see the face of the man who had given him the photo of Brenda and young Dylan, but without luck. There were thousands more to look at and he felt a headache coming on.

"I wish I could just remember who this guy was," he complained. Jake and the Chief, who were working in the same office, overheard him.

"So do I," they both said.

The Chief had been doing his bit to help the investigation, contacting witnesses, scheduling them to come in for another interview, tracking down the driver of the car that hit Jesse so he could get him to come to the station for an interview, and arranging to have Tommy Sanderson come in for an interview with the Deputies.

Jake had been burning up the phone and email lines, searching NCIC data bases and other information centers, hoping to get the various pieces of information they wanted. All the while he couldn't rid himself of the knowledge that he was conducting an investigation he wasn't supposed to be doing. While he was wishing he'd find some evidence vital to the investigation, he was also dreading what would happen when he did. He imagined all hell breaking loose in Denver, and then raining down on him and Connor.

CHAPTER THIRTY FOUR

TOMMY CHECKED IN with the Sergeant, like usual, before starting his shift.

"Got a call from Chief Armstrong," the Sergeant told Tommy. "He wants you to go talk to some Deputy Marshals. Seems they have something going here locally."

"Did they say what it was about?" Tommy asked.

"Nope," Ingram said. "I figured if they didn't volunteer the information I wouldn't get it if I asked, so I didn't bother."

"Ok, thanks," Tommy said. "I will stop by the station." He turned and walked away, trying to look calm. When he got to his cruiser the first thing he did was call Helen on his cell phone.

"We may have a problem," he told her. "There are U.S. Deputy Marshals in town and they want to talk to me."

"What are you going to do?" she asked.

"Go see them I guess," he said.

"What will you tell them?" she wanted to know.

"Nothing besides what's already in the reports," he told her.

After a few seconds of silence on the phones, Helen asked nervously, "What are you going to do, Tommy?"

"Haven't decided," he lied.

"You already know what you're going to do, don't you?" she demanded.

"Yes," he admitted.

"You going to tell me?" she asked.

"Later," he said. "I gotta go now."

CHAPTER THIRTY FIVE

DURING THE DRIVE TO THE PARK Dylan thought of another question for Connor. "Who took the picture?" he asked him.

"A friend of Jesse's," Connor answered.

The answer surprised Dylan. "A friend? What kind of a friend, a woman? How come you never mentioned that?"

"Yes, it was a woman friend. I never thought about it until you asked. You think it is important?"

"Are you kidding me?" Dylan was astonished, and even Brent was looking at Connor like he couldn't believe what he had just heard him say. It seemed unlikely that Connor, of all people, would not realize the vital relevance of Jesse having 'a friend'. Especially so soon after she relocated.

"Just wait, that's not what I meant," Connor tried to explain. "Of course it was – is – important. Any of her connections are, obviously. What I was asking is if it was important right now to this list of stuff we are 'analyzing'. Hell, for that matter is any of this shit important?" Connor said, obviously frustrated by the ethereal aspect of Dylan's plan.

"Sorry," Dylan replied, seeing the frustration. "I was just shocked, that's all. It probably seems especially odd to me because I don't recall her having many friends. Something that odd seems like it should be on our list of weird stuff. Ok?"

"Yeah, ok with me," Connor said, still edgy. He felt like having a drink. Something stronger than beer.

"Ok," Dylan said. "Now tell us everything you can remember about her."

"They met soon after Jesse was set up in the WITSEC program here in Montana. I didn't meet her until I came back here after you were born. Her name was Anna Johnston. She had a baby daughter named Joan, but that's all I ever knew about her. Jesse never discussed her, and I spent very little time with her. In fact, the only time I did spend with her was at the park, the day we took pictures."

Dylan's heart began racing. His girlfriend's, Joan's, mom was named Anna Johnston. He had never met her but Joan had mentioned her name. It could have been a different Anna Johnston, but it was hard to believe in that coincidence. He told Connor about Joan, and her mom. Brent and Connor stared at him with their mouths agape.

"How did my mom and Anna meet?" Dylan asked.

"I think they met at work. Your mom was working at World Imports and so was Anna," Connor told them.

More appalling news. More coincidence. More weirdness. Dylan didn't like it much. In fact, he didn't like it at all. It wasn't the fact that he and his mom both worked at the same store that bothered him so much. A big store in a small town, lots of people work there. An acceptable coincidence. What was unsettling was that she had never mentioned it. Add to that James' reaction to the mention of World Imports the night before, and the coincidence was not so acceptable.

"What are you thinking?" Connor asked.

"World Imports is where I work, or was working, maybe," Dylan answered.

"You work at World Imports?" Connor asked, wondering why that was a bad thing. Like Dylan, he didn't make much of the coincidence, since it was a big store in a small town.

"Yeah, but probably not for long," Dylan said. "I was planning on working with you guys instead of going back there. What bugs me, though, is that my mother never told me she'd worked there."

Just as they were arriving at the park Dylan said, "We need to talk to James about World Imports. When we're done here, let's stop by the station and see him."

"Why?" Connor asked.

"Something happened last night when I told him where I worked. He got a funny look, and I felt he was uneasy about something. I didn't think much of it at the time, but now I think he knows something he didn't say."

They got out of the car and walked into the park, arriving at the spot where the picture was taken. They looked, from that spot, in the direction of every point on the compass, but nothing significant jumped out at them. Brent stood in the spot from which Anna would have taken the picture and Dylan and Connor stood where, years earlier, Connor had stood with Jesse to pose for the photo.

From their relative locations they looked again in all directions, but still nothing noteworthy made its presence known to them. In truth, they might not have recognized it if it did, since they weren't sure what they were looking for.

Out of curiosity, Brent asked Dylan, "You think she would have kept the cut off part of the picture?"

"Hard to say, but it wouldn't seem likely since the reason it was cut out was to make sure that no one ever saw it," Dylan answered. In his soul there was something about it that was nagging at him. Not so much about his question, but about the picture itself. They continued to walk around the park looking for ......whatever, but Dylan could not stop thinking about the picture. The more he thought about it the more significant it became.

It was the only picture that his mom kept displayed in the house – so why did she choose that one? It was the only thing missing from the house. Again, why the photo? Worst of all was the recurring and exasperating question of why he never knew the truth about the photo until now. He might have understood why she would be reluctant to tell him about Anna and Connor – since she was obviously keeping the whole witness relocation thing a secret – but what was so grating to him, was that he had never even thought to ask her about it. He was never, for one second, even a little curious about it.

It was a small park, one of those local neighborhood kinds of parks for moms to take their kids to play, so it didn't take long for them to cover the whole thing. From there they expanded the search into the bushes surrounding the park, sparking some of Dylan's old memories.

"I used to come here with my mom when I was young," he said to the others. "Back then there were blackberry bushes around here, around the edges of the park. We picked them sometimes, but then they disappeared, like blackberry bushes do. I remember they were right over there." He pointed to a spot about twenty feet away. "I think that may have been the first berries I ever picked with her."

Other than Dylan's memory of picking blackberries, their inspection of the park yielded nothing so they returned to the station to talk to James.

"Ok, what did we get out of that?" Connor asked during the drive.

"For one thing," Dylan answered, "I remembered something about picking berries at the park that I hadn't recalled until now. We also have our suspicion about what James might know about World Imports. It is not a lot but it is something. Did any one else get anything out of it?" Connor answered with a very reluctant maybe.

"What was it?" Dylan asked.

"I remembered something odd that happened the day we took the photo. There was something strange about the way Anna was acting. She seemed uneasy about something, like she was in a hurry to leave the park. A couple of times I caught her looking anxiously into the bushes, and once, I actually turned and looked to where she was looking but I didn't see anything. Remembering that now makes me wonder what it was that was bothering her."

"Good enough," Dylan said, "add it to the list."

When they arrived at the station they pulled James off his task of looking at photos and dragged him into the conference room. Dylan got right to the point.

"Please tell us what you know about World Imports," he ordered.

James didn't act surprised by the question, but he didn't answer right away. "What makes you ask me about it?" he asked instead.

Dylan told him about Anna Johnston and Jesse both working at World Imports.

"No shit. Wow, that's some coincidence," James said. "I guess I should have said something last night when I found out that you worked there, but I didn't want to sound like I was making something out of nothing."

He told them what he knew about World Imports. In the old days, when he was dealing drugs, he heard a lot of talk about the store. The grapevine talk was that it had connections to the criminal world of money laundering, smuggling and other equally unwholesome activities. He related to them any stories he could recall hearing about the import chain.

When James was finished Connor asked him, "Did you ID your guy yet?"

"No, and if I don't do it soon, I'll go nuts." Connor nodded his sympathy, having been in his shoes before. James returned, unhappily, to look at more photos.

When James was gone Dylan said, "I really don't like all these coincidences." Brent and Connor agreed.

"What's next," Connor asked.

"We go back to mom's house," Dylan said.

"Ok, what are we doing there?" Brent asked.

"Same thing we did at the park," Dylan told him. "We look for clues. Pictures, letters, whatever. Anything related to the items on our list."

"Ok, let's go," Brent said.

When James returned to his task of looking at mug photos he experienced a jigsaw puzzle moment. A jigsaw moment happens when you have just spent some interminable amount of time staring at the pile of pieces of a jigsaw puzzle without successfully finding one that will fit into place. Then you stop looking for pieces to do a small task such as eating a meal, getting a drink, or going to the bathroom. And when you return to the jigsaw puzzle you immediately see some pieces that fit in. No one can explain how that works, but it always does.

In James' case, after he was questioned about World Imports and returned to searching through thousands of mug shots, the first picture he looked at was a mug shot of 'his man'. He shouted with joy and called Jake over to show him the photo.

Jake sent off the appropriate inquiries to find out the current details about the man in the mug shot. He wanted to know such things as his criminal record, etc., but mostly he wanted to know his current whereabouts.

CHAPTER THIRTY SIX

AT THE HOUSE, DYLAN concentrated on looking for more pictures. He found an envelope in the bedroom closet with some pictures in it, however there was nothing in them that seemed to help. Just some old school photos of Dylan.

They left the house, bound for the scene of Jesse's death. Dylan felt an intense dread when he considered being in the same spot that was not only the last place his mother had been alive, but the place she died as well. They parked the car near the scene and Brent and Connor walked the short distance to the exact spot of the accident. Dylan them from inside the car.

He considered whether there may be some therapeutic value to contacting the same space where the mayhem occurred, possibly helping to discharge his powerful emotions. It seemed likely but he didn't think he had the courage to face up to it at the moment.

Neither Brent nor Connor had any such qualms. They walked all around the scene looking for something that might indicate the possibility of the involvement of another person or persons. They found a large bush a few feet from the corner of the intersection where she was hit large enough to hide a person from view, which they suspected to be the case. Brent walked down the street to the approximate location the car that hit occupied just before striking her. Connor stood behind the bush and was invisible from Brent's view, thus proving the possibility that someone could have been hidden there.

They finished their examination of the site and returned to the car. Dylan was standing outside of it, leaning against the hood, watching them approach. Brent didn't like the way he looked.

"You ok?" he asked.

"Yeah. Well no, not really, but yeah," Dylan said. "You find anything?"

Brent told him about their experiment with the bush and the subsequent theory that it could have hidden a man from sight. It was only a theory, hardly a real breakthrough.

Connor took a moment to call the station. Jake informed him that James had finally ID'd the man who gave him the photo. Connor relayed the information to Dylan and Brent.

Dylan said, "Let's go back to the station, I want to see who this guy is."

At the station they found the others in the conference room, Jake visibly excited about James' success with the mug photos. The first really good news of the day. Connor congratulated James, then asked, "So who is he and what do we know about him?"

"Just his name and criminal record," Jake replied. "He is Richard, Ricky, Allen. Known alias Dallas West. Probably has other aliases. His record shows mostly drug charges. He did some time for dealing and got out of prison about a year ago. Unfortunately he has slipped under the radar, never made it in to see his parole officer, and no one knows where he is right now."

"They haven't been able to find him in a year's time?" Connor asked.

"That's the weird part," Jake said. "I asked both the Vegas Metro PD, and the Marshal's office that same question, and neither of them has ever tried to find him."

Connor frowned, unable to understand why they would let him go like that. "Did they say why?"

"Sort of. They said he's too small of a fish to waste resources on. They also said that people like him usually end up finding their way back into the system on their own," Jake explained.

Connor nodded, knowing the truth of that cycle of behavior. It wasn't uncommon for wanted persons to get caught on a traffic violation, or for pushing a little dope, or shoplifting in plain sight of a store detective or something else equally as stupid. "Where's he from?" he asked.

"Vegas," Jake said. "And something else you should know. He was doing time in Nevada state prison, at the same time, as the drug dealers that Jesse helped to convict."

Connor raised his eyebrows and said, "Curiouser and curiouser." Then he asked James, "Have you figured out where you've seen him before."

"Yes, I did," James answered. "I only saw him once before, and he looked a lot different then, which is why I didn't recognize him right away. He was a drug mule for the people who supplied my product. He brought me some dope once."

Dylan put a couple of things together and asked James, "Wasn't it dangerous for you to go back to Vegas after you got out of prison?"

"I thought about that a lot while I was inside. I thought I might be blamed for giving Brenda information that she used in her testimony," James told him. "But the thing is, I knew that if they wanted me they could find me, no matter where I went. So I figured if I went back to Vegas, like I wasn't afraid of anything, then maybe they would figure I didn't have anything to hide, so I wouldn't be considered a threat and they would leave me alone. Shit, I'm still alive so I guess it worked."

"Ok, so are we doing to track this guy down. Are all the bloodhounds in Las Vegas following his scent?" Connor asked.

Jake said, "We got Vegas PD to put out a BOLO, and we notified other local agency offices like U.S. Marshals, FBI etc. But even if we find him, will it help? I mean, do you think he would really tell us anything?"

Connor said, "Let's get him here and find out."

"Right," Jake said.

"What else have you guys got for us?" Connor asked.

"A couple of witnesses are coming in tomorrow to see us, and the state M.E. is scheduled for a phone conference. The driver of the car, Wayne Lefthand, has checked out ok with NCIC, his background is clean and nothing suspicious shows up. We've been trying to contact him but it's been hard. His car, which is still at the state crime lab in Helena, is registered to a relative, who is also hard to contact, and the address on record for him is a vacant lot. A neighbor says he sets up his TeePee on it when he isn't on the road going to Pow Wows."

"Alright, thanks. When the witnesses get here we need to know the precise spot where they were standing when they saw whatever they saw. We also need to know if they were moving, and if so, from which direction. And you need to run someone else through NCIC. Her name is Anna Johnston. She lived, or still lives, in Flatrock and used to work at World Imports."

"You got it," Jake said, then asked, "What did you guys come up with?"

"Anna Johnston's name was the only other lead we got," Connor told him. "There were some weird coincidences with her connection to World Imports, which you probably heard about already." Then he explained their theory about the bush at the accident scene, and the pictures they found at the house. He added, "The pictures didn't seem to help us much though."

Jake, belonging to a younger and therefore geekier generation, said, "Give the pictures to me. We should magnify them and go over them carefully for clues. Just in case." Connor handed him the envelope. Dylan was surprised by the idea of magnifying photos. He pictured an old Sherlock Holmes movie, where they hold up a big magnifying glass and looked at things with it for otherwise invisible clues.

"You guys still do that, use magnifying glasses and all?" he asked.

Jake laughed and said, "Yeah, in a way, but we use hi-tech computer programs now, not magnifying glasses."

The idea interested Dylan and he asked Jake, "Can I be here and watch when you do it?"

"Sure," Jake said. "We'll do it tomorrow. I'll wait until you are here before I start."

"Cool," Dylan said.

Connor wrapped up the meeting and set the plan for the next day.

The Chief looked suspicious and asked, "So is everyone going to The Outlaw now?"

Dylan said, "Not me, I've got something else I have to do tonight." He glanced briefly at Brent but they didn't speak. They didn't need to. "Come on, James," he said. "Let's go home." James said goodnight to the others, then he and Dylan walked out.

No one else looked particularly interested in going to The Outlaw so Connor said, "I think we'll skip it for tonight."

The Chief said, "Good," with a little more relief in his voice than he had intended.

As they all filed out of the station, Jake fell in step with Brent, waited until they were out of earshot of the others and said, "I'm going to The Outlaw, you coming with me?"

Even though Brent didn't have an urge to go to The Outlaw, he noticed that Jake was excited by the idea. It would be bad manners to disappoint Jake, who was, after all, a visiting dignitary of sorts, so he said, "Sure."

Dylan and James were standing on the sidewalk outside the station waiting for them.

"I thought you said you had something important to do," Brent said to him.

"I do, but first we need a ride home. I forgot, until I got out here, that I rode here with you."

"No problem, let's go," Brent said.

They made the short ride to Dylan's house, dropping him and James off, then drove to The Outlaw, and were soon settled into their beers.

"Dylan gave you a funny look back at the station before we left," Jake said to Brent, "you know what he's up to tonight?"

"I've got a good idea," he answered. It was really more than an idea but he'd become used to playing down the thing with him and Dylan over the years.

"What do you think it is?"

"He's going to see Joan."

Apparently the answer satisfied Jake because he didn't bring the subject up again. Nor did he bring up any business talk the rest of the night. The work day had ended and the recreation time had taken over. They spent the rest of their evening enjoying the club. Especially Jake. He relished the beer, the crowd, the noise, and the jolly atmosphere. Brent was reminded of the Toby Kieth song 'I Love This Bar'.

CHAPTER THIRTY SEVEN

DYLAN HAD SOME QUESTIONS for Joan, especially about her mom, who had just presented an entirely new chapter to the sudden appearance of secret pasts. On the drive to her house he found himself reconsidering his relationship with Joan. Lately he had found himself having to reconsider many things in his life, so it was no surprise that Joan would be one of them.

In Dylan's eyes, and many other men's, she was shockingly beautiful. Not tall, not short, long shiny black hair next to unblemished alabaster skin. Deep blue eyes that were full of mischief. She had a nearly perfect figure, and he often thought she could have been a model. He asked himself the same question he had asked himself a thousand times before. Why me? Why did she pick me? She certainly outclassed him. And not just in beauty.

And yet, he treated her like an old shoe, ready to kick her off at any moment. What was wrong with him? Why, he wondered, would any sane man do anything that might cause him to lose her. He liked her; hell he probably loved her. And, whatever her reasons for it were, he was pretty sure she had similar feelings for him.

He decided to try a little harder to make her happy as he knocked on her door. She answered it and, happily surprised to see him, she smiled.

"Come in," she said, stepping back to allow him passage.

"I'm glad you came" she told him after they were seated together on the couch. "I've wanted to talk to you since I left your house the other day." She sounded contrite so Dylan let her speak. "I feel really bad about my behavior there. I should have realized that you were going through a bad time because of your mom. I wasn't very understanding was I?"

Dylan hesitated for a moment. She looked stunning. Not her usual stunning, but a casual stunning that Dylan found very erotic. She wore a baggy oversized sweatshirt, without a bra, and she had on short sweat shorts. Her hair was very relaxed, not tied up with anything, and she had washed the make up off of her face, which only accentuated her natural beauty.

He forced himself to concentrate on the conversation and said, "Yeah, but don't worry about it, it didn't bother us."

She didn't know how to take that remark. Was she being forgiven or was she being dismissed as someone unimportant and insignificant? She didn't want to imagine that so she changed the subject.

"Why did you come?"

He wasn't supposed to talk about the Deputy U.S. Marshals and what he was doing with them so he had to be careful about how he asked his questions. He hesitated a bit while trying to decide the best way to ask. Joan took his silence the wrong way.

"Did you miss me?" she asked him, looking down demurely.

Dylan hesitated another moment, considering her question. It was true that he missed her, but it wasn't why he'd come to her house tonight. And he didn't think that telling her his real reason for being there would go along with his recent decision to try harder to make her happy. Again she misinterpreted his hesitation and said, "You can stay with me tonight if you want, I'll take care of you."

That statement stirred up some altogether different feelings. He realized, too, that she was making her own effort to make him happy.

"Sure," he said. "I'd like that a lot. Thanks."

She purred, mentally speaking, and moved closer to him on the couch so that their bodies were touching. Dylan liked the feeling and sat silently, enjoying it, while he thought about how to bring up his questions without spoiling the mood.

"How come I've never met your mom?" Dylan finally asked her.

The question surprised her. Was he going to finally get serious about their relationship? Was he planning on proposing? Did his mom's death shock him into being sensible, or did it shock him into insanity? She shrugged and said, "I guess the main reason is because she doesn't live here."

"Where does she live?"

"In Las Vegas. She moved there a couple of years ago, right after we met."

"Did she know about me?"

"Yeah, I told her about you. Why?"

Dylan wasn't too surprised by what he was learning so far, but neither did he like it much. Instead of answering her question, he asked another of his own.

"This being a small town and all," he asked her, "do you think she could have ever known my mom?" What he was really wondering was why, and when, his mom and Anna stopped hanging out together.

"That's always a possibility but she never said anything to me about it." She was becoming suspicious now. Why all these questions about her mom? It felt like something much more than a lead up to a proposal. Maybe he was looking for another mom to take the place of his. He probably missed having a mother figure in his life. It seemed kind of soon for him to be doing that, but you never know.

"Where is this going Dylan?" she asked him.

He knew where he wanted to go with it but he also knew that going there would include giving away the secrets of the U.S. Marshal investigation. He would have to clear that through Connor first.

So this is how he answered her question, "I don't know, I guess I've just been doing a lot of thinking about moms since mine died, and I wondered about your mom and all. You know what I mean." He said it like he was tongue tied and a bit embarrassed, hoping she would back off asking him any more about it. Then to get her off the subject he said, "Thanks again for asking me to stay with you tonight."

She grinned and said, "My pleasure." She was glad he wanted to be with her. It made her feel like he wasn't mad at her for what she did the other day.

The next morning Dylan was glad he'd stayed. She was true to her promise and took good care of him. Then again, sex with her was never disappointing. As he was leaving, he asked her if it would be ok if he called her later.

"Yeah, I'd like that," she said with a remarkably attractive smile.

CHAPTER THIRTY EIGHT

THAT SAME MORNING Brent drove by Dylan's house to pick him and James up. Dylan's car was gone and James was standing out front alone.

James got in the car and Brent asked him where Dylan was.

"Don't know, man, he never came home last night."

"I see," Brent said. He looked over at James who was smiling a sly smile. Apparently James also saw.

They drove on ahead to the station where they had all agreed to meet again that morning. Dylan was there when they arrived. Brent and Dylan looked at each other for a second and Brent could tell he'd gotten lucky with Joan. He gave Dylan a small smile and hoped that Dylan's lucky night would help him feel a bit better about life.

James watched the silent exchange between Dylan and Brent and felt a funny sense of pride in Dylan. He also felt, for the first time in his life, a vicarious emotion of happiness. A sharing of the happiness Dylan was feeling. He began to realize what he had been missing out on all these years.

To Dylan's ultimate delight they all had coffee and donuts, courtesy of Jake. Dylan couldn't wait to ask Connor for permission to include Joan in the dream team, so he started the meeting by telling everyone what had happened the night before, except for the sex part. He asked Connor what he thought about bringing Joan into the team.

"I'll trust your judgment about that," he said.

Dylan was happy with that answer but thought he better check with the others so he asked, "Anyone else have an objection?"

No one did so Dylan said, "I think we need to see her right away but she's at work and she's not fond of taking time off. It might work better if the Chief calls her and says its official police business and he needs to see her right now."

The Chief said, "I'll convince her, don't worry."

Then James said, "Ask her to bring a photo of her mom. You never know, maybe I've seen her somewhere in Vegas."

Now that they had settled the matter of Joan, they set plans for the rest of the day.

The Chief called Joan and convinced her to leave work and come to the station right away. While waiting for her to arrive, Dylan wondered how he was going to approach the subject with her. Their personal relationship might interfere with how she took it, and he worried that she might not entirely believe what he had to tell her.

He decided it would be best if the initial briefing was done by the Chief and Jake. They could brief her in a room that had a camera, so Dylan could watch it, and then be called when she was ready.

She arrived quickly and the Chief introduced her to Jake who took her to the briefing room. Jake started by explaining to her that what they were about to discuss was confidential and asked her if she would agree to keep the secret. She looked bewildered by his statement and uncertain about what to say. Jake, seeing her confusion, explained further that it involved a case in which she might possibly be of great help in solving.

That seemed to give her the incentive that she needed to make up her mind. She couldn't very well turn down a request for help.

"If I can help, I'd be glad to cooperate in any way I can," she said.

Jake needed more than that so he asked her, "Do you agree to keep everything we tell you secret?"

"Yes, I do," she answered. Dylan, watching from the monitor, could tell she was nervous.

Jake told her why they were there, about Jesse's past and what they suspected about Jesse's death.

Joan did something none of them expected, she started crying hysterically. Dylan had never seen her cry like that and was taken aback. Jake and the Chief looked at each other, neither one having a clue what to do. The Chief left the room, returning a moment later with a box of tissues. He gave her the box and she held some tissues up to her face and started collecting tears with them.

Dylan entered the briefing room with the others and put his arms around Joan to comfort her. She started to calm down and he handed her some fresh tissues. He wanted to say something to help her but found himself at a loss for the appropriate words.

When Joan was able to speak again she said to Dylan, "I'm really sorry. I feel even more guilty now because of how I've been acting toward you lately. Why didn't you tell me last night?"

"I couldn't without getting permission from the Deputies first. Sorry."

At that moment luck intervened on the Chief's and Jake's behalf and the first witness arrived to be interviewed. They both excused themselves and left Dylan and Joan alone in the room. Dylan didn't think that he wanted anyone watching them on the monitor, if they took a notion to, so he asked her to go for a walk with him. She agreed, grateful for the chance to get out.

As they were walking away from the station Joan said, "I'm sorry," over and over again. In an attempt to get her to stop saying it Dylan asked, "What are you so sorry about?"

"I don't know. Everything I guess. It's all just, so horrible sounding. Your poor mom. And then I was so mean to you guys the other night. I didn't really mean all those things I said you know. I don't know why I got so upset. I'm sorry," she said for the umpteenth time. Now that she'd brought it up, Dylan was curious to know why she did get so upset that night.

"What was it you were so upset about anyway?" he asked.

Dylan wasn't sure why she acted the way she did at his house either, but he had a suspicion. He knew if he could help her isolate her reasons, the future of their relationship could be a bright one.

"What were you really upset about?" he asked.

"I think I felt guilty about going to work instead of being with you, and when I went to your house to make up for it, and saw you and Brent, well I .... I just got jealous I guess." She hesitated for a second then added, "That's not entirely true. The truth is I've been upset about Brent for a long time. His resentment of me, combined with my jealousy of your close relationship with him, really upsets me." She got a little teary eyed after saying this, but was under control.

Dylan understood her reasoning, and she was right about a lot of it. He felt guilty now that he had not noticed how his complacency in their relationship might have made her feel. She was also right about Brent's attitude towards her and he felt bad about that too.

"Listen," he said, "I'm sorry I've not really revealed my true feelings to you. I guess I was insecure about us because I think you are too good for me. But I really care for you a lot. Even more than I care about Brent, but in a different way of course. And I promise to deal with his attitude toward you. OK?"

Joan didn't say anything, she just threw her arms around him and gave him a big, long, affectionate kiss. When that was done, she said, "Thanks for not being mad at me."

"I'd never dream of it," he told her.

"By the way," she said, "I've never thought of myself as too good for you, so stop worrying, OK?"

"Ok."

They held hands while continuing their walk and Joan said, "This thing with your mom sounds so unreal, it's just so hard to believe."

"Yeah, tell me about it."

Jake had never gotten the chance to explain Joan's mom's role in the current scheme of things so she asked Dylan, "So how come I've been brought here? How am I supposed to be able to help?"

Dylan still had the half a photo of him and his mom with him, so he took it out and handed it to Joan. She looked at it and then looked back at Dylan for an explanation.

"You know the park near my mom's house?" he asked her.

"Yeah."

"That picture of me, as a baby, and my mom, was taken there."

"Yeah?"

114

"By your mom." He let that sink in for a second then said, "They were close friends and they both worked at World Imports when the picture was taken." He could see the same look of shock on her face that he had felt when he'd gotten the news. Like him, she was not shocked by the context of news, but by the fact that her mom had never revealed such a vital piece of information to her.

"Is that why you were asking me about her last night?" she asked, frowning.

"Yeah."

"Wow," she said with a short embarrassed laugh. "I thought it was something else."

"What did you think it was?" he asked.

She was too flustered to tell him what she was really thinking last night, so instead she said, "I don't know, I guess I thought you were looking for a new surrogate mom or something." Dylan couldn't very well blame her for thinking that, since it was him who had given her that idea.

CHAPTER THIRTY NINE

THE FIRST WITNESS THAT JAKE interviewed was a middle aged woman with dyed blond hair, named Heather Vert. Heather lived in a single-wide trailer in a low rent trailer park near the store where Jesse shopped. She didn't own a car, and claimed she was walking home from the store when she witnessed the accident.

After asking her several questions it became apparent to Jake that Heather did not actually see the accident. She, maybe, heard something, like screeching tires and a bang. And she, maybe, saw Jesse lying in the street after she'd walked close enough to see around the bushes lining the sidewalk. Jake wondered why Patrolman Sanderson hadn't included those details in his report.

When another supposed witness showed up for their appointment, Jake did a similar interview with them, with basically the same results. They did not actually see the accident occur, although they were nearby when it happened and probably heard it.

He collected the notes, found Connor, and briefed him on the results of the interviews.

Connor nodded and said, "Not much to go on, but I guess I will go back the accident scene and see if any of this helps. How's it going with Joan?" he added.

"She came in and we told her about Dylan's mom. She started crying and Dylan took her for a walk, so we never got to tell her about her mom"

"Ok, I'll see you when I get back. Anything else comes up, call me." He collected James and Brent and they drove back to the accident site to see if they could use the locations of the witnesses to learn anything useful.

When Jake returned to his office the Chief had the state trooper, Tommy Sanderson waiting to see him. Jake took him into the office to interview him and the Chief went back to his own work.

The Chief had gotten approval to exhume the body and had given the order to get it done. The actual inspection of the body would be done at the Montana state crime lab in the state's capital city of Helena. Their little town of Flatrock, like most towns in Montana, was not equipped for sophisticated forensics or crime data bases.

For that same reason the car which struck Jesse had also been sent to the State Crime Lab. Forensics had finished inspecting the car and had sent in their report. The Chief read it over and didn't see anything new in it, but it didn't matter what he thought. This was the Marshal's show, just like Brent had said, and he would give the reports to the Deputies. Let them decide.

At the accident site, Connor sent James and Brent to the two respective locations where the witnesses were standing when they witnessed, in actuality, nothing. They repeated the experiment they had done the day before with the location of the car. The results were identical. If anyone was behind the bush on the corner, they could not have been seen by any of the witnesses.

They finished up their examination of the area by locating various locations from which a potential witness could have seen someone behind the bush. They were not very confident that the information would do them any good, but they did it anyway. They were right, it did no good at all.

Then Brent did something strange. He walked out into the street without looking, narrowly avoiding being struck by a car. He did it because he was drawn by an irresistible force to the exact spot where Jesse had died. He could no better explain what force was imposing its will upon him than he could his connection with Dylan.

He stood in the exact spot where Jesse was struck by Wayne Lefthand's car, welded to it by something beyond his control. While he was standing there, James and Connor diverted traffic around him so he didn't get hit. James had the traffic under control and Connor went to Brent.

"What are you doing, trying to get yourself killed? Get out of the road," he instructed Brent.

Brent stood trancelike, and unmoving, seeming to not hear Connor, who resorted to moving him bodily toward the sidewalk. Brent moved compliantly, but it was like steering a zombie around, and Connor didn't appreciate the sensation of it.

He got Brent back on the safety of the sidewalk and James joined them, letting the traffic flow again.

"Shit, man," James said, nearly terrified. "What were you trying to do out there?" Connor nodded and looked at Brent for an answer.

By then Brent was recovering from his trance and he had an answer, but he didn't think it was one that would satisfy James or Connor.

He had experienced an incident like this only once before in his life, and it involved Jesse then too. He was young then, maybe eight years old. He and Dylan were playing with a soccer ball in the front yard of Dylan's house. The ball rolled into the street, like it had several times before. Every time it had rolled into the street one of the two boys chased it down and kicked it back into the yard.

Except one time, when the ball rolled into the street and he and Dylan both stood frozen, staring at it as a car sped down the street and ran it over. The car was going way over the speed limit and had appeared suddenly, then disappeared just as quickly. When the grip of the 'frozen feeling' had dissipated, he and Dylan had looked at each other in horror. Then they turned their heads in unison and looked at the house. Jesse was in the window of the house looking at them with a fond smile.

The sensation of being frozen in place that day felt just the same as it did today.

Here is how he explained it to Connor, "I'm not sure. I just had to do it. I can't really explain. Sorry." He still looked a bit shaken up so Connor left him alone. Brent was glad he backed off because there was only one person to whom he was going to try to explain what happened; Dylan of course.

CHAPTER FORTY

JOAN HAD RECOVERED AND seemed ready to answer some questions, but, having just made a rather major improvement in their relationship, Dylan wanted to keep himself as detached from the questioning as possible. He took her back to the station, planning to find someone else to do the questioning. He suggested to Joan that she use the bathroom to freshen up, hoping it would give him time to get the Chief or Jake to handle the remaining questioning.

As he entered the conference room to make the arrangements with Jake and the Chief, Trooper Sanderson was just leaving. They said hi to each other as they passed. Tommy had a grim and determined look on his face, like he was upset, and more than a little worried. The term 'bloody minded' came uninvited to Dylan's mind.

Dylan went on through the door into the conference room and asked, "What's he so upset about?" Indicating Tommy with his thumb pointed back over his shoulder.

"Who?" Jake asked.

"Tommy."

Jake and the Chief gave each other a puzzled look. They both thought that Tommy had left the interview a happy man.

Jake said, "He seemed happy a minute ago. Why are you asking?"

"He looked upset when I passed him just now. Maybe more than a little."

Jake was still trying to make sense out of what Dylan had just said about Tommy, when Joan came out of the bathroom. Dylan quickly told Jake what to ask her.

Dylan escorted Joan to the conference room, Jake and the Chief following. They got seated around the table, while Dylan tried to make Joan as comfortable as possible. Jake began asking her questions, as instructed by Dylan.

He started off easy with, "When exactly did your mom move to Vegas?"

"About a month after I started dating Dylan, so twenty two months ago."

"When did you first tell her about Dylan?"

"Two weeks after we started dating. She had noticed I was dating someone and asked me who it was. I told her his name and that he worked at World Imports."

"Did you ever mention Dylan's mom to her?"

"Yes, when I told her about Dylan she asked me what his moms name was. I thought that was a little strange, but I told her." Joan was frowning now, as though she didn't quite like the little conclusions her mind was throwing at her.

Jake kept up the line of questioning, "How did she react to hearing Jesse's name?"

Joan took a minute to answer while she reviewed the memory in her mind, then said, "She didn't say a thing, she just turned and walked away. I remember thinking that her reaction was a bit odd, like she might know the name, and for some reason disapproved of her. You know, some sort of social snobbery." She frowned a little deeper.

"Did she ever mention Dylan or Jesse again?"

Again, Joan needed some time to review her memories, then said, "Just once, a couple of weeks later, she asked me if I had met Dylan's mom. I told her that I had, and she asked me if they, Jesse and Dylan, had mentioned wanting to meet her. I said no, the subject hadn't come up. Then she told me she was moving to Las Vegas." Then Joan started crying again.

Aware of Jake's discomfort, Dylan gestured to him to stay in the room. Jake scowled his own feelings about that but he stayed. Dylan helped Joan with tissues again until she stopped crying. It didn't last long this time and when it stopped she said, "Sorry."

"It's ok, we understand," Dylan said. Then he nodded at Jake to continue his questions.

Jake lost his interest in the questioning. He felt like a brute, having made her cry twice already. He hesitated and looked at the floor, unwilling to go on.

Dylan understood Jake's reluctance, but he knew Joan, and Jake didn't. He was sure that they weren't inflicting anything serious on her so he took over.

He asked, "Have you seen her or heard from her since she moved?"

Joan's tentative smile let Dylan know that she was thankful for him taking over the questions. So much for his theory of distancing himself from it.

"Sure," she answered. "We talk at least once a week on the phone. But I haven't seen her. I wanted to go to Vegas to visit, but I was always working so I never did."

"Did she ask you to go visit?"

"No."

"What phone number do you use for her?"

"The same cell phone she had when she was here. She never changed it."

"You have her address?"

"No." She frowned, like the fact had just occurred to her, and now seemed wrong somehow.

"When you were talking on the phone did she ever ask about me or my mom?"

"Yes, pretty normal questions like, 'How are we getting along?'. But right after Jesse died she called me and asked how we were dealing with it. At the time I wondered how she knew about it, since I didn't tell her. I thought that maybe she heard it from one of her friends in Montana."

"Was that the last time you talked to her?"

"Yes."

At this point Jake got up to leave the room. He gestured to Dylan to follow him outside so he could talk in private.

"Why don't you go freshen up and get some coffee," Dylan suggested to Joan. "I need to talk to Jake. Let's meet back here in about ten minutes, ok?"

Joan said ok and went to the ladies room.

Dylan and the Chief followed Jake to the Chief's office.

Dylan asked him, "You OK?"

"Yeah I guess so," he answered. "That was rough on her. I felt like an asshole when she cried like that."

"Yeah, I hate seeing women cry too. But she's not crying because of what you did. She's crying because of the shock of finding out stuff about her mom that was kept secret from her. I know that feeling, believe me."

"He's right Jake," the Chief interjected, trying to console Jake. "It's not your fault."

"Yeah, I guess so," Jake said, still not too happy. "I think we should warn her about talking to her mom again," he advised. "You know, in case she calls Joan, we don't want her saying the wrong thing."

He had a point. Until they knew how Anna fit into things, it was best not to give her any information about what they knew, or what they were doing.

"Let me handle that," Dylan said.

"Sure, thanks," Jake said, relieved.

"No problem."

When Joan came back into the conference room, Dylan said, "Joan, we really need your help, but it may involve doing some things you might not like. My mom's death was officially declared an accident, but we don't believe that. I think you might be starting to suspect it as well.

"It looks like your mom may have been involved in some way, but we don't know how, and we need to find out. Will you help us?"

Joan looked distressed, no doubt due to the possibility that her mom was involved in something that Joan would have a hard time accepting. She hesitated, like she might cry again, but she held it together.

Dylan gave her a little nudge, "What do you think?"

"I want to help, of course, but you said I wouldn't like it, so I don't know."

Dylan never said she wouldn't like it, he said there were some things that she might not like. However, any man with a lick of sense would never mention either one of those things. "Ok, I know how you feel," he said. "We'll leave you out of it. Your mom probably has nothing to do with it anyway so why make trouble where there is none. I'm sorry, we've probably over-reacted." He was trying reverse psychology, hoping it would work.

It worked pretty well actually. She said, "I'm sorry, I want to help, I really do. But what if you want me to do something that I just can't do?"

"Don't worry, if you really can't handle something, we will work it out. No one will force you. Ok?"

"Ok. What do you want me to do?"

He wanted to say, 'Tell your mom to drive to the Grand Canyon and jump off the highest cliff', but he thought she probably wouldn't like that. And besides, he wasn't really sure, yet, that her mom had done anything wrong.

So here's what he said, "It's more like what we don't want you to do. We don't want her to know that we suspect that my mom's death was not an accident. So if she calls, and if she asks about it, just act like you still think it was an accident. Can you handle that ok?'

"I really don't like hiding things from her. What if she catches on. What if she senses that something is wrong in my voice or something?"

There was a small degree of BS in that statement and Dylan let her know it, gently, by saying, "I might be out of line here but can you please list all of the things you have hidden from your mom in your lifetime?" He figured he had about a fifty-fifty chance of getting a straight answer to his question.

To everyone's surprise and obvious relief, Joan laughed. Then she said, "Sorry." Again. "But, as surprising as it may sound, I wasn't really that good at hiding things from her. She really might be able to tell that something was wrong." Then she laughed again and said, "I think I can pull it off though."

She was starting to lighten up, and she took his question well, but there was more required from her. He hoped his luck would hold.

"There's more, we may need you to ask her some leading questions. It might help us in our investigation. Will that be ok?"

"Sure, I said I wanted to help and I will." His luck was still holding. She sounded a bit anxious, but at least she was willing.

"Thanks, Joan," he said affectionately.

Joan sensed the sincerity in Dylan's voice and she smiled demurely, like women are wont to do, and said, "You're Welcome." What she really meant, and which she didn't say of course, was, 'Wow, if I had known he was going to be so passionate about this I would have been easier to convince'. Dylan, being Dylan, knew that anyway, and planned on taking full advantage of it later that night.

At that moment Connor, James and Brent, returning from the accident scene, walked into the room. Joan had never met Connor or James, so Dylan introduced them.

"Nice to meet you," they all said to each other.

"Do you have a photo of your mom?" James asked Joan.

She looked puzzled and said, "Not with me. Was I supposed to?" James looked devastated.

"Be patient, grasshopper," Dylan said. But behind the statement he asked himself why James was so bent on seeing a photo of Anna.

"Ok, sorry," James said, but didn't look it.

"Welcome to the team," Brent said to Joan. He figured that if she was one of them now, he might as well make it as pleasant as possible. Besides, there was something different about her. Or about how he perceived her. Or both. He could feel it in her, and in himself, and he saw and felt it in Dylan. It was a change for the better and he liked it, but it made him wonder a bit. How simple and easy it was to include someone who he, a very short time ago, had nearly erased from his life. He felt a bit treacherous for not including her in his life sooner.

"You ok with all this?" Brent asked her sympathetically.

"It's pretty weird, and kind of awful, but I'm going to try," she said bravely.

"Don't worry, I'll help you get through it. If you need anything, call me," he said surprising her and Dylan, who had been listening.

"Thanks, Brent." She appreciated that the usual tension between them seemed to be gone now, and felt even more gratitude for Dylan for taking care of Brent's attitude like he promised. Dylan, of course, was a lucky recipient of that undeserved praise, since he hadn't spoken a word to Brent about the matter yet.

Dylan said to Joan, "Why don't you go back to work now. I have to talk to these guys for a while. Can I see you tonight?" He said it because he knew it would make her feel better, but also because he really looked forward to it himself.

"That would be nice, yes," she said with a smile that Dylan was really beginning to appreciate.

When she left the station Dylan was smiling, marveling at how different his attitude about her was now. Instead of only seeing a breakup in their future, he now saw only her in his future. And it felt good.

"Come on, lover boy, we gotta talk," Brent said to Dylan. Then to the others he said, "You guys ok without us for a while?"

"No problem," Connor said. "We'll be here when you get back."

CHAPTER FORTY ONE

WHILE BRENT AND LOVER BOY were gone, Connor met with Charlie and Jake to get briefed about Joan's interview. In the middle of the briefing a call came in for the Chief, who excused himself to take it.

Jake wanted an opportunity to talk to Connor alone, so he gave James some money and asked him if he wouldn't mind getting them some coffee from the local strip mall.

James took the money and left, but he knew that there was coffee in the station, and he could sense that Jake wanted to be alone with Connor. He smiled at the thought that he could keep the money and come back with no coffee and no one would be the wiser. He didn't care about the measly few dollars, he was just amused at the shallow effort to get him to leave. Shit, all they had to do was say that they needed to speak in private.

One of the reasons Connor had chosen Jake for this assignment was because he knew that Jake had a slightly abnormal ability. Jake didn't normally reveal that fact to people. He especially didn't tell the U.S. Marshal's office, or put it on his resume`. But Connor had managed to discover his secret.

Some time back he was leading a search for an escaped prisoner, and not having much luck finding him. Jake came along and, following some strong 'hunches', found the escapee in record time.

Connor had noticed right away that Jake was not following what you would call leads based on hard evidence, and later he asked Jake about it in private. Jake tried to explain it away but his explanations were weak and Connor pressed him for the truth. Jake clammed up, not wanting to jeopardize his job. Connor promised him that the conversation would never be repeated and that his job would be safe, so Jake told him about his so called 'abilities'.

It turned out that Jake had, his entire life, had some unexplained way of locating lost or missing items, pets or people. In his youth, neighborhood residents would come to him occasionally for help in finding things or animals, and, rarely, a person. He never understood what the big deal was. Or, more accurately, he never understood why nobody else seemed to be able to perform such a simple function. To him finding things or persons required about as much effort as determining what color green grass or blue sky was.

Nevertheless he could do it, and as he aged he gained more understanding of the extraordinary nature of his ability. He also realized the problems it could create for him if revealed to the wrong people. Thus the initial reluctance to tell Connor.

After Connor had taken Jake's confession, he'd told him about his experiences with Jesse, and how it had changed his way of perceiving such phenomena. He convinced Jake that his secret was safe with him and from there forward they had worked together off and on with an implicitly secret kinship.

So, knowing why he brought Jake along on this assignment, Connor had a pretty good idea why he was setting up a private chat.

"What's up?" he asked Jake.

"A couple of things. Something is bugging me about the trooper, Sanderson. Our interview didn't turn up anything new. It was almost like he was quoting his original report word for word and didn't elaborate at all for us. That bugged me, but he seemed pleasant and cooperative so I left it alone. But then when he was leaving he ran into Dylan, who said that he looked upset. He never seemed upset during the interview. I just don't like it, and something was eating at my craw about him anyway. I can't put my finger on it but there's something funny."

Connor knew Jake well enough to take his suspicions seriously so he asked, "What do you want to do?"

"We ordered a background on him. Let's wait until it comes in and then decide."

Connor suspected that Jake had already drawn some conclusions about Sanderson but was not willing to declare them until he had some verification. His suspicion, however, was wrong this time.

Jake's unspoken reason for wanting to hold off on a plan for Sanderson had nothing to do with needing verification. Rather it had to do with the fact that, for the first time in his life, he mistrusted his 'feelings' about Tommy. He had heard what Dylan said about Sanderson, and he believed him. Dylan had no reason to lie about it. But at the same time he had a hard time doubting his own read of the man. And that read was that he was a dedicated white hat. The dichotomy unnerved him.

"Smart plan," Connor responded. "What's the other thing you want to talk about?"

"We aren't getting any breaks from the hard evidence. Everything seems to be checking out. So far, all we have been accomplishing is to prove that the original report was good and that it really was an accident. The funny part of that, though, is that the more proof we get that it was an accident, the less I want to believe it. It's backwards, but I think I know why I feel that way. I think it is because it's too clean, like someone made an effort to make it look perfect. No evidence of that, just a feeling." This part of his report contained no doubts on his part.

"I know what you mean, but all we can do is stick to our plan and see how it pans out. Anyone else come in yet?"

"No, just the witnesses and Tommy. Still trying to find the driver of the car." Connor gave Jake a questioning frown in response to this.

"I know. I'm supposed to be good at finding people. My gift. But something is wrong with this one. It's puzzling me." He shrugged.

"Ok. Let me know if anything changes."

CHAPTER FORTY TWO

BRENT AND DYLAN drove to The Outlaw so that Brent could calm himself with a beer while telling his story to Dylan. He ordered a pitcher. Dylan ordered iced tea. He said he didn't want to start on beer yet because he wanted to preserve his 'stamina' for later. Yeah, right, lover boy. Brent poured him a glass from the pitcher anyway, and Dylan drank it anyway.

When Brent finished telling Dylan what happened in the street at the accident scene, Dylan only had one question, "What did you hear?"

"When I was standing in the exact spot where her body was, I heard only one word. I heard the word 'bitch'."

"My mom said 'bitch'?" Dylan asked, amazed.

"No, it wasn't your mom's voice, it was a mans' voice. That's what is freaking me out." Dylan didn't blame him.

"Yeah, no shit," he said.

"I'm scared, man. I'm scared shitless," Brent said. "This is all getting way too big for me. I don't know if I can handle it. I mean, I walked out in front of moving traffic for Christ's sake. What is that all about? And hearing your mom's voice might be freaky, but at least I kinda get that. Now I'm hearing a mans' voice. A strange mans' voice. What the hell is that about? It would be one thing if it answered some questions for us but it doesn't answer shit. All it does is raise more questions, and cause me more heart failure. And what do we have to show for it? Nothing more than we had at the start. We still don't know shit." After an awkward moment of silence Brent said faintly, "There's one more thing."

"What's that?" Dylan asked, suspecting that the 'one more thing' might actually be the primary thing Brent needed to talk to him about.

"Do you remember when we were about eight years old, and we were playing with the soccer ball at your house? And the ball rolled into the street and a speeding car hit it?" He looked up, hoping Dylan would remember the incident in the same way he had.

"Yeah," Dylan said somberly. "I remember. I never forgot. I don't know what scared me worse, the fact that one of us could have – should have – been hit by that car, or the smile on my mom's face when we saw her watching through the window."

"Yeah, exactly. Do you remember the way it felt when you just stood there frozen in place watching the ball?"

"Yeah, it was pretty weird"

"Yeah, well that is the exact feeling I had when I stood in the street today. It is the only other time I have ever felt that."

"Wow, man," was all that Dylan could think of to say.

"Yeah," Brent agreed. "Only this time I was standing in front of cars coming at me. I came even closer to being killed." Brent was pensive for a moment and then asked, "Is this shit we are doing really worth getting killed over?"

"Are you saying that you want to quit?"

"I'm not sure what I'm saying, other than this is getting really hard to handle."

"You can if you want."

"What?"

"Quit." Dylan would certainly understand Brent having second thoughts, and he wouldn't stand in his way if he wanted to quit, but he hoped he wouldn't.

"No, I'm not quitting. It's just hard, that's all."

"It'll get easier soon," Dylan said, trying to bullshit someone he could never hope to bullshit.

"Bullshit," Brent said.

"But you can handle it can't you? You can cowboy up." It wasn't a question, it was more like an expression of his hope, his need, and his confidence in Brent.

The words 'cowboy up' touched Brent's manly pride button and he responded to it the way Dylan was hoping for.

"Hell yes," he said, steeling up his spirit. He held his glass up to a toast, a gesture which helped to reinforce his resolve. After all, if you hoist a beer to it, you have to follow through on the promise.

After a gulp of beer Dylan said, "I know it's going to be hard, but I need you. In a perverse way, finding out about my mom's secret past, and suspected murder, has given my life a real purpose for the first time. When I first heard about my mom's death, before the Deputies came along, I had no real life left. My future held only the promise of an irreducible minimum of mere existence until I, unhappily and without satisfaction, grew old and died. Now finding my mom's killer, and discovering her real past, have given me something worthwhile to live for, the only worthwhile thing. You are not in that same position, so your voluntary commitment means a lot to me, and I could never express my full appreciation to you for doing it." He raised his glass to another toast of commitment.

"You know you don't really need to say all that for me to know how you feel." Referring to their connection.

"Yeah, I know. Pretty cool huh?" Dylan said, smiling.

"Yeah, pretty cool."

CHAPTER FORTY THREE

"THIS JUST CAME IN," the Chief said, holding out a fax to Jake and Connor. Jake took it from him and read it. It was Anna Johnston's background report. It wasn't good. He handed it to Connor.

Connor read it and said, "It's not good."

The report included a criminal record, which was a surprise. She was arrested in Las Vegas many years ago for drug dealing. It was pretty small time stuff, with no priors, so she got a light sentence.

But the arrest record was not what was bad about the report. What was bad was that she had been dealing with Ricky Allen and his cohorts. She was connected to the bad guys. Very not good.

There was another unsettling coincidence. After she got out of prison she got a job in Vegas, was reporting to her parole officer on time, passing her drug tests and generally seemed to be doing well. No complaints to the P.O., just glowing reports.

Then, suddenly, it changed. She started complaining to her P.O. that she was scared, worried about reprisals from her old drug dealing buddies. She demanded a transfer of her parole to Montana, where she said she was already promised a job, and where she thought she could get away from her druggy friends. The complaints and the request came just after Jesse was set up there for witness protection, and the job she was promised in Montana was with World Imports.

Connor said, "We really need to talk to this broad."

"Yeah," Jake said. "But did you notice her present location in the report?"

"Yeah, Montana," Connor confirmed.

"So where is she really?" Jake wondered. He knew that she was off parole and no longer obligated to inform anyone when she moved around.

"Joan says Vegas."

"We need to verify that but I'm not sure how," Connor said.

"Ok, how about this," Jake suggested. "We get Dylan to ask Joan to call her mom and get her to agree to a visit. Once they meet up we will know for sure where she is."

"Good plan," Connor agreed. Then he had another thought.

"You don't know where she is?" He was referring to Jake's special talent. He worried about it after Jake told him it wasn't working on Wayne Lefthand.

"Yes, I think I do. But I have my reasons for getting Joan involved." Connor nodded, relieved that Jake still had his mojo. He was about to comment on it when James entered the room.

James set the coffee down on the table. In an effort to be facetious he carefully counted out the change as he laid it on the table next to Anna's sheet. There was a photo of her attached to the fax, which he noticed. "Holy shit," he exclaimed. Connor turned to see what the problem was.

"What's wrong?" he asked, aware of James staring at the photo of Anna.

"I recognize the broad in this photo. This is the chick that came with Ricky Allen when he brought me some dope one time. He never introduced her, she just stood with him like a sidekick. Who is she?"

"Her name is Anna Johnston. She is Joan's mom."

"No shit? Wow," he said, making a genuine understatement. "I knew I needed to see a picture of her."

"We really need to talk to this broad," Jake reiterated.

"If she was in Vegas, could you find her?" Connor asked James on a hunch.

"Needle in a haystack unless she is hanging out with the old crowd. If she is, there's a chance, but only a chance. If she's not, you are better off using the cops to find her."

"I don't think he needs to worry about Anna," Jake said to Connor meaningfully. Connor caught on and changed subjects.

"What about Ricky, could you find him?" He glanced at Jake for approval of the question. Jake nodded his OK.

"Yes, but I'd be risking my neck to do it." James said.

Brent and Dylan walked into the station just in time to hear James' answer.

"Risking your neck to do what?" Dylan asked, feeling a never before felt sense of worry for his father.

"Find Ricky Allen in Vegas," James told him.

"Why would you do that?" Dylan asked.

Jake said, "I just asked him if he could if he had to. We haven't decided if we want him to try yet. I was just running some ideas around in my head. Here, check this out." He handed him the fax on Anna.

Dylan read the report but didn't say anything. He handed it to Brent who read it silently then said, "We need to talk to her," and then looked at Dylan expectantly.

The other men looked at him in the same way.

Dylan got the picture. "Alright," he said, "I'll talk to Joan and see what we can find out."

Connor said, "We were hoping you would do that. This fax says she is still in Montana. But Joan says she is in Vegas. We need to know for sure which it is, so see if you can get her to call her mom and set up a visit. Maybe then we will know if she is still here or not.

One more thing you should know," Connor added. "James recognized Anna from her photo, and he says that she worked with Ricky Allen running drugs in Vegas."

130

Great, Dylan thought, more bad news. Then he thought of something he'd been wondering about and asked Connor, "Why do you think Jesse and Anna quit hanging out together, assuming they did stop hanging out, which seems to be the case?"

"I've thought about that too," Connor said. "But I'm not sure. Let's just find her first, then we can ask her."

"I think the answer to that question may hold a key to what happened," Dylan said, underlining the significance of it.

"I think you are right," Connor agreed. "And now," he announced loudly to the gang, "since we are all here I want to have a little meeting with everyone and get a status report. Let's all sit down and compare notes." Connor indicated the chairs around the table wanting the others to sit down.

Dylan started things off by saying, "Obviously, Anna may hold many of the answers we are looking for, so we should concentrate on finding her." He hesitated, waiting for someone else to contribute, or ask questions. When no one spoke up Dylan continued

"We need to find Ricky for the same reason," he said, then added, "Can anyone think of anything else?"

"Yes," Jake said. "I really need the NCIC report on Tommy as fast as possible."

"Good point," Dylan acknowledged. " And I have one more thing to add," he said. "I may be the only one who can do it, but we need to know what the hell picking berries has to do with all this. I know that may sound weird, but at the bottom of all the words we've heard from my mom is something to do with picking berries. I'm convinced that if I can make the connection, we will get some answers." The others merely nodded, unable to contribute anything sensible to what he'd said.

Connor said, "Ok, so let's focus our plans on the items Dylan and Jake just listed. Jake, you continue the actions you've started with NCIC. I will try to light a fire under their ass to get us a sheet on Tommy. Add to your list a request for all the information that the NCIC has on World Imports, and then interview the managers, past and present at World Imports. Try to find someone who was there when Anna and Jesse worked there and see what you can find out.

"James, I want you to figure out how you can use your Vegas contacts to help track down Ricky. Charlie, you mind helping Jake here at the store?"

"No problem," he replied.

"Thanks. Brent and I are going back to the accident scene," Connor said.

When the meeting broke up Jake approached Dylan and said, "We still have some time before Joan gets off work, you want to blow up some photos with me?"

"Yeah, that would be great."

CHAPTER FORTY FOUR

JAKE AND DYLAN sat at Jake's computer, scanning and examining the photos that were brought in from Jesse's house. They zoomed in closely on several of the photos, enabling them to see things previously invisible to the naked eye. Many details appeared as a result of the magnification, but it failed to reveal anything significant. Then Dylan handed Jake the photo that had been, temporarily, stolen from his mom's house.

"Here, try this one," he said.

Jake inserted the photo into the scanner and did his thing with the computer. They looked it over in tiny detail, and at first there was nothing revealing about it. Then something in the background caught Dylan's eye. He asked Jake to zoom in on the area of the bushes behind his mom. As the image grew larger, it became too grainy and blurry to identify. But that didn't slow Jake down, he zoomed in even closer, then used his special computer wizardry to clarify the image, allowing Dylan to identify what it was that had caught his eye.

It was a small pyramid of rocks that were carefully stacked by human hands beneath one of the blackberry bushes. Dylan sat back from the computer screen, thinking. Jake watched him and waited quietly. When Dylan started shaking his head Jake asked him, "What do you think?"

Dylan said, "There is something about that rock pile but I haven't quite placed what it is. It's on the tip of my brain but the light is just not clicking on. Whatever it is, I know it's important."

"Didn't you say that you used to pick those berries in that same park with your mom?" Jake asked him.

"Yes,"

"Did she make a pile of rocks there?"

"No, I don't recall seeing those rocks when we were there picking berries," Dylan said, concentrating in an effort to remember.

"Did she ever make piles like that before?"

Bingo! Dylan's eyes opened wide in surprise and he said, "Jake, you are a genius. Yes, she did do that once. But it wasn't in that park. It was a time when we went out in the woods, looking for blackberry bushes. We arrived in the woods and were ready to start picking, but instead of finding a bush and picking it, she did something that, at the time, I thought was weird. She took a picture locket out of her pocket, put it in a plastic bag and then buried it. Then she made a rock pile on top of it, just like the one in the picture."

"Do you know why she did that?" Jake asked.

"She said she was playing a game. I was pretty young then, so maybe she thought it would be more interesting for me if I thought of it as a game. But I think she was trying to teach me something. I think she wanted me to remember the purpose of the rock pile, which was to locate something buried. That pile we just saw in the photo means something is buried there."

"Wow," Jake said, putting the pieces together and seeing the possibilities. If Jesse had buried some significant clues under that bush, their jobs might have just gotten a whole lot easier.

"Yes. And you, my friend, are the one that asked me the right question that made it all click. Thank you," Dylan said, elated.

"You're welcome," Jake said. "Did you see the picture?" he asked Dylan.

"What picture?" Dylan asked back.

"The one in the locket. The one she buried when you were picking berries," he asked, wondering if whoever was in it might be of significance.

"No, she never opened it. She just dropped it in the bag and buried it. But, something way better. Now I understand why I was hearing my mom's voice saying 'Watch the ground for signs'."

Brent and Connor arrived at the accident scene with the intention of repeating the experiments they had done previously, this time armed with the information of where the witnesses had been standing when they witnessed the accident. But too late he'd realized the folly of the exercise. The so called witnesses had not witnessed a thing that could be considered useful.

But here they were, at the scene. And rather than waste the trip entirely, he decided to go ahead and make an effort at reenacting the witnesses points of view. Connor knew he was grasping at straws at this point, barely hoping that their project would reveal something to them, and so they were not too disappointed when it yielded nothing.

As they were preparing to leave, Brent felt the same strong urge that he had felt the last time he was at the accident scene. Only this time the urge took him to a spot behind the bush, a much safer place than in the midst of moving vehicles.

While standing in the spot he had been drawn to, he heard the same strange man's voice saying the same word; bitch. He didn't see anything or hear anything or think anything else. This time the duration of the trance – or whatever it was – was much shorter, and when he came out of it Connor was staring at him speculatively but was not as alarmed as he was when Brent stood amidst traffic.

When Brent saw the pleading look on Connor's face he sympathized with his need to understand what was happening to him. He apologized for not

133

explaining sooner, then went on to explain as best he could, with what little understanding he himself had, what had happened to him.

Connor's only response was, "Who was it?"

"Who was what?" Brent wondered.

"The voice. Who said the word bitch?"

"I have no idea," Brent admitted. "But I have the feeling that I will find out one day." He did not sound happy about the prospect.

"Wouldn't that be a good thing?" Connor asked.

"Good for someone, I suppose. Maybe good for everyone, but for reasons I can't explain, the concept of knowing fills me with dread."

CHAPTER FORTY FIVE

"I'VE GOT TO PICK UP JOAN FROM WORK," Dylan told Jake. "But it won't take long to tell her what we need, then we can go to the park and take a look for that pile of rocks. Tell Connor to meet us there."

"Sure thing," Jake assured him.

Dylan drove to Joan's office and parked out front. Picking her up in person turned out to be a good choice. When she saw him waiting for her just outside the exit she lit up. That excited Dylan and they were smiling when they hugged each other.

"I'm so glad to see you, what are you doing here?" she asked him.

"Wanted to see you, so here I am," he half lied.

"Sure. Why are you really here?" she joked.

"Ok, the truth is, I really did want to see you and I really am here. But I also wanted to ask you if you would come to the station with me. We thought of a couple of more questions. Do you mind?"

"No, I don't mind. It means I will be spending more time with you, right?" she asked hopefully.

"Damn right. Hop in my chariot and let's go."

They made the short drive to the station in Dylan's car. Once inside, Dylan found Jake and asked him, "Are the others going to meet us at the park?"

"They said they would," Jake told him.

"That's great, thanks." Then he and Joan went into the conference room.

After they were seated Joan asked, "What's up at the park?"

Dylan told her about the pile of rocks they had seen when they blew up the photo of him and his mom. Then he explained to Joan what they had found out about her mom, Anna, in the report from NCIC. Joan didn't cry this time, but she really didn't like hearing about her mom's arrest record.

"Wow," she said. "I had no idea about that. I wonder why she never told me about all these things."

Dylan knew exactly how she felt. Suddenly finding out that your own mom had kept a rather large secret from you your whole life is not exactly comforting news. But the fact of having this in common with her made him feel even closer to Joan.

Dylan knew that it would be better not try to rush her into dealing with the news, but he was anxious to get the information they wanted.

He said as compassionately as possible, "I know. Look at the secret that my mom had been keeping from me. I know exactly how it feels."

"Yeah, weird huh?" she said.

"Yeah it is," he replied. "But now that we know about it, we would really like to talk to your mom and see if she can provide more information. Can you call her and find out where she is? I think it would mean a lot to all of us."

"Sure," she said tentatively, her face a little pained, like she was still trying to figure it out.

"Something wrong?" Dylan asked.

"No, I just still can't believe it. All the secrets of our moms' past suddenly being revealed. What do I say to her?"

"When you talk to her don't let her know what we told you about her. Make it sound like you are just wanting to check in with her and to say hello. Tell her you are considering visiting her and you want to know where she is and how to get there. Try to find out if she is really in Vegas or somewhere else. Either way, try to get an address, ok?"

"Ok, but why are we being so secret about it?" she asked.

"I know it sounds kind of underhanded," Dylan explained it to her. "But until we know exactly what your mom's involvement is, or isn't, we don't want to tip our hand. We don't want her to get scared and go underground on us. Or worse, pass on the information to the wrong people."

She looked a bit hesitant but she took out her cell phone and dialed her mom's phone number. The call was not answered, at least not by a live human. It was answered by the electronic voice mail. Joan left a message saying that she was thinking of visiting and to please call her back. Dylan had another idea and asked Joan to wait for him for a minute while he spoke to Jake.

"Can we put some kind of a trace on either Anna's or Joan's cell phone," Dylan asked Jake, "and use it to locate where either phone is?"

"We can order it, yeah," he said. "I don't know why I didn't think of that. It's a good idea. Results aren't guaranteed but it could work. Give me the numbers and I will get it ordered."

Dylan gave Jake the numbers and then added, "Tell whoever you order it from that we left a voicemail from Joan's phone just now, and are expecting a return call from Anna's phone."

"Sure thing." Jake walked over to the phone and made the call, as requested, but he already knew where Anna was, and it was not Las Vegas. After all, it was his specialty to know where people were, and he knew she was close. He also knew that things might go smoother if her daughter was the one to bring her in. He found Dylan and Joan in the conference room and told them he was ready to go to the park.

"I will drop you off at your car on our way to the park," Dylan informed Joan. "Call me the minute you hear back from your mom please. And thanks very much for helping us out." He kissed her on the cheek.

"I don't think so," Joan told him.

"What do you mean?" Dylan asked, fearful that she may have changed her mind about calling her mom.

"I mean I am going with you to the park. I want to see what got buried there as much as you do. OK?"

"More than OK. Let's get James and the Chief and saddle up and go." I'm really starting to love this broad, he thought to himself.

They found James and the Chief in the Chief's office where they were happily burning up phone, fax and email lines to Vegas and other locations around the globe in an attempt to find Ricky. They were desperately hoping to get lucky soon and locate him, so when Jake asked them to go to the park, they begged off, preferring to stay behind and keep a watch for the expected responses.

Before Jake left, the Chief asked him to relay a message to Connor. "Tell him I have the autopsy report from the state capital, but that it contains nothing new. It looks like a car collision was cause of death."

Jake agreed to relay the message and then asked the Chief, "Anything come in on the trooper, Sanderson?"

"No, I haven't seen anything on him yet."

"Ok, thanks. Call us if anything comes in." Again he wondered about the delay and asked himself what it was about Tommy that was so bewildering to him. He shrugged and gathered up Dylan and Joan and the left for the park.

CHAPTER FORTY SIX

THE DARK HAIRED WOMAN, Anna Johnston, was parked near Joan's office building, waiting to see her come out at the end of her work day. She knew that seeing her without being able to talk to her, or hug her would break her heart, just like it had on previous days, but she couldn't help herself. She had to see her baby, make sure she was OK.

She was surprised when she saw Dylan arrive and wait near the exit. Romantic behavior such as this was not something she was aware of in him. She was even more astounded when Joan came out and lit up at the sight of him. They kissed and hugged like a couple of school kids under the influence of a serious crush. She caught herself smiling at the sight of them and was overcome with the pride and satisfaction that a mom feels when her daughter finds love and happiness in her life.

"My, my," she heard herself mutter. "Isn't life just full of surprises." A short burst of unexpected laughter erupted from her, followed by a brief giggle. Followed by a feeling of dread. She brushed a tear from her eyes as she followed them in her rented car.

She had a car of her own but it was parked in a rented storage unit where it couldn't be seen by somebody who shouldn't see it. Somebody like Joan, who thought her mom was in Las Vegas. Or somebody like Brent, who nearly noticed her when she had been parked across from Dylan's house, watching it, the other day.

Anna kept a fair distance behind Dylan's car so he would not be able to recognize her in his mirror. She followed them to the police station and then parked a block away, still in sight of his car and the station. She watched them go inside, and not much later she got a call on her cell phone.

The phone's caller ID told her that it was Joan calling her. At first she wondered how Joan knew that she was parked nearby, but she quickly realized that just because she was calling her, it didn't mean she knew where she was. Still, the coincidence was eerie and she was too nervous to answer. She decided to call her back later.

A few minutes later Joan walked out of the police station with Dylan and the young Deputy. The three of them got in a rental car, which she assumed was the Deputy's, and drove away.

Anna followed them from a safe distance. After driving only a few blocks she was able to figure out that they were headed for the park. She had been keeping eye on them since yesterday and had seen them go there once before. To avoid the possibility of being spotted, she took a different route to the park.

She parked a few blocks away from the park, and walked around to the edge of the woods surrounding it. Joan and the others hadn't arrived yet, but Brent and Connor were already there and they appeared to be waiting for the others to show up.

She had been dreading this very moment for a long time, the moment when someone would discover the park's secret. She was almost relieved that her long lived dread of discovery may soon be over. She stayed well back in the trees and watched the expedition of discovery.

Connor and Brent had gone to the park as requested and were waiting for the others to show up. Jake hadn't explained to Connor why Dylan requested them to be there, so they killed some time making guesses about it. They came up with a lot of crazy ideas, just as a way to keep from being bored. But out of all of the crazy ideas they came up with, not one of them included the idea that Jesse had buried something in the park under a pile of rocks.

While they were standing around waiting and conjecturing, Connor got the creepy feeling that he was being watched. He looked around a couple of times to see if someone was watching, but he didn't see anyone. He was reminded of the time when he was here taking the now famous picture with Anna, baby Dylan and Jesse. Only that time it was Anna who was looking hunted.

When Jake finally arrived, the first thing he did was relay the Chief's messages to Connor, telling him that, basically, they had struck out with the forensics people in Helena.

"Humph," Connor responded, "I'd thank you but I would have no idea what for."

"Tell me about it," Jake said. "This lack of information just confirms my feeling that we are being hoodwinked." Connor didn't want to discuss Jake's theories in front of the others, so he put it off until they could be alone.

"Ok, so what are we doing here?" Connor asked, changing the subject to one he hoped would yield something more helpful.

Jake showed him the print of the blown up photo, explaining to him Dylan's recollection of Jesse's lesson about watching the ground for clues such as this very type of pile of rocks.

After examining the photo, and hearing Jake's explanation, Connor knew that they had discovered a significant clue. For the first time since hearing about Jesse's death he felt a glimmer of hope. He instinctively looked for the spot in the park where the pile had been made, but because the print was narrowed in on such a small part of the park it was hard to pinpoint..

139

"Do you know where that pile was?" Connor asked Dylan.

"Yes," Dylan said, showing them the spot.

Connor looked to where Dylan pointed and instantly recalled the day when the picture was taken. He remembered how Anna kept looking into the bushes. He was sure now that she had been looking in the direction of the pile of rocks, and for the first time in many years some pieces of the mystery puzzle in his mind were starting to fall together.

Dylan walked to the spot where the pile of rocks had, allegedly, once been. He was followed by the others and they began looking among the bushes for some kind of a clue indicating exactly where the pile had been. Connors excitement was somewhat mitigated by the fact that there was no longer a pile of rocks in existence there. In fact there were no rocks at all, not even a scattering of what may have once been a pile. But after more than twenty years it would have been a miracle if there was still any sign of the little pyramid.

"What do we do now," Connor asked, "start digging up the whole area?"

"What if we tried a metal detector first?" Jake suggested. "If whatever Anna buried here had metal in it, it will make it a lot easier to find. If there is no metal, or if the idea doesn't work, then we can start digging up the area."

"Great idea, Jake. I'm glad I brought you along," Connor said. He called Charlie and asked him to send them a metal detector.

"Did anyone bring a shovel?" Joan asked.

They all looked at each other like they had just been caught doing something really stupid, which they had, then they laughed.

Dylan looked at Joan and said, "Not only are you good looking but you're a genius, babe."

Joan didn't answer him, but she thought that Dylan might get lucky tonight if he kept dealing out complements like that.

Connor called Charlie again and added a few shovels to his order. The Chief said he would not only send some shovels but would also send some pick axes, in case the ground was hard or rocky.

Connor said thanks and hung up. Then he considered what Charlie had just said and groaned.

"What's up?" Jake asked him.

"Charlie is sending pickaxes with the shovels," he whined.

"Yeah, so?"

"So I don't really look forward to chipping rocks out of the ground, that's what. I'm a little too old for that shit," he said, looking miserable.

"Yeah, I see your point," Jake said.

Not being sure if Jake was referring to his age, but guessing he was, Connor said, "What's that supposed to mean?"

"Nothing. Never mind. We'll do all the digging and you can supervise, ok?"

"Don't push your luck, Jake."

Jake held up his hands, palms out in the universal sign language meaning 'ok, sorry, I'm backing off'. But he was having a hard time hiding his smile.

Connor gave him a hard look.

The metal detector arrived, Brent grabbed it and started moving it back and forth over the ground hoping it would show something. After just a few minutes it whistled and whined like it had just discovered the titanic under the ground.

Brent and the crew got excited and now wished the shovels would hurry up and get there so they could dig up the treasure. But like always in such situations, due to the magnitude of their anticipation, time seemed to slow to a near stop while they waited.

After what seemed like a year but was really five minutes, the shovels and picks arrived. Dylan was anxious and grabbed one of each, rushing to the task.

He started with the shovel, but was making slow progress. The ground was too hard. He switched to the pick and started breaking up the dirt. Brent grabbed the shovel and used it to remove the dirt that Dylan loosened with the pick. The teamwork was successful and after several minutes of digging they heard a metal click against the pick.

Several ooohs and a few heys could be heard from the crew, who got excited by the sound of metal on metal and moved in for a closer look.

Dylan became a little more cautious and tried to pick around the object so that he wouldn't damage it. The others stood closely around the hole looking on in curiosity. A few minutes later Brent bent down into the hole and started using his hands to scoop the last bits of dirt out from around the object. The crowd held its breath when it finally came loose and Brent lifted it out of the hole. He held it up for all to see.

The first person to speak was Joan. She said, "What is it?"

"It's an old trap for trapping small fur bearing animals," Brent said.

The old trap was obviously not an object buried by Jesse, and the group felt let down, but they faced the reality of the situation and Brent started over with the metal detector. He covered a lot of ground with it but all he found was a couple of old cans, a few small coins, some parts from an old farm implement and a child's sand box shovel. They finally conceded that if something was buried there it was either not metal or it was too deep.

Plan B went into action and a few of them grabbed picks and shovels and started digging. The starting point that they chose for the digging was based on comparing the photo blow up with any land marks that still existed and roughly triangulating the location of the pile of stones.

Before they got very far with the digging Brent said, "You know, this would be a lot easier and faster if we used a backhoe. Why don't I go rent one? The rental shop is just down the road."

"Ok with me," Connor said with undisguised relief. The fact was that none of them were enthusiastic about spending hours blistering their hands with picks and shovels.

Connor knew, however, that Dylan would not stop digging by hand while waiting for the machine to arrive, no matter what anyone did or said. So, contrary to what he had said to Jake a short while ago, he decided to join Dylan's effort rather than stand around and watch him. Jake and Joan reluctantly agreed with Connor and sluggishly picked up their tools.

When Brent arrived with the machine, relief was plainly evident on the sweaty faces of the excavation crew. No one had found any buried objects and not much dirt had been excavated either.

The machine was a small affair, not one of those huge ones on tracks. Brent's reasoning in renting it was that they wanted to be somewhat delicate in the operation of digging up the ground so that they didn't inadvertently destroy the object they were trying so hard to obtain.

Brent, who once had a short-lived job operating heavy machinery, elected himself as the operator, while everyone else elected themselves supervisors and began giving him directions. That would have been alright if they had been in agreement about their directions, and if they'd given them one at a time. Desperate to do his job unmolested by his group of foremen he sent them off on little errands, like getting some yellow crime scene tape to keep people away from the hole, or getting some stakes to hold up the yellow tape, or getting some water for them, etc.

While Connor watched the operation, there were several more times that he felt like he was being watched. He looked around occasionally but still didn't see anyone.

CHAPTER FORTY SEVEN

ANNA WATCHED THEM in the park as they searched the ground around the old blackberry bush. Almost with a fright she realized that they did indeed know what they were looking for. For an instant she considered saving them the trouble of digging and telling them what they would find there, but she decided to wait.

She saw the metal detector arrive and shook her head. That would be a waste of time, but she couldn't walk down there and tell them now, could she? When they found something with the detector and started digging excitedly, she thought she wouldn't be able to remain silent any longer, it was so maddening to watch. But she managed to wait and eventually they had discovered that their hopes were unfounded. Maybe now they would get on with it. Either that or give up. She still had mixed emotions about which option she most preferred.

She noticed that the digging stopped and that they were standing around as if waiting for something. It made her curious and she thought about calling Joan to see if she would tell her what they were waiting for. But if she did that, Joan would realize that she was not in Vegas, as she had been leading her to believe.

About twenty minutes later she saw some heavy equipment arrive. They were getting serious now. While she watched the machine, she wondered what had tipped them off about something being buried there, and quickly concluded it was that damned picture.

She knew twenty years ago, when it was taken, that it would cause trouble. She remembered seeing the small pyramid of rocks behind Jesse and Connor through the view finder of the camera and it had made her very nervous. Once, Connor had even looked around behind him to see if he could see what was worrying her. She recalled how her heart had skipped a beat in a moment of panic when he did that. She'd gotten lucky that time and he didn't notice it.

After Connor had left town they developed the roll of photos and could see the pile of stones clearly in one of the pictures. She argued with Jesse to move the buried items to a different place, but Jesse was adamant about leaving it where it was. In fact she chose that very picture to frame and hang in her house. She said she had her reasons but wouldn't tell Anna what they were. Maybe now she was going to find out.

She watched the digging for another half hour and got bored, so she decided to return Joan's call and see what she wanted.

Joan was getting a bit bored with the digging activities herself when her phone rang. The caller ID said it was her mom so she motioned to Dylan to get his attention and then pointed at her phone to signal to him that it was her mom.

"Hi, mom," she answered, trying to sound cheery.

Dylan came quickly to Joan's side so he could listen in on the call. Joan was saying, "Yes, I tried to call you earlier. How are you?" After a couple of seconds she said, "I'm fine. I called because I wanted to come see you. I miss you. Do you mind if I come visit?"

Joan listened for a minute and then said, "Yeah, I understand, maybe later. I'd like to mail you a card or something, what's your address?" Then a second later, "I know it's not necessary, I just want to." Then, "Ok, I'll watch for it – love you too." She hung up the phone.

She turned to Dylan with a hurt and disappointed look on her face and said, "She said she had too much work and now was not a good time."

"What about her address?" Dylan asked.

"She just blew me off and said she would email it to me. I don't get it, Dylan, what's going on?" Joan sounded confused and looked like she was on the verge of going into shock.

"Joan, take it easy," Dylan told her soothingly. "This is not as terrible as it seems. I'm certain that your mom isn't involved in anything evil. You'll find out soon enough that it will all be ok." He was sure that what he said was true, even if he wasn't sure how to explain why he was so convinced.

"But how do you know?" The one question he couldn't fully answer. But he tried.

"In your heart of hearts," he asked her, "do you really think your mom could be up to something really bad?"

She hesitated and appeared to be deep in thought for a few seconds, and then said earnestly, "No, I don't." She gave Dylan a big hug, easing his worry about her.

His nerves didn't get a break for long, though. Jake, who was standing a few yards away with Connor, had caught his attention with a wave of his arms and motioned for him to come over. Dylan caught a brief glance from Jake to Joan which told Dylan that Jake didn't want her to come.

"Wait here," he told Joan, "I'll be right back."

"Do not to look around when I tell you this," Jake warned Dylan when he approached.

"Ok, I won't, what is it?"

"They got the trace on Anna's cell phone. She's here, in Montana, and near the park." Jake whispered.

"Wo! I'm glad you warned me not to look around," he said. "Holy shit!" he added.

"Yeah," both Connor and Jake agreed. Connor wondered if it was the reason he felt 'eyes' on him for the past hour or so.

"Now what?" Dylan asked after getting a little composure back

"Yeah, exactly," both Connor and Jake agreed.

"Boy, you guys are a lot of help."

"We better think of something quickly, here comes Joan," Jake said.

Dylan and Connor turned their heads in Joan's direction and Jake was right, she was walking towards them.

In a low voice Dylan said, "For now don't say anything about it."

"Is something happening?" Joan asked. Damn, Dylan thought, she must have seen the surprised looks on our faces.

"No, hon, we were just trying to guess what might be buried here and what we would do about it. We are kind of thirsty and tired, though. Would you mind, much, getting us some coffee?"

"No, I don't mind. Cream or sugar?"

"Both please, we really appreciate it, thanks," Dylan said and handed her some money.

Joan walked away to do what Dylan asked, but she didn't look happy about it. He looked forward to making it up to her later. The thought made him smile.

"Ok, so now what?" he asked again.

"Do we really want her right now, or do we leave her alone?" Connor asked, then explained his line of reasoning. "If we nab her now, we can't hold her, we have no charges. She may go into hiding when we let her go. On the other hand, if she decides to cooperate with us, now would be better."

Dylan already had the answer, "We have to get her immediately. She already knows we are on to her so if she is going to go under, she will do it now. Besides, I got a feeling she will help us."

"Good enough for me," Connor said. "Jake, go tell Brent to make a call to Charlie and have his cops hem her in. Tell them to be easy about it, we don't want to spook her." As an after thought he added, "And ask Charlie to run a make on her car so we know what she is driving."

"Won't that tip off the other cops to what we are doing?" Jake asked.

"You really think they don't already know exactly what we are doing?" They both knew what it was like to work in a police station. Secrets were hard – impossible – to keep. The other cops had seen them working in their station long enough now to have a pretty good idea about what was happening.

"Yeah, I guess you're right," he said, and then ran over and talked to Brent, who made a cell phone call to the Chief.

While waiting for Flatrock's finest to show up they began to slowly fan out, a strategy aimed at preventing any attempts she might make to escape in their direction. Jake got in his car and drove around to the other side of the park to watch the streets there.

Anna dialed Joan's number and then watched her in the park when her phone rang. She was startled when she saw Joan make hand signals to Dylan and call him over. For a second her mind froze up and she worried that her tongue might do the same. She considered hanging up before Joan answered, but it was too late.

When Joan answered with "Hi, mom," she was somewhat surprised to hear her own voice respond with, "Did you call me earlier?"

Now that she knew she was able to speak she had to think fast about what to say. Or not to say. The knowledge that Joan was cooperating with Dylan and the Deputies shouldn't have surprised her. After all she was here with them in the park, and had been to the station a couple of times. But this sudden discovery that she she had been trying to contact her on their behalf threw her off. When Joan asked to see her, and asked for her address, Anna quickly deduced her motives and made lame excuses to avoid giving the answers. She wanted to take a little time to think about it before deciding what to tell Joan, so she ended the phone call.

She watched Joan take some money from Dylan, then walk away from the park. Brent stopped digging in order to make a phone call, then the group spread out along the edge of the woods. She gasped when she realized that they knew where she was.

She only had two choices really, give herself up or run. And since they already knew where she was, running was out of the question. She would go to them, but not just yet. There was one thing she wanted to do before talking to them.

It was pretty obvious to Joan that she had just been excluded from something being discussed by Dylan and the Deputies. They were not very good at hiding their emotions and she could read their faces easily. She felt offended by the segregation, especially by Dylan because she had just begun to believe that they were bonding better than ever.

She arrived at a convenience store across the street, ordered the coffees and waited for the clerk to make them. By the time the clerk had finished making the coffees and had lined them up on the counter, Joan's anger had waned a bit.

146

She paid the clerk, then stared at the line of cups, trying to figure out how she was going the carry them all.

As she was reaching out to try picking up the cups, a voice behind her said quietly, "Let me help you with those." Her hand froze at the familiar sound of the voice, she turned slowly and saw the familiar sight of her mom's face as well. The sight of it was so utterly unexpected that her mind would not immediately accept it, causing a brief lag before she let out a loud gasp and then started crying.

Anna didn't seem surprised by her reaction. She put a gentle arm around Joan and said, "It's ok, it's just me, I didn't mean to scare you. It will be ok, don't worry." It had a calming effect on Joan and soon she stopped crying.

When Joan could speak again she said, "Oh my god, mom. What is happening? How did you get here? I thought you were in Las Vegas."

"Yes, I'm sorry," she replied. "I did go to Vegas, and have been there most of the time since I left. But I came back after Jesse died. I'm sorry I misled you honey, and I know you need a good explanation, and you'll get one. But if you don't take the coffee back to the others they will panic. They know I'm here and are looking for me right now. I think we should take them their coffee, then I can explain myself to everyone. Ok?"

"Ok," Joan said weakly. They grabbed up the coffees and left the store. As they walked Joan concluded that Dylan and the others had been hiding the news of her mother's proximity. She also concluded that she reacted to the news exactly like Dylan had anticipated she might, so maybe she could understand his reluctance to drop the news on her all of a sudden. So, he still cared for her after all.

Jake circled around the west end of the park to get to the north side, which is where the phone trace reckoned Anna's location. On his way around, Connor called him with a description of Anna's car. Jake hadn't seen one like it so far and continued looking for it until he reached the north side of the park. No car with that description was visible. And no woman of any description was visible. He saw the squad cars coming towards him from the east and when they met up they stopped to compare notes. The cops had not seen Anna or the car.

Unfortunately, the local cops were looking for a car fitting the description of the one registered to Anna, not bothering to look at the drivers of any of the cars not fitting that description. They were clueless when she drove right past them in her rental.

Jake called Connor and gave him the report that there was no Anna and no car. Connor called off the search and everyone returned to the excavation site, where they were met by Joan, carrying half of the coffee order, and Anna Johnston, carrying the other half of the coffees. The men were shocked, but pretended not to be, so they wouldn't appear outwitted.

"Hello, gentlemen, would you like some coffee?" Anna said calmly. The men reached for a cup, she smiled smugly at the satisfaction of having outwitted them.

First things first. Before drinking his coffee Connor asked her, "You plan on running?"

"I suppose if I really intended to run I would have done it long since, instead of hanging around here. So, no, I don't plan to run," Anna answered.

"Fair enough. Will you talk to us?"

"I will. You all deserve an explanation. It appears you were looking for me."

"Thanks, yes we do, and yes we were," he responded.

Dylan had noticed Joan's red eyes and knew she'd been crying. He went to her side like a loyal knight in champion of his fair lady, and watched Anna with a bit of a scowl.

"You OK, baby?" he asked Joan.

She felt infinitely better by being addressed as if she was a princess being worried over by her knight in shining armor. With a rascal-like smile she said, "I feel much better, my lord." Then she reached up and kissed him on the cheek. Dylan smiled back, blushing a little.

Anna watched the exchange with both a frown and a smile, happy but puzzled at the same time. She spoke to Joan but meant it for everyone when she said, "I apologize for springing my presence upon you so suddenly, but it seemed like the only choice I had, given the circumstances."

"Circumstances which you created," Dylan couldn't help pointing out.

"Quite right. Again I apologize. But when I explain, I hope you will not hold it so firmly against me."

Connor intervened, this was all very dramatic, but not very productive.

"Do you remember me?" he asked her.

"Yes, Connor, I would never be able to forget you. Jesse saw to that."

Connor got misty for a second but managed to keep the tears under control.

"That day in the park when you took our picture," he asked, "were you worried about the pile of rocks over there?" He motioned to where they had been digging.

"Yes, and I noticed that you were aware of my state of panic. You looked right at it once and, for a second, I thought you had caught me out."

"Well, I never did see it until today in the photograph, thanks to Dylan and Jake. Do you know what's buried there?"

"Yes, I think," she said with some hesitation. "That is, I knew back when we took that picture, but I can't be sure if it is the same now."

"Will you tell us?"

"I think it is something you have to see for yourself, instead of hearing it from me. You are very close to it now. Be careful that the big tractor doesn't destroy it."

Dylan had been studying Anna during her brief conversation with Connor, noticing the similarities between her and Joan. The dark, straight hair, same height and similar build showed plainly that they were closely related. But the similarities ended there, and that was what piqued Dylan's curiosity, causing him to look more closely.

What was different about them, other than age, was the emotional energy that he could sense about them. Anna was feeling hunted and was teetering on the verge of paranoia. She put on a good act of seeming calm, but he could see that she was really quite skittish. There were also physical clues indicating how she had been living recently. Her hair was out of sorts and her clothing was wrinkled as if it had been worn for a few straight days. Dark circles under her eyes and an obvious absence of make-up added even more evidence.

Oddly, he sensed that she was even more beautiful without make-up than she would be if she was wearing it. Few women are like that, but she was one of them. So was Joan.

He made an effort to look past Anna's recently acquired condition and could clearly imagine the underlying beauty lurking in the shadows of her dilemma. With just a miniscule stretching of the same imagination he realized that her type of beauty possessed the rare quality of hypnotic attraction, which when unleashed on an unsuspecting male victim would probably be irresistible. The mere thought of such a possibility made him question his own enthrallment over Joan. Was she beguiling him, he wondered. Did it matter?

In response to Anna's warning not to damage the buried artifact, Bent said, "Ok everyone, it's back to picks and shovels."

The concept of more physical labor pulled Dylan out of his wonderings and imaginings about Anna and the Fair Sex in general. He once again took up arms against the earth.

Excitement grew in the air at the prospects of success, knowing now that something really was buried there. Something significant, according to Anna.

Brent moved the machine out of the way, leaving the lights of the backhoe shining on the digging area, now that it was growing dark. The others picked up their various manual tools and took turns picking and shoveling. Even Joan pitched in.

CHAPTER FORTY EIGHT

THE CHIEF AND JAMES had their hands full with their own brand of labor, and had been working hard at the station while the others were working up a good set of blisters in the park. Instead of pick axes they were slinging telephone handsets and hammering keyboards, but so far no one in Vegas had been able to track down either Anna or Ricky.

The Chief heard that the trace on Anna's phone had located her in Montana but, not being so trusting in modern tech., decided not to cancel the search for her in Vegas until they actually found her. James went along with this decision but inwardly smiled at the Chief's old fashioned views.

James had called some of his old buddies in Las Vegas, to see if he could get any help from them in tracking down Ricky or Anna. The results were mixed. Most of his friends had no problem informing him that Anna had been seen back in Vegas, working at one of the small casinos off the strip. Ricky was a much different story.

Ricky was allowed a certain amount of protection from his fellow criminals, and anyone who gave up information about him could be in serious trouble. The way James' contacts responded to questions about Ricky told him that they would not tell him anything even if they knew it. And since no one had told him outright where Ricky was, their search for him was getting nowhere.

Soon after learning of the success of Anna's cell phone trace, her mortal existence was confirmed in a phone call from Connor. The Chief passed the news on to James.

"She's here, in Montana," he said. "In fact she is with Connor and the others in the park."

"You're shittin me," James said, openly confused. "You sure? All my dudes in Vegas told me she was there."

"I'm just telling you what Connor told me," the Chief responded. "But I doubt that he would lie about it." James shrugged. Not his pay grade to worry about it. In fact he had no pay grade at all.

Moments later, the Chief got a fax from the Vegas Marshal's office. He read it and knew at once that he had better tell Connor about it.

Connor listened blissfully to his cell phone's ring tone, thankful for the break from shoveling dirt. He had only been digging for a few minutes and he already had blisters. "Hello, Charlie," he answered.

"How did you know it was me?" the Chief asked.

"Caller I.D."

"Oh, yeah, I forgot about that," the Chief said. Connor waited patiently for Charlie to get to the point.

"Anyway, the reason I called, we just got a report from the U.S. Marshal's office in Vegas about Trooper Sanderson. I think you need to see it right away."

"We got something kinda serious going on here right now, Charlie. Can you give me the vital details on the phone?"

"Yeah, no problem. They haven't been able to get an NCIC response yet, but one of the Deputies there in Vegas recalled that Trooper Sanderson used to work for the Las Vegas Metropolitan PD. He said that a friend of his in the Vegas Metro PD had told him that Tommy had gotten in some trouble there and they let him go. So, curious, he called the Vegas Metro PD and asked if they knew anything. Vegas Metro confirmed that he used to be on the force there."

"What kind of trouble?" Connor wondered.

"You need to read the report for the details, but basically he was dirty. He was running with the same crowd that got put away on Jesse's testimony."

"Holy shit," Connor sputtered. The Chief heard a choking sound, then Connor was coughing.

"You ok?" Charlie asked.

"Yeah, I'm ok," he assured him. "Holy shit," he repeated.

"Yeah, no shit. What do you want to do?"

"We are about to dig up something in the park, and Anna says it's important. As soon as we have it I will come in and read the report, then I'll decide what to do about it. Ok?'

"Sure thing."

Connor had a last minute thought and before he hung up he asked Charlie, "What kind of clout do you have with the Highway Patrol?"

"Not much."

"Ok then, can you spare a man to keep a watch on Tommy?"

"No problem. It's not like we got a lot going on around here. Flatrock is not exactly big city. You want the cop that I assign to know what it's about?"

"Let's face it, Charlie, they already know what's going on. They would have to be dead not to know."

"Yeah, I guess you're right. I'll get a man on him right away. What do you want him to do?"

"Just have him make sure that Tommy sticks around. Tell him to report to you immediately if he starts to leave town."

"You got it. You need anything else at the dig?"

"Not yet, thanks." He hung up the phone at the same moment that Jake hollered to him that they had found something. He walked over to the dig and saw Brent lifting an object out of the ground.

As he held it up they all saw a small plastic box. It looked like a fishing tackle box and probably once was.

151

Connor asked Anna, "Is that it?"

"Yes, looks like the same box," she verified.

No one took a breath, watching anxiously while Brent brushed the last bits of dirt and dust from the box, waiting to see what was in it. Just when they thought he would open it and expose the contents, Connor said, "Let's take it back to the station and open it there. It's getting too dark out here. Anna, you ride with Brent."

"Are you kidding?" Dylan asked, exasperated. "We've been waiting for hours to see what's in there."

"No, I'm not kidding. You can wait a few more minutes. Besides, if you really want to see what is in there we need to be in a well lighted and protected environment, not out here in the open. The contents of this box, whatever they are, could be too important to take a chance with them," Connor reasoned. Dylan realized that Connor was right.

"You are right of course. I'm just too excited is all."

"I understand the feeling, believe me. Is everyone ready to go?"

"What about my car?" Anna asked.

"We'll bring you back here to pick it up later." He wanted her to ride with Brent because he didn't want to take a chance on her changing her mind and rabbiting on them.

CHAPTER FORTY NINE

AT THE STATION, the Chief and James were finally getting a few reports coming in. The first report was the background information on World Imports, but it was a dead end. The mob guys had quit using it when they were put in prison, which was before Anna started working there.

Ricky Allen, on the other hand, had been apprehended and was in custody in Vegas. They had found him accidentally during a drug bust, just as they had predicted. He wasn't talking about Jesse, Anna, Montana or anything else for that matter. But they had him cooling in a cell in Vegas.

They even got a report that they hadn't asked for. Tommy Sanderson's ex partner at the Vegas Metro PD had heard about the hunt for Anna and called the Chief to volunteer some rather interesting information. He said that Tommy had mentioned the name Anna Johnston to him just before he left for his new job in Montana a few years ago. He said he recalled Tommy saying it would be funny if he ran into her there. And the way he said it made it sound like he had a score to settle with her. At the time, he hadn't really understood the connection, but when he heard that someone was looking for both Anna and Ricky he noticed a coincidence he didn't like, and thought they should know about it.

James and the Chief gave each other a high five in celebration of having finished up their particular duties. Just as they were high fiving, Connor, along with the crew from the park, walked in and saw their mutual admiration in progress.

Connor said, "You guys look like you just won the lottery."

The Chief turned at the sound of Connor's voice. "In a way we did win a lottery. We just got a fax from Vegas Metro. They have Ricky in custody. And Tommy's ex partner at the Vegas PD has volunteered some rather interesting information." He told the crew what he had learned from Tommy's old partner.

"Great news, Charlie, You and James are doing a fantastic job here, thanks," Connor said. "Can you get Vegas to release him to us?"

"I'll get on it right now," the Chief responded.

"If they agree, tell them we'll send a Deputy over to take custody," Connor added. Then, to Jake, "Call the Vegas Marshal's office and ask them to be ready to send a Deputy over to the cop shop to pick up Ricky and bring him here."

"Yes, sir."

That taken care of, it was time to see what was in the box they dug up. Brent had put the plastic box on the table in the conference room, where the group had gathered. They stared at it, somewhat pointedly, while waiting for

Connor. The Chief was the only person not present for the opening. "Where's Charlie?" Connor asked.

"I'm here," the Chief announced as he entered the room. "I just spoke to the Vegas Metro PD. I asked if they would remand Ricky to the U.S. Marshal. Their answer was, quote, 'please take the scumbag and do the world a favor and lock him away for a few centuries'."

"Excellent. By the way, have you located the driver of the car yet?"

"No, not yet. Can't figure that one out for some reason," Charlie answered.

Unable to wait any longer, Dylan asked Connor, "So can we see what we have all been working so hard for and open the damn box now?"

"By all means. I think you should be the one to do it, Dylan."

Dylan wasted no time when he approached the box and pulled the top off of it. The others hovered around him, as curious as young kittens.

The contents were as mysterious as they were revealing. There was a gold picture locket which Dylan instantly recognized as the same one he had watched his mom bury when he was young. Since she had buried it in a different spot than where they had found it, he wondered how and when it got moved. There were also some photos and several pages of paper written in Jesse's handwriting.

The photos were not all of the same subject. Dylan looked at each one in turn and then passed it around for the others to see. Some were of Dylan as an infant with his mom and Connor, obviously taken on the same day as the one she kept framed in the house all these years. Others were of Jesse and Anna, probably taken around the same time by the looks of their age and the way they dressed.

The most interesting photos, all taken in Montana, were the ones of Tommy Sanderson, Ricky Allen and another man that no one seemed to recognize. These photos caused an overwhelming suspicion and raised some questions.

After he had passed on the last of the photos, Dylan opened the picture locket. The picture inside was a small close up of Jesse's and Connor's faces, cheek to cheek. He didn't pass it around to the others, but instead gave it to Connor and said, "Here, you keep this." He reasoned that his mom had included it in the box for Connor, and not as a clue to anything. It was her way of passing it on to him, since she could ill afford to keep it in the open.

Connor accepted it, opened it, looked at the photo and said, "Thanks." Then he left the room. From previous experience Dylan had a good idea where he was going. He only hoped that he wouldn't have another melt-down like the last one.

The others seemed curious about the locket and the exchange with Connor and his reaction, but they had the respect not to ask about it.

James, on the other hand, had missed the entire incident. He had been absorbed in one of the pictures Dylan had handed him. He had passed the other photos around to the rest of the group, but something about this one grabbed his attention so he kept it and continued to stare at it. It was the one of the unidentified man. He looked vaguely familiar to James and he couldn't help but feel that he had seen him somewhere before.

It would turn out that it was the one picture that Anna should have seen, but didn't get the chance.

The last item they pulled from the excavated box were the pages written by Jesse. Dylan picked them up and looked at the first page. "Do you want me to read it out loud?" he asked.

"Yeah, go ahead," the Chief answered.

At that point Connor returned to the room and Dylan looked up from the letter, noticing the Deputy's red-eyes. He looked back down at the letter and, noticing the date of it, said, "This is dated two years ago."

The significance of that produced various reactions. Anna frowned in confusion, wondering what had happened to the original contents that were buried there long ago, when the now infamous picture was taken.

Connor stiffened and said, "That means she didn't make a pile of rocks marking the location, it would still have been there. Or at least some trace of it would have been."

"You're right, Connor," Dylan said. "She must have buried the box without leaving any traces or hints. I suppose now we know why she kept only that picture around the house all these years. She knew it would be the only clue to lead us to the box she buried there."

"Wow," several of the group said.

"Shit," James said.

Dylan scanned the first few lines of the letter and doubted his ability to control his emotions. He handed the document to Brent, who, understanding Dylan's dilemma, began reading it.

To whom it may concern,

I am assuming at the outset that my son, Dylan, is the one reading this missive, since that is my passionate wish. However, there is the possibility that someone else has found this, thus the vague opening address. Not trusting entirely to mere wishes I have attempted to instruct him, in his life, in the various clues and perceptions that would lead him to the location of this letter and other objects. So if he, in fact, found my buried treasure I congratulate him and apologize for all the vagueness and cloak and dagger. By now he should understand the reason.

In any case, the fact that you are reading this indicates that the circumstances surrounding me are extreme. Perhaps more than extreme, since extreme circumstances seem to have defined my existence for some time now.

While it is my deepest hope that such circumstances do not include my own demise, I fear that it may be the case. It is against that very condition that I am writing this, for if I am gone, there may be no other way to convey the facts revealed herein.

I will begin with the unhappy facts and end with the more positive ones in hopes that it will put you more at ease by the time you finish reading this.

By now you know about my involvement in the witness protection program and the reasons that I am in it, so I will skip ahead of that story. In the unlikely event that you did not know about it, please contact Connor McDermott at the U.S. Marshal's office.

Recent events have caused me to become suspicious, if not certain, that my identity and location have been compromised. It started with spiritual disturbances. Dylan will know what that is. For others I can describe it best as 'chills up the spine of my soul for no immediately evident reason'. Some time after those feelings started, I began to see people from my 'other past'.

First I saw Tommy Sanderson, who was, in all unlikelihood, a Montana Trooper in our own town. I never knew Tommy, but I recognized him from a picture which appeared in the Vegas newspapers many years ago. The article in that paper said he was a crooked cop in Vegas and had worked for the same gang I testified against. I was astonished at how it could come to be that he was working in Flatrock, and the coincidence of it frightened me.

Then I saw a man whose name I never knew, but I recognized him from my courtroom testimony. I noticed him several times seated among the spectators in the courtroom during the trial. I wish I could provide more information to lead to his identity but I cannot. I feared that inquiries about him would only attract more attention to me. However I did manage, by some miracle, I believe, to get a photograph of him which you will find with the other photos. Possibly it will help in some way.

Connor interrupted Brent with a passionately expressed question, "Why in the hell didn't she contact me?" He seemed to be asking the question to himself and not anyone in the room, and was visibly distraught, making Dylan wonder if he would break down again.

Brent answered, "I think the next bit in the letter will explain that." He hurriedly continued reading, hoping to prevent Connor's continued downward spiral.

By now I can guess that whoever is reading this will be wondering why I didn't contact the Marshal's office. That is a most difficult question to answer, and I feel that Connor may take it hard that I never asked for his help. If he ever doubted my love for him, then no explanation will suffice. However, I feel confident that he knows better than to doubt it, in which case I can only say that contacting him would never have changed the unfortunate circumstances of our mutually unrequited affections, and could, quite possibly, have made them even more torturous. Please tell him how sorry I am for both of us.

By that same token I feel that I can no longer run and hide. I simply could not bear to relocate and change my name again. Since Dylan is a grown man now, any relocation would have meant losing him in my life, so, wisely or not, I chose to stay and take my chances. My apologies to all if this decision turned out badly. However, know this; I have taught you that there is more to life than mere flesh. DON'T FORGET THAT LESSON. If you do, you will disappoint me and, more importantly, yourself. I will always be around!

Joan and Anna were crying noiselessly, and James whispered, "Damn."

Dylan, however, was smiling, and if the others weren't so somber looking he felt like he might be laughing, but not due to psychotic glee. Rather, it was because he was thinking of how, even in her absence she could manage to scold him and instruct him all at the same time. And she was right, she was still around. He could feel her. Like fingerprints, no two people feel the same, and he was very familiar with how she felt. That familiar feeling was another reason he was smiling. It was a comforting feeling.

Brent kept reading:

To continue, the next person I saw was another friend of mine from Las Vegas. Her name was Helen Whelan. I only saw her once and she didn't seem to notice me. But it was another scary coincidence and I found it hard to believe that these events were unrelated.

I was, therefore, prompted to bury the artifacts that you now have. I hope the photos will provide effective evidence, or at least be of some slight value.

Now I must speak of my dear friend Anna. Anna is at the root of the entire situation I find myself in. She was the person who originally tipped me off about James. She also helped me a great deal in dealing with the whole mess. Hopefully she can explain the details of it. I must make a confession to her. There was never anything in the box we buried those many years ago. She was so worried about its discovery by Connor and I never had the nerve to tell her then. The entire purpose of the pile of rocks was to take a picture of it so that one future day Dylan would know what signs to look for when something would actually be buried there. For that same reason it is the only photo I kept displayed in the house.

I might as well make more apologies for yet more deceptive behavior on my part while I am at it. It seems, upon reflection, that there may be few, if any, persons in my life who have not become victims of my legerdemain.

James burst out, "For gods" sake. What the hell is a ledger da mane? This fancy talk has gone too far. I swear if she was alive I would send her back to school so she could learn to speak real English, which we would all be able to understand."

The others stared at him unpleasantly so he calmed himself a bit and said, "Sorry for the interruption, but at some point I would really like to be able to get what she is saying. Am I the only one?"

Anna explained calmly, for everyone's benefit, "Legerdemain is a word that means sleight of hand, like a magician. It refers to using the art of deception. It comes from French words meaning literally, 'light of hand'.

James said, "Thanks, Anna," in a sulky voice. Then he contritely asked Brent to continue, which he did.

You could call it parlor tricks of a sort really, and I fear that a full explanation of how it works would become far too lengthy to hold the attention of a sane man for its duration. Suffice it to say I seem to have been born with a gift to prevent others from gaining certain knowledge about me, from my mind, if I am so inclined. If I was not so good at it Dylan would long since have guessed what my life and history was truly about.

I hope he does not feel that I betrayed him in this regard. My intentions were wholly honorable. I felt it was bad enough that I had to live a life of looking over my shoulder, and could not bear the guilt of causing him to have to do the same. I was only trying to be a good thorn. Dylan should know not to hate the thorns.

I may have had a gift for stopping mind readers from reading my mind, but unfortunately I am not entirely able to stop someone from discovering my whereabouts. I wish with all my heart that I was.

I have digressed from the subject of dear Anna in my selfish attempt to purge my guilt. Anna has sacrificed her life for me. I know she had other reasons than just me, but I will not deny myself the knowledge that those other reasons were not strong enough to cause her to make the sacrifices she did. No, she did it for me, and for Dylan. I don't say this in a selfish manner, but rather as an expression of my admiration and appreciation. I have known no stronger friendship with another, and ironically it was the strength of our bond that built the wall separating us. We knew, many years ago that we could never continue our connection without jeopardizing our lives. So we vowed to never have contact with each other again.

At the time it was a very tough choice for us to make, and was heartbreaking beyond words. And now that I have the benefit of looking back on my life, I have decided that I made a poor trade by forsaking my ability to live in exchange for my corporal life.

When Dylan and Joan started dating it was utterly frightening, in the sense that it created a renewed risk. However, the beauty of their relationship was worth the risk and my heart sang with happiness for them. Through them I could at least experience the real joys of life, even if only as a voyeur. I hope that they have happiness with each other and that they are never forced apart.

All my love,

Mom.

PS. Tell Brent I may have led him astray when he was young. I told him that the hard ones were not worth it. It turns out I was wrong. They are always worth it. Tell him I apologize.

The room was awash with quiet mourning for several moments. Brent broke the silence by saying, almost to himself, "I knew she was full of shit." He said it matter of factly and it sounded like an 'I told you so'. He didn't look up or look at anybody after he said it. Instead he was looking inwardly, at something back in time.

His statement definitely garnered some attention, and when Brent was finished congratulating himself on his recent vindication, he looked up to see the faces of the others staring at him as if he was some kind of an evil freak of nature.

Dylan eyed his friend, wearing a faint smile of understanding.

CHAPTER FIFTY

IT TOOK A WHILE FOR CONNOR to recover from the reading of Jesse's letter, but when he finally came back to his senses he had transformed from a forlorn lover to a mad hornet.

He told Jake, "Get to work on the photo of the unknown man. Send it in to NCIC or wherever the hell you need to send it and let's find out who he is and get him here. Then track down Helen Whelan and get her in here."

Connor looked next at the Chief and said harshly, "Where the hell is Sanderson?" The Chief wasn't sure what to think of Connor's new persona, but Dylan liked the change.

"I got a man on him still. What do you want to do?" the Chief asked.

"Can we arrest him?" Connor asked grasping at any excuse to get Sanderson in for questioning.

"You tell me. Do we have any real charges?"

"No, damn it."

"All I could do," the Chief explained, "is ask him to come in and talk to us. As a Deputy U.S. Marshal you might make it a strong request to cooperate with an investigation but we still end up with the same result, no way to make him talk and no way to hold him until he does. And if we do put some pressure to him, he might go on the run. Especially if he is hiding something."

"Good point. I guess all we can do for now is to keep an eye on him. How good is your man at surveillance?" he asked, hoping that whoever it was wouldn't lose Tommy.

"He's no expert. He'll get spotted eventually if you ask me," Charlie said candidly. He didn't want to blow this deal any more that Connor did, but he had to be honest.

Connor thought about what Charlie said for a minute and made a decision. He looked at Jake and said, "Call the Vegas Marshal's office ask them to send us the best surveillance deputy they have. And while you are at it ask them when they will be arriving with Ricky. Oh yeah, tell them to bring whatever files they have on Sanderson." He turned to the Chief again and asked him, "What's your officer's name?"

"Officer McDonnell. Mitch McDonnell. We call him Mac," the chief explained.

"OK, do me a favor and get hold of Mac. Tell him to hang in there for a little while and do whatever it takes to make sure Sanderson doesn't see him. Tell him it is better to lose him than it is to get caught, so don't take chances. Tell him he'll be relieved soon."

Mac could have been reading their minds because at that very moment the Chief's phone rang and when he answered, it was Mac calling him. The others were not paying him much attention until they heard him yell, "You're where?" Then their eyes and ears were glued to him. After a short pause he said, "I'll call you right back, just keep going for now." He hung up the phone and looked over at Connor.

"That was Mac. He is following Sanderson on the I-15 south and they just crossed the border into Idaho." The Idaho border was about two hundred and fifty miles away from Flatrock. Mac had been following Tommy away from town for hours. "What do we do?" Charlie asked Connor.

"That's a good question," an extremely annoyed Connor answered, "What the hell happened to 'let us know right away if he starts to leave town'?" he demanded.

After seeing the Chief's blank stare Connor said, "Never mind, for now we keep Mac on him, but tell him not to hang back. We can't lose sight of him now, he could be headed for any one of a thousand different destinations."

The Chief was at a complete loss to explain Mac's behavior and could offer no kind of consolation to Connor. All he could say was, "I'll let him know. Sorry, Connor. I wish I could explain his actions but there really is no good excuse."

"Forget it, Charlie. At least he still has him in sight and that is the most important thing. Hell, even if he had called us right away, he would probably still be doing the same thing he is doing right now."

"I'm glad to see you feel that way," Charlie said. "Because there is one more thing you should know. There is a woman with him." He readied himself for another tirade from Connor.

"Fine. Just fine," Connor said. "Is there more, Charlie, or are you done spreading all your good cheer?"

"I'm done," Charlie said evenly.

"Gee thanks."

"You're welcome."

Moving on to the next order of business Connor turned to Jake.

"Jake, you call Tommy's boss at the Highway Patrol and see what he knows. Don't let on that we know where he is. Tell him we want to ask Tommy some more questions, and let's see how he responds."

Anna and Joan had been sitting quietly, watching the cops at work, and had almost been forgotten about until Anna volunteered confidently, "He's going to Vegas."

Connor turned to her and said, "How sure are you?"

"Positive." After she said it she realized that she really had no clear idea how she had arrived at the conclusion, or why she was so certain that it was correct. But for whatever reason, she did know and she was certain. She didn't think it was psychic thought. She had just put together a bunch of little bits of data, and they all clicked into place.

Connor, considering Anna's statement about Tommy, was about to tell the Chief to call Mac off the chase when he was interrupted by the ring of Jake's cell phone. He listened, hearing Jake say, "Got it, thanks for the call." Jake hung up and said with a hard voice, "Ricky got away. He escaped."

"That's unbelievable!" Connor shouted. "How could they possibly let him go?" His face reddened and contorted, transforming him from one mad hornet into a whole swarm of them.

The others were no less dazed. Just when things were starting to come together, they just as suddenly fell apart.

Anna reminded Connor, "You better call off Mac. If Tommy sees him it won't help us."

"She's right," Connor said to the Chief. "Let's get him out of there before Tommy spots him." The Chief made the call to Mac, who happily made a U-turn for home.

"I should probably tell you what I know before you make any other plans," Anna said.

"That would be great," Connor said. "I've been wanting to hear your story. In fact it's been one of our priorities to find you and try to get some answers from you. But you go ahead and say what you have to say. If we still have questions when you are done we'll ask them."

"Ok. You know from my record that I was connected to the wrong people when I was young," Anna started. "I did some stupid things, including drug deliveries. In fact I did some deliveries with Ricky, which is how James knows me. But what no one else except Jesse knew until right now, is that I'm the one who told her what James was doing."

So far her story was garnering plenty of attention from the listeners, portending the revelation of the truths they had been hoping for.

"I did it for two reasons," she continued. "The first reason was a selfish one, I wanted out. But I needed a way to get out without getting killed by the gang for leaving. The first time I met Jesse, on a delivery with Ricky, I noticed she was pregnant. She wasn't showing yet but a woman can tell. That's when I got the idea that Jesse might be able to help me.

"I knew that when she found out what James was involved in she would want to break away from the dealers, for the safety of her unborn child, and I hoped that together we could come up with a workable plan.

"My other reason was to help James get out. I could tell that his true nature was not the drug dealer type and I assumed he'd be happier doing something else. I guess I took a chance on that assumption but I hope I was right." She looked over at James for confirmation.

"Hell yes," James confirmed. "I always wondered how this all got started," he added.

"I'm glad of that," she said. "Anyway," she continued, "it was Helen Whelan, who was a friend of mine at the time, who had first talked to me about leaving the gang, but we both agreed that to do it without retribution would take an intelligent, and bold plan.

"We figured that our only way out was if the gang got busted. But we needed the right person up front, giving enough evidence to do the job of convicting them. Helen said she could supply all the damning intel on the gang, but insisted on being anonymous for reasons she wouldn't tell me. When Brenda, Jesse's name back then, came along we knew she was perfect for the role and we decided to ask her if she would do it.

"I set up a meeting with Jesse at a place where I knew it would be safe for us to meet. We met, and I told her about James, what he was doing etc., and asked her if she wanted to help us all get out. She did, and I told her to meet me at the same place the following week.

"After that first meeting I went to Helen and told her that Jesse agreed to help. We discussed out tactics for the next several days, then I met with Jesse again at the agreed time and place. The basic plan was for me to provide her with information I'd get from Helen, which she would then pass on as testimony at trial. She would be the front person, pretending to be the source of details she would give in her testimony. As far as she ever knew, I was her only source of the details. I didn't tell her about Helen, at that meeting or ever.

"I had even less information about the drug gang than Jesse did. It was Helen who brought me all the all the information, which I passed on to Jesse. I wondered where Helen got her information but she would never tell me. She said if she did she would have to kill me. But I'm getting ahead of the story.

"Whatever the source of the information was, it was Jesse who put herself out there in the open as the source. It put her at risk, while we hid behind the scenes, but she didn't care. Brenda had a set of balls on her for sure, so to speak of course. We had considered the option of me being the witness but we figured that I would not be reliable enough because I was 'dirty'. Even Jesse wasn't perfect, since she was married to a dealer, but she was new and had a clean record. She stood a better chance than anyone else we could think of.

"On the other hand there was the possibility that the drug ring leaders might figure out that Jesse was getting her info from me, via Helen of course. If they did we would all be dead women. The solution we came up with to avoid that possibility was for me to be included in the bust. Brenda would finger me and I would take a fall and do jail time. We figured that if I went down for something, then no one would suspect me of giving them away. It seemed to have worked.

"After I got released from prison and put on parole, Jesse contacted me. She said she could get me a job at World Imports if I wanted to get out of Vegas. It sounded like a good plan and I came here, got the job, and we hung out for a while. But the longer we were together the worse our paranoia got, until we felt like we were going mad. So as you just heard in the letter she wrote, we decided not to risk being together any more.

"I had known Tommy when I was running drugs," she continued, "and knew he had his hand in it, but wasn't sure how deep. I saw him rarely but he was definitely part of the inner circle."

Jake interrupted her, "Did you know his partner too? Was he involved?"

Her answer was surprising, "Tommy never had a partner that I know of, and I'm pretty sure I would have known." She frowned, wondering why he had asked that question.

Jake read the question on her face and told her about the call from the man who claimed to be Tommy's ex partner.

"I guess he could have had a partner without me knowing. It's not out of the question that's for sure," she responded. But the look on her face said that she still had doubts. After a few seconds she asked, "Did he say what his name was?"

"Brad Danison," Jake answered.

"I knew Brad," she said, "but I never knew that he was partnered with Tommy. I knew that he was on the gang payroll. He hung around, on the fringes. I saw him a few times, but only briefly. One time I saw him taking a package from my boss. I assumed it was money, but who knows. Whatever he was doing it did not involve me, or what I was doing.

"On the rare occasion that we were near each other," she added, "he would call me bitch. It was the only thing he ever said to me, and I never said anything to him. Obviously I didn't like him, and I damn well didn't like being called bitch. But I quit taking it personally when I saw him call a couple of other women bitch. I figured that he had some kind of complex and called all women the same thing. Not your Mr. Nice Guy.

"Yet he had to be involved with the boss somehow or he would not be allowed to hang around. And he was very clever, I'll give him that. He never let on about anything he was doing, and no one else talked about him either. So when the time came, I had nothing at all that I could pass on to Jesse about him. One thing I know for sure though, no cop is friendly with the boss without being on the roll.

"Yeah," Connor said, "he sounds like a real scumbag. Jake, we are going to need some help from the Vegas Marshal's office with this. See what they can tell us about this guy and find out if they will get a Deputy to check into Sanderson's history with Metro PD in Vegas and tell us what his story is. And have you found out what Tommy's boss here in Montana knows yet?"

"No, not yet," Jake told him.

"I will handle Tommy's boss," the Chief volunteered, "and you do the Marshal's office."

"You got it, thanks," Jake replied. Then he took the photo of the mystery man from James so he could get it run through NCIC. No one else in the group ever got to see it. If they had, Anna would have identified him, saving them a lot of time and grief.

"One more thing," Connor said to Anna. "Where do you live? We've heard it's Vegas, but you are here now."

"That's a reasonable question," she answered. "The truth is I'm in limbo. But I think what you're asking is where have I been. I did move to Vegas after Joan hooked up with Dylan. I was already paranoid about someone from the drug ring coming after me and Jesse, but I knew that they would come after Jesse first. And if they found her, they would find Dylan. And if they found Dylan they would see Joan and then find me. Anyway, like I said, I was paranoid. I stayed at some temporary places in Vegas, moved around a lot, you know, from paranoia. Then when Jesse died I came here and I've been living mostly out of my rental car."

"If you were so paranoid about being here," Connor asked, "why did you come back? Especially after Jesse got killed?"

"Yeah, I never said paranoia bred intelligence did I? I guess it really boils down to maternal instincts. I felt that Joan might be in greater danger and I had to be closer to her, to protect her. Although I have no idea how I would have accomplished that." Connor understood her motive, even if it was not strictly logical.

"I need some rest," Joan said. "Mom, are you coming home with me tonight?"

"Yes dear, I'd like that."

"Dylan?" Joan asked.

"You guys go ahead. You probably need to spend some time together, and besides, I've got a few things to wrap up before I go home. Call me in the morning." Besides, he thought, I won't be getting lucky with your mom hanging around the house. And if he wasn't going to get lucky then he would take advantage of the chance to get some needed rest.

"You're sweet," Joan said, "but that's not what I meant. You brought me here and my mom doesn't have a car either. We need a ride."

Brent said, "I'll take you guys, I'm going your way anyway. Besides, it will be nice to be in some good looking company for a change, instead of having to look at these barbarians all the time." He looked around at the rest of the group, smiling.

Joan walked over to Dylan and gave him a nice kiss goodnight. Then she gave him a look, right in the eyes and they made a 'connection'. It was the first time that ever happened to them, and what they both knew at that moment was that they were in love. That had never happened to Dylan before either. He kinda liked the feeling.

As tired as Anna and Joan were, they found it hard to go straight to bed. There were a few things that needed saying first.

"I can't believe you slept in your car, right outside my house," Joan said. "Why didn't you just come inside?" It broke her heart to know that on the very nights that she sat on her couch alone, missing her mom and wishing she talk to her, she was right outside her door. Anna's eyes filled with tears at the sight of the pain on Joan's face.

"I'm so sorry, honey. I wish I had come in, I really do. I missed you so much, but I was too scared. I believed that Jesse's death was no accident, and I didn't want to draw attention to you, in case the killers decided to go after you, or Dylan."

"So what about now?" Joan asked. "Am I still in danger? What if they followed you here?"

"Don't worry," Anna assured her, "if I thought it was dangerous I wouldn't have come to you in the park. It seems that whoever was here doing their foul deeds, has left. And no surprise with so many cops and Deputies running around. I think we are safe for the time being. But until we catch the persons responsible, there will always be a threat in our future. That's why I am going to try to help the Deputies."

CHAPTER FIFTY ONE

DYLAN WAS SITTING in the passenger seat of his car looking out the side window. He knew he was supposed to be driving the car instead of sightseeing, and he knew that no one else was driving the car. It was driving itself. Somewhere in the back of his mind he was aware that cars were not supposed to drive themselves, but he wasn't worried, the car knew what to do. Sure, he was aware that cars were inanimate objects and as such they couldn't really know anything, but the fact caused him no concern at all. He had something more important to worry about. If only he could remember what it was.

Shit! He forgot. How could he forget? It was important wasn't it? He knew what it was a second ago. Was he losing his mind? Damn it, he just had to remember. It was vital. It was a matter of life and death. What was wrong with him? "REMEMBER DAMN IT," he ordered himself.

He didn't notice getting out of the car, but there he was, standing on the curb watching the car continue on down the road without him. It could take care of itself, he thought. And even as he thought it, the fact that he had forgotten something important had simply disappeared from his awareness.

He decided to walk further down the sidewalk, toward the corner, but when he attempted to take a step, his foot was stuck to the concrete and wouldn't move. He tried again, harder this time. His foot still would not move. He tried again with the other foot . It wouldn't move either. Damn it foot, MOVE! He tried and tried to walk until he was out of energy. His legs were so tired from his attempts to walk that they were shaking, and he thought that they would not support him any longer. He started to sit, but his feet were still glued to the ground and this caused him to lose his balance and he fell towards the ground. He reached out with his hand, to break his fall, and felt, not the rough pavement but something soft and warm. He looked up and saw that it was his mom's hand.

She was smiling at him and he stared at her face for a long time, getting lost in it. He felt happy and serene, and had a floating sensation. He looked down to see if he really was floating, and he panicked when he saw that he was high above the earth.

He was frightened by the knowledge that he would start plummeting back to earth because..... well....everyone knew that it just wasn't natural for a body to float in the air. His heart raced wildly with the anticipation of the fall. Instead of falling he was held hanging by his mother's hand, and she was laughing at him.

Her laughing annoyed him, causing him to forget about his fear of falling. He tried to scold her for laughing at him, but his voice wouldn't work. Despite the fact that he had not said a thing, his mom said, "Hush now, and watch," then pointed at a spot on the ground below. He looked in that direction and saw a car. It was his car, and he was driving. He could not fathom how he could be floating in the air and driving a car at the same time. Had he gone insane, or he was in a coma and dreaming, or he was dead.

Oh my God, was he dead? His dread of his own unimagined death was interrupted by the sight of his mom on the sidewalk. She wasn't holding him up any longer. She was standing on the curb at the corner of the street. He was driving his car towards her. A couple of blocks behind Dylan was a highway patrol car with its flashing lights on. Did he do something wrong? Was he going to get a ticket? He watched the trooper, curious about what would happen to him.

Dylan the floater looked back at the corner to see what his mom was doing. Dylan the driver was just approaching the corner, and then his mom jumped out into the street in front of him. To Dylan the floater's total dismay, Dylan the driver never even had the chance to slow down before running over his own mother. His car never stopped. It just kept right on going.

He was staring so hard at the fleeing car that he almost missed seeing something else move out of the corner of his eye. It was a man. The man had been right behind his mom, and now he was running along the row of bushes that grew adjacent to the sidewalk. When he got several yards down the path he turned left and ran through a small gap in the bushes into a parking lot on the other side. He stopped running and started walking casually back toward the corner where his mom had been hit.

Dylan became angry with the man and wanted to smash him. He figured if he fell out of the sky and landed on him that would do a pretty good job of smashing the fellow. He willed himself down and his body began a fast descent. He aimed his projectile body at the walking man and started screaming angrily without stopping the entire way down. Just a half second before he would have hit the man he heard him half whisper the word 'bitch'.

"Wake up! Dylan, wake up! Come on man, its ok. Wake up!" James hollered. Dylan had been screaming bloody murder in his sleep for so long that he wondered if he would ever wake up. Out of desperation he shouted as loudly as he could, "Wake up you son of a bitch!"

That did the trick. Dylan woke up swinging, punching James solidly on the point of his nose. James fell backward onto the floor, not so much as a result of the punch as from his own reaction to the surprise of it, which was to jump back. Before he could recover from the fall, Dylan was on him like a crazed mountain lion. He was growling and swearing, snarling and spitting like a mad, wild animal. He had his hands around James' throat and an ugly, wild look in his eyes. Blood was flowing from James' nose and the sight of it seemed to further enrage Dylan who screamed with such violent insanity that James started fearing for his own life. Seeing it as his only chance for survival he knocked Dylan off him with a solid blow flush in the face. The blow knocked Dylan again he off long enough for James to get back up on his feet, prepared to defend himself from another attack. He eyed Dylan, waiting for him to mount another charge, but Dylan stayed on the ground and moaned. James remained poised, not yet trusting him.

Finally James said, "Are you ok?"

Dylan moaned again and rolled over, looking up at James blankly for a few seconds, until his eyes were somewhat focused. "What happened?" he asked. He saw the blood coming from James's nose and rubbed his own face wondering why it hurt.

James said, "You attacked me when I woke you up. First you hit me in the nose, and then you jumped on me and started strangling me. I thought you were going to kill me so I hit you."

"Why were you trying to wake me up?" he asked groggily.

"You were screaming bloody murder in your sleep. I thought you were having a nightmare." He had thought a lot more than that, but couldn't think of how to say it.

Dylan looked away, trying to regain his bearings. The last thing he remembered in his dream was wanting to smash some guy on the ground. The rest of the dream was not too clear but he knew it wasn't a good dream. He still felt a bit disoriented like people do when they are somewhere between sleep and awake. He got himself up off the floor and sat in a chair, rubbing his face.

James sat in another chair across from Dylan, watching him. Neither spoke. James because he didn't really know what to say and Dylan because he didn't have his senses completely about him yet.

Eventually Dylan asked, "Are you ok?" He had noticed James rubbing his neck, and saw too that it was swollen and red.

"I'll get over it, how about you?" James answered.

"I'll live."

Then they looked each other in the eye, made a connection and felt a new found affinity. A second later they both started laughing and almost crying at the same time.

When the laughing and crying wound down Dylan rubbed his face again and said, "You got a hard punch."

To which James responded with, "You got a hard strangle."

"Thanks."

"You're welcome. What was that all about anyway?

Dylan didn't fully understand what it was about. He had some good guesses, based on what little he had remembered about his dream, but he didn't feel like trying to explain it just yet. There was something significant about his dream, something he would have to work out at some point, but for now he told James, "It must have had something to do with whatever I was dreaming."

"Yeah, well next time you start dreaming like that I won't be bothering to wake you up. You'll be on your own." The clear meaning of which was that he hoped Dylan would not have any more bad dreams, but if he did he would still help him. Then he wondered why people sometimes do that – say the exact opposite of what they really mean.

Dylan just nodded his head up and down in acknowledgment and said," I guess we better clean ourselves up and get to the station."

CHAPTER FIFTY TWO

WHEN DYLAN WALKED into the station with James the first thing he noticed was the last thing he expected to see; Joan.

Likewise, when Joan heard the station door opening she looked up and saw the last thing she expected to see; Dylan and James, both with black eyes. Dylan had one rather swollen and angry looking black eye, and James had two, less swollen, black eyes and a swollen nose.

Everyone else in the room, the entire team, was just as surprised as Joan by the condition of the two men.

Joan and Dylan both tried to speak at the same time. Both started with the word 'what', and both stopped speaking when they heard the other speak. Then both said at the same time, "You go first."

Dylan was too tired to keep up this game so he shut up and waited for Joan to say something. Joan's first question was the most obvious question and the same question everyone in the room had on their mind.

"What happened to you guys?"

If Dylan and James had been thinking, they would have anticipated the questioning of their appearance and rehearsed some answers. But they hadn't been thinking and so they both answered with the first thing that came to their minds. And it just so happened that the first thing that came to both of their minds, and which they both stated at once was, "I ran into a door." They looked at each other with surprise and laughed. That made everyone else laugh, even if they weren't sure why.

Jake said, "Ok, so what really happened?"

Dylan said, "I had a bad dream," like that should explain everything.

Thinking that maybe Dylan's answer wasn't a complete explanation James added, "And I was part of the dream I guess," making a satisfied nod as if he had just cleared up the whole matter.

Joan, frustrated, said, "Will you please tell us what happened?"

Dylan didn't want to get into what really happened but he saw no way out of it so he said, "I was having a bad dream and James tried to wake me up. But instead of waking up totally, I hit him, thinking he was part of my dream I guess. Then I attacked him and tried to strangle him. He had to punch me in the eye to get me to snap out of it."

James was nodding his head up and down while Dylan spoke, in an attempt to confirm what he was saying, ending Dylan's story with, "Yep."

Joan walked over to Dylan and gently brushed his face with her hand and then asked, "Are you guys ok?"

Again, at the same time, they answered, "We'll live."

"What are you doing here?" he asked Joan. He had expected her to be at work, not here in the station.

"You think I'm going to let you guys have all the fun without me?" she responded, surprising him. She flashed him a big smile, looked him in the eye and he knew, without needing further explanation, that she was on board. She was one of them. One of the Dream Team. But even better than that -way better- was the connection, the oneness, and the love that passed between them when they looked into each others eyes.

Brent had not missed the exchange between his friend and Joan, and thought to himself, "Son of a bitch, Joan came through. Way to go man. Way to go." He was so happy for Dylan he almost got misty. Almost. He admitted to himself that he had been wrong about Joan, and he was never so happy to be wrong about something in his life.

Dylan noticed Anna tearing up and decided he better change subjects if he wanted to control his own tears. He put his arm around Joan, looked at everyone else and said, "What the hell are you guys standing around for? We got a killer to catch."

"He's right," Connor said, "Let's get to work. What have we got this morning? Or does Dylan need his coffee and donuts before we can begin working?"

"Oh, yeah, I'm glad you mentioned that," Dylan said. "I really could use some coffee after a rough night last night. And we might as well have a donut or two to wash down with it." He turned to James, "What about you James, you want some coffee and donuts to ease the pain in your nose and throat?"

"Shit yeah, sounds good," James said.

Brent said somewhat resentfully, "I am not going out for donuts this time. It's someone else's turn."

After hearing Brent's resentment, and taking one look at Connor's sour face, Joan volunteered. "I'll go. You guys get some work done."

"Thanks, babe," Dylan said to her happily.

"Now that we have the important stuff settled," Connor said, "I will ask again, what have we got this morning?"

Jake was the first to report, "Ok, Charlie talked to Tommy's boss at the Highway Patrol. He said that Tommy asked him for a few days off after hearing about Wayne Lefthand's suicide, so his boss authorized the leave."

Connor recognized Wayne Lefthand's name as the driver of the car that hit Jesse. But he knew nothing about a suicide. "What do you mean?" he asked Jake.

"Apparently," Jake explained, "Wayne's cousin called the Highway Patrol and told them that he had found Wayne in his TeePee, camped somewhere on the rez., dead from a self inflicted gunshot wound to the head. The cousin said Wayne couldn't take the guilt."

"Damn it!" Connor said. "It wasn't his fault. Why?" He wasn't asking anyone, and no one answered, but they understood how he felt. They felt the same as he did. It wasn't Wayne's fault whatsoever, and his suicide was a tragic waste of life.

"Why didn't he get help?" Connor asked in frustration.

"I asked the sergeant the same thing," the chief said. "He said that Wayne *had* gone for help. He felt depressed about Jesse's death and went to a Dr. He was given a prescription for the depression, and a few days later Wayne was dead."

"Jesus," Connor said.

"No shit," James agreed. "What the hell good is a Dr. anyway, if you end up worse after seeing one than before you went to him?" No one had a good answer for him.

Jake allowed a moment for the others to recover from the stunning news. Then he continued. "Tommy's sergeant said that Tommy took the news very hard. He said he muttered something about having seen enough, then asked for his leave."

"Charlie," Connor asked, "would you please go over there and brief the sergeant on what's going on? Then find out what, if anything, he knows about Sanderson's past?" The Chief nodded and left the room to carry out the orders.

"What else you got, Jake?" Connor asked, his mood somber.

"The Whelan woman is back in Vegas. Turns out she was here in Montana around the same time Jesse saw her. She stayed here until yesterday, when she turned up back in Vegas, staying in a cheap motel. She registered under her name, but the room was paid for with a credit card issued to Tommy Sanderson. We are still waiting for a full background on both of them from NCIC."

"Ah, the plot thickens," Connor quipped. "She must have been the woman that Mac saw in Tommy's car."

"It gets even better," Jake continued. "The Marshal's office in Vegas wasn't too happy when they arrived at Vegas Metro to pick up Ricky, only to find out he was no longer there. Seems like that little piece of negligence really ticked them off. They have been doing a little digging ever since, and came up with some interesting results.

"It turned out that Ricky's baby sitter at the Vegas Metro station, while they had him in custody, thought he was smarter than standard police policy. He thought Ricky was not a flight risk and took off his cuffs. Then he decided he could fully trust the scumbag to stay put while he went to take a leak. When he came back, guess what, Ricky was gone. He just walked out the door. Several cops watched him go, but they all figured that if he was walking around freely without cuffs he must have been released, so they never even thought of trying to stop him. But here's the interesting part, the cop who let him go was Brad Danison."

Anna's eyebrows went up but she didn't say anything.

Connor, however, did say something. He said, "That is interesting, to say the least. Isn't he the man you said was once Tommy's partner?"

"Yes he is," Jake agreed.

"And he just offered up some damaging information about Tommy?"

"Yes he did."

"So do we know the connection yet?" he inquired.

"The connection?" Jake asked, wondering what Connor meant by that specifically.

"Yes, the connection. There must be one. Between Ricky and Danison. You don't think a veteran cop like Danison would uncuff a prisoner and then leave him alone in a room 'by mistake – oops' do you?"

"Now that you put it that way, I guess not."

"Ok, so I will ask it again. Do we know the connection?"

"No," Jake said. "They have not reported a connection to me. But I will ask them to find one."

"What about Tommy? Have they come up with any files or reports on him yet?"

"No word yet, but they have Helen's motel staked out. Tommy would be crazy to show up there, but hey, you never know."

"Ok, Anna you got any idea where to look for Ricky?" Connor asked.

"Not really, it's been too long for me to be sure what he might do," she answered.

"Fair enough. What about Tommy? You seemed certain that he would be going to Vegas, any idea where he went specifically?"

"No, not really. Sorry," she said.

CHAPTER FIFTY THREE

MONTANA STATE TROOPER, sergeant Ingram was crossing the courthouse parking lot to his car, just after completing his shift, when ran into a brother in arms, Chief Armstrong. "Howdy Charlie," he said, reaching out to shake the Chief's hand.

"Howdy, Archer," the Chief said, returning the handshake. "You got a minute?"

"Depends. Is this official police business? If so, I just got off shift and I'm going home to a cold six pack. If not, I got all the time you need."

"Let's call it unofficial, and I'll buy you a beer while we talk," the Chief proposed.

"You got a deal. How 'bout we meet at The Outlaw?"

"You too, eh?" the Chief said. Archer frowned.

"What do you mean?" he asked.

"Never mind," the Chief said, not wanting to take the time to explain his comment, "I'll meet you there." He turned away before Archer could pursue further questioning.

At The Outlaw, the Chief filled Archer in on the details of the Deputies investigation, including what they knew so far about Tommy. At the end of the narration, Archer nodded his head several times, indicating that he wasn't surprised by the news.

"Tommy's been a special case from the beginning," he explained. "I got a call one night a couple of years ago from a government official, someone way up there." He raised his hand high into the air to indicate an alleged lofty elevation.

The Chief put on his best 'if you can't trust me, who can you trust' face and asked, "Who was it?"

"I can't tell you, Charlie. I wish I could, but really I can't. They put the fear of God in me when they swore me to silence and I don't think I will ever be a brave enough person to violate my oath. But what I can tell you is that they persuaded me to hire Tommy, sight unseen so to speak. He had the job before he ever set foot in Montana. Not that I'm complaining, he's been an excellent member of the team." The Chief felt a little swept away by the significance of what he just heard, like maybe he was getting in over his head.

"You ever notice him acting strangely?" he asked.

"Not until recently. Not until the day of Jesse's accident. I guess now we're calling it her murder. He was so shook up that day that I made him go home early and take some time to recover."

"What was he so shook up about?" the Chief asked.

"I assumed it was Jesse's death."

"That seems unlikely to me, to be honest. Wasn't he a veteran big city cop? I would think he could handle it better."

Archer nodded agreement. "I thought the same thing that day. But you should have seen his face, man was he out of it. Ever since that day he's not been quite the same. Then, as I already told you, he asked for some sick leave. And now you say he left town with his girlfriend."

"Yes," the Chief muttered pensively.

CHAPTER FIFTY FOUR

THE CHIEF'S REPORT created a meditative silence in the room. Sergeant Ingram's story about his late night phone call regarding Tommy was almost frightening. Connor knew that only someone very high up could intervene on Tommy's behalf, and have the clout to keep it so confidential. Possibly as high as the Attorney General's office. So why would people at that level be so interested in Tommy Sanderson? It didn't make sense to him, and the more he tried to make sense of it, the more confused he felt. To hell with this shit, he thought.

"Anyone got a plan?" No one answered.

Dylan had been trying to make sense of the news as well, wondering where it fit in with other facts they'd uncovered so far. There were his dreams about hitting his mom with a car and killing her, which he knew must be significant but wasn't quite sure yet how. There was the letter and other artifacts from his mom. There was Tommy, who fled to Vegas, with Helen. And then there was Helen. There was the almost complete lack of evidence or witnesses at the accident scene. There were the weird things happening at the Vegas Metro PD, such as letting a prisoner go free. Of all the things he had considered there was one that gave him some real hope. And that one thing was far from real evidence. It had to do, once again, with people hearing his mom's voice. He was just about to speak up about it when the fax phone rang.

Brent pulled the paper out of the fax machine, looked at it for a second and handed it to Jake. "It's for you," he said.

Jake took the paper and read it silently, all eyes upon him. He looked up and said, "Vegas Marshals office says they recognized the unknown man in Jesse's photo as a local Vegas cop. It's Brad Danison."

"He was here," Anna stated in a disturbed whisper, her face ashen.

Connor went beyond whispering. "Son of a bitch!"

James contribution was, "Yeah, no shit."

"What do you think it means?" Anna asked hoarsely. Joan stared at her mom with a mystified look on her face, perplexed by her sudden panic stricken appearance. She had never seen her mother act like this before, and she wasn't sure how to deal with it.

"Maybe he was coming here to find Tommy," James said. "Sounds like the guy suspected him of something, and maybe he was checking up on him." It was as good a theory as any, but Connor didn't agree.

"Maybe," Connor said. "Or maybe they are working together. They were partners back in Vegas at one time. Maybe they've kept a version of the partnership going here."

"Yeah, maybe," James replied.

Connor looked over at Dylan, wanting to ask his opinion on the matter. He changed his mind, though, when he saw Dylan leaning back in his chair with his fingers interlaced behind his head and his elbows sticking out, wearing a big grin.

"I just figured it out," Dylan declared.

All eyebrows went up with gleeful surprise. Connor was almost too excited to get the words out of his mouth when he asked, "You know who killed her?"

"No, but we're getting close," Dylan said. "We're on the right track, and we're going to Vegas."

You could feel the letdown, the disappointment that he had not named the killer. No one wanted to make an issue of it, but they did look at him expectantly.

In answer to the non verbal questions being so deafeningly asked by everyone, Dylan asked Connor, "Why did you bring Jake on this assignment?"

"A lot of reasons. What are you referring to?" Connor asked, wondering where Dylan was going with this.

"I'm referring to what you told me about his 'peculiar' ability," Dylan enlightened him.

"To find people," Connor said, getting the connection and smiling. Then he said, "Looks like we're going to Vegas."

James said, "Who's we?"

"Yeah," Brent said, "Who's we?"

"Yeah," Joan said.

"Yeah," Anna said.

"Yeah," said the Chief.

Dylan looked at Connor for the answer. After all, the Marshal's office would have to coordinate it, and probably foot most of the bill as well. Connor furrowed his brow, rubbed his chin and looked at each person in the room one at a time while considering how to handle this. After a few seconds he threw his arms up in a resigned manner.

"To hell with it, whoever wants to go is who 'we' is," he announced.

Several cheers went up at the news. Jake groaned.

The Chief said, "As much as I want to go I need to stay here with the station. Someone has got to run this damn place, and if Brent is gone I will need to cover his shift." That was his way of saying that Brent could go. It spared Brent the trouble of asking permission and the Chief knew that Brent would go anyway, even if he had to quit the department, which he didn't want him to do.

"Thanks, Chief," Brent said.

As Connor's junior, it was Jake's job to deal with the accounting, purchase requests, and other administrative duties. In normal circumstances a request up command channels for the extra money would probably not be approved. But this request would be far from normal. Connor was not even supposed to be conducting an investigation in any way, shape or form, much less involving five civilians in an excursion to Las Vegas.

"How are we supposed to get approval for all the expenses?" he asked Connor in an attempt to veil his actual reservations.

"I am counting on you to figure that out, Jake. That is the second reason I brought you along on this assignment, your ability to do the impossible and convince the Marshal to give us all the money we ask for," Connor retorted.

"That's not funny," Jake replied.

"It wasn't meant to be," Connor said seriously. "Now go get us the money we need."

"Great, thanks," Jake said. It's your funeral, he thought to himself.

"You're welcome," Connor said and smiled. Jake took a quick count of heads, then went back to filling out his forms. The more the deadlier; for Connor. And maybe him along with Connor

"Speaking of Jake's enormous abilities," Joan asked Connor, "Just why did you bring him on this assignment? Apparently you and Dylan understand the relevance of his peculiar ability, but none of us do."

"Sorry, I should have explained. The point Dylan was making is that the main reason I chose Jake to come along with me on this assignment was because he has an uncanny ability to find people who need finding; such as escaped prisoners and other wanted persons. And most of the people we need to find right now seem to be in Las Vegas. It seems to be the best place to find what, or who, we want. So that is why we are going there."

"Makes sense," Joan said.

"Look," Dylan said after deciding he needed to give an explanation. "Before we get moving I need to tell you more about what I figured out."

"Shit yeah," James said. "That would be really friggin decent of you. I mean we only been sittin here for the last ten minutes wondering what the hell you were talking about. At least I was anyway." He looked around at the others hoping to get their agreement, which he did.

"Hey, sorry," Dylan said, "but I am trying to tell you now, ok? When this all started, what was it that was guiding us? Guiding Brent and me? What one thing did all of us experience in common, except the Chief? And I don't know if Anna did because I never asked her."

Joan smiled and said to him, "Your mom's voice." She was getting the hang of this connection thing and she liked it. And she liked the smile from Dylan that it earned her too.

179

"Has anyone heard her voice lately," Dylan asked, "because I haven't." He *had* been having the dreams, but decided not to mention that. The dreams were not the same as hearing mere words, and would have to be dealt with by him alone.

"You haven't yet asked me," Anna answered, "but I gather you people have been hearing Jesse's 'voice'. And as a matter of fact, I've heard it too. But like you just said, not recently."

"Interesting," Dylan told her. "That verifies my theory. If I know my mom – and I do – her silent 'voice' is a sign," he said. "It's a sign signifying that we don't need any more 'nudges' from her. It's a sign that we are on the right track and closing in.

"I know how her mind works. My whole life she tried to get me to figure things out on my own. She would only help me with hints and nudges up to the point where I was able to reason things for myself, then she would back off.

"Recently I was getting her voice, and you guys were too. It was telling me to watch the ground around the berry plants. But ever since we found her buried things in the park no one has heard her voice again. Get it? We figured it out, so now the voices have backed off." He waited and looked around to see if they understood it, and could see by the excitement on their faces that they put it all together.

Dylan looked at Connor and asked, "So how do we work this? I, for one, have almost no money left and probably no job and….."

Before he could finish, Joan interrupted, "You never have any money, even when you have a job." She said it with a faint smile.

"I know, ain't that cool?" He smiled faintly back at her. There were hidden innuendos going between them now and Dylan was enjoying it as much as Joan was.

"NO," she said, "it ain't." She emphasized the word 'ain't' sarcastically, but had a smoldering look in her eyes. The kind of look that made Dylan think he might get lucky. Maybe even get lucky in Las Vegas. In a hotel room. Now that would be cool.

The sexual tension between them was so strong that Connor worried they might jump on the floor and start doing it right now, right there, in front of everyone. He precluded the possibility with a gentle reminder, "You were asking me something, Dylan?"

"Oh, yeah. Let's see, what was I asking? Oh yeah, who's going to finance this expedition?"

"Don't worry about it, we will all have food and a roof over our heads," Connor told them all.

"And travel expenses?" Dylan asked.

"I have a feeling we wouldn't get there otherwise, so don't worry about it. Jake is handling it, ok?"

"Cool," Dylan said.

"Yeah, cool," Joan verified, and went back to staring at Dylan with her smoldering come hither look, in which Dylan once again lost himself.

Connor couldn't take it any more. "For Christ's sake, why don't you two just stay here in Flatrock and bunny hump for a few days and we'll go to Vegas to solve this thing without you."

Both of their heads snapped up, looked at Connor and said, in unison, "What? Huh?" Their bewildered looks resembled two people who had just been brought out of a state of hypnosis with a snap of the fingers, now wondering what had just happened to them.

"That's my boy," James said with a proud smile.

"Sorry, Connor. We're coming, don't worry about us," Dylan said, not wanting to be left behind. He tried to avoid looking at Joan, though he couldn't wait to be alone with her in a hotel room in Las Vegas.

Brent, who witnessed the exchange between Dylan, Joan and Connor, was extremely amused and laughed out loud for some time, in spite of Dylan's threats of what he would do to him if he didn't stop.

CHAPTER FIFTY FIVE

TEN MINUTES AFTER JAKE submitted his request for funds to the District Supervisor, Dennis Wheeler, he got a phone call. It was a short conversation because all Dennis said was, "Get Connor on the phone."

"Hi, Dennis," Connor said when he picked up the phone. He guessed what was coming and struggled for an explanation that would get approval from his supervisor. Not having much hope for that plan he tried to remember how much room he had on his own credit card.

"What the fuck, Connor," Dennis started. "I thought we had an understanding here. Next thing I know I'm looking at a request for approval of funds for two deputies, a local cop and four civilians to fly to Las Vegas, rent a car and two hotel rooms. What the fuck," he repeated.

"It could be worse," Connor replied, hoping to raise a comparison that would make his request look insignificant. He didn't get the chance.

"No it couldn't," Dennis preempted him. "It's already the worst it can get. What the hell are you thinking?"

"Sorry, Dennis. Look, I need to explain a few things."

"More than a few," Dennis snorted.

"Yeah, you're right. But give me the chance. If you want to bust me out of here after you hear me out, that's fine. But please listen."

"Make it good," Dennis said after a hesitation.

"Thanks." Connor proceeded to give Dennis the unabridged version of what had transpired since he arrived in Flatrock, including the psychic mumbo jumbo. Now he was at the mercy of his supervisor. Sink or swim. Aim high, he was always told. Now he wondered if there might be such a thing as too high.

"You know what you've done here, Connor?" Dennis replied quite unhappily. "You put us both in the same trap. I gave you a bit of a long leash, and you took off running. Now I can't rein you in without putting my own ass in a sling for letting you off the leash to start with.

"And now that you are so deep into an investigation, unofficially I might add, it's too late to call in another team. You already have too much headway going. And to be honest, you've done a good job.

"So I'm stuck with you. Tell Jake he'll get expense approval." Connor heard some under the breath swearing from Dennis but, to Connor's relief, the man didn't reverse his position.

"I think it was Confucius that said, it's better to ask forgiveness than it is permission," Connor said to Dennis.

"Fuck you, Connor," Dennis said, then hung up. Maybe I had that wrong, Connor thought. Maybe it wasn't Confucius. Then he wondered if he was too old for a career change.

The flights were scheduled to board in two hours. It was a twenty minute drive to the airport, giving them less than an hour to get packed and ready to go. Each member of the team of travelers raced home, threw some stuff in a bag and raced back to the station. When they had all returned, the Chief had a couple of his cops ready with their cruisers, to transport them to the airport.

Connor supervised the loading of the police cruisers and made sure everyone was accounted for. Assured that all members of the Vegas bound team were present and seated in the police cars, he moved toward his place in one of the cruisers. He hesitated a moment, looking back toward the station entrance, where Charlie was watching them leave. He walked back to the door and took Charlie's right hand in both of his hands, gave a firm grasp, and looked him in the eye.

"Couldn't have gotten this far without you," Connor said to him. "You are a real asset, Charlie, and I'm sorry you can't come along with us. I hope you will still be available to help us here locally if we need it."

"You can count on me. Anything you need, you just call," the Chief responded. Then he added, "You gonna keep me in the loop while you're there?" He was hoping for a blow by blow coverage of their mission, but would be happy to compromise with a few progress reports.

"You got it. See ya." Connor turned back and climbed in the cruiser.

"Take care of my boy," the Chief yelled as Connor was closing the patrol car door.

When he turned to go back into his office, he was surprised by the tears welling up in his eyes. He had been part of this thing from the start and was disappointed that he had decided to stay behind. The more he thought about it, the more he regretted his decision not to go.

And then there was Brent, who added a host more reasons for his regrets.

CHAPTER FIFTY SIX

BECAUSE OF THE SHORT notice booking of their flight, they were not seated together, which made it difficult for Connor to give last minute instructions to the others during the flight.

In the old days, before September eleventh, Connor could have flashed his credentials and gotten any kind of seating he wanted, but not any more. Even a U.S. Deputy Marshal could not trump the Homeland Security regulations.

But Connor was sure that some kind of planning was necessary before landing in Vegas so he was forced to wait for the fasten seat belt sign to be turned off. When that happened the team migrated to the flight attendants' station at the back of the plane and huddled there. They had to flash some badges at first just to be allowed to do that, even momentarily.

At the first such meeting, Connor instructed the others not to discuss any 'psychic shit' in front of any of the cops, deputies, or any other law enforcement types in Las Vegas. He also informed them of the primary mission strategy, which was to turn Jake loose with his bloodhound-like locating talents. His primary target for location was Tommy Sanderson. Secondary was Ricky Allen. Connor's job would be to work with the local Deputies to investigate Brad and Tommy, and maybe Helen. There was still a staggering lack of data coming up on these three people. Data they vitally needed.

It was during the strapped in periods, when Dylan was able to concentrate without distraction, that he finally got the nerve to consider the bad dreams he had been having.

Even ordinary dreams were hard to remember after awakening. And even harder to understand. And his recent dreams were not ordinary dreams. He had to struggle to recall them, but he knew the dreams were the key to his understanding of recent events so he made the effort to do so.

It wasn't until just before the plane landed that he made a breakthrough and recalled a part of a dream that he hadn't remembered before. It was an important part. It was the part about seeing someone flee from the scene and evade detection by squeezing through the bushes and into a parking lot.

He also recalled the man saying the word bitch. The same word Brent had heard at the accident scene, making the connection obvious. But what the connection indicated was not so evident. He decided he would talk to Brent about it when he had the chance and see what they came up with.

Moments later their plane landed in Vegas. They were met at the end of the ramp by two local U.S. Deputy Marshals who escorted them through the airport to two waiting black limos. For Jake and Connor this kind of treatment was standard operating procedure, but for the others it was far from ordinary treatment and, at least for the moment, they felt like celebrities.

Ok, the black cars weren't limos, they were federal Crown Vics. But they were black and they came with drivers. Close enough.

Unfortunately their ride in the black, make believe limo was short. Very short actually. They only took them as far as the airport car rental depot, maybe a mile, and dropped them off.

The Montanans were astonished by the fact that the car rental depot was like an airport terminal in its own right, except it was dedicated to autos and not jets. There were international airports in Montana that were not nearly as big this car rental station. They commented on it to each other while the deputies dealt with the red tape of renting a couple of cars.

Economy models. Not even close to limos. It would have been nice if they could have rented more than two cars, but Jake had more than a little trouble getting approval for the two. The only reason he got approved for two was that seven people were one too many for one car.

When all the paper work was completed the group was led to their cars, where they loaded their luggage and bodies and drove away from the terminal. They made their way towards the U.S. Marshals office, with Connor leading the way in one car, and Jake following in the second.

The route took them along most of the Las Vegas strip. For the Montanans, who, except for Anna, had never been to Vegas, the sight of the strip was overwhelming. It was like a fantasy land to them and they gawked at every strange sight they encountered, and there were a lot.

There was a constant stream of comments coming from them such as; oh, look at that; did you see that guy; hey that looks like the empire state building; wow, everyone is drinking beer out in the street; how high do you think that building is; what's a hooter; I've never seen so many Elvises, etc.

And then there was the traffic. Driving in this kind of traffic, in this big of a city, was a new experience for the Montana people. There was a constant stream of thousands of cars coming at them from all directions. The sensation was frightening.

And the rate of travel they managed to achieve felt to them as if they were making no progress at all. It took them a half hour to cover five miles. The only time it takes someone half an hour to travel five miles in Montana is when they are walking. Slowly.

When they finally arrived at the U.S. Marshals office, they were greeted by the Marshal himself, who looked at the size of Connor's entourage and tried, unsuccessfully, to keep his resentment from showing.

Connor saw his troubled look and said, "Sorry for the crowd but they are all essential at this point."

The Marshal grunted and introduced himself as Grant Curran. "Let's go find a bigger briefing room," he growled. "The one I had in mind isn't going to work."

They found an adequately sized room and got settled into their chairs around a conference table. Brent couldn't help but notice that it was a bona fide fortune five hundred conference table. Nothing like the one they called a conference table in Flatrock.

Connor introduced each member of his team by their names, but didn't offer an explanation of their roles. The look on Grant's face said that he wished none of them were there, he asked Connor if he was sure he wanted them all to hear his briefing.

Connor hadn't even known that there was going to be a briefing, but instead of saying so he told Grant that he did, indeed, want his team to hear it. Grant in response, by way of covering his own ass, said that the briefing would contain 'sensitive, classified' information and that if any of his guys leaked it, he would hold Connor responsible.

Connor said, "I'm totally comfortable with that."

Most of Grant's briefing was not new information to the Dream Team. But there was one thing that he said that got them thinking. He said that when they tried to pull Tommy Sanderson's jacket, access to it had been blocked.

When Connor asked what he meant by that exactly, Grant said, "Usually when we run into that response to an inquiry it means that the person is either deep undercover, or under investigation by an agency with more pull than we have."

Connor thought about that. It certainly explained why Jake had been having trouble getting any information on the trooper. And he knew that access to law enforcement personnel files is sometimes hard to get, but only for local level agencies, and typically not for the U.S. Marshals office. He'd had to create blocks to such files for the protection of their witnesses, so knowing a bit about the process, he surmised that the block to Sanderson's file was probably created at a very high level. He would have to get himself into that upper loop if he wanted to find out what was going on with Tommy. He asked Grant if he would help him get into that loop.

"I have a few friends in higher places that I can ask, but no guarantees," Grant said.

"Thanks," Connor said. "What about Brad Danison and Helen Whelan? Any news on them?"

"Still working on those," he told Connor. "I'll let you know when we get something."

CHAPTER FIFTY SEVEN

THE HOTEL WHERE THE MONTANA team was billeted was not one of the big ones on the strip. It was a somewhat cheaper one south of the strip and a little west, but it was still beyond anything the Montana people had ever experienced. They had booked two rooms; one for Anna and Joan, and one with two double beds for all of the men except James, who stayed in his own house.

Dylan was not too upset about the room arrangements. They were here to get a job done. A very important job. But it would have been nicer if he could have bunked with Joan.

The male quarters were officially dubbed HQ, which triggered a memory in Brent and he began to think of himself a little like a member of *The Dirty Dozen*. After a brief meeting in HQ their plan of action got under way.

Jake drove Connor back to the Marshals office and dropped him off. Then he put his nose to the ground and started following the trail of his prey.

He started by visiting the Las Vegas Metro Police Department. He couldn't say why he started there, but he knew it was the right place to begin. His 'special talent' told him so.

James' task was to hang out in his apartment, make some contacts in the neighborhood, and keep his eyes and ears open. This was assuming that he still had some of his old connections in the world that exists below the law. He had serious doubts about the accuracy of this assumption, but duty compelled him to make the effort. If he heard or saw anything important he was to call Brent immediately. No problem. He could handle that.

In fact the entire team was instructed to contact Brent. He was the information clearing house. Everyone reported to him, and he passed the reports on to the appropriate person or persons as needed. That way someone always knew what was happening with every aspect of the operation and could keep it coordinated.

He had a cell phone and a land line, as well as a fax machine and a laptop with an email address. Every team member had been issued a new cell phone, for business use only, compliments of the U.S. Marshals office. The cell phones could do more than just handle phone calls. They could send and receive texts and emails. They could be used as a GPS, or surf the web. Even take and send pictures and videos. And if you set the ringer to vibrate and called yourself over and over you could get a massage with it. All of this available to those who knew how to operate them. Dylan definitely did not know how, and had to be instructed.

They were ordered not to use their personal cell phones. And they were also ordered not to use their new Government Issue phones for personal calls. Apparently personal calls were forbidden altogether. So much for the massage app.

Anna and Joan were given the official title and task of 'expeditor'. As the word implies their duties were to do whatever was asked in order to expedite and or assist the actions of the others. In private Joan complained to her mom that they were really just gofers. Anna rather agreed with her but advised against mentioning it.

Dylan received no official posting, which left him free to do whatever he desired. In short he was a loose cannon. The term loose cannon usually being reserved for use as a derogatory label describing someone who has gone astray and is functioning outside the group.

However, in Dylan's case they were hoping for a somewhat more positive connotation. He was free to follow up on his own ideas or hunches, or he could be called on by one of the others for help, or he could call on one of them for help. He was a floater and was expected to operate in a fashion very similar to Jake.

And so it was that the unusual and nearly modern vigilante team from the wilds of Montana set out to find beloved Jesse's vile killer in the wild concrete jungle of Las Vegas.

CHAPTER FIFTY EIGHT

THE DRY AIR OF VEGAS MADE DYLAN THIRSTY, and he decided that a cold beer would take care of his thirst just fine. He went to Joan's room to see if she wanted to go with him. His rap on the door was answered with, "We're unpacking. Will come out when we are done."

"No problem," he shouted back through the door, as if he really knew what the hell she was talking about. Were they unwilling to open the door because they were changing clothes, and were only half dressed? Did they have all their underwear spread out on the bed? He shrugged. Whatever. He got in the elevator and pushed the lobby button.

The bar was not a bar in the sense that Dylan had grown used to in his life. It was more like an arcade. There were hundreds of slot machines, all being played at once, and the musical sounds that they made combined into a cacophony that had the effect on him of 'white noise'. The result of which was that in the midst of a large, noisy, and active crowd, he could yet feel strangely isolated. He was surprised how easy it was to think in these surroundings, and he silently sipped on his beer, reflecting on the upcoming task.

After only seconds of deep reflection he came to his first official conclusion – the beer in Las Vegas was very cold. He assumed that this fact must have something to do with the searing heat the town experienced, and he found such reasoning to be quite sound.

However, his first official decision in his new and official capacity of loose cannon, was that he would return to the room so he could have his little chat with Brent. With Connor and Jake gone, and the girls locked up in their room, it would be the first chance they had to be alone since they left Montana.

He finished his very cold beer and took the elevator back to the room. He walked in without knocking, both because it was his room too, and because it was a standing rule that any member of the team could come in without knocking whenever they wanted to. The dress code for inhabitants of the room were also dictated by this rule, as one could imagine.

Brent greeted Dylan, who sat in a chair across from him and said, "I need to bounce something off you. I have had a couple of dreams about my mom. In one of them I dreamed that I was watching my mom get hit by a car that I was driving."

"Whoa!" Brent said. "That's something that can only happen in a dream."

"Yeah, it was eerie. Anyway, in the dream I was floating in the air, watching as she got hit, and I saw a man walk away from the scene right after I ran her over. I mean right after someone ran her over. It was me in the dream. Never mind that part. The important thing was that when I descended and got real close to this guy, I heard him say the word bitch."

Brent understood right away why Dylan was telling him about this. "Interesting," he said. "What do you think it means?"

"Not sure, that's why I wanted to bounce it off you. Got any ideas?"

"Maybe. Where exactly was the guy standing when he said bitch?'

"It was a dream, so 'exactly' might be hard to achieve. But I think he was walking toward the corner where my mom stood before she jumped. He was about twenty feet away from the curb and approaching from the west; from the parking lot. Mean anything to you?"

"It might. But first let me ask you why you used the word jump. You said Jesse 'jumped' off the curb. That's the first time I've heard it described that way."

"You're right. I hadn't thought of that before. But that was what she did in the dream. That's why I said it."

"Ok, just curious," Brent told him, then he shared his own experience.

"When I heard the word 'bitch' at the accident scene I turned and looked at the very spot you described. And both times it happened I expected to see the man who said it standing in that spot. The first time I looked, I saw no one, instead, due to a sudden and intense panic, I ran out into the street, almost getting hit by a car." Brent's story explained some things for Dylan but he knew that Brent was holding something back and said so.

"Yeah," Brent conceded, "but I'm not holding back on purpose. I just can't quite figure out how to say it out loud. There is something about that first time, when I walked out into the street, that bothers me, but I'm not really sure how to describe it."

"Give it a try," Dylan encouraged him.

"The panic I felt was something that didn't make sense. I mean, at that very second, right then when it happened, I was panicking but I couldn't understand why.

"I remember wondering about it – wondering what caused me to experience the panicked reaction. Nothing had happened that should frighten me in the least bit, but there I was in a total panic."

"Ok. I think I can follow that," Dylan responded. "Tell me something else, did you hear any other words, at any time, besides 'bitch'?" Dylan had a hunch and he wanted to search it out.

Brent thought about it for a minute. "Wait, yes I did. I heard something just before I heard 'bitch'. I heard your mom's voice say, 'Brent, don't stop'." He shrugged. "I really don't know what that means."

"I'm not sure either, but try this on for size. Could the panicked feeling be my mom's emotion, not yours? Maybe you were feeling her feelings?"

190

It was a bizarre theory, but Brent felt that there may be some inherent truth in the idea. Not an explainable kind of truth, but a kind that someone might just plain 'know'.

"Yeah, that could explain it," he offered. "It did kind of feel that way, like it was not really me who should have been feeling that way."

"Ok," Dylan said.

"Does that help?"

"I think it just might be what I was looking for," Dylan said. He was about to explain further when Brent's BC rang. BC meaning, of course, his Business Cell, their Government Issue cell phones.

Brent answered his BC with, "Brent here."

CHAPTER FIFTY NINE

WHEN HE WAS FINISHED with his phone call Brent looked up to see Anna, Joan and Dylan all looking expectantly at him. He hadn't noticed Anna and Joan come into the room, but he was certainly glad they were there because they were holding coffees and sandwiches. He took one of each.

"That was Connor," he told them. "Vegas Metro PD has Ricky back in custody. The idiot got pulled over for running a stop sign and they brought him in. Connor is on his way to the police station to pick him up and bring him back to the Marshal's office. Hang on, I have to call Jake and let him know."

"You think he'll talk?" Dylan asked, after Brent made his call.

"Not sure, but I don't think he'll get away again. And the more important question is does he really know anything, even if he did want to talk." Brent's BC rang again.

"Brent here." He spoke briefly to James and hung up.

"What did he say?" Dylan wanted to know.

"He said that he's been hearing rumors about Tommy being back in town. Everyone seems to know about it and they sound scared. I gotta call Jake again." He passed the information on to Jake and went back to work on his coffee and sandwich.

Dylan found himself thinking about what James had just reported, realizing that he must still have some of his old connections and was already busy working them. He was surprised by a feeling of mild pride in James.

There wasn't much more for those in HQ to do at that moment except to wait for more reports, so they got comfortable on the cushy chairs in the hotel room. Joan sat next to – almost on – Dylan in one of the bigger chairs and put her arm around him.

The room remained quiet, Dylan deep in thought, concentrating hard on something in his mind while his eyes were looking into the middle of the room at nothing. After about fifteen minutes he muttered the word 'bitch'.

Joan removed her arm from Dylan's shoulder and said, "Pardon?"

"Sorry," Dylan said, now aware of his mistake. "I didn't mean you. I was thinking about something else. I wasn't aware I said anything out loud."

Anna had heard Dylan say the word 'bitch' as well, and was startled by the sound of it. "This may sound bizarre," she said, "but when you said the word bitch it sounded exactly how I remember Brad Danison saying it to me." She shuddered. "It still gives me the creeps."

Dylan looked over at Brent to see if he had taken note of the fact. He had.

Dylan said to Anna, "That's interesting." He considered telling her about what he and Brent had just been discussing, but decided to wait. "I never got a chance to ask you," he said instead. "What did my mom say when you heard her voice?" Anna brightened at the question.

"The berries are all yours, treat them well," she said.

Dylan made a grunting sort of laugh and said, "Yeah, sounds like her. You understand it?"

"Sort of...maybe.....I'm not sure," She said. But Dylan knew the truth; Anna was absolutely sure of the significance of the words. And so was Dylan. She just needed a little more time to get comfortable with the idea of inheriting another child.

While the others returned to silently waiting, Dylan returned to thinking. A few minutes later he stood up suddenly and walked to the door.

He said to Brent, "I got something I need to do. I'll check in with you later." He grabbed the rental car keys from the table and walked out without another word, not even a goodbye, not even to Joan. Joan stared at the vacant doorway with disbelief.

Brent read the worry and insult on Joan's face and said, "Don't worry, he'll be ok." Not because he believed it, but because he was trying to console her.

CHAPTER SIXTY

CONNOR INTERROGATED RICKY for over an hour without getting a single word out of him. Ricky had too much at stake to talk. He had his life at stake, and he wasn't feeling like dying.

Connor grew tired of being in the same room with the scumbag and decided to take a coffee break. He left Ricky sitting in the small room with handcuffs on. He didn't say anything to him, he just got up and walked out.

He sat in the break room drinking coffee, considering the various options for dealing with Ricky. So far his favorite option was to leave him in the small room without food or water until he was dead, but he doubted that wish would come true. While daydreaming about extremely painful treatments for Ricky, Grant walked in and sat next to him with his own cup of coffee in hand.

"Any luck?" he asked.

"No. You?"

"Not yet, but I've made some calls to some people in know in higher places. Left messages for them to call me. I'm not too optimistic they will help me, assuming they can. I probably wouldn't if I was them. But hell, you never know, maybe we'll get lucky."

"We will. One way or another we will. We have to." Connor's intensity made Grant curious.

"This thing personal?" Grant asked.

"Yes and no."

"Same thing as yes."

"Yeah, I guess." Even though Deputies were not supposed to get personal with their witnesses, everyone knew that it happened. But it usually wasn't talked about.

"It happens," Grant said, thinking the same thing as Connor.

"This time it is different."

"It's always different."

"Yeah, I guess so. But this one is different."

"If you say so."

"I do."

"OK, I hear ya. I'll do whatever I can."

"Thanks, Grant. I appreciate your help."

"No problem," he said. "By the way, I got a call from Dennis in Denver."

"No doubt," Connor said. He didn't need an overactive imagination to guess what Dennis had said. "You're supposed to watch my ass, right? Keep me out of trouble."

"Pretty much," Grant admitted. "I got the idea he was not your biggest fan."

"Yeah, well," Connor said.

Grant opened the office door to let himself out, but the door was blocked by another person, who was trying to enter.

To Connors complete and pleasant surprise, the man entering was Charlie Armstrong, the police chief from Flatrock, Montana.

CHAPTER SIXTY ONE

JAMES WAS TRULY SCARED. Maybe more than scared, though he didn't know what 'more than scared' would be called. Frightened? He didn't think so. Frightened sounded less than scared to him. Terrified? Yeah, that was more than scared. Was he terrified? Shit yeah, he was terrified.

He had managed to lay low for all those years, but it now appeared that his amnesty was over. He shouldn't be surprised. He wasn't surprised. He knew he was taking a risk the minute he decided to call the U.S. Marshal's office and report the photo he had been given by Ricky. But he did it anyway, so no he wasn't surprised. But he didn't like it any better just because he expected it.

Maybe he should do something. Yeah, he should do something, but what? Call the cops? Yeah, right. Half the guys waiting outside his apartment right now were probably cops. He knew one of them was for sure. He recognized him. So what should he do? Call Brent on his BC? What was Brent going to do? Call the cops? Brent was a cop, it's the first thing he would think of. Maybe.

A sharp rap on the door made him yelp, jump out of his skin and arrested his heart for a couple of seconds. He froze. No way he was opening the door, and saying come in didn't seem much wiser. There was another knock and then he heard a voice from the other side of the door.

"James, you home? You in there? Let me in." It was Dylan. Shit.

Afraid that if Dylan stood by his door much longer he would be killed, James hollered, "Come in, come in, hurry up!"

Dylan barely had his foot in the door when James shouted, "Shut the door, shut the door, hurry up!"

Dylan shut the door as requested. James looked like he'd gone totally bananas. Or maybe he decided to finally try out some heavy drugs and was on a bad trip.

"What the hell are you doing here? How'd you get here?" James demanded.

"I came to see your place. I drove the rental car. What the hell's going on?"

"Now we're both screwed. I wish you wouldn't have come here," James whispered.

"Please tell me what's going on," Dylan pleaded.

"Did you see the men waiting outside?

"No, what men."

"The men who are waiting to kill me."

CHAPTER SIXTY TWO

JAKE DIDN'T EXPECT to get much cooperation from the Metro LVPD and he was not disappointed. In fact he counted on being ignored completely, leaving him free to explore the cop shop unmolested. He'd known that he couldn't waltz into the place and say, 'here I am, a U.S. Marshals Deputy and you will give me your total cooperation and confidence'.

So he played the game of 'local uniforms don't like suits'. He asked a bunch of stupid questions, annoying everybody in the place, proving to them how fucked up the feds really were. He was told several times to stop bothering them, eventually making a show of giving up, making them think they had put him in his place. Now contritely silent they ignored him completely, gladly leaving him free to roam around as he pleased, which was what he really wanted in the first place.

He wandered the station unmolested, looking for clues about Tommy and Brad. As expected, any trace that Tommy Sanderson had ever stepped foot in the building had been completely erased.

Brad Danison, on the other hand, was evident in many parts of the station, and he found himself wondering if Brad might lead him to Tommy. There was a catch to that plan though. Brad was an active cop, and if Jake decided to run surveillance on him he would normally be required to get permission. Maybe he could clear it through Connor, let him worry about the red tape issues.

CHAPTER SIXTY THREE

HELEN SAT IN HER MOTEL ROOM watching TV, and wishing she could do just about anything other than what she was doing. She was starting to get the heebie jeebies from being locked up in the room for so long, and she couldn't help feeling hunted. In fact, she was inclined to believe that she was not in any better of a situation than a sitting duck.

Tommy had made it clear that it would be unsafe for her to be seen in the streets, and made her promise to stay in her room Meanwhile he gallivanted off into the city to conduct his 'mission'. She promised him she would stay inside, but now was beginning to wonder if it was worth it, the urge to get outside starting to outweigh her fear of danger.

Here was the problem: if she was a sitting duck just waiting in the room for someone to come along and shoot her, then she should get out. But on the other hand, what if she was actually safer by staying in the room out of sight, and going out would just get her spotted? It was a conundrum. She hated it, but it could be worse. She could be that O'Connor woman – Jesse.

CHAPTER SIXTY FOUR

BRAD DANISON HAD HEARD THE RUMORS. More than rumors actually. If Bennett Alivio, the biggest drug importer in Las Vegas and Brad's 'other boss', said Tommy was back in town, it was probably more than a rumor. Brad had never been able to find out how Bennett received such information, but whatever the source was, it was a damn good one.

He wondered what Tommy's appearance in Vegas implied. It could be nothing, or it could be everything. It depended on why he was here, and Brad intended to find that out. But first he had to find him, which would not be easy. Not if Tommy didn't want to be found, and Brad assumed that to be that case. Not easy maybe, but not impossible, because he knew Tommy. Oh yeah, he knew Tommy very well.

They had spent a lot of time together. Partners. That's what partners did, they hung out together. They got to really know each other. They got to know each others' routines and their habits. Their little idiosyncrasies. Their likes and dislikes; their sexual preferences; their favorite foods and restaurants; their family members and friends; and maybe even their favorite hiding places.

Brad knew that, as well as he knew Tommy, Tommy knew him. Tommy was a smart cookie, he would avoid his usual habits and haunts, hide himself from Brad's circle of contacts and informants. He would not be found in a normal or logical place. Oh yeah, this was going to be fun. You can run Tommy, he thought to himself, but you can't hide. Not from me.

Brad knew about Helen, knew where she was right now, but going to her would be fruitless. Tommy would expect that move for sure. She would know nothing about Tommy's location, and Tommy knew not to come near her. Brad couldn't use her for bait because there was no way to inform Tommy that Helen was on the hook.

He the word out on the street, to his network of snitches, promising a reward. Not too much money, because offering big bucks produced too many false claims from people desperate for money. And not such a small amount of money that no one paid any attention to it. He didn't expect to get any real leads this way. Tommy was too wise to let himself be seen by any of Brad's snitches. But he did it anyway, on the off chance he might get lucky.

He asked Bennett if he would keep him in the loop in case some news about Tommy's whereabouts might come to him. For that little service he knew he would have to pay big, not in money but in some currency more valuable to Bennett.

Brad sat at his desk considering Tommy's options. Where would he hide out? Would he even hide at all? Maybe he was just driving around town and playing slots at the big casinos. It is easy to blend in with thousands of people playing thousands of slot machines. No he wouldn't do that. Too many people knew him in those places. Security people, convicts, snitches, and other cops. And he wouldn't be staying in the industrial area, because a lot of drug dealers and snitches worked those areas as well.

What about out of the city – in the desert or mountains? Very unlikely; he might not be seen by anyone, but at the same time he would not see anyone himself. And whatever reason Tommy had for being here, it was not for a desert or mountain vacation. He had to be close to the city. That meant he was nearby, but not in the main hotels or casinos, and not in any drug ridden neighborhoods. That narrowed the possibilities down to only a few hundred in a thousand square miles.

Come on Tommy, where are you? And more important, what are you up to?

CHAPTER SIXTY FIVE

"BRENT HERE," he answered into his cell phone, a minute later saying, "Got it, I'll call you right back."

Anna and Joan overheard the call, were anxious to know what was happening, but Brent ignored them and immediately dialed a number on his phone. They listened as he spoke to Connor.

"Hi, Boss, its Brent. I just got a call from Dylan. He is at James' apartment and he says that some bad guys are staking the place out and James is freaked. He wants to know if you can do something to roust out the bad guys."

"Do they know who these bad guys are?" Connor asked.

"James says that at least one of them is a cop but the rest are 'some bad dudes'."

Connor hesitated and then said, "If one of them really is a cop, that could complicate matters, rules out useing the local PD for help. What's the address?" Brent gave him the address and Connor promised to call back as soon as he came up with a plan. "Meantime," he said, "I have someone here you should talk to."

Brent was surprised to hear the Chief's voice on the line. He asked him, "Hey, Chief, are we on a conference call or something? How are things at home?"

Charlie laughed and said, "No conference call, Brent. I'm here in Vegas at the Marshals office." Brent was elated.

"Welcome to the party," he told the Chief.

Anna, overhearing the conversation, perked up noticeably at the news that Charlie was in town, Brent and Joan silently noticing the fact.

"Thanks. Connor needs to talk to you again, here you go," the Chief replied. When Connor came on the line he said, "I've got an idea. Let's get the fire department to help us."

"Ok, how do you want to do it?"

"Call Dylan and tell him to make some smoke come out of the window and then call 911 and report the fire. But tell him to wait ten minutes before he starts. I need time to contact the fire department and devise a plan with them."

"You got it. What's the Chief going to do?"

"Not sure yet. If you get any ideas let me know." Connor hung up without waiting for Brent to respond.

Brent called Dylan and explained Connor's plan to get the fire department involved in their rescue. Dylan asked him what they were supposed to do after the firemen arrived.

"Connor is concocting some scheme with the firemen but I'm not sure what it's going to be," Brent explained," "Just make some smoke and be ready."

"Got it, Thanks."

Brent's next call was from Jake.

"Tell Connor I'm going to be following Brad. Since he is a Metro PD cop, I figured he should know," he told Brent.

Brent passed the message on to Connor.

The next call he got was from the Chief, who asked if someone could give him a ride to HQ. Brent happily promised to arrange it.

"Anyone want to pick up the Chief from the Marshal's office?" Brent asked Anna and Joan. Anna quickly volunteered for the job, but her jubilation disappeared when she realized that Dylan had the car, and she reminded Brent of the fact.

"So he does," Brent admitted. "I guess we better get those boys out of James' apartment and back here."

"Yes, how are we planning to do that?" Anna asked him.

"Connor has a plan. It's set to go into motion in about ten minutes. Dylan will be back soon and then you can go get the Chief," he reassured her with a knowing grin.

Anna didn't miss Brent's grin and she felt mildly embarrassed about it. But only mildly. She also felt something she had not felt in a long time, aware now how much she had missed the feeling. She smiled again at the thought of Charlie.

The plan Connor had come up with was explained on the phone to Chief Mel Lewis at Clark County Fire Station number twenty eight.

"Yippee!" Mel responded to Connors plan.

"So you are up for this?" Connor asked him.

"You bet I am. It's been kind of boring here lately, and I love doing creative things. This will be fun." Mel told him.

"Ok, Mel. Have a ball, and thanks," Connor said.

"I will, thanks for the call," Mel said back.

When Connor hung up he found himself smiling without knowing why. Mel was just one of those kind of people who naturally left people feeling better. Apparently there are a few people like that left in the world.

Mel's phone conversation had grabbed the attention of several firemen, who were as bored as Mel and looking forward to hearing about his fun plan..

"Ok, gather round boys," Mel announced.

CHAPTER SIXTY SIX

CONNOR FINISHED HIS CALL TO MEL and went back in the room with Ricky to try, once again, to get some information out of him. Unfortunately Ricky's resolve had not eroded during Connors coffee break. So instead of wasting more time with him, Connor decided to let him cool off a little longer, leaving him in his cuffs alone in the room again. Maybe he would check in on him again in the morning. If he felt like it. Which, right now, he doubted.

He was back in the break room drinking more coffee and wondering what he might be able to work on besides Ricky when Grant entered and said, "I got more bad news."

"Great," Connor said sarcastically.

"The file on Danison is off limits. We can't get anything on him. And I've already tried my connections and got no help."

"Him too?" Connor asked. "What the hell is with these guys?"

"I wish I knew, Connor. But there is more. Helen's file is out of bounds too. Just like the other two," he said, resigned to the fact that they were not going to get it.

Connor not as prepared to accept defeat in the matter as Grant was, evidenced by his reddening face. "Shit. We need that information," he said. Desperate times required desperate measures, and he was a desperate man. If normal channels didn't work, he was ready to go outside normal channels. He would do whatever it took.

"What non conforming methods can you suggest?" he asked Grant.

"If you are asking me if I know some ways to get my ass in a sling, the answer is forget it," Grant asserted.

"I don't blame you for wanting to keep your job, and your ass, intact, but what I'm asking for is help getting my own ass out of a sling. I just need ideas. I will take all the actions and leave you out of it," Connor said.

"Yeah, OK, I get it," Grant said. "I wish I could help. But the only way I know of getting into their files is if someone with enough authority to access them. And that person would have to be willing to risk his job by revealing them to us. Not a likely scenario." He thought to himself that he was obviously not as desperate as Connor, because if he was he knew exactly who he could go to for help.

"Yeah, doesn't sound promising," Connor agreed. "If I knew someone with that authority I would ask them anyway. But I don't know anyone I could even ask. Do you?"

"No, sorry," Grant lied, but revealing his source in high places was not an option.

Connor brightened suddenly, saying, "What if we get them to come to us?"

"Who? How?"

"Whoever gave the order to seal the files. That person has to know what's in the files, right?"

"Ok, that's logical, but how on earth would you magically get them to come to you?" Honestly the idea sounded absurd to Grant and he wondered if Connor's desperation hadn't destroyed his logic.

"We interfere," Connor said with a diabolical smile, "We make enough noise that they have to come to us to get us to back off. Then at least we will know who it is that's running the blockade on these guys. And maybe we can get some intel from them."

Grant saw where Connor was going with this and he wanted nothing to do with it. "Who's us?" he asked.

"Ok, I'll make the noise and leave you out of it," he promised.

"Fine, but what if they show up and tell you to back off and that's all you ever get out of it, besides trouble?" It was the most likely scenario, and Connor should realize it.

Connor did realize that Grant was right, but he didn't care. The moment James arrived in Montana with the photo given to him by Ricky, he'd decided that if he didn't find Jesse's killer he was going to quit his job at the U.S. Marshals, so he had nothing to lose. "I'll take the chance," He told Grant.

Grant admired Connor's determination and it gave him a change of heart. He decided he would help, but he wouldn't go to his top source yet. He said, "Ok, I'll help, but keep my name out of it if the pot starts to boil over."

Connor blew out a breath of relief. "You got my word on it, Grant, thanks."

"No problem, I hope. So what's the plan? How do we do this interference thing anyway?" Grant asked.

"We burn the wires with inquiries about Tommy and Brad. We put it out to everyone, DEA, FBI, Secret Service, ATF, Homeland Security, Border Patrol, Customs, Immigration, TSA, Nome Alaska Sheriff, and anyone else we can think of. We tell them that we are running surveillance on the two men and that we plan to bring them in for questioning. We say we know where they are and that we want any and all information about them that the various agencies can supply us. It's mostly true, we do know where Brad is and we know that Tommy is in Las Vegas anyway."

"Ok," Grant agreed. "But can we run the wires out of your home office in Denver? And tell them to forward responses to you here? That gives me a pretty good buffer between the brass and my ass."

"Sure, I have no problem with that. Thanks," Connor told him.

CHAPTER SIXTY SEVEN

JAKE HAD BEEN WAITING OUTSIDE the Vegas PD station for an hour when he finally saw Brad leave through the main exit. He waited for Brad to drive out of the parking lot, following him at a safe distance. Brad stopped to fill up his car with gas, then drove another few miles to a restaurant. Jake watched him enter the restaurant from his car. Ten minutes later Brad came back out. He hadn't stopped there to eat, so why did he stop there, Jake wondered.

Over the next couple of hours Brad stopped at six more restaurants, three bars, two strip joints and a beauty salon. Jake smiled, certain now that he was looking for Tommy.

Late into the night Brad stopped at an apartment building where he parked his car and entered one of the apartments using a key. Jake guessed that it was Brad's home, and if he was right, Brad would not come back out until the next morning. It was at that point that Jake realized a flaw in his plan. He couldn't stay awake forever. And he was getting hungry.

He called Brent and explained his situation.

"Does it look like Brad is bedded for the night?" Brent asked him.

"Looks that way," Jake answered.

"Ok, I have an idea." He explained that the Chief had come to Vegas to be part of the team and recommended that he be Jake's replacement.

"Yeah, fine with me," Jake said.

"Ok, but you are going to have to pick him up from the Marshal's office and bring him with you to the hotel."

When the Chief arrived at the room with Jake he was welcomed like a long lost relative, with plenty of hugs and handshakes going around. Jake had already reacquainted himself with Charlie during the ride to the hotel so he excused himself to get something to eat before going to bed. On his way out he handed Anna the keys to the rental car.

When the greetings were finished Brent briefed the Chief on the set up at HQ, gave him a cell phone and called Connor, getting his approval for the Chief to replace Jake.

"Welcome to the madhouse," Brent told the Chief. "You go on duty immediately. You'll be taking over for Jake on a surveillance. Anna has the keys to the car, but before you leave Jake will give you a briefing. Tomorrow morning you return here for some sleep and Jake takes over again. Any questions?"

"Yeah, how's it feel to be the boss for a change?" He was making a joke of it, but inside he felt a sense of pride for Brent that he might feel for a son of his own, if he had one. He wished he might some day get the guts to express his paternal feeling for this young man.

"You're still the boss, boss," Brent told him. But it did feel strange to him to be directing the Chief.

"Sure thing, I'll see you tomorrow," he said.

At that moment Anna was by his side with the car keys. She led him to the hotel restaurant to meet up with Jake, who was eating before getting some sleep. They found Jake seated at a small table in the back of the restaurant and took the two remaining chairs. Jake told the Chief what he needed to know and sent him on his way. Anna gave him a goodbye kiss on the cheek.

After the Chief and Anna left the room, Joan asked Brent, "Did you notice the way my mom was looking at the Chief?"

"No, how?" Then two seconds later, "No, really? Are you serious? I was kinda wondering about that earlier when she first heard that he was here. Did you notice something then too?"

"You're right, that's how it looked to me." She shrugged and Brent chuckled.

"It's not funny," she said but was trying not to laugh. Then she changed the subject and said, "I feel useless just waiting around here. Isn't there something I can do?"

"I have a feeling you won't be bored much longer." As if on cue the phone rang. "Brent here. Howdy Dylan, what's up?" He listened for a few minutes and then hung up. To Joan he said, "Ok, you're up. You need to go pick up James and Dylan at the fire station. He said to have you bring some of his clothes. Apparently he needs them."

Joan looked puzzled and Brent said, "He didn't tell me and I didn't ask. All he said was to have you bring some clothes. His bag is on the bed over there."

She took some clothes out of his bag and then asked, "How do I get there? He took the car." A second later she asked, "So why does he need a ride?"

"Oh yeah, good question. I wish I knew."

Charlie was opening the driver side door when he was grabbed roughly from behind. The assailant had a thick and very strong forearm around his neck, pulling him to the ground. Charlie was not a ninety pound weakling, and could hold his own in most physical contests, but he was no match for this man. The man had speed too, and Charlie was taken down so fast he barely noticed the cuffs being strapped to his wrists. He'd thought he was being mugged and the cuffs surprised him, they weren't a normal accessory in muggings.

The assailant lifted Charlie off the ground and stood him up, facing him. The man looked as big and as strong as Charlie had imagined, except much uglier, and he'd imagined a pretty ugly guy. He had the definite look of a thug, except that he was dressed well. Probably a high-priced thug.

"Come with me," the thug said and began leading him back into the hotel.

Having no choice in the matter Charlie went along. The man did not fear being seen leading a cuffed man through a crowded lobby and Charlie wondered if he wasn't an agent of some kind, and not really a thug. Or he could be both. It happens.

As they traveled through the hotel, Anna intercepted them on her way back to their room. She was overcome with anguish at the situation but could do nothing but follow them.

CHAPTER SIXTY EIGHT

BEFORE BRENT COULD come up with a mode of transportation for Joan there was a knock on the door. A knock on this particular door was not a good sign. Since they had an open door policy for team members it meant there was a stranger at the door.

Brent hollered, "Who is it?"

A short silence and then, "Officer Butler, please let us in." It was a polite request but it told him all he needed to know. He could tell by the way they spoke that it was some sort of law enforcement person but something about it didn't sound right. And it bothered him that they knew his name.

Not wanting to risk endangering Joan, he sent her into the bathroom with her cell phone, in case she needed to call for back up. He went to the door and opened it, letting in two men in black suits.

The two men stood just inside the door and Brent introduced himself, "I'm Brent Butler, gentlemen, how can I help you?"

"We need to talk to Jake Tillman." It wasn't a request in the traditional sense that it begged a response. In this case it was a request that expected compliance. A request made by people who were used to getting what they asked for without resistance. Brent wondered where they were from and considered asking to see their badges but decided against it. Then he wondered what he should or shouldn't tell them about Jake. He considered lying to them but decided against that as well.

The fact that they already knew that Jake was in Vegas and where to find him, told Brent that they would probably know if he was lying to them. When he finally spoke he said, "Jake is on his way here now. Should be here any minute. Have a seat. Want something to drink?" They'd be better off refusing the offer, Brent thought. The only thing he had to offer was Vegas tap water. Better to go thirsty.

They stood there without responding. They didn't sit and they didn't drink. What they did do was be creepy. They did that very well. Brent's cell rang.

"Brent here," he answered.

"Brent, its Connor. Listen close. Ask those men for their ID's. Don't respond to me or say anything, just ask them."

Brent was surprised that Connor knew what was going on so quickly, but he took the phone away from his ear and asked the creeps, "Can I see your ID's please?" They looked at each other but didn't speak or reach for their ID's. Instead they asked, "Who's on the phone?"

"They want to know who you are," Brent said into the phone.

"Tell them," Connor assented.

"It's Deputy Connor McDermott, U.S. Marshals," he informed the creeps.

"Tell him we are waiting for Deputy Tillman," the biggest creep said. The other creep wasn't speaking, which made him more creepy.

Brent relayed the message. Connor said, "Ok, no more games, ask them for ID's. Tell them I said to produce them or I am pulling Jake in and they won't find him."

Brent would have done just that except that at that precise moment Jake walked into the room. So instead he said to Connor, "Here, why don't you talk to Jake directly." He handed the phone to Jake, walked across the room and sat on the bed.

The two creepy gentlemen turned and stared at Jake while he talked to Connor on the phone.

"Hi, Connor, I just walked in. What's going on?" Jake inquired.

"You have visitors. The two men in your room were asking to see you, but they are refusing to identify themselves. I don't really know if we can make them present badges but we have to try. Do whatever you can, but in the end agree to whatever it is they want and then call me when they leave."

Connor was upset when he hung up. If this had been a response to his plan to get the upper levels to come to him, he would have been happy, but it was too soon for that.

Jake hung up and introduced himself to the gentlemen. Then he asked them to return the favor and tell him who they were. Their response was, "We appreciate your desire to know who you are talking to, but in the interest of not endangering an ongoing investigation we need to remain anonymous." Again it was the big creep talking.

"So, I assume from your reference to an investigation that you are some sort of law enforcement agents. Mind telling me which branch?"

"Yes I do mind, as a matter of fact, so quit prying," he said smugly.

"But if you are law enforcement personnel," Jake persisted, "aren't you obligated by law to identify yourselves?"

"No, not any more. The Patriot Act changed all that," big creep explained.

"How convenient," Jake snarled.

"You got it," big creep answered.

"So what you are saying is that this is going to be a one way street," Jake asserted.

"Now you are starting to understand. You must be a bright guy," the creep said.

"I guess I'm not that bright, because I still don't get it. You could be anyone. You could be terrorists or mafia or just about anyone as far as I'm concerned. So if you want me to listen to you, you have two choices. You can cough up an

ID or you can go back through channels and have my superiors order me to do whatever it is you want me to do." He sounded tough, but he was pretty scared. He really didn't know who they were. What if they were really bad guys?

Their response was, "Actually, there is another choice. We can take you with us and make sure you don't see the light of day for a while, courtesy of the Patriot Act again. How does that sound?"

They were playing it tough, and Jake knew they were right about the Patriot Act. He'd read it, like every other employee of a law enforcement agency in the country had. But he wasn't ready to give up yet so he told the alleged agents, "If I disappear, one of the others on the team takes over. They all know what I know. We have a deep bench, and if you keep taking them in, you'll end up with a crowd after a while." At least he wouldn't be alone if they called his bluff.

"They all know what you are doing?" the big ugly one asked, surprised by the news that so many people knew what was going on.

"Yes, they know everything that I know," Jake said, noticing a chink in their armor and hoping to take advantage of it.

"They aren't Deputies," big creep said with wonder. "Most of them aren't even cops. What the hell is going on here?"

"We are looking for a killer. What are you doing?" Jake told them sarcastically.

The big one motioned to the other creep to sit and they both sat down. They seemed to lose some starch and relaxed a little. The big creepy one said, "You were following Brad Danison."

"Yes," Jake said, and at that moment the hotel door opened and the Chief was led into the room in handcuffs, by another creepy gentleman, who did not look like a cop. He looked more like a thug. A well dressed thug, but a thug nonetheless. They were followed by Anna who was visibly upset. Brent went nuts.

"Ok!" he hollered, "What the fuck is going on here. Get him out of those cuffs right now. I SAID RIGHT NOW!" As he rushed the man holding the Chief, the two creeps jumped up off their chairs. Jake went for those two but after taking only a step he noticed they were holding guns and that stopped him.

Brent had seen the guns as well and stopped moving, purple-faced with anger. "Will someone please tell us what is happening!" he hollered. "Because right now I'm thinking we are being hit by the mob. And if we are, you guys are buying more trouble than you want."

For a moment there was a silent standoff, a stare-down where each was waiting to see what move the other was going to make next. The silence was shattered by an extremely obnoxious high pitched screech, accompanied by strobe lights. It was a fire alarm and it was wailing throughout the entire building, like it was supposed to do. It was also sending an alarm to the fire station and firemen were rushing to respond and put out the fire.

They heard the sounds of doors opening up and down the hallway. The hum of people's voices mingled with the barking of orders from hotel employees, ordering people to leave the building. It wouldn't be long before police and firemen arrived.

It didn't take long for the creeps to make up their minds. They uncuffed the Chief and prepared to leave. Before they left they told Jake, "Meet us at the Marshals office." The way he said it did not sound like he was extending an invitation to share tea and crumpets. He thought it might have sounded more like an invitation to his own execution.

After the assumed agents left the hotel room Joan burst out of the bathroom in tears. "Oh my god. Are you guys ok? I was so scared," she shrieked. Anna ran to her and put her arms around her protectively.

"Everyone's fine, pretty much," Jake said, without really knowing more about it than that no one was dead, in spite of coming close to it. As for the rest, he was left with a lot of questions and damn few answers.

"Does anyone know why the fire alarm went off?" Jake asked, "Shouldn't we be getting out of the building now?" He had considered it a fantastic stroke of luck when he first heard the alarm sound. But now he was considering the possibility that his luck could change for the worse if they got trapped in a burning building.

Joan understood Jake's concern and said, "Don't worry about it," she said, holding up a cigarette lighter. "I set it off from the bathroom. I always carry one with me for emergencies."

"Thank God for that," the Chief offered. He sat down on the edge of the bed, looking like he hadn't quite gotten all his ducks in a row yet. It was probably the first time he had ever been 'arrested'.

"Yes, indeed," Brent said to Joan. "Not only are you beautiful but you are brilliant. Dylan is a lucky man." He was dialing his cell phone as he spoke.

"Why, thank you, Brent. What a lovely thing to say. Does that mean you don't hate me any more?" Brent didn't mind the mild reproach, he deserved it. And he didn't miss the impish smile on her face.

"As a matter of fact," he responded, "I think I love you now..... NO not you, Connor." Connor had answered his cell phone at just the right, or wrong, time.

"Those guys are on their way to see you," Brent told him. "They want Jake and the Chief to meet them there. How did you know they were here anyway?" He listened for a moment and then said, "I see. I'll send them over right away." Brent hung up and looked at Joan again.

"Now I'm sure I love you. You called Connor from inside the bathroom," It was the second complement from Brent in five minutes time and Joan was flattered by his newly acquired attitude toward her.

"Someone had to do something about those goons," Joan chided. "But I didn't call him, I texted him. I didn't want to risk being heard," she said proudly.

"You rock, girl!" Brent told her delightedly. "Speaking of goons," he looked over at Jake and the Chief, "you guys better get over to the Marshal's office. Joan and Anna will drop you off on their way to pick up Dylan and James."

Anna didn't hear him. She was talking to a hotel employee at the door. She explained to him how the alarm had been set off. The hotel man looked neither happy nor satisfied with her explanation and promised to return with the fire marshal, who would 'take care of the matter'. Anna thanked him and went to Charlie, who was still sitting on the bed, and plainly not happy about going to the Marshal's office with Jake. "You ok?" she asked him as she put her arm around his shoulders.

"Yeah, I'm ok. Wounded pride is all. I've never had to deal with people like that before. I'll take ordinary violent street criminals over those guys any day." Anna noticed that he was starting to get some color back, and she kept her arm around him without saying anything.

"Come on, we gotta go," Jake said to the Chief. Unlike the Chief he was anxious to get to the Marshal's office and find out just what the goons were all about.

Anna and Joan led Jake and the Chief to the door. As they opened it they encountered an impasse. Two firemen were blocking their exit. Anna assumed, incorrectly, they they had come to 'take care of things'.

The first fireman said, "Hi there, my name is Mel Lewis. And this," he said, motioning to the fireman next to him, "is Philip Beauchamp." Anna was about to introduce herself when Mel and Philip stepped aside, allowing Dylan and James to enter the room. Joan rushed past them and threw her arms around Dylan.

"How did you get here?" she demanded. "I was just on my way to pick you up."

Jake was in a hurry and not willing to wait for an emotional reunion to complete itself. He grabbed the car keys from Anna, motioned to the Chief to follow, and walked out. Anna gave Charlie a brief hug on his way out and then turned back into the hotel room.

Joan, Anna and Brent stared openly at Dylan, and for good reason. He stood in the middle of the room wearing nothing but a bath robe. Joan was highly amused and Brent was trying pretty hard not to laugh – with moderate success.

"What the hell are you wearing?" Joan finally managed.

"A bath robe," Dylan answered with false casualness.

"I can see that. But why?" Joan asked.

"Because one of the firemen took pity on me and was nice enough to loan it to me. Then when they got the call to this hotel, they were nice enough to give us a ride." Another one of his famously inadequate explanations.

"That's very nice dear, and you look wonderful in the robe. But I think what I was asking is where are your other clothes? You know, the ones you left here wearing?"

"Ah, I can explain that," Dylan said, undaunted.

"So can I, but I can't wait to hear your version," James muttered sarcastically. Mel and Philip excused themselves, saying they had to check in with the Captain. Probably they had already heard Dylan's story and once was enough.

Dylan gave James a dirty look and then continued his story. "Did you know that fires are not necessarily all that easy to start? I would never have guessed it myself. One always assumes that you have to be so very careful around combustibles lest they combust with almost no encouragement. But have you ever tried to start a fire? It's not as easy as you think. For example you'd think a roll of paper towels ignited with a match would be adequate to get a good sized blaze going. But I can tell you from recent experience that it's not. You would also think that holding a cigarette lighter at the bottom of a set of drapes would do the trick, but no. However there was one thing that I was fairly confident would burn well; alcohol. So when I threw a bottle of rubbing alcohol on the smoldering paper towels it worked a bit too well. Dozens of flaming pieces of paper towel, combined with drops of alcohol landed on my clothes and James had to rip them off of my body. I'm lucky he acted so quickly or my skin may have suffered a great deal of burning." Satisfied with his rendition of the incident, he glanced at James.

"Idiot," James muttered.

Dylan gave James another dirty look, but he knew when to make an exit and he said, "I think I will go change my clothes now. If you will pardon me please." He grabbed the clothes that Joan was carrying and went into the bathroom.

While Dylan was changing, Joan asked James about their escape from his apartment, hoping to get a better explanation.

"It was cool," he told her. "Once the fire got going well, thanks to Dylan's little cocktail, the firemen came rushing in with all their hoses and equipment. They had hidden two sets of fireman uniforms inside of their own uniforms and gave them to us when they got inside. We put them on and then walked out to one of the fire trucks. We sat in the cab of the truck while they cleaned up the fire in my house. Then they drove us back to the fire station. It was a great plan. I hope the landlord had insurance."

"What happened to the bad guys?" Anna asked him.

"They scattered like cockroaches as soon as they saw smoke and heard the alarm."

Dylan returned, properly dressed, and put his arm around Joan, satisfying his yen for a little reassuring physical contact after his ordeal at James apartment. He asked her, "What have you guys been up to here while I was gone?"

Joan re-lived the ordeal with the creeps and thugs, including the part where she saved the day by calling Connor from the bathroom and tripping the fire alarm. Dylan was duly impressed. "You're incredible babe, maybe I should marry you." Joan blushed.

"You better hurry," she responded, "I think Brent is falling in love with me."

"You don't say?" Dylan pondered. He looked over at Brent who had been watching the exchange.

"She's a keeper, mate," Brent offered by way of an explanation.

Dylan was surprised by Brent's thorough change in attitude towards Joan. It was only a few days ago that he was hoping she would go away. But then, Dylan hadn't been all that far behind him in his own opinion. Funny how things change.

"Oh yeah," Joan remembered, "something else happened while you were gone. My mom was looking at the Chief in a very special way." She raised her eyebrows conspiratorially.

"Special how?" Dylan asked. No one answered, they just looked at him with a 'you know' kind of look. Dylan recognized their look and realized what they were talking about.

"No way. Really?"

"Really," Joan said.

CHAPTER SIXTY NINE

THE MEETING AT THE MARSHALS OFFICE started out with a transparent pretense of social pleasantries but quickly dwindled into reality. The goons, or rather the guests, were anything but pleasant. Now that the social pleasantries were abandoned, Grant reminded them that they were in his office without being invited and without properly identifying themselves. The reminder failed to produce and ID's and several minutes of questioning got zero information at all from them. It appeared to Connor, who'd been waiting patiently, along with Jake and Charlie, that the two guests were stalling, and he thought he knew why.

Connor figured that they were waiting for authorization to give out information from someone higher up. He almost admired their adherence to the secrecy of their mission, and when the big goon's cell phone rang, he hoped it was the call they'd been waiting for. The man listened to the phone briefly before saying, "yes, sir," and hanging up. Little did the Marshals know that there was no superior on the other end of the phone. It was a hooker that Big Creep had paid ten bucks to call him at a pre-arranged time, all a part of his charade.

"I'm special agent Duvall, FBI," Big Creep said. "This is special agent Thompson." He indicated his partner, who was much younger and looked more like a surfer dude than an agent. A surfer dude in a black suit. A surfer dude who never spoke, at least not to anyone in the room so far.

"Nice to meet you. You already know who we are," Grant said, in a way that clearly expressed that he was still miffed at the lengthy charade they had to play.

"Yes, but what I don't know is why you are following Brad Danison," Duvall said.

The penny dropped and Connor figured out what happened. The FBI had been tailing Brad already and had spotted Jake following him around. What great luck, Connor thought. Maybe now they would find out something about Danison. Maybe the agents would fill them in, especially now that they had gotten permission. From a hooker, but he didn't know that.

"We are trying to locate a murder suspect," Connor explained. "Our investigation led us to two people of interest, Tommy Sanderson and Brad Danison. We found Brad easily enough since he was still active with the Vegas Metro PD, but Tommy eluded us somewhere in the city. Now it's your turn. Why are you watching Brad?"

"He is a person of interest in a federal investigation. We have been hoping he will lead us to the head of an evil snake. We don't want it to get messed up. Understand?" Duvall said brusquely. Connor was disappointed by the further attempts to stonewall them.

Jake was the type of man who thought that giving up on something without really trying would make him look like a sissy. Or maybe he just really wanted to find Jesse's killer. But for whatever reason he was not ready to give in to the agent. He tried taking another tack.

"Look, we don't want to interfere with anything you are doing. We don't necessarily know if Brad is involved in our murder. What we really want is Tommy. And I think Brad is going to lead us to him. How bout you just call us as soon as Brad meets up with him, and then we can follow Tommy and leave you guys alone to keep doing whatever it is you're doing with Brad?"

"No," Duvall said.

"No what?" Connor asked.

"No, we won't tell you if Tommy shows up, and no, we won't let you follow Brad."

"So basically we are back to square one. You aren't going to tell us anything and you won't let us watch Brad." Connor said. Jake noticed some color building in his face.

"That's right," Duvall said smugly.

"No, that's bullshit," Connor declared. His face had become a dark purple cloud, and Jake feared the storm it had the power to generate. He intervened before Connor had a chance to get the agents mad enough to pull their guns again.

"Let it go, Connor," he said. "We gotta do what they say. You know the rules." He looked directly into Connors eyes and Connor could tell that Jake was up to something, so with no trifling amount of willpower, he stayed quiet. Still purple faced, but quiet.

Jake turned back to the agents, "Sorry to cause you all this trouble. We'll stay out of your hair. And thanks for explaining things to us." He walked with them toward the exit as he was talking, and saw them through the door. Then he turned back to Connor and the others.

Grant was the first one to speak.

"So what was that all about?" he asked Jake.

"Yeah," Connor asked, "what was that about?"

The Chief, during his entire career in law enforcement had never seen anything like what he had just witnessed, and he decided that whatever was going on, it was best left to those with the higher pay grades and more experience, so he wisely remained silent. Horrified, but silent.

Jake said, "It was getting nowhere. They were just wasting our time, and we don't have time to waste on them. Brad is getting close to Tommy and I don't want to miss him because of the time we are spending with those assholes."

"So what's the plan?" the Chief wanted to know.

"The plan is we go back to following Brad. We blew it last time because we didn't know to watch out for the feds. So now that we know about them, we avoid them. And we don't have to do it for long because Brad is going to lead us to Tommy very soon."

"How does he know that for sure?" Grant demanded of Connor.

The Chief, having become a bit of an expert in the matter, said, "You don't want to know."

CHAPTER SEVENTY

TOMMY SAT IN A BOOTH, back to the wall, and watched the entrance to the all-night diner while waiting for his food order to arrive. He had ordered his favorite meal; cheeseburger with no mayo, fries and a chocolate shake, without whip cream. The diner wasn't exactly five star, but it was the best place he could find at this time of night, or rather morning now.

Lots of people order the same thing that Tommy had just ordered, but not very many of them enjoy the meal the same way Tommy does. Tommy has a unique way of eating his favorite meal. In fact it was the way in which he ate it that made it his favorite meal.

After the waitress brought his order, she went behind the kitchen counter and watched him eat it. The cook and the bus boy joined her. They watched him dip a corner – or would it be called an arc - of his cheeseburger into the milk shake and then take a bite. Then he took a few fries and dunked those into the chocolate shake and ate them. Then he took a drink of the shake. Then he repeated the process over and over until the meal was devoured.

The waitress came back to his booth and cleared the table. Tommy asked her to bring him a cup of coffee, which she did. He sipped on it, still watching the entrance to the diner.

He chose this diner based only partly on its proximity to his favorite meal. The other reason was its location, Boulder City. It was near Vegas, but because it had no casinos, the normal network of snitches, dealers, pimps, hookers and crooked cops didn't reach it. His hope was that if a man was really looking for him, he could, eventually, find him here. As previously stated, away from the network of his kin. He hoped he would come soon.

CHAPTER SEVENTY ONE

JAKE WAS EXHAUSTED AND HUNGRY. His rest had been interrupted by the arrival of the nice FBI men, and their polite invitation to accompany them to the Marshal's office. But he still had a few things to do before he could eat and then sleep. He drove back to the hotel with the Chief and immediately drafted Anna into his new plan.

The plan for following Brad without alerting the FBI agents wasn't that difficult, really. The agents would be looking for them in the same rental car they had used earlier today. And they would be looking for the same men, Jake and Charlie. So Jake had Charlie rent an older car from rent-a-wreck, while he and Anna bought some wigs of various colors. Anna applied a wig and some make up to the Chief which turned him into a red head with pale skin and freckles. Quite different from his dark hair and unblemished complexion. Jake would get his makeover in the morning before relieving the Chief.

Jake finished giving the Chief last minute instructions then grabbed a few slices of the pizza Anna had ordered for them. He finished eating and went to his room to get some sleep. The Chief started out the door to begin his stakeout of Brad, but Anna stopped him. She handed him a room key. He took it, looked at it a second and then asked, "What's this?"

"It's the key to our new room," she said demurely.

"Our?" he asked.

"Yes, after you showed up I took the liberty of getting another room, for just the two of us. I couldn't imagine you being crowded in with all those other guys in one room, especially since you will need to be sleeping at odd hours. And I have a feeling that Joan and Dylan would like more privacy, judging by how they have been acting lately. The simple solution was to get another room for you and me. Hope you don't mind." Charlie took on look at her disarming smile and knew he'd had it.

"Not a bit," he said. "See you in the morning. It will give me something to look forward to." I'll be a son of a bitch, he thought to himself, surprised at what he was feeling, and thinking.

She gave him a kiss on the cheek, and then went to her old room to pack up and move. Charlie walked out the door smiling.

When Anna entered her old room, Dylan and Joan were already there, asleep on the bed, thankfully with all their clothes on. She packed up quietly and moved her bag to her new room.

CHAPTER SEVENTY TWO

DYLAN LOOKED OVER THE EDGE towards the street below. He must be atop the highest building in Las Vegas because the street was a long way down. Looking down made him feel dizzy and he feared he might fall off the rooftop, so he looked up he saw an amusement park, which frightened him almost as much as looking down. Above the amusement park was a tall needle-like structure pointing toward the sky. He concluded that he was hallucinating – or dreaming – because it was not very sensible that there would be an amusement park on the roof of a tall – very tall – building. And yet there they were; roller coasters and scary rides just like the ones he used to ride in amusement parks when he was a kid.

He looked down briefly to ensure that his footing was secure, and was shocked when he saw that his toes were hanging over the edge of the sloped roof. The rest of his feet were slowly sliding the short distance toward the edge of the roof and there was nothing he could do to stop it. Doomed to fall a very long way, he expected to feel panic and the accompanying rush of adrenaline. He expected to see his life flash before his eyes. He expected to soil his underwear. But instead of any of those things, he felt only calm, as if there was not the slightest bit of an emergency.

He sat down on the sloping roof with his feet dangling over the side in mid air. Fortunately, when he sat he stopped sliding and became as secure as if he was sitting on level ground. The stability he felt on the slope was real and he was confident of its continuation in spite of the fact that it defied all of the laws of physics. He admitted to himself that he was quite happy that he was not falling, even if he didn't understand it.

He wasn't happy for long, soon realizing that if he stood up again, or moved at all, he would indeed slide all the way off the roof. He was confronted by a tough choice. He could sit there in one spot until he died slowly of dehydration or starvation, or he could move and then fall briefly, if speedily, to a sudden death.

"Not much of a choice is it?" he heard his mother say. She turned out to be sitting next to him on the roof. He hadn't noticed her until she spoke and he wondered how long she had been there. He wondered how long he had been there. It could have been a very long time or no time at all. It was impossible to know for sure.

Instead of answering his mom he asked her, "How long have you been here?"

"Been where?" She seemed not to understand his question, which seemed simple enough to Dylan.

"On the roof," he said as if it was the most obvious thing in the world.

"What roof?" she demanded.

Dylan looked back over the edge of the roof, expecting to see all the tiny cars and people a million feet below, so that he could point it out to his mom and thereby demonstrate 'what roof' they were sitting on.. He was expecting it with such utter conviction that he almost jumped six feet back when he saw the pavement just a few feet from his face. He was, in fact, sitting on a curb with his feet right up against the asphalt. Had he been hallucinating? Wasn't he, just a moment ago, sitting way up above the world on a tall roof? Yes he was, he answered himself. And if he was, then where was his mom? Was she still up there?

"I'm right here, dear," she said from next to him.

Dylan turned at the sound of her voice and saw her sitting there next to him like before. Like him, she was sitting on the curb.

"How did you get here?" he wanted to know.

"Ah, now that is not a very easy question to answer. It may take a very long time to answer it, but then I have all the time in the world. How about you? Do you have time for the answer?"

Dylan could not fathom her response. He just wanted to know how she got down to the street from the top of the roof. He was hoping she'd explain it, but couldn't imagine it taking a long time to do so. He asked her again, "How did you get down here from the roof?"

"What roof?" she demanded again. "You keep insisting that I am on a roof when obviously I am not." She seemed annoyed about it.

Something was very wrong, and since his mom had never been that unstable, it was probably him. He must be losing his mind. He had occasionally worried slightly about his sanity, and the idea of losing it really scared him. Now that it had finally happened, it felt worse than he had ever imagined it would. The worst thing about it was that he was extremely embarrassed that his mom had to witness it.

"Don't worry," his mother said. "You are not crazy. You will never go crazy. You are not that kind of person. You're too strong." She was very reassuring and Dylan lost all concern about his sanity. If mom said he was sane, then by god he was sane.

"Thanks, mom," he told her.

"You're welcome. I have to go now. Don't forget anything I've said. I love you," she said affectionately.

"I love you too." He looked over towards her but she was no longer sitting on the curb. Instead, she was standing up and looking back away from the street, toward something behind her. Dylan turned to see what she was looking

221

at. There was a man there, just a few feet away. He looked familiar but Dylan could not quite place his face. He got up from the curb and walked toward the man, intending to introduce himself and see if the other man would tell him who he was. He held out his hand in greeting. The man reached his hand out toward Dylan but when Dylan looked down at it, it was holding a gun.

Dylan was stunned. He was so stunned that his voice would not work. In fact he could not even draw a breath. He had a gun pointed at him and he could not breathe. One way or the other, he determined, he was going to die.

The overwhelming certainty that he was about to meet his maker caused Dylan to feel calm again. He lost all his fears. He was ready. Ready to die. But when he looked down in anticipation of the blast of the gun, it was no longer pointing towards him. It was pointing at his mother. He felt paralyzed and tried to scream and nothing came out.

Why was he so helpless? He had to move. He had to do something or his mom would be killed! MOVE DAMN IT! DO SOMETHING! He willed himself to act. Nothing. He was frozen. He watched helplessly as the man said, "The boy dies." What did he mean by that? What boy? Why? Then the man said one more word in a venomous voice, "Bitch."

Something about the word 'bitch' triggered something in Dylan and he overcame his paralysis. He lunged at the man and started slashing at the gun to knock it out of the man's grasp. He swung his arms as hard as he could but they had no effect on the man, like he was a ghost and his arms passed through the other man's arms as if they were mist. The man smiled a cruel and satisfied smile and looked in the direction of his mom. Then he turned and walked away without firing the gun.

Relieved, Dylan turned to look at his mom expecting to see her alive and well. But when he looked, she was gone. He looked past the place he had last seen her and noticed her lying in the street, bleeding. He looked up and down the street, hoping for some help. It was a street he recognized from Montana and that puzzled him. Wasn't he in Vegas now?

He watched as a Montana Highway Patrolman drove up the now familiar street and parked his car in front of his mom's body. He felt her neck for a pulse, and then shook his head indicating that there was none.

Dylan refused to believe it. What happened? He was talking to her mere seconds ago. How had this happened? He started screaming. He kept on screaming. He didn't intend to stop. He screamed as long and as loud as he was capable, the sound of his own voice muted, and his vision dark. He was disappearing in a sea of black, an unending scream that he somehow knew was his, growing more and more faint, more far off. Before becoming erased in the sea of blackness he thought he heard another faint but familiar sound. Concentrating on the new sound, he heard it again, and it was Brent. He could *barely make out what he was saying. He listened closer. There it was again, faintly, "It's me, Brent, please stop screaming. It's me."*

It had been such a muted sound that he forgot he'd been doing it. He stopped.

CHAPTER SEVENTY THREE

JOAN AWOKE WITH A VAGUE FEELING that something was wrong. Slowly emerging from the grips of the half-real world between dreamland and consciousness, she realized that the bedclothes were soaking wet. Not merely damp, but literally soaked. She looked over at Dylan expecting to see him awake, considering it unlikely for someone to sleep through something like that. However unlikely, Dylan was was still asleep, and any attempt to rouse him were futile.

Baffled by the condition of the bedsheets, she looked around the room for a leak or some other source of water. Finding nothing, she turned to Dylan again, trying to wake him. When he still would not wake up she became frightened, and tried harder to wake him up, but with no success. Worried that he may be dead she ignored the wet bedclothes and checked his vitals, determining that he was still alive. So why wasn't he waking up?

Panicked, she pounded on his chest hoping it would wake him. After only a few blows to his chest Dylan started screaming, and at first Joan was happy, thinking that he was awake. But he wasn't awake, and his screaming continued, unbridled and not seeming likely to stop.

When she heard pounding on the hotel room door, and recognized Brent's shouting coming from the other side of it, she opened the door, thankful that help had arrived.

"What's wrong?" Brent asked excitedly after entering the room. Without waiting for an answer he walked across the room, drawn by the screaming Dylan, staring at him helplessly.

She walked on shaky legs alonside Brent, toward Dylan, with the avid hope that Brent would know what to do."I don't know," she said. "He wouldn't wake up when I tried to wake him, and then he started screaming and wouldn't stop. And now I can't wake him up or stop him from screaming."

Having no idea what to do, Brent asked Joan, "What should we do? We have to wake him up somehow. Or we at least have to shut him up before he wakes up the entire hotel."

On cue more people showed up at the room, no doubt due to the loud, obnoxious wailing emanating from it. Jake was among those who had arrived, looking sleepy eyed and dazed. Anna was right behind him, and behind her was a hotel employee. Probably a security guard from the looks of his suit and the radio he was carrying.

Brent leaned over Dylan and began talking to him. "Dylan it's me. Wake up," he yelled. "Stop screaming." He looked over at Joan and said, "Why is the bed soaked?" Joan shrugged. Brent continued talking to Dylan, "It's me, stop screaming. Wake up."

The screaming stopped, which relieved the people in the room, and probably everyone in the hotel. On the other hand Dylan did not wake up. Instead, he thrashed around on the bed with a contorted, tortured look on his face, and he was sweating profusely. Brent guessed that was why the bed was so wet. He didn't know a body could contain that much water.

He told Joan to get a bottle of water ready for him. Thankfully, Dylan soon stopped thrashing and his face looked calmer. A minute later he opened his eyes, looking uncertain of his surroundings, and not recognizing anyone in the room. His eyes roaming around the room, looking at people in hopes of recognizing someone, stopped on Joan.

"You look frightened," he said. "Are you ok?" Joan sighed with undisguised relief.

"Yes, I'm OK," she said. "You scared me is all. You wouldn't wake up and you were screaming. Were you having a nightmare?"

After gathering himself a bit more he realized it was true, he did have a bad dream. He recalled screaming in the dream, which seemed like a dream itself. A dream within a dream. The worst kind.

He looked up at Joan again, "Yeah, I think I was having a nightmare," he managed to say weakly. "Why is the bed soaked?" He sat up and put his feet on the floor.

"We don't know for sure but we think it is your sweat. Here, you want some water?" She held out the bottle for him. He took it and drank some water.

The others drifted out of the room, thinking, correctly, that the possibility of impending danger was over and that it was better to leave them alone.

Joan got Dylan into some dry clothes, then changed the sheets and blankets on the bed. She made them mediocre hotel coffee with the complimentary hotel mediocre coffee making machine. They sat for a while, drinking coffee and getting their nerves back.

Dylan grew tired but was afraid to go back to sleep. Joan, drained her of energy, snored softly with her head in Dylan's lap. He looked at her face in his lap and admired her serene beauty as she slept. He wondered how a bum like him had ever gotten so damn lucky as to have a girl like her fall for him.

CHAPTER SEVENTY FOUR

CONNOR DECIDED IT WAS TIME to check on Ricky, who was still in the room where Connor had left him. He had his head down on the table and was snoring. Connor woke him up. Ricky complained that he was not only tired, but hungry, and thirsty as well. He started to say something about having some sort of rights, and Connor wasn't supposed to deprive him of water and...... And Connor left the room again without saying anything.

He was tired of Ricky, but Ricky had been right about one thing, it was time to eat. He walked to a nearby deli and got a coffee and sandwich. He had lost any interest in talking to him, but wasn't sure what to do with him. By the time he finished his sandwich and coffee, he'd come up with a plan for dealing with him.

He walked through the office and straight into the room containing Ricky. Without a word he approached Ricky and unlocked his cuffs.

"Thanks," Ricky said.

Connor said, "Fuck you. Go home now."

Ricky was leery. "What do you mean go home? You turning me loose?" he asked.

"Yep, good luck," Connor said and smiled. It was a funny smile. Maybe a maniacal one.

The funny smile made Ricky more suspicious. "Why are you doing this?" he asked.

"Don't need you any more. Goodbye." Connor smiled again. Same maniacal smile.

Ricky began to sweat. "Why not?"

"We got what we wanted without your help. But they won't know that will they? They will be very certain that it was you who helped us bust them. Especially after you spent so much time in here. Thanks. See you later." Again with the smile.

"You're lying. You'd be lying. You can't do that," he said, the fear beginning to show in his voice.

"Not my problem is it? You can go now. See you later. Have a nice life. What's left of it anyway." Connor was smug, like the proverbial cat that ate the unfortunate proverbial canary.

Ricky stared at Connor for less than a minute, taking him only that long to figure out the implications of what he was saying. Somehow the cops had made a case against his friends without his help. That would explain why they had left him alone for so long and then suddenly let him go. And now Connor was threatening to give Ricky the credit for ratting on his friends. An act which would guarantee the termination of Ricky's life. He might not be very smart, but Ricky was not suicidal. He decided he better do whatever it took to keep Connor from executing his scheme.

"Ok, I'll talk," he said. "I'll do whatever you want me to do. But you got to promise to leave my name out of it totally. And I won't agree to testify in open court. Let's face it, once I talk I will be a marked man, so I want to be in your program. I want you guys to hide me. But I don't want the whole world knowing where I am this time. Look at what happened to Brenda."

"We already have all the information we need," Connor lied smoothly. "But if you have something to say, I'm listening. If it is useful, then we will talk about a deal. If not, then you can leave and you are on your own." Connor heard his body say all this, but inside he was seething. Ricky's last statement about Brenda – Jesse, had set something off in his brain that could have fatal consequences for Ricky. Connor had to muster a hell of a lot of willpower to control his urge to strangle him. Or much worse.

CHAPTER SEVENTY FIVE

BRENT CALLED CONNOR, telling him about Dylan's nightmare, and in turn Connor told him about Ricky. He said Ricky was just starting to talk and he would call back when he was done with him. While waiting for the return call, Anna kept Brent company, bringing him coffee and some food, which Brent was grateful for.

She asked him, "You heard from Charlie?"

"No, but he hasn't been brought back here in handcuffs yet, so I take that as good news."

Anna managed a laugh at that. "Yeah, I guess you're right. Can I ask you something?"

"Sure."

"How come Charlie isn't married?" She asked it carefully. She knew Brent was fairly close to the Chief and she didn't want to cause any hard feelings by prying.

"He was once," Brent said easily. "A long time ago. Didn't last long. She wasn't very understanding of military police work and Charlie was not very understanding of anything but his work. And I guess he hasn't found anyone else who is understanding of it yet."

"I see," she replied. She debated whether or not she should tell Brent how she felt about Charlie, then made up her mind and said, "I like him, Brent." She watched him for his reaction to that, but he didn't seemed shocked by her admission.

"Yeah, we noticed," Brent said. "And we also noticed that he doesn't seem to mind." Anna nodded acknowledgment. She knew that Brent was important to Charlie and wanted his opinion.

"Do you mind?" she asked.

"I like the arrangement. Especially if he likes it," he answered. They both fell silent, and a moment later Brent was asleep. Anna went back to her own room to get some rest herself.

The Chief began his shift by doing a drive-by of Brad Danison's house. Brad's car was not in its assigned parking space, meaning he had left his house while Charlie and Jake were undergoing the changing of the guard. The Chief checked the police station but Brad wasn't there either. He checked Brad's house again, in case he'd only run a short errand before returning home, but he wasn't there.

Unsure where else to look, the Chief had Brent wake up Jake and ask him for advice, but Jake had not been able to give him any hints. Brad could be anywhere in the city, or anywhere outside it for that matter. More likely, though, that he was still local, so the Chief took a chance on one of the bars that Brad had visited earlier when Jake was following him. Jake had told him about the place, saying that it might be part of a regular route for Brad.

He parked his car far enough away from the bar so that he wouldn't be seen easily. And he waited. And then he waited some more. He drank a lot of coffee to stay awake. And he waited.

The sun started coming up and he was still awake, and waiting, but getting tired. He recalled what had Anna said about length of his shift, 'I probably won't see you again until this afternoon.' He wondered if he would last that long. Maybe some breakfast would help.

He scanned the area for a fast food place and spotted a Rebel gas station that had a convenience store attached to it. It was the type of place that had prepared and packaged hot meals that almost passed for food. Better than nothing. He started the car and drove to the gas station.

The store was nearly empty, it was too early in the morning for the breakfast rush hour crowd. There was one other person inside and he was looking over the same fare as Connor. Probably trying to make the same decision, which food item would be halfway tolerable. The Chief didn't look too closely at the man, concentrating instead on finding something to eat. He finally picked out a sausage, egg, and cheese muffin, reasoning that a sandwich like that would be hard to screw up. He took his alleged food to the cash register to pay.

The other shopper was ahead of him paying for his own meal while Charlie waited for him. When he finished paying he turned around to leave and Charlie got a good, close up look at him and almost fainted. It was Brad.

He had no time to avoid being seen by Brad, so trusting his disguise he said, "Morning," like any fellow shopper might say, then walked past him to the check out counter, hoping for the best. He was tempted to turn back to see if he'd been made but resisted the temptation.

Charlie payed for his food and walked out the door. He had just spotted Brad getting into his car when he realized that he might be seen by the federal agents if they were watching Danison. His disguise would keep his face from being recognized, but if he looked like he was following Brad it would attract attention. He pretended that he forgot something in the store and turned around and went back inside. From inside the store he watched Brad drive away, and then he watched to see if any feds were following Brad. If they were, they were too good for Charlie to spot.

He waited another minute and then went back out to his car. He had to make a guess at where Brad might have gone. He guessed home. He drove back toward Brad's house and saw his car parked outside. He parked in the same spot he'd used earlier and ate his breakfast while watching the house. He had been wrong about the inability to screw up a sausage, egg, and cheese muffin.

CHAPTER SEVENTY SIX

ONCE RICKY HAD DECIDED THAT COOPERATING with Connor was in his best interests, meaning it might keep him from getting killed, he talked a lot. Unfortunately he said very little. By the end of his tale Connor had to admit that Ricky knew almost nothing about Jesse's death. Except for one small but important fact. The person who gave him the picture from Jesse's house was Brad Danison. It was an important fact for obvious reasons, but more importantly it provided Connor with the hope that it was not his own visit to Montana long ago that had directed attention to Jesse. Brad was not in jail when Connor made that trip, and if visit was what had tipped him off to Jesse's location, he could have gone after Jesse over twenty years ago. But he had gone to Montana only recently. Maybe it was still possible that his visit gave her location away, but it seemed much less likely now.

The only other useful thing Ricky talked about, in his desperation to save his own hide, was Ben Alivio and his organization. Connor knew that Grant and the Vegas Marshal's office would love to have the information. so he remanded Ricky to Grant, glad that Brad Danison wouldn't be able to come anywhere near him. Ricky wasn't happy about the arrangement, being under the impression that Connor had promised to take care of him and put him under protection. He mentioned it to Connor.

"Hey, not my problem," Connor told him and left.

Dealing with Ricky had worn Connor out and, deciding he was done for the day, he headed back to the hotel to get some rest.

When he got to his room he saw that Jake was already asleep, so he tried to get into bed without waking him. He thought he was successful at it until he heard Jake say, "Time is it?" groggily.

"Early, or late depending on how you look at it. About seven AM. I wake you up?"

"No, I heard you come in. I was already awake. Sort of. Heard from the Chief?"

"No."

"You been up all night?"

"Yeah." He wasn't happy about the fact.

"How'd it go?"

"I'm too tired to tell the story. I'll tell you in the morning.... Or whatever it is when I wake up." He was practically asleep before he finished saying it.

CHAPTER SEVENTY SEVEN

HELEN COULDN'T TAKE BEING LOCKED up like a prisoner any longer. Better to be dead, she thought. Or at least better to be given a chance to fight off death hand to hand, rather than let it kill you of boredom. She showered, got dressed and walked out the door. She was a bit nervous, but in spite of her nerves she had the brave thought, "OK bring it on, I'm ready."

She looked around as she shut the door behind her. Nothing unusual yet. She headed for the stairs and looked down the stair well in case someone was waiting. No one there. She walked down the stairs and onto the side walk. She stood on the sidewalk, looked up and down the street, saw nothing threatening so started walking.

Her plan was to walk a couple of blocks to a drug store and buy some personal items she needed. Then she would walk a couple of blocks further on and get something to eat at a nearby coffee shop.

She arrived at the drug store without incident. No cars had followed her, no people followed her, no one shot her or attacked her or kidnapped her or did anything at all to her. She bought what she needed. She exited the store, looked around again but still saw nothing threatening. She walked on down the road toward the coffee shop, anxious to eat a real breakfast, not the same old granola bars she had been forced to eat in her prison cell – a.k.a. her motel room.

She made it safely to the coffee shop, found a booth she liked and sat down. She hadn't ordered any coffee, but a cute young waiter brought some coffee to the table anyway. Her paranoia got the better of her and she wondered why he would bring her coffee without asking first. Her imagination went wild. Was he an undercover agent? A hit man? Was her excursion outside motel life about to come to an end, without even a chance at a decent breakfast? The waiter reappeared with his order pad.

"Why did you bring me coffee? I didn't ask for it," she said accusingly.

The waiter thought that she may be some kind of drug addict who was experiencing the paranoia of coming off of drugs. She didn't look like one of the crazy hookers that often came in after a hard nights work, but you never know in Vegas.

"It's our policy," he explained to her. "We automatically bring coffee during breakfast hours. See the sign?" He pointed to a small tent shaped sign on the table that said, 'Bottomless coffee during breakfast hours. Please inform our wait staff if you don't prefer it.'

She felt silly and was certain that the poor waiter thought there was something wrong with her. Not sure how to correct the situation she merely said, "OH, sorry I didn't see the sign."

"That's ok, it happens a lot. If you don't want the coffee I'll take it away," he said with a very friendly smile.

"I'll keep it, thanks." The smile he gave her did not go unnoticed, he was coming on to her. Or maybe he was just working on earning a bigger tip. Maybe she'd been locked up so long that she thought every guy who smiled at her was coming on to her. Maybe she was just hungry.

"What's the biggest breakfast you got?" she asked.

"The lumberjack," the waiter said, again with a broad smile.

"I'll take it."

He wrote it on his pad and winked at her then walked back to the kitchen.

What do you know, she thought. The son of a bitch was coming on to her. She smiled to herself.

She finished off the whole lumberjack breakfast and a couple of cups of coffee. While eating she had shamelessly flirted with the waiter every time he came to her booth. Her hunger and ego both well satisfied, she left some money for the check, plus a generous tip. Apparently, flattery might get you nowhere, but it will get you a big tip. She'd have to tell Tommy about her flattering waiter. That would get him going.

Thinking about Tommy reminded her of the reality of her situation, and she began to wonder again why no one had bothered her. It was possible that they were only watching her and didn't want to talk to her or kill her, or whatever. If they were watching her they were pretty discreet about it.

She stood outside the coffee shop and took a minute to make up her mind what to do next. She did not look forward to going back to her room. Ever. But she had to, at least long enough to drop off her shopping bag and get ready for the town. Back in her motel cell she cleaned up and changed clothes, then called a cab. Before she left she wrote a note for Tommy, saying where she would be, in case he finished his business and showed up.

The taxi dropped her off at the Silverton Hotel and Casino, where she walked directly to the bar and ordered the house specialty drink, a Bloody Mary. They made the best ones she had ever tasted.

She sipped on her drink and roamed the casino looking for a game that would interest her. The choices were limited by the fact that her finances were limited. No high stakes poker or craps. No five dollar slots. Unhurried, she watched other people gamble for a while, thoroughly enjoying both the human company and the excellence of the drink.

Eventually she found a quarter machine that she liked, sat down and put in twenty dollars. She bet four credits at a time, then wondered why she didn't just play the dollar slots. She justified her choice by telling herself that she would have the option to slow the betting down to a quarter at a time if she wanted to. But even while telling herself that, she knew she would never bet less than four quarters. So why the hell don't I just play dollar slots, she asked herself again.

CHAPTER SEVENTY EIGHT

THE EASTERN SKY WAS TURNING predawn gray when Tommy finally concluded that Brad was not coming. He went back to his room at a cheap motel on the Boulder City side of Henderson. He needed some rest but couldn't afford a full day's sleep, so he gave himself three hours on the alarm clock, undressed, and went to bed.

Three hours later the alarm clock sounded. Tommy got out of bed, freshened up in the bathroom,then went out to get some coffee and a sweet roll. He brought the coffee and sweet roll back to his room, deciding to give Brad another chance. He consumed his food and waited. Several hours later there was still no sign of him. Maybe he'd been wrong about Brad looking for him. He was going to have to change tactics, instead of waiting for Brad to find him, he would have to find Brad.

Finding Brad was no trick, he could be easily located at the police station. The trick was finding Brad at the right place, the place of his choosing. His best chance at making that idea work was to use Helen. He hated exposing her, but he couldn't come up with a better solution. It was a tough choice to make, but he had to make it.

He drove to Helen's motel, slowing down as he approached, watching for signs of a stakeout. He saw no one so he parked his car, walked up to her room and knocked. He looked around while waiting for her to answer, but didn't see anyone. When there was no answer at the door he knocked again, a little harder. Still no answer. A bad sign.

He had one of the two keys they had been issued when they registered at the motel and he used his to get in. He walked through the door cautiously, wary of an ambush. He checked the room and bathroom but they were empty.

He looked around for some sort of clue explaining her absence and found a note. After reading it he was pretty pissed off. She knew the rules and she had agreed to them. So she had either broken the rules on her own decision, or someone had forced her out of the room and made her write the note to cover their tracks. But the note didn't feel forced to him, the handwriting was too normal. No, he decided, she had changed her mind about the rules on her own.

Damn it, his plan would not work if she got nabbed. He tore the note off the pad, stuffed it in his pocket and strode out the door.

CHAPTER SEVENTY NINE

BRAD SPENT THE ENTIRE NIGHT LOOKING FOR Tommy without success. Tommy was making it hard, as he expected. And to make it even tougher, all the punks and wise guys knew that something big was happening with Tommy, and it scared them. They avoided Brad and even if Brad tracked one down they wouldn't talk. Hell, he could tell they didn't know anything anyway, so he didn't push them. He returned home at seven a.m., tired and needing rest. He set his alarm for ten a.m.

When the alarm sounded he groaned, hating having to get up after only a few hours sleep. He picked up the phone and called in sick. The captain started to give him a hard time but he interrupted him and said, "Oh god, sorry I got to run to the toilet and throw up," then he hung up the phone. He didn't care if they fired him. If he didn't find Tommy he might be in worse trouble.

While drinking his wake up coffee he decided on a new plan. It was one that he'd previously considered then discarded. Helen might be the only way to get to Tommy after all. They couldn't stay apart forever. And maybe Tommy was hiding in her room under the assumption that no one would believe he would do something that dumb. He wasn't sure it would work, but it was worth trying.

He assumed Helen was being watched by the feds, the U.S. Marshals, the local PD and some wise guys. Hell, she could be billed as the top attraction in the City of Las Vegas. His plan wouldn't work with the whole world looking on so he decided to do a little recon and find out if she was being watched, and if so by who.

He drove to one of those large building supply places that advertised that professionals shopped there, but was really used mostly by do-it-yourselfers. He went to the one that he had used several times before, when doing repairs on his house.

He left the store fully equipped to disguise himself as a construction worker, with clothing and a hard hat and tinted safety glasses. After donning his disguise he surreptitiously covered a large perimeter around Helen's motel, looking for signs of a stakeout.

There were no cops, no feds, no Deputy Marshals, no wise guys, no nothing. He was glad of it, but found it almost unbelievable. The only explanation he could come up with was that nobody believed Tommy was stupid enough to show up at her room, and no one believed Helen would know anything on her own. The same as he had believed all this time. He laughed at the thought.

He knocked on Helen's door but no one answered. He expected that – even if she was in the room she would not answer the door if she had any sense at all, so he brought out his master key, one he had paid a clerk a hundred bucks for during a bust earlier in the year.

The room was empty, a fact that he had not expected. He looked around the room carefully for evidence that might tell him where she had gone. He saw a motel note pad on the table with a pen next to it and examined it closely. He could see that someone had written on the pad and then torn the sheet off the top, leaving a faint impression on the sheet beneath it. After careful examination of the impressions he could only make out enough of the letters to know it was a casino, but several of the letters in the name of the casino were too faint. He could make out the first letter. It was an S. He could also make out a T and an O. He started mentally listing all of the casinos he knew of that started with an S. Each time he thought of one he wrote it down on a piece of paper he tore off the back of the motel notepad. He wrote Sahara, but it didn't have a T or an O, so he crossed it out. Then he wrote Silver Dollar, but had to cross that off too. He went through a few others before finally writing down Silverton Casino. It matched.

CHAPTER EIGHTY

THE CHIEF, SOMEHOW MANAGING to stay awake, finally saw Brad leave his house and get into his car. He started his own car and waited to see which direction Brad would drive. If Brad drove in the direction of the station, the Chief's plan was to take his own, different route to get there, in hopes of not getting spotted by the federal agents. But Brad drove off in a direction away from the station so the Chief was forced to follow him.

He waited for Brad to get a few blocks away and then pulled out behind him. He watched for the feds but didn't see them. If they were watching, he could only hope that his plain car and clothing disguise would shield him from their discovery of him.

Brad was pretty easy to follow despite the speed of traffic on the surface streets. In his first few hours of driving in Las Vegas Charlie had been terrified at the fact that people drove nearly as fast on surface streets as they did on the freeways, and after being flipped off several times for only going a mere ten miles over the speed limit, he decided to start driving fast enough to at least keep up with the flow of traffic.

Now, a bit more comfortable with the M.O. of Vegas drivers, Connor managed to keep several cars between them while still keeping Brad's car in sight. A few miles later Brad pulled into a home improvement store and parked. He went inside for about twenty minutes and came out with a shopping bag. Then he got back in his car and drove another couple of miles where he parked on the side of the road. He stayed in the car for several minutes and the Chief could not see what he was doing in it. When he got out of the car he was dressed like a carpenter. He even had on a hard hat and dark glasses, obviously trying to disguise himself for some reason.

The Chief stayed in his car and watched as Brad walked around a motel, covering a perimeter of a couple of blocks. Then he walked up to a motel room door and knocked. After waiting a minute he took out a key and opened the door. He didn't walk in right away, but instead looked through the door and scanned the room. Then he entered slowly, warily.

After Brad disappeared into the motel room Charlie scanned the motel complex and grounds. There was something about the motel name that sounded familiar to him, and after a few minutes he recognized it as the motel that Helen was checked into.

CHAPTER EIGHTY ONE

DYLAN WOKE UP AT TEN A.M. Joan was still asleep with her head in his lap. She woke up shortly after him and stretched and yawned. She noticed that the TV was still on.

"You been watching TV this whole time?" she asked.

"No," he said. "I fell asleep watching it. I didn't think I would fall asleep after having that dream, but I guess I was wrong." Joan noticed that he was still a bit pallid.

"You're still tired, let's get some more sleep," Joan suggested.

"I am tired, but today is a big day and it's already ten. I'm going to clean up and go across the hall to see Brent."

"OK. I'll clean up after you're done and then come meet you there," she said. She wondered what he meant by a 'big day' and momentarily considered asking him, but let it pass.

Dylan stood under the hot water of the shower enjoying its soothing effects. It relaxed him enough that he thought he might try to remember something from his dream. He knew that there was something in it that was important. Something key to what they were doing here. He wished he had a little more time and rest before tackling the memory, but he couldn't afford the time.

He took a deep breath and started looking back, in his mind. The first thing he recalled was Brent's voice asking him to stop screaming, which made him wonder why he was screaming. From previous experience he deduced that it had something to do with his mom. Possibly he ran her over again, but he didn't think so. He would have remembered that. He remembered it the first two times he dreamt it.

The gun! He recalled that there was something about a gun in the dream, and that it had freaked him out. He replayed the scene in his mind in which he swung wildly at the gun, but without effect. As if he, or the gunman, was a ghost. And he recalled the gun pointed at his mom, but never firing.

Cold water on his body pulled him out of his reverie. He made adjustments to the faucets by turning down the cold, but after turning it all the way off the water was still only lukewarm at best. He stood in the shower for a moment longer while debating whether he should get out and dry off. He was just about to turn off the hot faucet and exit the shower when he felt the water getting hot again. He turned the cold water back on until he got the temperature he wanted, wondering if that was typical of hotel water systems.

It was at that moment that he heard someone say the word 'bitch' so clearly that he flinched and turned around to see who had said it. There was no one there. He had heard it only in his mind, and it sounded just as it did in his dream.

He returned to recalling the dream and finally remembered the missing part of it, the face of the man who held the gun, and who had also said the word 'bitch'. It was Brad. Brad Danison, and he spoke. He said 'The boy must die'. He remembered Brad saying those words in the dream and then everything fell together. The tough choice. The gun. The boy must die. No gun shot. His mom dead in the street. It all lined up and he got the explanation he was looking for.

A moment later he heard a noise and took his head out from under the water to listen more closely. The shower curtain was too thick to be able to see anything through it so he reached up for it just as it slid back. Joan was standing there wearing nothing but her good looks. Her good looks were quite unavoidable and Dylan felt a new wave of emotions.

"You were taking too long," Joan said as she entered the shower and closed the curtain behind her, "and I missed my man."

They embraced under the hot shower. The feeling of her bare skin against his was incredible. The sensations that the naked physical contact aroused in him made him want to hold her for eternity. He needed to hold her for eternity. And the emotional and spiritual passion, and the connection between them intensified the experience to unbelievable extremes, and he clung to her with the same survival instinct as he would summon to cling to his very life. He knew the feeling was mutual because at that moment their feelings were inseparable. All of the emotions of recent days, all of the mysteries, and the latest answers and understanding, the incredible love that Joan had for him, they all combined into an inexorable tide that threatened to sweep him away. He felt the tears coming unchecked and unstoppable. They mixed with the shower water and ran down Joan's back. They were tears of equal sorrow and happiness. Tears of equal relief and apprehension. Tears of equal love and anger. Tears of revenge and very little mercy.

They stood in their watery embrace for several long and lovely minutes. Dylan's tears abated and his emotions leveled themselves out to become something natural. Something approaching normal. He started to come into touch with his body again, and his body was reacting naturally to the circumstances of their bare embrace. They began a session of unbridled, passionate, and yet patient love making that was completed, eventually, in the hotel bed.

As they lay there entwined together in the bliss of the afterglow, Dylan could not help thinking how grateful he was that his dream about Joan and him in a Las Vegas hotel had come true. He was even more grateful that it had happened in a way that far surpassed his dream. Joan expressed both of their feelings succinctly when she whispered to him, "I'm so happy, Dylan. And I love you so much. Can we just stay here and not move? Ever?"

As wonderful as her suggestion sounded, Dylan knew it couldn't happen. Events were moving forward without him. Important events, and he couldn't let that happen. Now that he finally understood what was happening, what had happened to his mom, he knew what had to be done.

"I wish I could, babe," he told her. "I really wish I could. Maybe when this is over we will stay in bed for a week. Maybe more. For as long as you want. Ok?"

"Sounds good to me," she said dreamily. She moaned with disappointment when Dylan made a move to get up, and clung to him with a fiercer grip. Dylan gave in easily and remained wound around her for a while longer.

CHAPTER EIGHTY TWO

EVENTUALLY DYLAN AND JOAN extracted themselves from each other and Dylan made his way across the hall to see Brent, Joan clinging closely at his side.

James, freshly showered, greeted them when they arrived. He took on the self assigned responsibility of bringing them up to date.

"Morning, guys," he said. "Something big is happening. Jake just got a really important call." He conveyed the news with all due seriousness, which piqued Dylan's curiosity.

"Oh yeah," Dylan asked, "what is it?"

"I have no idea. I just heard him on the phone. It sounded like real bad news though. After he hung up he went into the bathroom. He's still in there so I have no further information." He shrugged.

Joan and Dylan looked at each other in disbelief and raised their arms palms up. Sign language for 'I don't get it'. At that point, Brent emerged from the bathroom, hollering at the slumbering Connor and Jake, who sat up slowly, rubbing the sleep from their eyes.

Dylan noticed that they were dressed in street clothes, reminding him of himself the morning after the funeral. Except they were probably not hungover. More likely, they kept their clothes on due to the open door policy. That and the co-ed status of the team, not wanting to be seen semi naked by a woman. So much for women's rights.

Brent looked at Dylan and furrowed his brow in concern.

"How you doing?" he asked.

"I'm ok. Still a bit tired and shaky, but ok. I figured something out this morning, and we need to talk about it. But first tell me what the big news is."

"You really freaked me out you know," Brent said instead of answering Dylan. "I mean it was really intense. I thought you might actually end up dying. It was way more than just a hangover like the other day. Are you sure you are ready to go back to work?" His own doubt showed plainly on his face.

"Under other circumstances I'd say no," Dylan answered. "But this is different. Events are coming together now, and things are going to start happening. And they are going to happen fast. I don't have the time to wait until I'm better. I am just going to have to cowboy up." He looked Brent in the eye so that he would know there would be no compromising on his decision. And also to let him know how much he appreciated his concern and caring for him.

Brent said, "Fair enough, but you let me help you. You keep me posted, and you promise you will come to me if things start getting rough." His cop tone of voice again.

"I promise. Now what's going on?" Jake came out of the bathroom at that moment and looked expectantly at Bent, wanting to hear the explanation as well. Connor stood by, listening in also.

"Ok, I just got a call from the Chief," Brent informed them. "He said that Brad went to Helen's motel and that he used a key to let himself into her room. He said he never saw Helen, but he suspects that she wasn't in her room. At the time of the call Brad was still in the room."

Connor knitted his brow, a bit puzzled, then asked the question that was on all of their minds, "Wasn't she being watched?"

"Not by us," Brent answered.

"Why not?" Connor asked. The color in his face made it clear that his temper was rising.

"We assumed everyone else was watching her. In fact I'm sure the Marshal had a man on her. I heard Grant say so yesterday," Brent explained.

Connor got on his cell phone and called Grant. When Grant came on the line Connor did not mince words. He asked, "Did you have a man on Helen's motel room?"

Grant noticed the urgency in Connors voice and hesitated a moment before answering. In that moment of hesitation a great many things went through his mind. He deduced that something went wrong at Helen's motel. He recalled calling off the watch on her room because he didn't see the value in it and he needed the manpower. He recalled that when he made the decision to call off the watch, he also decided not to tell Connor about the decision. And he remembered dreading this very moment, when Connor found out. His mistake was that he did not expect or anticipate something going wrong with Helen. And now apparently it had.

"We did for a while, but I pulled them off last night," he explained.

It was Connor who hesitated this time, but his hesitation was caused, not by a thinking process, but by shock. When he spoke, what he said was not intelligible, sounding something like, "I....you.....what.....but.....Jesus....damn it........why...I mean...say that again."

"I said I took the watch off of Helen last night. I needed the man for something else and I didn't see the value in watching her. I'm sorry, ok? I can tell by your voice that something's wrong and that means I screwed up. So tell me what happened and I will try to fix it. I promise. Ok?"

"Brad Danison went to her room and let himself in," Connor told him. "Apparently she is not in her room. We don't know what happened to her yet."

"Shit. Sorry, Connor. OK, here's what I'm going to do. I'm sending a Deputy over right now to search the room and see if we can figure out what happened to her. But we have to wait for Brad to leave first. Are you sure that she isn't in the room with him?"

"No, actually. It appears that when he went in the room it was empty. But we have no way to be certain. The only way to know for sure is to go in the room and look."

"Ok, is Brad still in the room?"

"Just a minute." He told Brent to call the Chief and find out if Brad came out of the room yet. Brent did as he was told and found out that Brad had just walked out the door of the room alone. Connor relayed the information to Grant.

"Good. I will have a Deputy check the room and find out if she is in there or not. If not, he will go in and see what he can figure out. What else can I do to help?"

"That's it for now. Thanks." He hung up and looked at Brent with an expression of terror mixed with outrage.

"Tell the Chief not to let Brad out of his sight. Tell him I don't care if he is spotted by Brad or the Feds or anyone else, just don't lose him," he ordered. Then he went into the bathroom to take his turn at cleaning up.

Brent made the call and forwarded Connor's instructions to the Chief as ordered. The Chief informed him that he had already begun following Brad and gave him his current location, based on a couple of street's name signs.

"Thanks," Brent said. "Keep me posted."

"You got it."

CHAPTER EIGHTY THREE

U.S. MARSHALS DEPUTY SAMSON was dispatched by Grant Curran to the Starlite motel, room 112. He was instructed to confirm the presence, or absence of one Helen Whelan. He was not to apprehend or interrogate. He was to observe and report only. He was to use his own judgment as to the optimum methods to use in the execution of his instructions, but be discreet.

Deputy Samson arrived at the Starlite Motel and knocked lightly on the door of room 112. He waited the appropriate amount of time but nobody answered the door. He knocked again. No answer. He used a key that he had been given by the desk clerk to let himself in. The door swung open and Samson entered cautiously. A few seconds later he was certain that there was no one in the room. He called Grant and reported the results of his search.

"See if you can find anything in the room that would indicate where she is. If you do, call me back," Grant instructed him.

Samson searched the room, looking for anything that held the possibility of being a clue. He saw a shopping bag from a local drug store, but the only thing it told him was that she had been to the store, and had obviously come back or the bag wouldn't be in the room. He saw that her suitcase and clothing was still in the room so she wasn't planning to leave permanently. Same thing in the bathroom; all of her toiletries and make-up was still there.

He decided to give up the wild goose chase. On his way to the door he saw a pen on the table. Deputies were always doing too much paper work, and therefore they were always looking for pens. He walked over to the table to grab the pen as a souvenir. When he reached down for it he saw a piece of motel notepad paper sitting next to the pen with a few Casino names written on it. All of the names were crossed off except for Silverton, which was circled.

What do you know, he thought, she left a damn clue. No one had told him about Brad, so he could not have known that it was really him that left the clue, but what does it matter? A clue is a clue. He called Grant and reported what he had found.

Grant knew right away who really wrote the list of casinos, but instead of saying so he just thanked Deputy Samson, then hung up the phone and called Connor.

CHAPTER EIGHTY FOUR

WHEN CONNOR HUNG UP THE PHONE his face was a whole new shade of purple, and the HQ room was silent. It was one of those pregnant silences that actually spoke of something, like, 'what the hell has gotten into Connor'. But Connor never gave then the chance to ask before disappearing into the bathroom.

He emerged from the bathroom a short while later, and gave them the explanation they'd silently hoped for.

"I finally got Ricky to talk," he told them. "He only said one meaningful thing. He told me that Brad Danison was the one who gave him the picture from Jesse's house." He let that sink in a minute, waiting to see if anyone had a response. No one did. They understood the implication.

"We've got to try to get ahead of him," Connor continued. "Get Charlie back on the cell phone. Tell him to stay on the phone while he follows Brad and relay every move he makes." He wanted to see if he could get an idea of Brad's general direction of travel and then possibly head him off. Brent made the call and put his cell phone on speaker mode so that everyone in the room could listen.

By now the HQ room was crowded. Every member of the team was there except the Chief, and even he was there via a speaker on Brent's cell phone. They listened closely as he gave his blow by blow report of Brad's travels. At some point, in the description of streets they were driving, Anna thought she knew where they were headed.

"It sounds like he is headed for the Silverton Casino," she said. "It is the only major destination in that direction."

Connor nodded at the information, and was about to respond when his phone rang. It was Grant, who proceeded to tell him what Deputy Samson had discovered at Helen's motel room. The information confirmed Anna's deduction that they were going to The Silverton, and it explained why as well. They were following Helen.

The others continued to concentrate on the Chief's reporting, ignoring Connor's conversation. Dylan took advantage of their single-minded focus and lightly tapped Joan's elbow to get her attention. When she looked at him he put his finger to his lips to indicate silence, and then he tipped his head toward the door. Together, they quietly inched their way in the direction of the exit. Before they reached the door Dylan scooped up the rental car keys from the dresser.

After speaking with Grant, Connor had a far away look in his eyes. Anna noticed, and it worried her. "You ok?" she asked.

"Yeah, yeah, just trying to figure all this out. Something is coming down and I don't like it. And I don't like not knowing what it is. It's out of control. Out of my control."

"You still want to try to get ahead of Brad?" Anna asked him.

"Yes, that's right," he said. "Thanks for reminding me, I'd forgotten."

"No problem," Anna said.

"Jake," Connor said, "hurry on over to the Silverton and see if you can get there ahead of them. Check in with us when get there."

Jake grabbed the car keys and ran out the door.

That taken care of, Brent looked around, ready to hear what Dylan had to say to him about his nightmare the previous night. However, Dylan was not standing where Brent last saw him. He looked around the room in case he had moved, but didn't see him anywhere in the room. He checked the bathroom but it was empty.

Anna hadn't been paying quite as much attention to the phone call with Charlie as everyone else, and had seen Dylan leaving with Joan, grabbing up the car keys on their way out. She had no clue what they were up to but she wasn't about to get in their way. If she was sure of anything about Dylan it was his instinct. He had uncanny instincts at times. Almost as good as his mother. She had admired Jesse's abilities and she had never interfered with her when she was 'off on a hunch'. When she saw Brent looking around the room she didn't need any super-human instincts to know that he was looking for Dylan.

"He left," Anna told Brent.

Brent looked at her, bewildered, and said, "Left? What do you mean left?"

"I mean he and Joan walked out that door about fifteen minutes ago." She pointed toward the exit.

"Why? Where were they going?" he asked with a look of disbelief on his face.

"I don't know, I didn't ask them. But if I was a gambling woman I would bet that they were going to the Silverton."

"Shit, that's all we need." He called Dylan.

"So what happened to your promise to keep me informed?" Brent said when Dylan answered. He paused for the answer and then, "Yeah, whatever. What the hell do you plan on doing there?" he listened to Dylan's answer, visibly upset by his freelancing. "You don't have a plan, that's beautiful. So why are you going there?" Dylan answered him again, apparently, and Brent said, "You do that," and hung up, still pissed off.

Connor asked Brent, "What did he say?"

"He's going to The Silverton," Brent said unhappily.

"Great," Connor complained, "we've got Jake, Charlie, Helen, Brad and now Dylan and Joan all going to the Silverton. What the hell is going on over

247

there? It's got to be something. Did Dylan say why he was going there?" he asked.

"Dylan said he was going there because Brad was going there," Brent answered. "And he wasn't sure why he needed to be there but he knew that he did. I don't know what that means exactly, Connor, but I wish I did."

"He's probably right you know, based on past experience," Connor said in a resigned tone of voice.

"Yeah, that's one of the things that pisses me off. But he shouldn't be there alone. It worries me."

"Shit, Brent, he's hardly alone," Connor said. "Everyone in the damn world is there. He'll have Jake, Charlie and Joan to back him while we just sit here and whine."

James, who had been almost invisible due to his unusual silence, interjected, "Do you think Brad and Helen are in this together somehow?" The sudden change of subject took the others off-guard. Once they started thinking about it, however, they decided that it was a reasonable question. Brad was obviously going to The Silverton to meet Helen, so why couldn't they be in it together?

"Good question, James," Connor admitted, "but I don't really know what the connection is."

Anna had been considering James question as well and thought she might have at least part of an explanation.

"You guys are missing something," she informed them.

"What's that?" Brent asked.

"Why was Jake following Brad?" she reminded them.

"To find Tommy. So what?" they asked her.

"Apparently you guys didn't get enough sleep," she accused.

"That's no great secret you know," Brent responded, his patience beginning to deteriorate. "Why don't you just tell us what it is that our sleepy heads don't get."

"Ok," Anna responded. "Jake was following Brad because he was sure that he would lead us to Tommy. And he was sure it would be very soon, right?" She still couldn't believe they didn't see it.

"Yeah, right," the three men agreed in unison, then continued to stare at her waiting for her to explain it.

"So maybe soon is right now. Maybe he is leading us to Tommy. Who is the only person who might know where Tommy is?" She wasn't going to wait for them to figure it out any more, so she answered her own question, "Helen Whelan. And even if she doesn't know, someone may be able to threaten to hurt her unless Tommy comes out of hiding. It's a possibility."

"Shit, she's got a good point don't she?" James asserted.

"I'll say," Brent agreed. "But what do we do about it?"

248

"I've got an idea," Connor said. He picked up his cell phone and called Grant.

.

CHAPTER EIGHTY FIVE

AS SOON AS THEY WERE OUT of the room and in the hotel hallway, Dylan whispered to Joan, "Come on, we have to be at the Silverton casino when they arrive." Then he quickly made his way down the stairs with Joan right behind him. Once they were in the lobby, and could speak in a normal volume, Joan asked him, "What if they don't go there?"

"They are going there. Trust me. I am sure of it."

"Ok. If you say so, I believe you."

"Thanks."

"You're welcome," she said with an impish, rascally smile that Dylan happily returned.

Dylan went to the front desk and asked for directions to the Silverton Casino. The clerk explained the route to them and they thanked him and exited the hotel.

They found the car in the parking lot and pulled out into the street following the directions they were given. Joan was thrilled by all the secrecy, urgency, and knowledge that something big was approaching. Plus, of course, the knowledge that they were being naughty.

A half mile down the road Joan said, "Now tell me what's going on."

To Joan's surprise and delight Dylan gave her a complete explanation.

"This morning in the shower, before you showed up that is, I figured some things out. I know that my mom jumped in front of the car on purpose, but Brad was responsible for it. It wasn't a suicide. It was a sacrifice. For me. She killed herself to save my life." Joan was amazed by the news, but she wasn't quite following his logic.

"How did her jumping off a curb save your life?"

"In my dream I was trapped in a situation that had only two solutions, and both of them resulted in my death. How do you decide what to do when you know you will die no matter what? My mom told me, in my dream, that it was a tough choice, and then everything changed. My dream changed and suddenly I was watching her stand on the curb with a gun pointed at her. The man with the gun was Brad. He told her that if she didn't jump, he would kill me. She made the tough choice and jumped off the curb." His eyes were starting to water up again, and he looked more determined than ever.

"Oh my God," Joan said.

"Yeah, oh my God is right. And there is more. Tommy was there when she jumped. He was right there in the street, driving his patrol car. He probably saw what happened. I'm not sure if he was part of it, but since he never said anything about seeing Brad, we can assume he may be in on it with him. When I catch up with Brad, I intend to find out."

She loved Dylan unconditionally but that didn't make her foolish. She had serious reservations about his ability to prevail in a confrontation with Brad. And if he somehow managed not to get himself killed, and figured out a way to kill Brad instead, he would go to prison for the rest of his life. She didn't know if Nevada had the death penalty or not, but if it did, Dylan could even be executed.

"You don't plan on trying to kill Brad yourself do you?" she asked.

"No. At least not yet I don't. But I promise you that I won't stop until I see appropriate justice served," he answered. The statement did little to relieve Joan's concerns, and she imagined several kinds of trouble Dylan could get himself into.

In order to be prepared for what she may have to do to save him from himself she asked, "So what do you plan on doing?"

"I don't have a plan. Per Se." He avoided looking at her after that admission.

Oh great, Joan thought to herself. Men!

They took the east entrance into the Silverton parking lot a few minutes after Brad had driven up the west entrance, the Chief close behind him. The casino structure rose up between the two entrances, blocking their view of each other. Dylan parked within view of the east entrance to take up surveillance of it. Brad and took up separate parking spots, both in view of the west entrance, but out of view of Dylan and Joan. A few minutes later Dylan got out of the car and stretched for a few seconds. Then he walked toward the casino to look for a bathroom.

CHAPTER EIGHTY SIX

GRANT CRINGED WHEN HE WAS TOLD that Connor was on the phone for him. He picked up his phone and spoke cheerfully, hoping for the best, "Hi, Connor, how are you?"

"I need another favor," Connor said without answering Grant's question.

"Sure, what do you need?" So much for cheerfulness.

"Can you set up a meeting with those two feds, Mutt and Jeff, whatever their names are? I need to talk to them again. Tell them to come to the hotel room. They know where it is, they've been here before." Grant agreed to do so, of course, just as Connor expected him to.

"What are we going to talk to those nice gentlemen about, exactly?" Brent wanted to know after Connor hung up.

"We are going to get them to help us."

"We've tried that already, twice," Brent said, "and it didn't work."

"I know." Connor replied. "But things have changed. Maybe they will shut us out again, I don't know. But we have to try. We need to know what the story is with Brad, he's the key. Think about it. He used to be Tommy's partner. Jesse took a picture of him in Montana. He gave a stolen picture of Jesse to Ricky, who gave it to James. He let Ricky escape from custody. The FBI is watching him and doesn't want us near him. His file is sealed. Today he went to Helen's motel, then followed her to the Silverton."

"So what's changed. Why would they decide to help us now?" Brent wondered.

"The damn Silverton Casino is what changed. Look what's happening there. Helen arrives there, Brad tracks her down, the Chief follows him in, Jake tries to head him off, Dylan and Joan head out there on their own. I think that when we tell them that we followed Brad to the Silverton, looking for Helen, and that four of our team members are there, they may change their minds about cooperating with us."

"Ok, so after we tell them all that," Brent wanted to know, "and they get really pissed and ruin our careers, or maybe shoot us, then what?"

"If they do that then we are screwed. But I'm gambling that they won't do that. I'm gambling that they will realize that it is too late, and that we are already too spread out and too much in play, and that they can't do anything to us until after we've done what we came here to do. And if that happens then I think they will either help us or stay out of our way. Most likely they will have to help us, just to make sure we don't screw up their investigation." He looked hopeful if not confident.

Brent wasn't entirely confident either, "Won't their investigation be screwed the minute they let us get involved?"

"Probably, but they will want to minimize the damage. I hope."

"I hope so too, but either way, once this is over they can ruin us." In spite of that, he agreed with Connor, it was worth the risk. Connor shrugged.

"So are you in?" he asked.

"I guess that's why I came to Las Vegas. How bout you guys?" Brent asked Anna and James.

"Damn straight," James answered for both of them. Anna laughed and clapped her hands in agreement, which made everybody laugh.

"Ok, in the meantime what do we do?" Brent wanted to know.

"Call Dylan and see what's going on."

Brent didn't have a chance to make the call before Connor's phone rang. It was Grant. He told Connor that the two FBI agents would be at his hotel room in fifteen minutes.

Agent Duvall hung up his cell phone after talking to Grant and laughed. "I can't believe those clowns," he said to agent Thompson. "They want to se us in their hotel room. This is working out better than we had planned. What you wanna bet that they are going to ask us for help?" He laughed again.

Agent Thompson laughed nervously along with Duvall while driving. "Yeah, that's a good one," he agreed. "Help them back to Montana maybe, where they can play with sheep. Baa, Baa." They both laughed again and Duvall turned the car around, toward the Montana team's hotel.

"What do you want to tell them?" Thompson asked.

"Same thing we told them before. We keep them out of the loop."

"But they ignored us last time. They followed Brad everywhere he went. They are following him right now. What if they find out?" Thompson was a nervous type of man under normal circumstances, but now he was really on edge.

"I told you, they won't find out. They don't even care about Brad. They are looking for Tommy. The more we mess with them, and try to stop them from following Brad, the more they may become suspicious of him. So, we let them follow Brad around for a while, and pretty soon they'll catch up with Tommy and forget all about Brad. Ok? Feel better?"

"Not really," Thompson whined.

"Tough shit. We do it my way. Got a problem with that?" His anger scared Thompson. When Duvall was pissed he didn't just get a little angry, he went totally psycho, and anything or anyone in his path was not likely to survive. Thompson had only seen him kill once, but he concluded that there had been other times that he didn't know about. The one time Thompson had witnessed, Duvall had killed an informant with his bare hands in a fit of rage because the informant was five minutes late for a meeting.

"No problem," Thompson said.

CHAPTER EIGHTY SEVEN

BRAD HAD PARKED IN THE very back of the Silverton parking lot, where the buses and RV's usually parked. He considered looking for Helen in the casino but decided it would be too reckless. There were still some unknowns, such as Tommy, and he didn't feel like being surprised.

He picked out a berm at the edge of the parking lot that was raised three or four feet higher than the lot itself, and walked to the top of it. He could see more of the lot from this vantage point, but he was also a more visible target. Taking cover behind nearby light post with a big rock next to it, he couldn't help thinking of the cartoons he watched as a kid. The one where a big fat bull tries to hide behind a skinny tree.

Jake arrived at the Silverton mere moments ahead of Brad and Charlie. He watched Brad park in the RV section and walk to the far edge of the lot. Charlie parked closer to the building. Jake drove up alongside his car, stopping when his window was even with the drivers window of the Chief's car. "Hey, Charlie," he said as the Chief rolled down his window.

"Hi, Jake," Charlie said. "How did you get here so fast."

"We were tipped off by your description of Brad's travel route that he was headed here, so I ran on ahead." Charlie nodded understanding.

"What's the orders now?" he asked.

"Don't know," Jake said. "Why don't you call in a report and see what they say."

"Ok," the Chief said. "Where's Brad now?"

"At the back of the lot, behind a light post." Jake pointed in Brad's direction and the Chief spotted him.

"What's he doing there?" the Chief asked.

"Not sure. So far he's just watching the casino entrance."

The Chief called in his report to Connor, telling him that he'd met up with Jake and informing him what Brad was doing. Connor instructed him to return to the hotel.

"Roger that," the Chief said, although he had no intention of returning to the hotel. Wild horses couldn't keep him from sticking around to see what the hell was going on here. "What about Jake?"

Connor didn't answer immediately. He took a minute to consider and then said, "Tell him not to approach Brad. Keep an eye on him but mainly I want you to watch for Tommy to show up. I want to know immediately if he does."

"Got it," the Chief said. He hung up and relayed the instructions to Jake.

" What are your instructions," Jake asked.

"Go back to the hotel," Charlie answered.

"Yet you are still here," Jake observed.

"That's right," the Chief confirmed.

Jake thought for a minute, wondering how to deal with Charlie's little insubordination. While he considered it he spotted a familiar car in the parking lot. It looked suspiciously like one of their rental cars.

CHAPTER EIGHTY EIGHT

JOAN ANSWERED DYLAN'S PHONE, "Hello. Oh hi Brent. Yeah, Dylan is in the casino looking for a bathroom. No, I'm not sure what's going on, he hasn't exactly explained it to me. No, we haven't seen Brad yet. No, we haven't seen Jake or the Chief either. Ok, I'll tell him. Bye."

When Dylan returned from the casino Joan relayed Brent's instructions. Dylan seemed not to hear, "I saw Helen," he said. "I was looking for a bathroom and I saw her playing at a machine. I wasn't sure whether or not she knew what I looked like, so I turned away and fled."

"You know what she looks like?" Joan asked. "You've met her before?"

"No," he said. "I never met her. But I've seen her with Tommy before. Back in Flatrock. You know, small town and all that."

Joan asked him, "Is she alone?"

"Yes, as far as I could tell. I ran out kind of fast."

"Do you think she knows about me? Knows who I am or what I look like?"

"It doesn't seem likely, but it's possible. You know, small town and all that," he reasoned.

"But even if she knew me, she would think that I don't know her, right?" She was leading up to something, Dylan could tell. Not because he was psychic, or smart, but because she said it in a way that any idiot could tell.

"I suppose. What are you thinking?"

"I'm thinking why don't I go in and sit at the machine next to her and gamble. Then I can work up a conversation with her. You know, like a couple of fellow players chit-chatting. Even if she recognizes me she won't be able to admit it because she can't reveal that she was in Montana. She'll have to play along, wondering, but not knowing for sure, whether I know her or not. Most likely she will think I don't know her and that it is some amazing coincidence." She hesitated for a moment and then continued, "The only thing is, I don't know why I would be doing it. What would it achieve?" She looked over at Dylan for the answer.

"I'm not sure either. But she is a link to what's happening here, and what else are we going to do? We can't just walk away from her now that we know she is here. Maybe Tommy will come see her, who knows. Do you have your phone with you?"

"Yes."

"Ok, go ahead with your plan. If you need to talk to me, go to a bathroom and call me. By the way, the bathrooms are just to the left of the aquarium in the back of the casino." He leaned over and kissed her. "I love you babe."

257

"I love you too." She got out of the car and walked into the casino. Dylan watched her walking away. Nice view, he thought.

Connor groaned when Brent told him what Joan had said on the phone about Dylan.

"This is killing me," he said. He remembered that Anna had come up with a couple of helpful insights recently, and he had nothing to lose by asking her for another one so he said, "You got any other ideas or insights Anna?"

As a matter of fact Anna did have some ideas. She told Connor, "Yeah, I think that Charlie should be back by now. Since he's not, it means he's staying there. The question you should be asking yourself is why?" She looked at them briefly as if waiting for a response.

"You gonna tell us this time or are you really asking for an answer because you don't know?" James asked, trying to head off another one of her lessons.

"I'm really asking this time," she said. "I've made some guesses of my own but I wouldn't mind hearing what you guys think about it."

"I ain't got an answer to that one. Sorry," James said. He didn't believe that she didn't already have an answer figured out, and figured that whatever answer he gave her would just be refuted as unacceptable, so why bother telling her anything. He smiled at her and waited for her to say what her own 'guesses' were, or for some other unsuspecting person to take the bait and tell her what they thought. Brent took the bait.

"I know why," Brent said. "He feels something. He knows something is going to happen and he wants to be there. He can't know exactly what it is that's going to happen, but he knows *something* will."

"I agree," Connor said.

"Me too," Agreed Anna.

"Yeah, me too. Sounds right," James conceded, thinking how Brent had gotten lucky this time.

CHAPTER EIGHTY NINE

DYLAN WAS STILL STARING AT JOAN'S assets when a tap on the car window frightened the wits out of him. As soon as he came back to earth he looked at the window and saw the Chief. Next to him was Jake. He rolled down the window and said, "Hey guys, what's up?"

Jake said, "Well, we're here, and so is Brad. We are keeping an eye on him and waiting for Tommy to show up. But we haven't seen him yet, have you?"

"No, not yet. But I saw Helen. She is inside playing a machine. Joan is in there playing a machine next to her so she can keep an eye on her. What do you think we should do?"

"All we can do is watch and see. After that......well, after that is after that," Jake said uncertainly. "I only know that this is where we are going to find Tommy, so be ready."

"Ready to do what?" the Chief asked.

"We want to take him in and talk to him, but I'm not sure how best to accomplish that. We don't know exactly where he will appear."

"I've got an idea," the Chief said. "We spread out." What a cliche, he thought to himself. The line had to have been used in every western movie ever made.

"What I mean is we divide the parking area. Dylan stays here, I go to the west side of the lot and Jake goes to the east side. We all have our phones so we can stay in contact. That way, no matter where he appears, one of us is more likely to be close to him.

"We report to each other if we see someone or if something happens, and I pass on the reports to Brent at HQ. If an opportunity presents itself we regroup and come up with a plan to deal with it. Everyone ok with that?"

Dylan and Jake were both happy with the Chief's plan, such as it was, and they each went to their respective positions.

CHAPTER NINETY

GRANT HAD TRIED ALL MORNING to get some work done but he couldn't stop thinking about what was happening with the team from Montana. They had a real case on their hands, and he repeatedly found himself wondering about all of their unanswered questions, instead of concentrating on his own work.

What really bugged him was the blockade of information on all three of the main suspects, Tommy, Brad and Helen. Something about that didn't smell right.

He had told Connor that he would ask his up-line contacts to help him find out what was happening with Brad and Tommy and Helen, but he had lied. Or rather he'd half lied. He did ask around at higher levels but he had known that the persons he asked would not know anything. And even if they did he knew they didn't have the authority to reveal what they knew to him. Permission would have to come from much higher up.

Grant knew somebody in just such a position but had been intentionally refraining from calling him. His contact was so high up that he would only call him as a last resort, not wanting to abuse his relationship with the man and thus lose his cooperation in the future.

This morning he decided that the situation qualified as a last resort and had made a call to the only person he knew who was capable of knowing why the information on their subjects was being kept secret. Even if he didn't know, he could easily find out. No one in the country would refuse his request for information.

He had a code he used with his contact if he wanted to talk to him without worrying about big ears listening in. He would call the man's secretary and left a message. The message was the code and the message was: Grant needs new orders. His contact would return the call when he could, and in return leave a coded message for Grant. Grant didn't know exactly what the message would be in advance, but he knew that whatever it was it would be clear enough to him so that he would know what to do. Right now he was waiting for that message.

He kept himself busy with office duties for what seemed like forever. Finally a message came. The message from his contact said: you have your orders already, just follow them. To another, the message would seem like a normal order from a senior to his junior. But Grant knew that there was another meaning to the message. The real meaning was that he was to use the same method of communication he had used the last time they talked.

The last time they talked he had used a pay phone in one of the smaller casinos near the Marshal's office building to call a phone number in Washington DC. He had no idea where in DC the phone was, nor what kind of phone it was. He only knew the number.

Grant knew how busy his contact was, and knew he would be using some of his valuable time waiting for Grant's call, so he hurried to the pay phone. On the way to the phone he wondered how they got such complete control of an apparently public pay phone as to make it a secure line.

Grant traveled the few blocks to the designated pay phone on foot. He made the call without having to enter any type of payment into the payphone; another baffling concept. The Assistant U.S. Attorney General, Tom Lapke answered with, "How are you doing, Grant?"

"Doing well, Tom," Grant said. "How about you?"

Tom said he was doing fine and they talked for a few minutes, catching up on all the latest social BS.

Few people, if any, knew about their lifelong friendship. More than a friendship really. They were more like brothers, but not by blood.

Grants parents had been close friends with Tom's parents. At the age of ten, Grants parents were killed in an airplane crash, and Grant had no other family. Tom's parents took him in and got him through high school and two years of junior college. Then Grant had decided to go to the law enforcement academy. Tom decided to go to law school and then got into politics and they got separated geographically but otherwise remained close. In spite of remaining fast friends they spoke only occasionally over the years. Both had become embroiled in their respective vocations and were mired in the heavy schedules demanded by them.

The infrequent times that they did correspond it was rarely about business; especially secret business like this. But the few times that secret business such as this was required, they used this same clandestine method.

With the pleasantries of the phone call dispensed with, Grant told Tom what it was he wanted help with.

"I figured that was what you were calling about," Tom said. "I've heard some grumblings around the office that you were making inquiries. Seemed to upset a few of the boys who thought no one should be able to see behind their secret curtain. I already did a little checking around for you and found out what I could. I have to warn you it's complicated. It was complicated before you guys got involved and now it looks like it is getting even more complex.

"I wish I could tell you to just stay away from it, but the fact that you called me tells me that it means a lot to you, and you would probably not listen to that particular bit of advice, so I'll do what I can. But I would like to impinge upon you the fact that this deal is big enough to get me in trouble if anyone finds out that we talked about this." He waited for Grant to give the correct response to this statement.

"I hear you, Tom. You know I won't do anything stupid, I know the risks for both of us," Grant told him, knowing it was want he wanted to hear. But what amazed him was that people higher on the food chain than Tom were aware of the people Grant was inquiring about. The Assistant U.S. A.G. doesn't have many people higher up the ladder than him.

Apparently satisfied by Grant's answer, Tom said, "We got a double blind invest going on. Now pay close attention here because this is where it gets a bit intricate. Take notes if you have to. We are trying to make a case for a couple of corrupt federal agents who are working for the Zorros in Las Vegas. But the trick is this: who do you use to watch a federal agent without running the risk that someone within the agency tells them that they are being watched? As you well know people in law enforcement like to watch each others backs. Even when they are doing something wrong. And believe me these two boys are doing something very wrong.

"So we had to get a little resourceful, and it just so happens that we received a little bit of Intel about a Las Vegas PD detective who, it turns out, has also gone corrupt and is working for the very same drug dealers. You know him as Brad Danison. The two agents are Duvall and Thompson. I believe you have the pleasure of knowing all three of them."

"You bet we have," Grant replied. "I can't wait to hear what you have to share with me about these characters." His curiosity had reached an all time high as a matter of fact.

"Ok, hold your horses. I'll get to it all eventually." He continued, "Believe it or not, Brad never knew anything about the agents being employed by the druggies, and neither did the agents know anything about Danison. The Zorro's leader, Bennett, likes keeping their contacts very secret, even from each other. He's not what you would call a trusting soul I guess.

"So here is what we did. We told Brad about the agents and we hired him to investigate them and bring in the evidence. We told him that we needed an experienced and honest cop to help us out, someone who could keep his mouth shut, even within the department. He took the bait hook, line and sinker, thinking he had hit a big payday. He could feel free to move around in the underworld with impunity because he had the defense that it was in the line of duty. And of course we were fairly confident that he wouldn't blab because he would want to keep his own activities a secret.

"On the other hand we did not tell the agents that we knew Danison was working for the same boss that they were. Instead we gave them a special assignment to run surveillance on a Las Vegas cop who we 'suspected' had been corrupted by an 'unknown' underworld organization for a long time. That person is, of course, Brad Danison. We knew it would not take them long to figure out who Brad was working for. So those two agents now have to watch Brad without making him suspicious of being watched, and without letting on to him that they also work for the same guy. They don't dare bust him either, because if they do, it will piss off Bennett, who's paying them a lot of money."

Grant interrupted the narrative with a question, "So how do you know that they will actually bring you the evidence you are hoping for, so that you can bust them and have a real case in court?"

It was a reasonable question and Tom had been expecting it. He said, "That worried us for a while too. But think about it; they have to turn in something or risk raising suspicions about themselves. Even if they turn in phony evidence it will still make a case and by the time it goes to trial their lives are over whether they get convictions or not."

"How do you figure that?" Grant wondered.

"Because once they are busted the mob will be worried stiff that one of them will start talking in order to save his own hide. They will either be looking over their shoulders the rest of their lives or actually get whacked. Their careers will be destroyed too. What life would be left to them after that?"

"Good point," Grant conceded.

Tom continued, "They will all take the fall eventually. The only thing that can go wrong is that they find out that we hired both the agents and Brad to spy on each other. If that happens the whole house of cards comes down. And even if that happens we have a back up plan. But that's another story for another time. It's a risky strategy but we couldn't think of any other way without running the risk of them finding out that we are on to them. Needless to say, there are numerous law enforcement personnel, in every branch, who get paid off by the mob to pass on intelligence, and if one of them somehow caught on to what was going on and spilled the beans we would be in trouble. So we are running this from the top and trying to keep it as confidential as possible."

"Let me see if I got this right," Grant said. "You enlisted a Vegas cop to go under cover in the drug ring in order to help you bust two FBI agents who are working for the drug ring. But you knew the cop was also working for the drug dealer already, which makes him the perfect guy to do it."

"That's right," Tom confirmed.

"And then you enlisted the two already corrupted agents to help you bust the cop," Grant said.

"That's right," Tom confirmed.

"But neither the cop nor the agents are going to want to bust each other because it would piss off Bennett and get them killed," Grant said.

"That's right," Tom confirmed again.

"But they have to report something to you to make you think they are doing what you recruited them to do. So whether they report the truth to you about each other, or whether they make it all up doesn't matter. You can still use it as if it is reliable intel because they are all bona fides in the system," Grant said.

"You're getting it," Tom confirmed.

"So you can pull them in when you are ready and whether the intel stands up in court or not, they are toast."

"You got it," Tom said.

"Brilliant," Grant said, "now I can see why you want to keep it under wraps. What about Tommy Sanderson?" Tom hadn't said anything about him, yet Connor seemed to consider him to be the main suspect. And his file was placed off limits as well.

"Sanderson is out of it. He moved out to Montana some time ago and joined up with the Highway Patrol." He knew that there was more to it than that, but he figured that since Tommy was safely relocated and working in Montana, he didn't need to tell Grant the whole story.

"Yeah, I know that, but now he's a prime suspect in the case of a relocated witness who was run down by a car and killed. Just when the Deputies assigned to the case were about to start moving in on him, he left Montana and came here, to Vegas." He would have thought that Tom knew all this and was surprised that he didn't.

"Are you telling me that Tommy is in Vegas right now?" He seemed surprised, but even worse than that, he seemed upset by the news.

"That's what I'm telling you. He's here and so is his girlfriend. She was holed up in a motel room for a while but just rabbited a short time ago and went to the Silverton Casino. She is there right now gambling and we have some men watching her and waiting for Tommy to show up, assuming he might be looking for her." There was a long silence on the other end of the line. When Lapke spoke again he was visibly shaken by what Grant had just told him.

"You got a hell of a situation on your hands, Grant. Tommy used to be Vegas Metro PD, but we recruited him to work for us as a double agent to get inside the organized crime drug racket in Vegas. He is the person who found out that Brad was working for the bad guys. One day he contacted us and said that he thought his cover had been blown. He said that they had been asking funny questions and treating him differently, making him suspicious. Then one of the drug dealers told him that he had heard some things about him. Not good things. He had heard that Tommy was trying to bust the mob, and that the mob was going to 'deal with him'.

"Tommy wanted out. He wanted to get far away; out of Vegas Metro PD and out of the state. But you know the saying: no one gets out of the mob and lives to tell about it. He was worried that he would have been a marked man for the rest of his life, which could have been short, if he just walked away. So we concocted a story that he was dirty and busted him off the force. We made it very public; lots of news stories in the papers and on TV. Made a real villain

264

out of him. We made it look like he got fired for working for the mob, and then run out of town on a rail. It was hoped that Bennett would accept that as proper grounds for letting him go.

"It worked. He went to Montana, of all places, and I put in a word to the head of the Highway Patrol there when Tommy said he wanted to work for them. He's a good man Grant. One of the best. And now you are telling me that he is mixed up in the death of a protected witness? It just seems too incredible for me to believe."

"Yeah, well there is more. The dead witness testified against the same mob that Tommy had infiltrated for you guys." A fact that Grant, just moments ago, would have thought Tom already knew about.

"Jesus, Grant! What the hell is going on there? Has everyone just gone nuts all of a sudden? I never would have figured Tommy would end up on the wrong side. But if he did you have one hell of situation going there," Tom said, more than a little worry in his voice.

"Yeah, well, I think I need some advice here, Tom. What should we do?"

"Now that you've told me about Tommy, I'm not sure I can tell you what to do. I'm going to have to re-evaluate things before I can give you any advice. I'll be quick about it, just hang in there."

"Should I tell the Deputies that are working on the Montana case?"

"I know I said that this was all highly confidential, and it is. But there are certain things that those guys may need to know for the sake of their own safety as well as their case. I am going to trust you, Grant. You use your best judgment to decide who should know what. Just try not to blow our case, OK?"

"You got it, Tom. Let me know what you think I should do as soon as you can. Things are coming to a head out here. And thanks very much for calling me back and filling me in. I really appreciate it. I owe you." He knew that he would never be able to do for Tom what Tom could do for him. He just was not in the same position as Tom was. But he could try. Who knows.....maybe one day.

"You owe me big time. I won't be holding my breath though." He laughed and said good bye and hung up the phone.

Grant immediately called Connor.

"Listen, Connor," he started without preamble. "I've just been given some interesting information about those two agents you asked me to send over there. Are they there yet?"

"Not yet," he answered, noticing the stress in Grant's voice. What's up?"

"I don't have time to explain everything. Just trust me and get rid of them. Make up some excuse, or ask them a couple of dummy questions or something, but don't spend any time talking to them. And don't tell them anything. Don't mention Helen, or what you guys are doing. Don't say a thing. I mean it," Grant asserted.

"Ok, I'll do what you say, but you better fill me in afterward."

"Don't worry, I'll call you. Good luck."

Connor told the others in the room what Grant had told him.

"Let's make a plan before they get here," he suggested. "James you answer the door when they knock, but don't open it all the way. Just crack it open a few inches and ask them what they want. Then, after they start whining, let them in. I will do the rest, but the rest of you pay attention and follow along with what I tell them. Try to read me and play along. I will explain everything after they leave. Whatever you do, don't tell them anything about what we know or what we are doing."

CHAPTER NINETY ONE

DUVALL AND THOMPSON DROVE THE remaining few miles without speaking. Thompson was too afraid to speak – what if he said the wrong thing and Duvall got pissed off? Duvall was silent because he knew that he had frightened Thompson and he didn't want him to go berserk on him.

When they reached the hotel Duvall said, "We're here. Let's go in and take care of these clowns. Play it just like before."

"Ok," Thompson responded cautiously.

They knocked on the door of HQ, which unknowingly told the occupants who they were. James opened the door a few inches, as they had planned earlier.

"What do you guys want?" James demanded. It was his role of bad cop in their variation of the good cop, bad cop routine. It was their fervent prayer that it would not become dead cop, dead cop.

The greeting from James was unexpected and the two goons looked at each other with surprise mixed with impatience.

"You asked for us and here we are, now let us in," Duvall said in his best tough guy voice. It seemed to work, James opened the door wide and let them in.

"What do you want?" Duvall asked.

"Thanks for coming," Connor said with a smile, hoping to make them more relaxed. "Have a seat gentlemen. This won't take much of your time, I know you are very busy. But our case is a critical homicide case and I just had to take one more try at asking for your help." Duvall looked over at Thompson with a snide smile, as if to say I told you so.

"Forget it. Is that all you wanted?" Duvall snapped.

"Well, yeah. I guess that was all. You sure you won't do anything at all to help us? I was hoping for a little bit of inter-departmental cooperation." He didn't want to give in too easily, in case it might raise suspicions. In fact he would have to remember to act angry when they denied his request, which they undoubtedly would.

True to Connor's prediction Duvall said, "The only cooperation that is going to happen here is if you stay out of our way. We will consider that cooperating." His smirk indicated an all too deep satisfaction with himself for inflicting his delusional power over imagined inferiors.

Connor went into his pissed off act, "Bullshit, cooperation goes two ways. So either you help us or there is no cooperation." He hoped that the anger would camouflage his anxiety.

Duvall lost his smirk quickly and replaced it with a burning look that truly frightened Connor. There was something incredibly disturbing about the guy, and for a moment Connor had some serious doubts about the wisdom of acting angry.

Duvall began to act the part that the others in the room had just been silently attributing to him and asked, "Are you threatening us? You intend to interfere. Is that it?" The intensity of the malice in Duvall's voice caused Connor's heart to race.

Brent's heart jumped too, and he perceived something sinister in agent Duvall that the others probably didn't completely appreciate. They may or may not have noticed that he was not a nice guy, or even worse, but he was pretty sure that none of them could see as deeply into his intentions as he could. Brent had, unfortunately, made an uninvited and equally unwelcome 'connection' with the man, and the result was ugly enough to make him regret his ability to do so. He had seen not only what the man was capable of, but also what inhuman acts he savored, and undoubtedly had committed in his life. Brent could describe it in one word – mayhem. Actually it would be better described in two words – beloved mayhem.

Thinking that things weren't looking too good at the moment, Brent decided he better act. He jumped up and addressed the two agents.

"Sorry guys, we are just a little frustrated with our case. We aren't intending to interfere with you. We promise to cooperate. Sorry we wasted your time." He was moving toward the door as he talked, and he held out his hand for a handshake to indicate that they could leave now. The sooner, and the further, he could put distance between himself and the agents the better.

The agents walked toward the door with Brent. Duvall ignored his hand and sneered.

"You need to keep that guy on a leash," he said, nodding his head toward Connor. Brent couldn't help thinking that the only inhuman being in the room was agent Duvall, and a leash would be severely inadequate to restrain him.

After the door was shut Brent asked Connor, "Why did you egg them on like that. We're lucky they didn't pull out their guns again."

"No shit, Sherlock," James said in his most nervous voice. He had an uncanny tendency to remain silent when things got tense, but then had no problem voicing his opinions once it was safe. "I was wondering the same thing as Brent. I mean that Duvall dude was a super bad ass. I ain't sure if I know any of that psychic shit like Dylan and all, but I do know that I don't want to be anywhere near that psycho mo fo again, and the last thing I would ever do is try to piss him off. You got some rock hard cajones, Connor. That's all I can say."

"I did it on purpose," Connor tried to explain. "I didn't want to raise suspicions. If I had taken their first 'no' and said ok see ya later, they would have wondered why I was giving in so easily. Especially after I made the effort to get them down here to see us. But yeah, they scared the shit out of me. No doubt about that. As to my cajones, I think I may have just used up whatever was left of them."

"Yeah, I see your point. That was a good act," Brent told him.

"Thanks. Now I just hope Grant calls me and tells me why the hell I had to put myself through all this insanity."

CHAPTER NINETY TWO

BRAD WATCHED THE PARKING LOT and the casino entrances from his not very well concealed hiding place on the berm. He was looking for Tommy but he soon began to see other people, ones he didn't expect and that he didn't like seeing.

First he saw two cars side by side with the drivers speaking to each other through their windows. Then they drove across the lot and stopped near another car, where they got out of their cars and walked up to the window of the other car. He recognized them when they exited their cars. It was one of the Deputies and the hick police chief from Montana. And they were talking to another person from Montana, that dip shit boy of that bitch Jesse.

He wasn't sure why they were here but he was sure that he didn't like it. Their presence here could only be a good thing if they just happened, coincidentally, to be on a Vegas vacation, but he didn't believe that for a second.

As he watched them, the Deputy and cop got back in their cars and drove to two opposite sides of the lot and parked. They waited in their cars, which meant they were not going inside the casino. Which meant they were watching it instead. Which meant what? Were they on a stakeout? Did they know about Helen? You bet they did, Brad figured out. They were doing the same thing he was, waiting for Tommy.

CHAPTER NINETY THREE

TOMMY SANDERSON MADE HIS WAY to the Silverton Casino in search of Helen. He approached the building from behind the Bass Pro Shop, walking slowly, carefully, around the corner of the wall, where there was only a driveway and no parking lot, making it easier for him to spot someone if they were watching the building from that side. If they were watching from the main lot he wouldn't see them, but they wouldn't see him either.

He took his time scanning the area for a trap, well aware of Helen's possible role as bait. There were no obvious stakeouts visible from this part of the building, but his experience in his profession had taught him a thing or two, so he knew that someone could be waiting inside the building, watching Helen. He avoided any of the main casino entrances, using the less used doorway to the Bass Pro Shop. He was familiar with this Bass Pro Shop and knew he could enter the casino through a hallway attached from the store. Fortunately for Tommy, nobody had thought of watching the back side of the building or the Bass Pro Shop entrances, so his caution kept him from being detected by the very people he wanted to avoid.

He inched his way through the connecting hall into the gambling area and saw the slot machines across the room. He didn't see her so he moved laterally to change the angle of his view. He spotted her playing a slot. At least she was still alive, he thought, and not kidnapped, or worse. But there was the possibility that she was planted there as bait, so he decided to keep an eye on her for a while.

He took up his vigil behind a nearby large aquarium and, looking back toward Helen, he noticed Joan, playing a slot next to her. They were talking to each other off and on, like they were friends, but Tommy was pretty sure that Helen had never met Joan. He wondered how Dylan's girlfriend made the connection with Helen. There was little chance that she was here on a holiday and just happened to sit down next to Helen by accident.

CHAPTER NINETY FOUR

AGENTS DUVALL AND THOMPSON ENJOYED a drink while watching an exotic dancer practice her particular art form on a stage. Duvall, now in a good mood, was free with his tips, which he stuffed into the dancer's artistic costume – a G-string. He bought Thompson drinks, attempting to cheer him up.

He slapped Thompson on the back, laughed and said, "What did I tell you? I knew they were going to ask us for help again. Those fools couldn't find a pussy if it was sitting on their face, much less find a pro like Tommy. I bet they were crying like babies when we left." He laughed again at his own joke.

Thompson seemed less interested in Duvall's crude jokes, or the dancers and drinks, and more interested in the problem going on inside his head. Ordinarily, naked dancing women and free drinks would successfully distract him from his daily worries and the vagaries of life. But today his problem was not ordinary. It was special.

"What is it with you," Duvall snapped. "Here I am making a good effort to have some fun and cheer you up, and you sit there acting like your mamma just died or something. Come on, loosen up. Have another drink, you'll feel better." He motioned to the topless waitress to bring another round.

"I don't like it," was Thompson's response.

"Don't like what, the club? Fine, we'll go somewhere else. This is Vegas, there's a thousand strip joints. What's your favorite one?"

"No, not the club. The club is fine. I just don't like the whole thing. The whole situation we are in now. I feel like I'm being sandwiched between a runaway train and a brick wall. We are supposed to be on assignment to bring down Brad, but we aren't doing it. And at the same time we are supposed to be working for the drug boss and we aren't doing that either. Some day it will catch up with us. Some day that train will run us down." He was a bit pale and clammy looking.

"Jesus that was depressing. Can I blow my brains out now before the train squashes me?"

"I'm serious man."

"I know you are. That's what makes it so damn depressing. Come on, you're looking at it all backwards. The whole point is that we are on easy street only for as long as we do nothing. We will only get in trouble if we bring Brad down, so we can't do that. And we can just tell the Justice Department that Brad has been a good boy and we ain't got nothing on him. No one gets mad and we can just skate. What do you think? Pretty nice gig, eh?" The fact that he actually believed this story scared Thompson even more.

"It's going to catch up with us. You watch," he said morosely.

Duvall gave up on him and walked to the stage apron to put some money in a G-string. When he came back to the table he said, "I'm tired of this place already. Let's go to the Silverton for lunch and then do some gambling. They got the best machines there, and I feel lucky today."

CHAPTER NINETY FIVE

TIME WAS RUNNING OUT, Grant knew. The situation at the Silverton was building fast. If he waited much longer for Lapke's phone call, it may be too late. He didn't know what issues Tom was facing that might prevent him from calling, but he knew that with a man in his position there were plenty of possibilities. Damn it! He needed that call right now.

He decided not to wait, and moved quickly. He phoned in an order for pizza, left the station and picked up the two large pizzas on his way to Connor's hotel. He went to the HQ room and knocked on the door. No one had told him about the open door policy.

Inside HQ they heard the knock on the door and stared at it, wondering who could be on the other side, silently hoping it was not the two creepy feds again. No one moved until Anna finally got up, looked at the others as if they were a bunch of wimps and looked through the peephole.

When the door opened all they could see were pizza boxes and they wondered who had ordered pizza.

"Hi, Grant, come on in," Anna greeted him. Grant entered, dropping the boxes on the first bed he ran into.

"Wow, pizza!" James exclaimed. "Is that for us?"

"You bet. I thought you might be getting hungry by now, and we are going to be very busy very soon, so chow down."

The ravenous crew grabbed up slices like they were free super bowl tickets. When appetites felt a bit sated, and the feeding frenzy abated, Connor spoke to Grant. "What did you mean by 'busy soon'?"

"Glad you asked me that, Connor." He found an open spot on the edge of the bed and took a seat. "I know you are already a little pissed at me about canceling the surveillance on Helen, but be prepared to be even more angry at me. I lied to you about my connections in high places." He waited for the backlash from Connor but there was no response, which told him he was right, he was more pissed now.

"But I am going to make it up to you," Grant said. "I made a call to a contact I have who is very high up. But before I tell you who it is, and what he said, I want to make sure that you understand that what I am about to tell you is confidential. Are you willing to be responsible for the crew's ability to keep a confidence here?"

"You bet I am. Lay it on us, we've been waiting." Connor smiled for the first time in a while.

"Ok, listen up," he said, then he proceeded to tell them what he had learned from Tom Lapke that morning, about Brad and Tommy, and the FBI agents.

"Well, that explains a lot," Brent said in awe.

"Yeah, no shit," James added.

"Wow, it really does," Anna added.

"But what," Connor wanted to know, "does all that have to do with us being so very busy soon?"

"What are you going to do, sit around this hotel room forever and talk on your cell phones? I think it's time we go on over to the Silverton Casino. That's where all the action is."

The others in the room looked around at each other, all wondering if one of the others had any real objection, and secretly hoping they didn't. No one said anything so James took that for a majority approval and said, "What are we waiting for?"

"Good question," Connor said. "Let's move out."

CHAPTER NINETY SIX

TWO THOUSAND MILES AWAY IN Washington DC, Tom Lapke had already boarded a private jet, bound for Las Vegas. What Grant had told him on the phone had convinced him that it was time to pull the plug on the Duvall - Thompson case. It was a weird operation to start with and Tom had been uncertain that it would work from the beginning. Now he hoped that he hadn't waited too long to shut it down. He acted so quickly he didn't even take the time to call Grant back. He would see him in person soon enough, and could explain then.

He'd hand picked a special ops team from the L.A. Office, ones he knew wouldn't have a problem busting another agent. Most agents don't like taking down one of their own, but Tom had confidence that the team he picked would do the right thing, whether they liked it or not.

His team would be flown to Vegas by an agency helicopter, arriving there in over an hour. Tom was much further away and would arrive a couple of hours behind his team. His instructions to the special ops team was to wait for him at the airport. Once he got there he would brief them and go over the tactics.

CHAPTER NINETY SEVEN

JOAN HIT IT OFF PRETTY WELL WITH Helen and she didn't get the feeling that Helen knew who she was. They played slots and chatted like every other tourist in the place, which was nice, but not very productive. She couldn't help wondering if she should be doing something more effective, like asking leading questions designed to elicit revealing pieces of information.

She made a couple of weak attempts, one time asking Helen where she was from. Helen said Vegas. What did she do for a living. Between jobs. What was her occupation? Anything that paid money. Did she do any traveling? Not much really. Got a boyfriend? Yes. What is he like? A great guy. Basically, she got nothing out of her. Nothing useful anyway.

The casino cocktail waitress must have been bucking for a good tip because she kept bringing them free drinks. Joan didn't feel like drinking any alcohol but she did drink a lot of iced teas, and now she had to use the bathroom. According to Dylan, the restrooms were by the aquarium, which was so large it was hard to miss.

She rummaged in her purse for her phone on her way to the bathroom. She found the phone and pulled it out, looking around for the restroom entrance. An odd movement caught her eye, a man had ducked behind the glass and turned his face away just as she looked up. The attempt to avoid detection was the very act that caused her to suspect him. She didn't have a chance to see him clearly, but she felt there was something familiar about his face.

She stared at his back as she made her way to the women's bathroom, hoping that he would turn his face toward her again, but he never did. She entered an empty stall and called Dylan.

"Hi, I'm in the bathroom," she whispered to him. "I don't think Helen recognizes me. We have been doing a little social chatting, but I haven't been able to get any real information from her. I feel stupid. What the hell am I supposed to be doing here?" She paused for a minute, wondering why she was whispering. Too many spy movies.

"Oh, and I saw someone I recognized," she continued. "He was trying to hide his face behind the aquarium glass." Pause. "No I don't know who he is." Pause. "Yeah, I know I said I recognized him, but that's not what I meant." Pause. "I meant that he looked familiar to me, and he must have recognized me too because he turned away." Pause. "No, I didn't try to talk to him, I just came into the bathroom." Pause. "Because I didn't know what to do, I wanted to call you first." Pause. "OK, I'll go right now." She hung up.

Dylan had told her to confront the man and try to identify him, so she rushed out of the bathroom and took a turn in the direction where she had last seen him. He wasn't there. She looked around the aquarium perimeter trying to catch sight of him. He was not near the aquarium. She glanced around the casino but could not see him.

She called Dylan. "I lost him." Pause. "OK." She hung up, returning to Helen as instructed. Helen was still there, playing her machine. Joan must have been slightly frightened by what had just happened because when Helen looked up at Joan she frowned.

"Are you OK?" she asked.

"Uh, yeah, I just drank a little too much I think. I'll be OK," she lied.

CHAPTER NINETY EIGHT

TOMMY SWORE AT HIMSELF, calling himself a damn fool stupid rookie stupid son of a bitch. It was hard to admit that he had made such a stupid mistake, but on the other hand it was impossible to deny it. Joan had walked right up to him before he noticed her, and his sudden attempt to hide his face had only increased the chance that she had seen him.

He had fled to the mens room, shut himself in one of the stalls and sat on the toilet, still beating himself up for making such a stupid mistake. He knew he'd better come up with a plan soon, he couldn't sit on the toilet for the rest of his life, and if Joan was waiting for him outside the bathroom it wouldn't be wise to simply walking out the door. He left the stall and cracked the men's room door open and peeked through it in case she was there. He didn't see her.

Getting out of the casino seemed like the smartest thing for him to do so he left the bathroom and walked as fast as he could to the Bass Pro Shop. The panic of seeing Joan must have clouded his judgment and he looked for the nearest exit, choosing not to use the same, safe, door that he used when he entered. He used the main entrance and exited into the main parking lot where he instantly recognized Jake sitting in a car. For the second time in ten minutes was forced to make a sudden u-turn in order to hide his face.

Damn it, damn it, damn it, damn it, he swore to himself while re-entering the Bass Pro Shop. He aimlessly wandered the isles of the store, unable to believe that he had been so stupid again. He wondered momentarily if he was losing his mind, or coming down with some other serious malady. Maybe he was just getting too damn old.

The unexpected appearance of known acquaintances in the casino had created a new wrinkle in his mission. He was going to have to regroup, but he would have to do so calmly, or risk making more mistakes in his haste. Needing to lower the risk of being recognized, he came up with an idea.

He grabbed some fishing shorts from one of the store racks, then he picked out a fishing shirt and a fishing vest to go along with the shorts. To complete the disguise he found a fishing hat and some dark glasses. He paid for the items and returned to the dressing room, where he changed into his disguise.

He wrapped his gun and shoulder holster in his old clothes and put them in the shopping bag that the new clothes had come in. He stood back and looked at himself in the mirror. Something was terribly wrong. The black Italian loafers with black silk socks were not cutting it.

He went back out into the store and bought some hiking boots and some white socks. He changed into the new boots and socks and added his Italian items to the shopping bag with the rest of his old clothes. Again he looked in the mirror. Much better this time. It was a good disguise, and might work, if he was lucky. He was just about to dash out of the dressing room and out the side exit when he thought of something else.

Finding one of the sales clerks he asked them, "Do you have any other exits to this store besides the main entry and casino entry? You know, like a stock room door for deliveries or something?" He discreetly held his badge so that only the clerk could see it.

"Yeah, we got a delivery door that goes out to the back lot. It's locked though, the manager has the key." Tommy noticed that he looked a bit uncertain, maybe scared as well.

"Look," he said casually, hoping to calm the clerk, "I'm doing a bit of an undercover gig and I need a way out so that I don't blow my cover. I'm not supposed to tell you about it, but I need help, and you look like an honest guy. What do you say?" He held a twenty dollar bill next to the badge this time. The clerk appeared righteously offended by the offer.

"I am an honest guy. I don't need bribes to do the right thing," he said.

Tommy slipped the money back in his pocket. "Yeah, I can see that. Sorry, I'm just desperate is all. What's your name?"

"Willy."

"You'll help then?"

"Wait here," Willy said. He went to the front desk and spoke to a middle aged man that Tommy assumed – hoped – was the manager. The man nodded and handed the clerk some keys. The clerk walked past Tommy and while he was passing he said under his breath, "Follow me, quickly."

Tommy didn't need to be told twice, he stepped in right behind the clerk and followed him through a door next to the dressing rooms. It led to a stock room. They crossed the stock room and came to an outer door. The clerk hurriedly opened it with his key and held it open for Tommy to leave.

"I owe you, Willy," Tommy said as he slipped out.

Once Tommy was out the door he backed up to the wall of the store and took a quick look around to see if anyone was watching from this side of the parking lot. There were no cars, just a few delivery trucks. He felt lucky that no one was covering the area but at the same time he wondered how it was possible. They should be smarter than that, a fact that made him even more suspicious. It might mean a trap. Or....... no it couldn't be. Could it? He laughed. They didn't know he was here. That meant that Joan hadn't recognized him and Jake hadn't seen him. He got lucky twice. He doubted that the luck would hold for a third screw-up. But still, if they were waiting for him to show up because Helen was here, they should have covered all the entries, even the stock door he just came out of. Their mistake, his gain.

He inched to his left with his back against the wall. He wanted to make it to the part of the building that projected closest to the boundary of the parking lot. That would create the shortest amount of open space between the building and the street. It would still leave about fifty yards of open parking lot he would have to cover. He hoped, with his disguise on, if he walked nonchalantly they would not recognize him.

He made it across the lot and walked slowly down the sidewalk. The Silverton was on the outskirts of Las Vegas so, unlike the Vegas Strip, the sidewalks were virtually deserted. His plan now was to circle around the outside perimeter of the casino parking lot and come up from behind a small knoll on the opposite side of the building. He would gain a small amount of altitude there, and some slight cover, and then he could watch the lot.

Just as he started up the sidewalk he happened to glance at a car that was getting ready to turn into the Casino parking lot. He was surprised to see agents Duvall and Thompson in the car. He wondered about them for a minute and then hatched a great idea. He took his cell phone out of his pocket and dialed a number from memory.

CHAPTER NINETY NINE

WHEN TOM LAPKE GOT OFF THE PLANE, his special ops team was waiting for him in the baggage area as planned, ready to go.

Tom gave the proper coded greeting, showed his ID and they moved quickly from the baggage area, through a guarded exit marked VIP to where a van was waiting for them at the curb. It was a special ops van, custom equipped to meet the needs of special tactics operations. The paper trail on it, if someone was to check the plates and registration, would show that it was rented through one of the mainstream rental agencies under a cover name.

They seated themselves in the van and drove to an empty warehouse that had belonged to Howard Hughes at some distant past. Various businesses had rented it over the years and now it was empty. Due to nothing other than a damn convenient piece of luck it was not too far from the Silverton, west on Blue Diamond Road and then a short ways off the road in an otherwise bare patch of desert. The present owner was the U.S. government, although the property documents showed otherwise. Just a couple of hours prior to Tom's arrival a team had scoured it for bugs. They didn't expect to find any and didn't.

They drove the van into the warehouse and closed the doors. Once inside they unloaded the baggage and geared up while Tom briefed them. It was a tough briefing to give because the objective hadn't been completely formulated yet. They were operating on the fly, since too much information was still not available to them. All he could tell them was the background of the situation and who the main players were. He handed photos around so that each man would know how to identify the different personnel involved. He took special time to identify the friendlies so that they didn't get taken down by mistake if things got hot, and so that they could be protected if needed. The primary subject of protection would be Tommy Sanderson and each team member was given a photo of him.

Since Tom had inadequate intelligence as to who would be there, and what exactly would happen, it was impossible to compose a detailed plan. The overall plan was for the team to stand by, and act only if needed, and only on orders from Tom.

There was a secondary objective however, which was to bring in Brad Danison if he was spotted. Each member of the team was instructed to pay very close attention to the photos of him and to remember what he looked like. If Duvall and Thompson showed up they were to be brought in as well. Covertly if possible. With prejudice if not.

Tom had used his clout to check with the local FBI office to get the current whereabouts of Duvall and Thompson. He was told that they were at the Silverton Casino. He also knew about the gathering of the Deputy U.S. Marshals and the team from Montana at the Silverton so had decided that it was the place to be.

He provided the team with plot maps, floor plans of the casino, schematics, topo maps and several photographs of the facility so that they could familiarize themselves thoroughly with the playing field. Questions were answered, last minute details were seen to. These men were the best of the best and were on their mettle. The briefing ended and they piled back into the van and drove to the Silverton.

CHAPTER ONE HUNDRED

CONNOR, BRENT, JAMES, ANNA and Grant piled into Grant's car, which was parked illegally – but legally since he was a Deputy U.S. Marshal – at the curb in front of the hotel entrance. They made their way through the traffic to the I – 15 and drove south to the Blue Diamond exit. Grant drove off the freeway and then went the short distance to the Silverton parking lot. He found an empty spot and parked.

They sat in the crowded car silently wondering what the hell they were supposed to be doing, and what to look for. After waiting several minutes without speaking, Connor caught a glimpse of a familiar car.

"Isn't that Jake's car over there?" he asked, breaking the silence.

The others in the car looked to where Connor was pointing and saw Jake's car at the east end of the hotel parking lot. Soon after that they spotted the rental car that Dylan and Joan had run off with. It was parked at the west end of the parking lot. Jake was sitting in his car and Dylan in his, but Joan was not to be seen, and that worried Anna.

"I'm going to find Joan," she said as she made a move to get out of the car.

"Wait," Connor ordered her. "It might not be such a good idea for you to expose yourself right now. Let's see what we can find out first." He held up his cell phone for Anna to see, indicating his intention to take advantage of its convenience. She nodded agreement and sat back in the seat.

Instead of using the phone personally, Connor deferred to Brent – whose job it was – to call Jake on his cell phone to see if he knew where Joan was. Brent made the call. Jake informed him that they did indeed know where Joan was, she was watching Helen inside the casino.

Brent relayed the information to Anna who was relieved at first, but then the more she thought about it the more she started to worry again. She feared that Joan's proximity to Helen might put her too close to danger. And then there was Charlie, no one had mentioned him yet, so Anna did.

Brent called Jake again. "Hi, it's me again. You seen the Chief?"

"Yeah he's around the corner watching the west side of the lot," Jake answered.

"Ok, thanks. By the way, we are here in the lot at the Silverton. We are behind you and can see you and Dylan. What do you want us to do?"

"Ask Connor, he's the boss."

Bent hung up and relayed the answer to Anna. "Feel better?" he asked.

"Yes and no. But thanks." Everyone she loved was putting themselves in harms way. She admired it, but it still scared the shit out of her. "I need to go to the bathroom," she said. "Where is it? Anyone know?"

"I do," James volunteered. "And I have to go too. I'll go with you." They both got out of the car and walked toward the casino. Connor let them go. He didn't like the idea of them going into the casino but gave up any hope that he could stop them.

"Did Jake have a plan for us?" Connor asked after James and Anna had gone.

"No, he said to ask you. You're the boss."

"Great," Connor replied, frustration well displayed on his face.

CHAPTER ONE HUNDRED ONE

BRAD GREW TIRED OF WAITING, and was beginning to wonder if he was wasting his time waiting for Tommy show up. Even the bitch's whelp and the other two had been sitting there for hours doing nothing. He hoped that they were as bored as he was.

He knew that if Tommy had even the slightest suspicion that Helen was being watched he would not come near her. He knew that from the beginning, and took a roll of the dice, betting that Tommy might show up. Maybe he was wrong. Maybe the dice came up seven and he just crapped out. Maybe, but since he didn't have a better plan yet, he decided to stay put until he came up with one. Maybe, just maybe he would get lucky and Tommy would show up.

A short while later he caught himself daydreaming, which is not a good thing to do when you are supposed to be paying attention. That's why he almost missed something. What he almost missed was a car with five people in it.

He didn't almost miss the car or the five people though. He had seen it arrive. What he almost missed was the fact that no one got out of the car. One of the passengers made a couple of cell phone calls, but no one got out.

As a cop and investigator, Brad was trained to notice things that were not there. In this case what he 'didn't see' was people getting out of a car and walking into the building to which the parking lot belonged. That would have been something one would expect to see. And furthermore, five people in a car was kind of crowded. You wouldn't think they would want to just sit there. Unmoving cars in Las Vegas tend to get a bit warm. And when filled with people it has got to be uncomfortable. So why? It might be more surveillance, but five people? He had never heard of that.

Only a few more minutes passed when two people got out of the car. Two people he knew. James and Anna. He'd always known of them separately, and never pictured them together. He didn't even know that they knew each other. And yet here they were. Them and all those other people who were watching the building. Not a coincidence. He watched them walk across the parking lot and into the casino and wondered who else was in the car. He watched, and waited, to see if any of them would get out.

CHAPTER ONE HUNDRED TWO

DUVALL PULLED THE CAR INTO THE Silverton parking lot and picked a parking spot as close to the entrance as he could find. Thompson was still chasing his own tail in his own mind and Duvall was trying hard to pretend that he wasn't even there. He wanted to get away from the paranoid fool for a while and couldn't wait to get in front of a machine and gamble while Thompson played blackjack.

The two agents got out of the car and were walking towards the entrance of the casino when Duvall stopped mid stride and stared at one of the parked cars. He had a worried look on his face that made Thompson scared enough to pee his own pants.

"What!" he asked. "What the hell is it?" He looked around, trying to identify the cause of Duvall's fright.

"Get back in the car. Hurry," Duvall told him, then turned and walked briskly back to the car. Thompson followed, looking like he might start to cry at any moment.

They got back into the car, Duvall wearing a perplexed expression. Whatever was worrying Duvall, Thompson knew it was not good. He asked again, "What the hell did you see?"

CHAPTER ONE HUNDRED THREE

"WELL, WELL, WELL," BENNETT ALIVIO said as an answer to Tommy's phone call, "I thought you were gone for good, Tommy? How are you, amigo viejo?"

"How did you know it was me calling?" Tommy hadn't even spoken yet which meant Ben knew who it was before he answered, which also meant he knew Tommy's private cell number. All of which pissed him off.

"You know better than to ask that, Tommy. Besides, you got my number don't you? Seems only fair I got yours." He was right of course. In a way.

"Ok, so we're even," Tommy said, still unhappy.

"So to what do I owe the pleasure of this phone call, old friend? Looking for some drugos?" Bennett laughed at his own joke.

"And you know better than that, Ben," Tommy shot back.

"Just trying to lighten the mood, ol buddy. Don't get your panties in a bunch. So what's up?" he asked more seriously.

"Payback time, 'amigo'," Tommy said.

"What are you talking about? You threatening me?" Bennett sounded a little pissed.

Tommy laughed. "No, Ben. Other way around. I owe you, remember?"

"I don't forget things like that. You know that, Tommy."

"Neither do I. I always pay my debts, and I got something for you that will make us even."

"That's what I like about you, Tommy. You were always a stand up guy. Maybe you were on the wrong side – the other side – but you always played it straight. That's why I gave you safe passage when you decided to leave. I knew I could trust you to do the right thing."

"You beat me fair and square, Ben, and that's why I had to go. But I always appreciated the safe passage. It showed good sportsmanship and good character. That's what I owe you for and that's what I want to pay back now." That wasn't his true motive of course. What he was really hoping for was to get Bennett to unknowingly lay down some cover at the Silverton that would help him carry out his plan.

"Lay it on me, brother. What you got for me?" Tommy had got him interested now.

"You know about Duvall and Thompson?" he asked.

Bennett was leery. He didn't want to say anything to give away his secrets. "What about 'em?"

"They're playin you. The feds have them working on bringing in Danison because they know about his 'special association' with you, and Duvall and Thompson have been gathering evidence. They plan to bring him in with the evidence today, and after that they are planning a sting on you." He knew that this news would get Ben's interest.

"Is that right?" Bennett asked.

"Yes, that's right."

"Ok, so if we assume I am interested, how is it you can help me?" Tommy had him hooked.

Here came what Tommy hoped was the winning card, "I know where they are, and how you can catch them in the act. They are waiting in the Silverton parking lot to nab Brad. You will find them sitting in their car, and at several other parts of the lot you will see Marshall's Deputies waiting in their own cars. It's a set-up."

"I'll check it out. If you're right, consider your debt paid brother. You have a nice life up there in Montana." Bennett hung up, and Tommy prayed he had done the right thing.

CHAPTER ONE HUNDRED FOUR

BRAD WATCHED THE TWO FBI AGENTS, Duvall and Thompson, park, get out of the car, stop, turn around and get back in it. What the hell, he wondered to himself. Nothing about what he was seeing made sense. Why they were here didn't make sense. Why they jumped back into the car didn't make sense.

He laughed to himself as he considered the developments at the Silverton. When he followed Helen here he never imagined he would see anything like this. Things were getting more and more complicated, and he didn't like it.

He decided he was done waiting here for Tommy, he was getting the hell out. There were too many coincidences, too many people he didn't like, and too much just plain weirdness. Best thing to do in this case is leave it alone. Tommy would have to wait.

He stayed low and inched his way back down the knoll from which he had been watching the casino, standing straight up only when he was back on the narrow dirt access road. He turned to his left to leave and stopped in his tracks. There was a van parked on the road just fifty yards ahead. Several men were getting out of the van, and they were not just ordinary men. They were fully equipped federal agents.

Fully equipped meant that they were in full tactical uniform and were fully armed. Whatever they were here for, they meant business, and Brad didn't want any part of it.

A few seconds ago he didn't think it was possible for things to get any more out of hand. He was wrong. He kicked himself for not leaving several minutes ago, when he first thought about it.

He didn't think any of the agents had seen him and he wanted it to stay that way, so he turned quickly around and started walking in the opposite direction. They were still piling out of the van and getting set up for business, and he hoped they would be too busy to notice him. But just in case, he walked as quickly as possible while still trying to look casual.

———————————

Tom Lapke's recon of the Silverton had been thorough. He had chosen a position for his team that would give them cover, but at the same time give them a position from which they would have a clear view of the casino and its parking lot. He directed the driver of the van to turn onto a narrow dirt access road that skirted the outside of the parking lot. There was a berm of dirt about eight feet high separating the parking lot from the access road. It provided a barrier behind which the team could remain unnoticed. In addition to the cover that it provided, they could use it to gain a slight bit of altitude while watching the building.

The driver parked the van as instructed and the team piled out of it. Then they got to work setting up their gear and getting into position. One of the first men to exit the van was a veteran agent named Ken Clawson. As he was stepping away from the van to allow room for the men behind him to get out of the van, he caught a motion out of the corner of his eye.

When he looked in the direction of the motion he saw a man walking away from them. He was walking casually, as if he had been on a stroll along the access road. It seemed innocent enough, but he couldn't help feeling like the man been walking towards them when he had first caught sight of him out of the corner of his eye. The trouble was he just couldn't be positive about that. He stared at the man as he walked away from him, trying hard to recall exactly what he had seen at that first perception of the man. He was still staring when he heard Tom say, "Everything OK Ken?"

"Yeah, no problem. I'm ready to go, what's next?"

CHAPTER ONE HUNDRED FIVE

DYLAN COULD NOT UNDERSTAND HOW cops could tolerate a stakeout. He had been sitting in his car for hours, and he hated it. He hated the waiting. He hated the watching. And most of all he hated doing nothing. The only thing there was to do was think, and he did a lot of that while sitting in the car doing nothing. He did altogether too much thinking as a matter of fact.

He found himself thinking things that he didn't want to be thinking. He started doubting himself, wondering if he was doing the right thing. If he was in the right place. If he shouldn't be somewhere else, doing something else. He wondered if he was wrong about Tommy showing up like he originally thought he would. What if he was wrong about that and Tommy was on the other side of town, or back in Montana already. Should he just keep sitting and waiting, or should he make another plan? What would the plan be? He didn't have one.

Thoughts spun around in his head driving him crazy. He tried not to think, which only made things worse. The harder he tried not to think, the more he found himself thinking. It was useless. The only solution he could come up with was to do something. But what should he do? That question brought him full circle and he once again found himself lost in doubt.

He let out a loud sighing moan of frustration and held his head in his hands. At the precise moment that he gave up utterly on any type of solution he was struck by a mysterious impulse to get out of the car and go for a walk, which he promptly did and immediately felt better.

He began walking without any conscious aim, going in no intentional direction or to any known destination. He was just walking. After a dozen or so strides he realized that he was walking away from the casino. He wondered, momentarily, if it was wise to be going away from the building he had been watching for so long, but then he knew that it was exactly what he should be doing. He had been drawn in this direction like metal to a magnet. It was no accident that he decided to get out of the car and walk. And it was not coincidence that he walked in this particular direction.

As he walked, his mind was absorbed in attempts to know the upcoming events of his immediate future. He had never been good at reading futures, but he had a spectacular ability to speculate about it. Dreamily he passed cars parked randomly around the parking lot. In one of them he scarcely noticed a man behind the wheel, reading what appeared to be a smut magazine. He had a fleeting and detached criticism of the man and quickly rationalized it as 'only in Vegas'.

Agent Duvall had retreated to his car, along with Thompson, after seeing what looked like a stakeout. He had noticed Deputy Curran and some of the people from Montana in a car watching the casino and he didn't feel like being seen going into the casino. He watched from his car, curious as to why they were here and what they were looking for.

He glanced around the parking lot for others on the stakeout and noticed another car with someone sitting inside it, watching. He tried to get a good enough look at the man through the windows to know whether or not he recognized him but it was difficult.

He scanned the parking lot again and saw another man approaching from the east, heading straight for their car. He did recognize this person. He was one of the younger men from Montana, and the son of the woman who testified against the drug ring.

"Duck down under the dash," he said to Thompson. "Someone is coming and we don't want him to see us."

The panic in Duvall's voice caused Thompson to dive under the dash like he thought a missile was coming at them. If he had been scared when Duvall turned back to the car, he was hysterical now. He was nearly curled up into a fetal position on the floor of the car when he whispered, "What? Who is it? What the hell is going on? Let's just get the hell out of here."

Duvall had grabbed a girly magazine that was laying on the car seat, and held it close to his face so that he wouldn't be seen. He told Thompson with undisguised disgust, "Just shut the hell up will you? I'm tired of your mealy mouthed whining. We are not leaving." Dylan had passed them by so he lowered the magazine and said, "You can get up off the floor now, he's past us."

Thompson was sweating when he climbed back on the seat. He felt a little embarrassed by his behavior so he attempted to sound casual when he asked Duvall, "Why don't you explain this to me? What's our plan?" Secretly he hoped that the plan was for him to get him into the witness protection program.

"No plan. There is a stakeout going on here and I don't like it. I want to know what's going on, so we are going to stay here and watch," Duvall told him.

"Oh god," Thompson responded with the complete resignation of someone who is certain he is about to die.

"Just sit there and shut up." Duvall never looked at him while he spoke. He just stared straight ahead through the windshield.

"Great," Thompson responded.

Duvall turned his head slowly and gave Thompson a withering look. Thompson got the message and didn't say another word.

CHAPTER ONE HUNDRED SIX

DUVALL WAS NOT THE ONLY ONE who worried about Dylan's trek across the parking lot. Connor, and the others in the car with him, saw him get out of the car and walk away from the casino. It confounded them. Connor told Brent to call Dylan and find out what he was doing. Brent made the call but Dylan didn't answer the phone, so Connor told him to call Jake, or the Chief, to see if they knew anything about Dylan's unexplained sortie.

Brent asked in obvious frustration, "What the hell was the sense in giving him a damn phone if he never uses it?"

"How should I know", Connor replied. "He's your friend not mine."

"What's that supposed to mean?" Brent demanded sourly.

"Just do me a favor and call Jake and the Chief," Connor repeated, ignoring Brent's foul mood.

Brent made the calls but neither Jake nor the Chief knew what Dylan was up to, so Brent decided to try Joan. When Joan heard her phone ring, and saw from the caller ID that it was Brent, she turned away from Helen, answering in a hushed tone.

Brent told her about Dylan's little journey across the parking lot and asked her if she knew anything about it. Joan reported that she had not spoken to Dylan in a while and knew nothing about it.

Brent had a sudden idea and asked Joan, "Tommy hasn't shown up to see Helen has he?" He wasn't sure why he asked the question, other than out of desperation.

"Oh my god," Joan shot back. "It was him. It was Tommy I saw earlier by the restroom. I never connected it until you asked me."

"Where did he go?" Brent asked her.

"I don't know. When I came out of the bathroom he was gone and I haven't seen him since," she replied.

"Ok. Go back to the car now, I'll stay in touch." Joan hung up and prepared to leave the casino.

Helen had recognized Joan shortly after she sat at the machine next to her. It took her a few minutes to connect her with Montana, but when she did she recalled that she was Dylan's girlfriend. She tried not to let on that she'd recognized Joan, supplying vague answers to her questions and pretending to concentrate her attention on her machine. During Joan's phone call, Helen managed overhear her say Tommy's name. She deduced from that that Joan expected Tommy to come here to find her, and was waiting for him to show up.

She admitted to herself that there could be other reasons, but this was the most likely one, and the one that worried her the most.

"Look, it was really nice meeting you and gambling with you," Joan said to Helen after hanging up, "but I have to go now. That was my boyfriend calling and he is looking for me. Good luck with the slots. I hope you hit the big jackpot." She smiled and held out her hand for a handshake.

Helen shook her hand and said, "Nice meeting you too." Then she turned her eyes back to the machine, but her attention remained intently upon Joan. Using her peripheral vision while printing out her win ticket on the slot machine, Helen watched Joan until she got to the exit, then got up and followed her. She put the slot receipt in her pocket so that she could cash it in later, and looked cautiously through the glass doors before walking outside.

She watched Joan walk across the parking lot and get into the passenger seat of a car. There was no one in the driver seat. Helen went back into the casino and stood behind the glass doors, so that she could keep an eye on Joan without being detected.

Way across the lot someone familiar attracted Helen's attention and when she looked beyond the car, toward the person, she also caught sight of Dylan walking away from the building. He was a little more than half way across the lot and was walking very slowly toward the other person. She would not even have noticed Dylan if he wasn't walking directly toward Tommy. She exited the hotel and started following him.

CHAPTER ONE HUNDRED SEVEN

LAPKE'S TEAM WAS IN PLACE AND spread out along the berm bordering the parking lot. Ken Clawson took up his position and peered across the lot toward the casino. He watched Dylan leave his car and start walking toward them. Shortly after that, Joan exited the casino and got into the car that Dylan had just vacated. A minute later, Helen exited the casino and followed Dylan. Ken had signaled Tom to take a look and he'd seen the activity through his binoculars.

At first Helen appeared to be following Dylan, but her attention was not directly on him. She was looking at something past him and just to his left. Tom and Ken swung their binoculars in the direction of her gaze to see what she was looking at. It was a man dressed like he was going fishing. He wore sunglasses and a hat which made it difficult to identify him.

Helen did not have the same difficulty recognizing the man. Tommy had a particular and unique demeanor and way of walking. She would know it anywhere, and it was his peculiar movement that attracted her attention to him. Never having known him to do any fishing, she surmised he was trying to disguise himself. She continued in his direction, glancing at Dylan occasionally to see where he was headed.

Ken watched the fisherman for a moment. He was headed toward the berm which concealed them. Out of curiosity he swung the field glasses to his right to take another look at the man he had seen a few minutes earlier, walking away from them. Something about him was disturbing and he wanted another look. As soon as he had focused on the man's back the man had turned around, and for a second, looked right at Ken, then turned back and continued walking away. The binoculars gave Ken the advantage of seeing the man's face close up this time. There was something familiar about it, maybe from one of the photos that Tom had shown them. He pulled the photos out of his vest pocket and shuffled through them.

As soon as he came to the photo of Brad Danison he used his radio to inform Tom of his discovery. Tom acknowledged the report but issued no instructions other than, "Thanks, stand by."

When Jake, Joan, the Chief, and the others in Grant's car saw Helen leave the casino, they got out of their cars, working their way in the same direction as Dylan and Helen. No one really understood why they were gravitating away from the building, especially after learning that Tommy was inside, but they did so nonetheless. Drawn by natural instincts similar to the morbid curiosity humans have when they see an accident, or an ambulance, or police activity, they ambled on.

Shortly after Dylan passed by Duvall's car, Duvall noted that Helen was following him. Shortly after that, Deputies Curran, McDermott, and Tillman, and the other Montana people exited their cars, from their various locations around the parking lot, and aimed their bodies in the direction of Dylan as well. The way they were moving reminded Duvall of the slow deliberate way that zombies sauntered in the movies. He snorted a short laugh when he pictured that. Where the hell were all these zombies going? There was nothing but sand and cactus in the direction they were headed. Didn't make sense, and that worried him.

Duvall was not considering whether or not things could get any worse at that moment, but it happened anyway. Things got much worse when his 'other' boss, Bennett, walked out of the casino. Bennett's prescence here begged the question 'why'. After some brief consideration, Duvall decided that there was no reason for the boss to be here that did not include something dire for him and Thompson.

Little did he know how right that was. Unbeknownst to Duvall, Bennett had not just lately arrived. He had been there long enough to search the parking lot and find Duvall and Thompson sitting in their car just like Tommy had said. And he had also found the U.S. Marshals Deputies sitting in two different cars, just like Tommy said. Tommy had been right, and had done right by telling Bennett. His debt was paid. Soon, so would Duvall's and Thompson's.

Bennett *wanted* Duvall to see him exit the casino, to know that their time on this earth was coming to an end, and to be unable to do a thing about it except watch it come.

Duvall's survival instincts told him that he should leave. Leave now, leave fast, and go somewhere far, far away. But then there was that pesky and morbid human curiosity that drew people toward a fire, when they should be running away from it. And, seeing the smoke that promised fire, he succumbed to that disturbing human compulsion. He waited until everyone had meandered past the car and then said to Thompson, "Get out of the car, we are going to see what's going on."

"You serious?" Thompson was astounded. Duvall had a fatal problem with his brain. He didn't have one. "Didn't you see the boss coming our way?" he demanded.

"I saw him." Duvall seemed unworried. This worried Thompson.

"And yet you are still here," he said in amazement.

Duvall got out of the car, held the car keys out for Thompson to take and said, "You want to run, here you go." Duvall seemed serious about the offer and Thompson wasn't going to question it, he grabbed the keys, slid over into the drivers seat and sped off toward his destiny. A destiny that he had sealed long ago by being too cowardly to take the necessary steps to stop Duvall, or at least be shut of him.

He drove on desperately, but it was too late. The boss had already cast a net around the hotel and it was about to catch Thompson.

Duvall followed the other zombies across the parking lot like a moth flying inexorably toward the flame, keeping an appointment with a unique destiny of his own. A destiny no more, or no less dire than Thompson's, but one much longer in the making. It could be theorized that Duvall's fate was defined on the day of his birth, and that Thompson, despite deciding his own destiny, was yet taken victim of Duvall's madness.

With both horror and bewilderment Tom Lapke and his team watched all of the zany mob migrate in their general direction. What sort of madness is this, he wondered. What is it about man that he would take such obvious ill advised actions? And yet he saw it done routinely and throughout history. He prayed that someone with enough wisdom, or perhaps just plain sense, would soon come to solve the riddle of man's behavior and take away a lot of misery from the world.

While Tom prayed for the future salvation of mankind, team member Ed Hendrix had noticed through his spotting scope the appearance of the head of the local drug mob, Bennett Alivio. Bennett's appearance on the scene made Ed wonder how Bennett knew about what was going on here, and why he would care. Determining that it was not his pay grade to answer such complex questions, he reported the sighting to Tom Lapke, who received the news and asked himself the same questions as Ed.

CHAPTER ONE HUNDRED EIGHT

THE WINKER MAN HAD AN IMPRESSIVE reputation as a sniper. No one knew how he got the name Winker Man, and it was well known that it was unhealthy to ask him about it. The rumor was that he got it when he was in the military but so far no one alive had been brave enough to verify that rumor with the Winker Man. It's been said that there are a few dead people who asked him about it. But those are just rumors, it being impossible to verify the fact with the dead person.

The story goes that he got his sniper training as an elite member of a special forces team. Which team varies with the story and who is telling it. But there is no story or rumor that explains his unique moniker. Many debates and discussions had taken place as to the possibilities of the origin of his name, all well out of earshot of Winker Man of course.

As his reputation for killing grew, so did his list of friends in convenient places. Whether friends by choice or by coercion made no difference, they still would do whatever he asked. He just happened to have one such friend who worked at the Silverton, and it was he who had unlocked the access panel to the roof of the casino, which was how Winker Man had managed to position himself on the roof with his rifle laid across the top of an air conditioning unit, aimed in the general direction of the parking lot.

He had not been in position long when he saw one of the targets he had been ordered to watch for. The target was one of the FBI agents, who was driving towards the parking lot exit. He leveled his rifle toward the moving car and moved the weapon smoothly, keeping the cross hairs centered on the driver's head. He watched through the scope as Ben's ground men blocked the parking lot exit and intercepted Thompson as he tried to drive out. Bennett gave him the signal indicating not to shoot and he watched them escort Thompson out of his car, into one of Bennett's cars and then drive off with him. Poor slob would have been better off if the Winker had shot him. Oh well, Ben had his reasons.

He turned his attention back to the parking lot and soon spotted another one of the named targets. Once again he placed the rifle's cross hairs on his target and watched through the scope as he walked away from the casino and across the parking lot. He had a clear and easy shot right now, but he had orders to wait for Ben to give the nod before pulling the trigger. No nods came, and this time none of Bennett's men were anywhere near the target. He wondered what Ben was waiting for but withheld his shot, reasoning once again that Ben had his reasons.

Hendrix was getting good with his spotting scope, and moments after reporting the appearance of Bennett he made another important find and reported it to Lapke. "Got a sniper on the casino roof, just above and a little to the right of the Bass Pro entrance."

Tom picked up his binoculars and looked in the direction indicated by Hendrix. He saw the man holding the rifle and aiming it out into the parking lot. It was difficult to tell who he was or who his intended target was, but by now Tom was starting to feel pretty darn vindicated for deciding to come here with a team. He replied to Hendrix, "I see him. You stay put."

Lapke contacted another agent, Tony Tolliver, who had the nickname 'Sneakers' because of the amazing stealth he could use when approaching one of his victims, most of whom never heard or saw him coming, and were very surprised and more than a little embarrassed to find themselves on the ground being cuffed as the first indication of his presence. "Tony, you there?" Tom radioed.

"I hear you, even without your radio. You might want to be a little quieter," he said. He had difficulty, generally speaking, understanding people who could not operate quietly.

"Yeah, thanks for the reminder." Smart ass, he thought. "Did you hear Hendrix' report about the sniper?"

"Yeah, who didn't?"

"Fine," Tom responded. "So you going to get him or what?"

"I never said I wouldn't get him. Where do you want me to deposit him?" he asked.

"Just hold him up there on the roof and wait for further instructions. You can handle that can't you?" He asked this last question as if it was too easy of an assignment, in acknowledgment of Sneakers ability, and not in sarcasm.

"Tsk, tsk, ye of little faith," Sneakers replied goodheartedly, and then disappeared around the end of the berm. The rest of the team, who had been eavesdropping on their radios, watched in amusement, to see if he would re-appear on the other side of the berm. They all smiled and shook their heads in familiar amazement when, instead of re-appearing, he seemed to vanish into thin air.

Tom was just as amused by Sneakers abilities as the rest of his team, and watched him as closely as they did. But he was the leader and so he gently guided them back to business by speaking into his radio, "OK men, lets stay alert."

CHAPTER ONE HUNDRED NINE

TOMMY WAS APPROACHING THE BERM at the back of the parking lot when he noticed something unusual about a number of people walking in the same direction he was walking. There were no cars parked in the back of the lot, so why were so many people walking away from a casino and towards an empty lot?

On closer inspection he saw the familiar face of his girlfriend, Helen. Not more than a half a second later, he saw Dylan walking just a dozen yards ahead of her. It took only a few more seconds to realize that he knew just about every person out strolling across the lot. Many of them from Montana.

Not only was he was surprised to see Helen among them, but he was none too happy about it. It was obvious by the way she was looking at him that she had recognized him too, in spite of his disguise.. He surmised that she must have recognized Dylan as well, since it looked like she was following him. But why were Dylan, and all the others headed for the back of the lot? A question which had no desirable answers.

One thing that he saw that he did like, though, was Bennett and his men, who were set up at the front of the lot near the casino. For some reason they were not walking across the parking lot like the others, which made their migration seem even more strange.

Wanting to find cover Tommy headed for the berm as quickly as possible without looking too unnatural. He had about another hundred yards to cover before he could make a right turn leaving the side walk, gaining the cover of the berm. The sooner he got behind it, the less the chances were that someone else, besides Helen, would see him and recognize him, in spite of his disguise. Dylan had already glanced in his direction a few times with a suspecting frown on his face, but Tommy didn't think he had made the connection yet. At least he hoped not.

CHAPTER ONE HUNDRED TEN

FOR OBVIOUS REASONS, BENNETT did not like being around anyone who belonged to any kind of law enforcement organization, and in the past few minutes he had seen several such persons on the premises of the Silverton. It was making him uncomfortable, and he felt the unusual sensation of his skin crawling with the realization that he could become a hunted person. If he was going to do anything here, he wanted to do it quick and get out fast.

Just as Sneakers was making his way toward Winker, Bennett decided that now was the time to act. Any further waiting would only increase the chances of Duvall escaping and would put him in a vulnerable situation of getting nabbed by some cops or feds. He looked up at Winker on the roof. As soon as Winker looked down at him and caught his eye he gave the signal.

Winker nodded in return, then looked back through the scope of his sniper rifle. He placed the cross hairs of the scope on the back of Duvall's head, let his breath out slowly and squeezed the trigger. At almost the same instant that he pulled the trigger, two things happened. Actually a lot more than two things happened, but there were two majorly significant things that happened. The first was that Duvall lost his mind. And his brain and the front half of his face etc. It was too awful for a detailed description.

The second thing that happened was that Sneakers took Winker down so fast that it seemed to take his brain a week to catch up with what had happened to him. When he finally reconciled with the reality of his new situation he experienced the same emotional response as every other person ever taken down by Sneakers. He felt thoroughly abashed.

Bennett had started moving as soon as he gave the nod to Winker Man. He was already in his car and driving away when he heard the gunshot. He wasn't worried about the Winker Man. He figured he would catch up with him later. He figured wrong. He gave the driver of his car instructions to take him to the warehouse. The warehouse was a building in an industrial complex several miles out of town. It was a noisy sort of area and no one paid particular attention to strange sounds, such as men screaming in pain. It was also where Thompson would be waiting for Bennett. Thompson would soon be making a lot of strange and loud sounds.

A, driven by Adair Brown, AKA Snake, one of Tom Lapke's most experienced team members, followed Bennet's car out of the lot. Adair Brown. The moniker 'Snake', was derived from some of his fellow agents, who got into the habit of shortening his first name to Adder, a type of snake, which soon evolved into 'Snake'. Snake was a top hand at following other vehicles without being detected, so Tom had him steal the rental car that Jake had been driving and use it to follow Bennett.

———————

At the sound of the gunshot there was the usual response of the private security guards hired by the casino to protect its patrons, employees and premises. Those guards who did not have a heart attack hid behind the nearest large and solid object before getting on their radios and asking each other what happened. The complete compliment of the on-duty security force burned about five minutes establishing the firm agreement among them that a shot had been fired somewhere outside the casino building, probably from the roof. During those five minutes not a single guard did anything that could be construed as an action taken to protect anyone in the hotel, lodge, casino or store. No one other than themselves that is.

Once the guards were agreed that a shot had been fired, it took another five minutes for them to agree that one of the guards should call the police. It was a unanimous assignment that the lead guard was the one who most deserved to be chosen to handle that momentous responsibility. The lead guard took his responsibility as the leader of his force seriously and dialed 911 immediately.

"Yeah, this is Mr. Vincent Sousa," he reported to the 911 dispatcher, "the foreman of the Silverton Lodge and Casino security department. I would like to report....."

The 911 operator interrupted him, "If you are reporting a gunshot from the roof of the Bass Pro Shop we have already had a couple of dozen calls. You got anything else for us?"

"Uh, no ma'am, that was it." The next sound he heard was the click of the 911 operator hanging up on him.

In a few minutes the place would be swarming with all kinds of cops and other emergency responders. No sense him putting his ass on the line if the police were on the way. He would wait for them in his safe little cubby hole.

———————

Tom was watching Duvall through his binoculars when he saw Winker's bullet hit his head and put him down. He felt bad about Sneakers getting to Winker too late. It cost Duvall's life, but he had acted as quickly as he could.

304

He hoped they would not be too late to save Thompson. After all, they wouldn't be able to imprison him for the rest of his life if he was dead.

After Duvall went down, and Tom was sure that Winker was out of action, he sent two of his team members out to the tarmac to check the body. Assuming Duvall was indeed dead, and Tom felt certain that he was, he and Thompson were more or less taken care of, which left only Danison to deal with. He sent agents Ken Clawson and Ed Hendrix after him.

The gunshot that reverberated across the parking lot startled all of the people who were, wittingly or no, following Dylan across the parking lot. Most of them instinctively stopped walking and ducked their heads and looked for cover. There were no cars in this part of the lot, which left the berm ahead of them as the nearest refuge. Most of them instinctively ran toward the berm, but Joan spontaneously ran toward Dylan, worried that he'd been the target of the shooting.

Helen ran toward Tommy for the same reason. In spite of their intentions they both ended up following their man over the berm, since that is where the men were headed.

Winker had accomplished one thing for sure. He had sped up the events unfolding at the Silverton. No longer were individuals or groups of people meandering like zombies. No longer was anyone practicing caution. They were practicing one thing – survival. Or call it panic if you want. It was the same thing at this point.

Brad and Tommy were not excluded from the increased acceleration of events. They both started running while looking in the direction of the gunshot. Neither of them saw the other coming until they were facing each other, barely thirty feet apart, at which point they both stopped moving and stared at each other.

At first Brad didn't realize he was facing Tommy because of Tommy's disguise. But then Tommy said, "Hi, Brad, I've been looking for you." And he reached into his shopping bag.

Helen saw Ed and Ken approaching Tommy with their hands on their guns.

305

"Don't shoot," she yelled. "It's Tommy." She shouted these words over and over, desperately hoping Tommy wouldn't be shot.

Jake, Brent, Connor, the Chief, and Grant were all running over the top of the berm and shouting at Dylan, Joan and Helen, "Stop, get back!" In fear that they would get hit by stray gun fire, or worse - mistaken for the wrong people and shot intentionally.

Anna was alternately shrieking at Joan to get down, and at Charlie to do the same. James on the other hand, had lain on the ground at the sound of the first gunshot, held his hands over the back of his head and stayed there. He was the only one who wasn't yelling or running.

Ed and Ken were moving in quickly on Brad when they noticed another civilian coming towards him. The man looked like an out of place fisherman and Ken thought there was something both strange and familiar about him. He looked more closely at the man, but before he could determine who the weird fisherman was he saw him pull a gun out of his shopping bag.

Both Ed and Ken drew their weapons and trained them on the fisherman. They were about to open fire on the man when they saw others running at them and shouting. The people were getting dangerously close, but what made both men lower their weapons was that one of the runners were shouting, "It's Tommy, don't shoot!"

CHAPTER ONE HUNDRED ELEVEN

BRAD RECOGNIZED TOMMY'S VOICE and realized who he was facing. He tried to play it cool and while Tommy was fishing around in his shopping bag Brad said, "That makes two of us. I've been looking for you too."

Brad was unprepared when Tommy produced a gun from his shopping bag. That proved to be the worst and last mistake of Brad's life.

Tommy leveled the gun at him and said, "You found me, Brad, see ya later," and pulled the trigger. The bullet went right through his heart, killing him before he hit the ground.

From the first instant that Tommy saw Brad he was so focused – so obsessed, or possessed – that he never saw nor heard the others nearby, running and shouting. In fact, when he found himself lying on the ground with his hands behind his head, it was a mystery to him how he had gotten there.

The two federal agents, Ken and Ed, were the first to reach Tommy, but by the time they got to him he had already put his gun down on the ground and lay down on his stomach with his hands locked together behind his head. By some instinct he must have known that it was his best chance at not getting shot. The agents quickly frisked Tommy for weapons, and then wire tied his hands behind his back. For good measure they wire tied his ankles as well.

They found his ID when they frisked him, and when they verified that he was indeed Tommy Sanderson, they called Tom for instructions. After watching him shoot another man it was unclear to them whether they should be protecting him or arresting him.

"Just wait for me to get there. I'll be there in thirty seconds," Tom instructed them.

The shouting stopped and, with the appearance of the agents' guns the others stopped moving, worried about getting shot.

Ken and Ed, seeing that those people were no longer moving, told them to stay where they were – just in case they changed their minds and decided to leave, or interfere. The two agents who had checked Brad's body moments earlier- and found it to be lifeless indeed – had joined Ken and Ed at about the same time as Tom and the rest of the team, except for Adair, who was still following Bennett.

The sound of sirens – lots of sirens – was beginning to fill the air when Tom recognized Grant standing behind the dirt bank with the others. He walked over to him and shook his hand saying, "Good to see you, Grant." He looked around at all the other people standing around. "Looks like we have quite a party here. Who are all your friends?" Indicating the others with a nod of his head.

"Good to see you too, Tom. Very good. I had no idea you were coming, but I'm certainly glad that you did," Grant replied. "Let me introduce everyone. First, the law enforcement personnel. There are U.S. Marshal's Deputies Connor McDermott and Jake Tillman from the Denver office." Each of them shook hands with Tom. "These two are the Chief of Police from Flatrock Montana, Charlie Armstrong, and one of his officers, Brent Butler." Tom shook their hands as well.

"The rest of the party are civilians," Grant continued, "but have made invaluable contributions to our investigation." He pointed out each one of them and told Tom their names with brief descriptions of how they were involved. Tom nodded at each of them in turn as they were introduced.

"And this," Grant said, pointing to Tom, "Is the Deputy U.S. Attorney General, Tom Lapke." That introduction raised quite a few eyebrows, but, not knowing what to say, they wisely remained silent.

"These are some very enthusiastic party goers you invited here, Connor," Tom said, sarcastically referring to their silence.

"The shyness wears off once they get to know you a little," Connor joked in return.

Then, almost as if it had been rehearsed, everyone's eyes drifted over to look at Tommy lying on the ground all trussed up like a hog being readied for the spit. They expected an explanation from him, but knew they would not get one from him at the moment, causing them disappointment.

The silence around him got Tommy's attention, and with some difficulty, due to his present state of packaging, he looked up to see what was happening. The looks on their faces were comically pathetic, portraying the thought, 'Poor guy, if only he could talk.' "I'm not dead you know," he blurted out.

His statement seemed to break a spell. Helen slowly approached him cautiously, eying the agents who continued to aim their weapons at Tommy. She calmly said, "Does he have to stay on the ground like that? Can he at least stand up?"

Tom cocked his head slightly, considering what to do. He looked at Tommy for a second and then looked up at Ken Clawson and said, "Stand him up please, Ken, and untie his feet. For right now hand ties are enough."

While Ken was untying Tommy's feet and standing him up, Tom looked back at Grant and said, "A minute ago you mentioned an investigation that all these people were allegedly involved in. Suppose you tell me just what this investigation has to do with what happened here today."

308

Grant hesitated and looked over at Connor, Jake, and then Dylan. The others took turns looking at each other, and then back at Connor. The exchange silently elected him to do the explaining, but Tom noticed Connor's and suspected that there was something going on here than met the eye. He was about to nudge Connor into talking when he heard Ken say, "Please stay away from the prisoner ma'am." He looked over and saw Helen trying to approach Tommy.

"It's OK, Ken, I'll be responsible. Let her go to him," Tom instructed softly.

Helen walked over to Tommy and brushed some of the dirt off his cheek. She took his sunglasses off, which had been knocked cockeyed when he was on the ground. It wasn't until then that the others started wondering why he was dressed so strangely.

"You OK, Tommy?" Helen asked affectionately. Tommy nodded yes.

Lapke got a hunch that he might not get a story out of Connor until after Tommy gave his own explanation, causing him to consider something that he had never considered before in his entire career in Law Enforcement. He started considering doing something that most definitely did not conform to standard procedures, policies or protocols. Possibly not even the law. He walked away from the group, the distance giving him a measure of objectivity from which he hoped to make a more rational decision.

He returned to the waiting group a moment later. "You know where the old Howard Hughes warehouse is, a few blocks from here?" he asked Connor.

"Yes," Connor answered.

"Meet us there and hurry it up." He said, frowning at the arriving hordes of cops, firemen and EMT's. Connor followed Tom's gaze and appreciated the reason for Tom's rush.

"I doubt that we will be able to return to our vehicles," he told Tom. "At least not without being seen by all those cops."

"Yeah, I can see that, and I don't think we can all fit in the van."

"Excuse me, sir," Grant said. "But I think I know a way."

"Let me hear it, Deputy."

"I think if I go alone I can convince those cops that I'm on the case here and will be allowed to drive away in my car without anyone questioning me. Then I can come around the berm here and pick up as many as I can fit in the car."

"That's a good plan, Deputy...OH SHIT!" He said as if he just remembered that he left his stove on at home. "I forgot all about Sneakers!"

"Yeah, I noticed that," Tom heard just over his shoulder. When he turned and saw Sneakers there holding Winker, he just about fainted.

"Damn it, Sneakers, you trying to give me a heart attack?" No one had seen or heard Sneakers arrive.

"No, sir," Sneakers smiled.

"And how in the hell did you get past all those cops out there with this guy in tow?" Tom demanded.

"You really want to know, sir?" Sneakers asked him.

"On second thought, never mind" Tom said. "Just get that guy in the van fast." He turned to Ken and his teammates and said, "Get Tommy, and as many others stuffed into that van as you can. The rest of you wait for Deputy Curran to show up and meet us at the warehouse. Grant, get moving."

"Yes, sir." Grant ran off and there was a flurry of motion as the team headed for the van.

CHAPTER ONE HUNDRED TWELVE

SOMEHOW, AND FOR whatever random reason, Joan and Dylan were grabbed up by a couple of Tom's team members and stuffed into the very back of the van. They were packed in so tightly that their bodies were in close physical contact. In spite of the crowded condition of the van, or because of it perhaps, they felt a weird sense of privacy. Joan's face was only a couple of inches from Dylan's when she whispered, "You scared me back there. I was freaking out when you started walking across the parking lot and then when that shot went off....... Dylan, I thought someone shot you and I felt so......" She was fighting down tears too intently to finish, but Dylan knew what she wanted to say.

"Sorry, babe," he said. "Sorry I worried you. I just did what I thought I had to do. If I had even suspected the sniper and the rest of it, I might not have gone out there." Neither of them believed the veracity of that.

Dylan and Joan were not the only ones who took advantage of the short break in the action, nor the close quarters. Anna and Charlie had also been randomly chosen to ride in the van. Anna, close to tears, whispered to Charlie, "God, I was so worried about you out there when the shooting started. And Joan......... it was all so terrifying."

"Yeah, me too," Charlie whispered back to her. "When I heard you calling my name I panicked, thinking that you'd been hit. I didn't know what to do, to be honest with you, but that short lived realization that I may have lost you made me feel........., well, I felt something I have not felt in a long time." He started to look a little blushed, but Anna was smiling faintly.

Tommy and Helen were smitten by the same mood as the other couples in the van, but refrained from speaking verbally. Instead they held hands and looked at each other with significant expressions. What they wanted to say to each other was a bit more 'intimate' than what the others had said, and they were just a bit too shy about it to risk being overheard. More accurately, Helen felt shy. Tommy was more worried about the ribbing he would take from his fellows for the rest of his career. A career that was most likely ended forever now.

But the time for romance ended quickly when the van completed its very short trip to the warehouse and stopped inside of its doors. It took three more minutes for Grant to arrive with the remainder of the group.

There was not much in the way of conference room furniture in the old building. In fact there was not much in the way of any kind of furniture in the old warehouse. There was a small pile of pallets in one corner, which they drug to the center of the room, then draped an old tarp over the top of it. This served as a 'conference table'. Chairs were more difficult to invent. The one and only folding chair that was left in the building was given, without discussion, to Anna. Some of the federal agents used their equipment bags to sit on. Joan and Helen were allowed to sit on the floor of the van just inside the open side door, with their legs dangling onto the warehouse floor. Charlie stood behind Anna and used the back of her chair for some support. Everyone else was happy just to stand, or lean on the vehicles for some support.

Winker Man was hog tied, his mouth covered with duct tape, and laid out on the floor of the back seat of Grant's car looking extremely undignified. The doors and windows were shut so that he couldn't hear them talk, and more importantly so no one would have to look at Winker.

Tom was anxious to make his case, but he needed to know a few things first. "Grant, what was the status at the Silverton when you left the lot?"

"The normal organized chaos. Firemen trying to find a fire and or prevent the possibility of one. No panic, just going through the motions of their training. I suspect Pops – that's what we call the Fire Chief – was using the incident as an opportunity to run some training exercises."

"What were the cops doing?" Tom asked him.

"Same as the firemen more or less. They were running the routine per the manual. Only difference for them was that they had dead bodies to deal with. They had the scene crime taped and forensics was doing their gig. More forensics was up on the roof. The exits are sealed and no one is allowed to leave without clearance," he answered.

"So more or less under pretty good control?"

"Right."

"OK, we'll need to brief them, but it can wait until we remand Winker to LVMPD." He said Winker's name like he was trying to get a bad taste out of his mouth. "Let's get our business here over with first. Tommy," he said, "it is time for you to explain yourself. I think we all need to know what the hell you were thinking."

Tommy looked down at his shoes for a minute and then looked back up and looked around the room at each of the individuals, all of whom anxiously awaited his tale. His eyes stopped on Dylan's and held there for a minute. There was deep sadness showing in both men's eyes. "I am really sorry about your mom, Dylan," he said. "She was a real hero."

"Yeah, thanks," Dylan responded, then looked down at his feet.

Tommy hesitated again before speaking. "I'm not sure if I should say anything here, Tom. I mean, if I go to trial over this, it might go against me if I give up any information right now."

"Look, Tommy," Tom said to him, "I can't tell you what is going to happen when we leave here because I don't know yet. You may be right, and you may be going to trial. But I will make you this promise; whatever is said in this room by anyone, including myself, doesn't leave this room." He looked up at the rest of the group and added, "Agreed, everyone?"

They all agreed, and Tommy was about to speak when Lapke's radio chirped, "Tom, can you read me?" It was Adair Brown.

"Yeah, go ahead," Tom answered.

"I followed them to a warehouse near the concrete plant. Thompson is inside one of the buildings and Bennett is just now going inside. Any instructions?"

"Did you get the address of the place?"

"Affirmative."

"Then call 911 and make an anonymous report that you saw the sniper leaving the Silverton, and you followed him to the warehouse. Give them the address. Then come back to the Howard Hughes warehouse as fast as you can."

"Sir....uh, what sniper sir? I thought.."

Tom interrupted his query and said into the radio, "Just do what I asked. I will explain it when you get back here."

He set down the radio and looked back at Tommy.

"Sorry about that. Go ahead." He stared, just like all the others in the room, at Tommy expectantly.

CHAPTER ONE HUNDRED THIRTEEN

"IT ALL STARTED A LONG TIME AGO when I was a rookie with the Vegas Metro PD," Tommy began. " For whatever reason, Brad Danison latched on to me and took me under his wing. Looking back on it, I guess he saw something in me that I never saw in myself. He felt it was his duty to fill me in on the details of police life in the Vegas Metro PD.

"He took me on some stake outs, introduced me to some of the local and more colorful citizens around town, and eventually he let me talk to some of his CI's, confidential informants. It soon became apparent that he was doing some business with them on the side.

"He never actually told me what he was doing with them, but it was clear that he wanted me to know or he wouldn't have taken me along, and after a while I started feeling uneasy about it. I saw myself going down a path that I didn't want to be on, but it was not easy to distance myself from Brad by then. Rookies don't have a lot of say in what they do on the force, as a lot of you know.

"Eventually he got me assigned as his partner. That's when dropped the news on me that he planned to bring me in on his extra curricular activities and make me a partner in his dark arts as well. I knew that if I let it get that far, there would be no way out for me, but I had no idea what to do.

"Brad had connections in Internal Affairs, but even if he didn't I couldn't go to them for help. You guys know how that works. A squealer gets branded and shunned by the rest of the force, or even worse punishment. So I played along for a little while hoping that I would think of a solution. I never did think of one, but after a short time I was approached by one of your guys." He looked over at Tom, who nodded his agreement. It was also an unspoken approval for Tommy to reveal their secret operation.

"They asked me to go under cover in Bennett's gang. After thinking about it, I thought it might provide me with a way to get away from my involvement with Brad, so I said yes. Getting inside the gang was easy. They're always looking for bad cops to get on their payroll to help them avoid the law, and to help them if they get caught. You guys already know that drill. Anyway, we made up a story to tell Bennett.

"I told him that I needed some money to cover gambling losses and that I was for hire. I'd spent three months prior to that doing a poor job of gambling and losing a lot of money. I'd borrowed so I could gamble some more, and I fell behind on the repayment. All on purpose of course, because we knew that Bennett would check out my story. When my story checked out he hired me on

314

a probationary basis. I did a few short jobs for him and he paid me well for the services. I guess he liked how I worked because the jobs grew more regular."

"Things soon fell into a routine with Bennett, and it wasn't long after that that I found out Brad was on the take with Bennett too. I came up with a way to use that knowledge to get out of my partnership with Brad. I told Bennett it would be too suspicious if both of us were working for him while we were partners. He agreed, and after he had a little talk with Brad we separated as cop partners.

"I did a good job for Bennett and he gained more and more confidence in me, and conversely I grew less and less certain that I could handle it. I felt like I was playing Russian Roulette; eventually he would find out my true role and I'd be a dead man.

"About that time Helen came to me, telling me about Anna. She told me that Anna had been dropping hints to her that she had objections to being in Bennett's gang, and would be happy if she could find a way out. She also mentioned to Helen that James wife Brenda, Jesse to you guys, was pregnant and unaware of what James was doing. Anna wanted to help her and James get out as well. That gave me an idea and I started working on it.

"First, I got Helen to have a chat with Anna to make sure that she would go along with the idea. Naturally, Helen had to leave me out of the conversation and never divulge my involvement. Anna told Helen that she would be glad to do it. So next we had Anna talk to 'Jesse'. Once Jesse was signed on we got to work. I started feeding Helen incriminating info about Bennett. Helen passed it on to Anna who passed it on to Jesse. It was risky but I knew it would work, if we didn't get caught.

"When the time was right I contacted the FBI, who had been waiting for my call. They arrested Bennett, James, several of the top dealers, and of course, Anna. Jesse was put under the protection of the U.S. Marshals. The reason for Anna's arrest was, of course, to cover up her role as informant, and she and the FBI both knew she would be doing very short and easy time.

"Unfortunately, the case against Bennett was weak. I can tell you from experience he is a shrewd man. He was careful at all times not to carry dope on him and not to be near any of the drug exchanges. Attempts to get him on financial charges, like fraud and tax evasion, also failed. He was too savvy in the world of money handling. When the bust went down he was carrying a tiny amount of weed, so he ended up with only a conviction on a minor possession charge.

"He did two years and was released, returning to his former position and occupation, like he never left. He called me and we were back in business, which gave me another chance to gather enough evidence to make a bigger case against him.

"Brad became suspicious about that time, and knowing that he'd developed a serious dislike of me, I worried that he would make trouble for me. Somehow I managed to dodge that bullet for a while, and continued to do a good job for Bennett. But Brad finally got a wedge between us when he found out that Jesse was hidden in Montana. He told Bennett that I was the one who set her up there, and for some reason Bennett was inclined to believe him."

James interrupted Tommy at this point. "How come Brad didn't like you anymore. I mean, it sounded like you were his pet project there for a while?"

"Yeah, I was his fair haired boy, that's for sure. I couldn't figure it out at first, but later I concluded it was jealousy," he explained.

"What'd you do, steal his girlfriend or something?" James asked, having a worldly awareness on such matters.

"No, nothing like that. I think it was professional jealousy."

"You mean like the dude was so good at being jealous that he was a pro? Man, that's some serious shit there man." James noted, grateful for the expansion of his worldliness.

"Not exactly," Tommy explained patiently. "It's more like people in a certain profession are sometimes jealous of others in their same profession. In this case Brad was mainly a goldbricker. He goldbricked for the PD and he goldbricked for Bennett. I, on the other hand, worked hard and tried to do a good job, for both people. Bennett saw that in me and so he treated me better than he did Brad, and that made Brad jealous."

"I get it. Brad was pissed cause you was better than him. Happens to me all the time." That was met with widespread laughter, and Brent and Dylan high fived.

Tom's patience had been used up by now and he wanted to get on with it. But first he had a question of his own.

"I get why Brad had a hard on for you," he said, "but what I never did understand was why, all of a sudden, Bennett started believing the jerk after all those years of trusting you more than him?"

"That's easy. It was because I had started traveling to Montana frequently. I was trying to keep an eye on Jesse because I had heard rumors that she had been tracked down by the mob. Turns out I was right about that and when, with Brad's help of course, Bennett connected the dots between Jesse and me he was not happy. That is when I decided it was time to get out."

"Well, that explains it. Thanks," Lapke said.

"Hold on a minute," Connor said. "I have a question. Something you just said got my attention. You said you were worried about Jesse because of rumors that the drug mob had tracked her down in Montana."

"That's right," Tommy verified.

"Do you have any idea how they did it? How they found out where she was?" Connor asked. He was shaking when he asked it, and his palms and face

316

were sweaty. If Tommy knew the answer to it, it could either provide him with profound relief, or with utter defeat, and he had barely mustered the nerve to ask it.

"Like I said they were just rumors at the time. But reliable enough to make me worried," Tommy began. "Later however, just before I was so-called busted from the Vegas PD, I found out the facts, not just rumors. It was purely accidental actually. One of Bennett's suppliers was bringing in some meth from Canada and he drove through Montana. He stopped in Flatrock for gas and saw Jesse. Very bad luck. "

"Thanks," Connor said sadly. He was off the hook, but took little relief or pleasure in knowing it.

"Sure," Tommy said. "So the only thing left to figure at that point was how to save my own skin. You know all about this part already, sir," he said to Tom. "But for the others benefit; Brad was stirring things up and Bennett was suspicious of me, so with Tom's help, I set up a sting. A sting on myself. I pilfered some of Bennett's drugs and tried to make a sale on my own. Of course I was busted, as planned. Bennett lost a lot of expensive product due to my bust and he got even more pissed at me.

"My bust was well covered in the papers and on TV, where I was heavily vilified, all according to prepared press releases. Mayors and Police Chiefs and other civic leaders were calling for my beheading and so on. The purpose of the negative PR campaign was to convince Bennett that I was a dirty cop. Like all headlines, after a short while the public found something else to be outraged about and my heinous crimes faded into the background. It was then that I was released from custody, but suspended from the force.

"After my release I walked into Bennett's office and, before he had a chance to shoot me, I threw down a wad of money, repayment for the money he lost on my bad deal. That cooled his jets pretty good, and when I told him I was going to have to leave town and keep my head low, he said he understood. As far as he knew I was hated by the D.A, every law enforcement agency in the state and the public at large, making me a walking target. He knew I would have to disappear if I wanted to stay on the right side of the grass, so he gave me safe passage. Safe passage meaning I had permission to leave his gang, without him putting a contract out on me."

Lapke came up with another question, "Hang on a minute, Tommy. You just reminded me of something I've been wondering about. Do you know why Bennett showed up at the Silverton today?"

Tommy looked a little sheepish. "Yeah, I know why he was there. I called him and told him what was going on. That is, I sort of told him. I might have altered a few of the detail, and maybe I fabricated a few of the pertinent facts. But I only did it so that I could be sure he would show up. I made it sound like Duvall was setting him and Brad up for the big bust. I knew that when he got to the Silverton parking lot and saw all the stakeout personnel, including Duvall and Thompson, he would think that what I told him was true. I guess it worked." He held up both of his palms up in the gesture that universally conveyed, 'Hey, what else could I do, sorry'. His palms only got as high as his stomach, being limited by handcuffs, but the message was not lost.

Tom seemed about to comment on Sanderson's answer, but changed his mind. "Well, that clears up that mystery," He said.

"Yeah, let's see, where was I? Oh yeah, so like I said, the rumors were flying around that Jesse was in Montana, and Brad used the rumors to connect my travels there. By the way, my sorties to Montana confirmed the rumors that Jesse was there. I figured that Brad and Bennett were likely to know she was there as well. I felt responsible for Jesse because it was my plan that got her into the whole mess, and I knew that Bennett would hunt her down. So I decided to move to Montana and keep an eye on her. And that is why I moved there and joined the Highway Patrol. Tom didn't know any of this when he helped me get the job, I wanted to keep it as low key as possible. To my everlasting regret, I was wrong about keeping it to myself, I couldn't handle it alone." He paused, hanging his head.

He lifted his head and cleared his throat, prepared to continue. "I tried to watch her as much as I could without actually leading someone to her myself. I'm sorry to say it didn't work. It almost worked. I was just a block away when she got hit. If I had been just a little closer I could have stopped him."

Dylan just about shot out of his seat when he heard Tommy's last sentence. "You mean you saw someone? You saw what happened?" he demanded.

"Yes. I saw Brad Danison speaking to Jesse, and then, to my horror I watched as she turned and walked off the curb. There was nothing I could do, I was too late. Brad had disappeared quickly and completely. I knew I would never catch him there at the scene so I decided to stay and deal with Jesse's murder scene and deal with Brad later. I bided my time and planned my move to go after him in Vegas. You all saw the end result of that," he admitted.

That raised the eyebrows of many of the Montana people and Dylan was reminded of his dreams. In his dreams he had seen Tommy in the patrol car; had seen Brad sneaking off; had seen his mom with a gun pointed at her. A gun held in Brad's hand. And Tommy had seen it all too. But not in a dream. He had seen it as real as his mom had seen it. And after many days of unexpressed emotion, a dam finally gave way and he buried his face in the crook of his elbow, walked away from the group and wept. He wept powerfully; for his mom, for himself, for all of his close, dedicated friends in the room and for all of the unsung saints of the world. Joan followed him, and placed her cheek lightly on his shoulder but said nothing.

The Chief watched Dylan walk away wrapped in his sorrow. He turned to Tommy and narrowed his eyes in an intense glare. "You mean, you lied to us

318

back in Montana when we were trying to find out what happened?" Tommy took a step back. "Are you saying you just stood back and watched us working our guts out trying to solve what happened and never said anything? You just let us spin our wheels, when you could have cleared the whole thing up in a few minutes?" Tommy backed away in fear from the advancing Chief, whose eyes raged and body trembled.

Connor walked toward Charlie just in case he needed to prevent another murder. Anna, softly but intensely said, "Charlie, please." Her meaning was plain.

From Tommy's perspective the look in Charlie's eyes could not be taken lightly, especially when his hands were cuffed. He looked pleadingly at Lapke hoping he would get the Chief under control before something bad happened. Something bad to Tommy. He raised his hands palms out. "Hold it, Chief," he said. "Let me explain it. I had reasons for that."

The Chief stopped, put his hands on his hips and stared at Tommy. It wouldn't have surprised anyone in the room if they saw smoke shooting out of his ears. He didn't tell Tommy to speak his piece but his stare conveyed that unquestionably.

Tommy took the cue and spoke up in a hurry, before Charlie could change his mind. "Look, I know how you feel, and I wanted to tell you in the worst way. A couple of times I almost did, but I knew I had to deal with it the way I did.

"Think about it," he continued, "you really think Brad would ever have been subjected to any real justice? To start with, the case against him would have been so weak you would be lucky if he even got indicted. You know yourself how little evidence there was. And he would have had iron clad alibis all lined up. Some of them probably from bona fide, upstanding police officers. And your only witness would have been me, a man who was busted off the force for working for the mob. Not very reliable am I? And all that assumes he doesn't run, which would be another option for him. I know Brad, and if he decided to go under, you would never find him. So the chances were that, one way or another, he would get away with murder, and I couldn't let that happen."

Tommy had not been assaulted by the Chief yet so he kept talking, "Jesse was a saint. And I mean a real Saint. Right up there with Peter and Mother Teresa and the Pope. That kind of Saint. She didn't deserve what happened to her, and she sure as hell did not deserve for Brad to get off Scot-free. I was partly to blame for her situation, and I wasn't about to watch Brad walk the earth as a free human being. I'd rather go to prison myself. So here I am. Sorry you got the wild goose chase, but Brad is gone and I'm not sorry for that." He stared back at the Chief as if to say 'if you still want to kill me, go for it'.

The Chief stared back at Tommy, hands still at his hips, face still purple, eyes still daggered up, but he was thinking. He was thinking the same things that the others in the room, who had started this investigation in Montana, were thinking. He was thinking about how hard – impossible really – it was to come up with any hard evidence of Jesse's murder. Tommy was right about that. He was thinking about the time when they all sat around a table at the Outlaw Bar in Montana, and he had told all the others that he would do whatever it took to avenge Jesse because she was such an incredible woman, who deserved to be avenged. Tommy was right about that too. He remembered when they had first found out about Tommy's history and thought that he was the scum of the earth, the same way anyone was liable to think of him. Tommy was right about that. And he wondered what he would have done if he was in Tommy's shoes, but not for long because he knew exactly what he would have done. He would have done mayhem in Brad's world. The kind of mayhem it was not good for a human's mind to consider for too long of a time.

Anna had silently approached Charlie and she very tenderly put her hand on his arm and led him away. Tommy let out an audible sigh. Several others in the room quit holding their breath, including Tom Lapke, who could tell what they were thinking just by inhaling the atmosphere in the room. He motioned for Grant to follow him and then led him outside the warehouse.

CHAPTER ONE HUNDRED FOURTEEN

"I FIND MYSELF IN A BIT OF A STICKY situation here, Grant," Tom said once they were out of earshot of the others. "You came to me for help when you were in a tough spot with this little party here in Vegas, and now I'm coming to you for help. You are the only person in the world I can trust with this. I think you know what I mean."

Grant did know what he meant. He only hoped he could live up to the trust.

"I'm the Assistant AG for Christ's sake," Tom continued. "I should never even be on a mission like this, let alone doing what I feel inclined to do right now. I can explain going on the mission to my boss if I have to, but I'd never be able to explain what is going to happen next in that warehouse."

Grant frowned. "What's going to happen in there?"

"You tell me," Tom answered, giving him a conspiratorial look.

Grant was though he knew where this might be going. "It seems to me – and everyone else in there – that justice will not be served by taking Tommy to jail." He waited for Tom's reaction to that.

Tom's reaction was, "Really? Isn't that interesting? Do you have any thoughts about the best way to serve justice in this instance?" Grant's guess had been right, he was sure, now, where Tom was going with the conversation.

"Yes, I think I have a very good idea. And I think it would be a simple matter that would no longer require your services, or those of your team. I think the attending U.S. Marshal's deputies are more than capable of 'dealing with' Mr. Sanderson."

"Funny, that is exactly what I was thinking. I think I will go back inside and round up my team and get the hell out of here. Thank you, Deputy."

"No, thank you Mr. Lapke." They smiled at each other like the old friends that they were and shook hands.

Back inside, Tom said loudly, for all to hear, "OK team let's secure these quarters and get you back to your regular duties. We've been gone long enough. Grant, this is your jurisdiction more than it is ours. I remand this prisoner into your capable hands. Please see that justice is served." Then he got busy with the packing up of the gear into the van and preparing for departure.

The others in the room looked on, mouths a gawp with disbelief. They looked at Grant for an explanation but it was clear that he did not intend to give one. Instead he took Connor and Jake outside, to where he and Tom had just come from, leaving the rest standing there with blank stares.

A few moments later the two Deputies came back inside but stood silently, still not offering an explanation. The motionless silence disappeared rapidly when the van left the warehouse. In a blur of motion Jake approached Tommy and used a Judo maneuver to throw him to the ground, and at the very moment Connor pulled out a handgun and shot a round into the air. The others in the room were terrified and shocked about what they were witnessing. The world had suddenly gone mad. OK, maybe not the whole world, but for sure Jake and Connor.

Jake laid atop Tommy, as planned, and spoke closely into his ear, then stood up again. Tommy remained motionless on the ground.

Seconds later the overhead door opened and the van roared back into the warehouse. The agents flooded out of the van in a readiness for warfare. Lapke shouted, "What the hell happened here?" And he really did look genuinely baffled.

Before anyone else could speak up and declare the two Deputies officially loco, Grant said, "Sir, Deputy McDermott just shot and killed this prisoner." He pointed to the motionless body of Tommy on the ground. The little sparkle in his eye conveyed an alternate story to Tom.

"Good God, don't just stand there, arrest him immediately." He ordered Grant.

"Yes, sir," Grant replied, and went ahead with the arrest, cuffing Connor. Then he said, "Under control now, sir. I guess the trial will be a different one than we expected. Sorry for delaying your departure."

"I should hope so, Deputy. OK, men let's get the hell out of here." They complied and the van left again. This time for good.

After the door closed, Jake lifted Tommy off the floor and Grant cut the wire ties from his hands. Then he unlocked Connor's cuffs and lifted him off the floor.

A wide-eyed James was the first to speak. "Wow, that was awesome. What just happened?"

"Yeah, good question," Brent agreed. "What the hell is going on?"

Dylan had been frightened out of his grief and was staring in astonishment like all the rest.

"Alright, everyone, listen up," Grant ordered. "I don't want to shout across the room so come in close." They complied and crowded in around Grant.

"Here is the deal," he continued. "I had to give the Assistant U.S. Attorney General and his team a credible story to take with them, one that would take them completely out of any involvement in what we are about to do here. What we have already started doing actually. And before we go any further I have to make sure we are all in total agreement about what we are doing."

"What, exactly, would it be that we are doing, Grant?" Brent asked.

"Letting Tommy go," Grant stated.

Instantly upon hearing that, all eyes swung to Tommy. Helen had her arms around him, looking hopeful.

"And how are we supposed to get away with that?" the Chief asked.

"There is a way," Grant began. "But before we get that far we need to agree that letting Tommy go is morally OK? In other words, would anyone have a personal problem with it?" He waited for a response but got none.

"I interpret your silence for approval in the matter. Therefore, here is the simple plan: We put out the story that Brad was shot by Bennett's hit men. Two different shooters who hit two targets simultaneously. One with a long range rifle, and the other close up with a pistol. By now they have found Brad's body, not far from agent Duvall's, and already assumed that they were both targets of a hit, so it should not be much of a chore to sell the story. In fact we probably don't even need to do or say anything, investigators are likely to come up with this story on their own."

"Speaking of hit men, what do we do with the asshole all trussed up in the back of the car?" the Chief asked, indicating Winker in Jake's rental.

"That is the beautiful part. We drive him to some street corner nearby and Tommy calls the cops and says he ran into the killer as he was fleeing and took him down. The cops show up and Tommy has him all wrapped up, like a good cop would and he looks like a hero." He smiled proudly at himself.

"Won't work," Tommy said flatly, raining on Grant's proud achievement.

"Which part, why not?" Grant wanted to know.

"Couple of reasons. First because Bennett will think that I betrayed him, and I've worked too hard all this time to stay on his good side. Second, the cops still think that I betrayed them and won't like it that I am back in town, much less putting collars on a big time hit man."

"You mean like more of that professional jealousy shit?" James interjected.

"Exactly, James!" James bobbed his head, broadcasting his rightousness.

"Yeah, I guess I never thought of that," Grant said.

"But I have an idea," Tommy said. "I happen to know the security foreman at the Silverton. He would do anything for me, especially this. We get him down here and put Winker in his car and let him take in the collar. It will drive everyone crazy. Bennett, the cops, and especially Winker. He will be the laughing stock of the Hit Men United Union. The first one to be taken down by a rent a cop." Everyone laughed at that idea, which meant that it was unanimously accepted.

"OK," Grant cut in. " We go with Tommy's plan. And Tommy returns to work at the Montana Highway Patrol. He tells his boss that his business in Las Vegas is taken care of and that is the end of it. Agreed?"

"AYE!" everyone shouted.

"Wait a minute," Tommy said. "Aren't I supposed to be dead? Shot by Connor?"

"That was just a cover story for Lapke. So that he could insulate himself from letting you go free," Grant explained. "Now that he is gone, we can do what we want and if any shit hits any fans he can blame whatever happens on us."

Loose ends tied up and all present matters concluded, Dylan said, "I'm starving and I need a drink. Come on, I'm buying. Where do you want to go?" Jake grinned.

"The Outlaw!" he announced. Dylan didn't hesitate.

"Let's go," he said.

CHAPTER ONE HUNDRED FIFTEEN

THE NEXT DAY'S LAS VEGAS SUN newspaper ran a front page article about the 'Silverton Incident' as it was now being called. Tom Lapke read it at his desk and shook his head in wonder. He was wearing a broad smile, partly because of the story itself, but mainly because it was written by a woman who he knew Grant was sweet on, and he could only imagine how they had collaborated on the article.

The article detailed – according to credible but unnamed eye witnesses and reliable but unidentified sources – a mafia style assassination of two law enforcement personnel. One was a highly decorated Las Vegas PD detective named Brad Danison. According to the extremely accurate and highly reputable newspaper report, Detective Danison was working deep under cover in a Vegas drug ring and his cover had been discovered by the drug lord, who had him shot by a professional hit man. They had made Danison out to be a real hero. Yes sir.

The other victim was an FBI agent who was working in cooperation with Detective Danison. The agents name was being withheld pending family notification. Obviously another rare and worshiped American hero. By God.

Miraculously, this agent had a partner who survived the ordeal. His name has also been withheld. Reliable sources say that he had been kidnapped from the Silverton and taken to an industrial warehouse a few miles away where he was to be executed. Just moments before he was to be killed, police received an anonymous phone call informing them of the agent's location. Police immediately responded to the site and saved the agent, arresting the leader of the drug ring, Bennett Alivio, in the process. Alivio is to be arraigned on one count of attempted murder, one count of kidnapping and one count of conspiring to commit murder. Chances are that he will be in prison for the rest of his life.

The lucky agent was recovering in the hospital from beatings he had taken before his rescue. Plans were already being drawn up by the Chief of Police and the Mayor to make a very public presentation of awards for heroism to the surviving agent. One more American pillar of heroism. My Lord.

The police and FBI had responded quickly to the scene of the crime and began an immediate pursuit of the assassin. However, they were unable to immediately locate the suspect, who seemed to have vanished into thin air. Within an hour they had set up a drag net operation throughout the city in hopes of preventing his escape and tracking him down for an arrest. The operation had barely begun, however, when police received another call informing them that the sniper had been apprehended.

To the amazement of…..well….everyone, the sniper had been caught and collared by the head security guard at the Silverton Casino. The sniper goes by the name of The Winker. Authorities say that they have been hunting for the contract killer for some time. The Sun will be publishing a detailed account of how the security guard finally brought him down in this Sunday's edition. Be sure to read it.

Tom couldn't wait to see that concoction.

He continued reading; This reporter made significant requests and inquires for more details and background information, and was told by the Police Commissioner that further information would not be forthcoming at this time because there were still ongoing investigations in drug dealing in Vegas and he did not want to compromise those investigations. He assured me that as soon as they had completed their roundup of drug lords I would be the first to get the report. And you know that means that Sun readers will also be the first to know.

Tom finished reading the article and called Grant.

"You see the article in the Sun?" he asked when Grant answered.

"Yeah, I read it. Nice piece of fiction isn't it?" he quipped.

Lapke laughed. "Yes it is. I don't suppose you had anything to do with that did you?"

"Wouldn't say that I did, and I wouldn't say that I didn't. But I will say that I make a mighty good 'reliable source' when I want to be."

"You didn't have to sleep with that reporter to get that story across did you?" Tom asked.

"You know me better than to ask that, Tom," Grant said. "Of course I did, and it was worth it too. She told me so."

Tom laughed again and said, "If you guys ever need help getting bailed out again, do me a favor and call someone else."

"Yeah, right," Grant said. "Speaking of which, I have one more favor to ask you."

"Jesus, Grant," Tom replied. "You don't give up, do you?"

"Sorry, but this is important. Connor got his ass in a sling by going rogue on this little mission. He pulled off a success, or his ass would be beyond saving. But he's still in some hot water with his super, Dennis Wheeler, in Denver."

"Ok, I get the picture," Tom told him. "I'll make the call. Tell Connor not to sweat it. Are you done with me now?" he asked without malice.

"I'm done with you for now. Thanks for looking after me, big brother."

"That's my job. See you later."

Connor and Jake were sitting across the desk from Grant when he took Tom's call, and they heard the entire conversation.

"Thanks for getting him to help me," Connor told Grant. "He really your brother?"

"Sort of. Not by blood, but by everything else. His folks took me in when my parents died. I was ten, he was eleven. We were close up until I went to the police academy," he explained.

"Nice friend to have," Connor commented. Grant agreed.

"So where are your friends?" Grant wondered, referring to the Montana folks, who had yet to make it to The Outlaw due to the limited flights to Montana.

"Waiting for us at the airport," Connor answered Grant.

"Why?" It didn't make sense to Grant that they would be waiting for Connor. They were capable of traveling on their own certainly.

"Jake and I are booked on the same plane," Connor said, hoping Grant would figure out what that meant exactly.

Grant did and said, "I guess we better get you to the airport. You packed up and ready to go?"

"Yes," Jake said. "Our bags are in the rental car."

"We'll take care of the rental," Grant said. "Grab your bags and meet me at my car. I'm taking you myself."

After Jake and Connor left to get their bags, Grant picked up his phone and called one of his Deputies.

"Ralph, please book me a seat on the same plane to Montana that Connor and Jake are on. It is scheduled to leave soon so do it right away please. As soon as you're done with that get the car and be ready to drive us to the airport."

Grant put the phone down and began to pack a bag. In his type of business it was not unusual to be called away at a moments notice. For that reason he kept a bag, some spare clothing and a spare toiletry bag at the office.

At the airport, Charlie paced, looking at his watch at regular intervals. When he wasn't looking at his watch he was searching the walkway for Connor and Jake. "Have you seen them yet?" He asked Anna for the hundredth time.

"Sit down and quit worrying," she said for the hundredth time. Charlie returned to pacing. Anna gave up and sat next to Joan and Dylan and read a book.

Joan and Dylan presented a completely different picture than Charlie. They were sleeping with their arms interlaced and Joan resting her head on Dylan's shoulder. They were not looking too worried.

CHAPTER ONE HUNDRED SIXTEEN

DYLAN WAS SAT ON THE FRONT PORCH CHAIR of his mother's house. He had a good view of the mountains and, for some reason, could not take his eyes off of them. Literally, he could not move his head or his eyes. He didn't mind seeing the mountains. They were very nice to look at. But being unable to move ones eyes or head was a little unsettling. He tried again. No good, he was still looking at the mountains. Oh well, he surmised, might as well look at the mountains. They are *pretty.*

"I couldn't take my eyes off them," his mother said. Dylan flinched from the unexpected sound of his mother's voice coming from the seat next to him. He turned to her, unaware that he was now able to move his head. She was looking at the mountains.

"The first time I came to this house, I could not stop looking those mountains, so I figured I better stay." She giggled then, sounding like a little girl. Dylan looked more closely at her. She looked like a little girl for the briefest moment before looking her real age. Her countenance faded in and out, from a little girl to adult, making her appear to be all ages all at once.

In her young form she giggled again and said, in a young voice, "It was the first house Connor showed to me. I could have had a much nicer house with at least as good of a view." She giggled again. "But I was happy in this one, and never regretted choosing it."

Dylan tried to ask his mom a question but his voice wouldn't work. Frustrated he kicked at the porch railing, but it was too far away for his foot to reach and he forgot his question. Damn it, it was a damned important question. But damn it, he had no idea what it was.

His mom seemed not to have noticed his frustration when she continued, "You'll be happier here though. You can live free now. No need to be looking over your shoulder any more. You took care of that. All of the choices I made were made so that could happen. All of them. And now those tough choices are all vindicated. I rest in peace. Only I'm not really 'resting'." She little girl giggled again, then excitedly pointed, giggled again and said, "Look, Dylan! Look who's coming. Look! They're here. Look!" She tugged at his arm and he felt himself falling out of the chair.

Dylan opened his eyes just in time to avoid tripping over the backpack he had set on the floor. Joan was pulling on his arm and pointing down the walkway. "Look!" she said, "They're coming." She was pointing at Connor and Jake. Grant was with them.

Thinking about the dream he was just having made Dylan laugh, and Joan looked at him like he was crazy. "What's so funny?" she demanded.

"Oh nothing, I'll explain later," he said, trying to sound more serious. They walked toward the three men and greeted them with relief.

All calm, cool and collected, the Chief strolled up to them. "Thought you wouldn't make it for a second there," he said. Anna shook her head and smiled. God she loved that man. Him with all the status, strength, power and authority of a police chief, and yet a gentle giant of a human.

Brent had torn himself away from the stewardess he was getting to know, just long enough to say hello to the Deputies, before returning to his task. It was apparent from the look on the face of the young woman that she was impressed by Brent. Dylan shook his head, but for once in his life he was not jealous. He had the only woman he would ever want. Some day, he knew, he would have to tell her so. Some day soon.

Connor had only just noticed the bag that Grant was carrying. "What's with the bag?" he asked.

"Didn't I tell you, I'm going on vacation? I put in for the time off a month ago."

"Good for you," Connor said. "Where are you going?" He looked around at the other gates nearby as if he could spot which one Grant would be going to.

"I'll be on the same plane as you, Connor. For some reason Montana sounds like an interesting place to visit. Besides, I have just got to see where all this hoopla started. You don't mind do you?" Grant asked.

"Hell no, I think it's a great idea."

EPILOGUE

DURING THE PLANE RIDE BACK TO MONTANA, Connor had a chance to speak privately with Dylan. He asked him something he had been wanting to ask for a while.

"I was hoping that one day, before I go back to Denver, you might find time to take me berry picking." He asked it a little uncertainly, worried that he might not get the answer he wanted.

Dylan grinned widely. "I'd love to, Connor. And I think it will make my mom smile."

"I think so too," Connor agreed.

A short time later James took advantage of one of Joan's trips to the head and sat next to Dylan.

"Hey, man," he said to him, "that was some heavy shit you did back there in Vegas. I mean it took some real balls. And....,well, I'm just really proud of the kind of man you are." He laughed nervously and added, "Shit, you know what I mean."

"Yeah, I do, James, and I appreciate it. Thanks."

"Hey, no problem. Look I gotta ask you something. What did your mom mean by 'be a good thorn'?"

Dylan had wondered if James would ask him about that.

"She meant that parents are like thorns in a way." he answered. "They are designed to protect their children. I guess she was telling you to be a good father."

"Shit, she's always got to make it so complicated don't she?" he said shaking his head. Dylan smiled, recalling his strange dreams about his mom.

"Yeah, she does, doesn't she."

The plane arrived, they gathered their bags from the claim and walked out to the curb. In Montana airports, such walks are very short, and when they got to their destination, awaiting them was none other than Tommy Sanderson.

Tommy had decided to drive his car back to Montana with Helen and had left Vegas immediately after being set free at the Hugh's warehouse, thus arriving there shortly before the others landed. He and Helen had wanted the time alone together, and the long drive provided that opportunity. Besides, Tommy had to get his car back home somehow.

Now here he was, driving his patrol car and Helen was in the passenger seat. Parked behind him were two more patrol cars. Half the fleet.

330

James was the first one to approach Tommy, and seeing the group of Highway Patrol vehicles he asked, "You guys got a bust going down here or something?"

Tommy gave a short burst of laughter and said, "No, James, these are your limousines. Jump in one of the cars. I promise it won't take you to a jail."

"Thank God for that." James gave him a high five and got into the back seat of one of the cars.

The arrivals were all seated in the patrol cars, but Tommy stayed at the curb. They watched him greet another arrival, one they didn't recognize. Tommy loaded the stranger and his bags into the car and they departed.

Joan and Dylan ended up in Tommy's car and he asked, "Where to, Dylan?"

"Mom's house. Please."

"You got it," Tommy said, and the convoy made quick time to the house.

Dylan went to the chair on the porch and sat looking at the mountains. Next to him was Joan, who followed Dylan's gaze toward the mountains. Dylan considered mentioning the dream he'd had about them at the airport, like he'd promised Joan, but he decided to wait. There was something else that had to come first.

The others were milling about the house and chatting idly. Most of the conversation revolved around the 'Silverton Incident' and the events of the past few days. During the re-living session one of the local Flatrock policemen showed up. Peter Gilman was holding a small brown package. He approached Brent and held the package out to him.

"I've come to bring you this." He handed Brent the package.

"What is it?" Brent asked.

"Open it and find out. But first you should get Dylan and Joan in here to watch."

James volunteered for the chore and went out the door to retrieve Dylan and Joan. When they came back into the house Brent held up the package and said to them, "Peter brought this for us."

Brent opened the package and grinned. Rather than display the item to the others, Brent walked over to the mantel and placed the object in the blank spot where a photo used to stand. He stood back so the others could see it.

When the group moved in to have a look they saw the once-missing photo of Jesse holding baby Dylan. Except that now, by some mysterious miracle, standing next to her in the photo was Connor. A much younger Connor. Somebody in the room sobbed.

Brent asked Peter, "How the hell.....?"

"It wasn't easy, but we used computer photo editing to combine the torn photo of Jesse and a photo of Connor."

"How in the hell did you get that old picture of me?" Connor badly wanted to know.

331

"That was the hard part," Peter looked sideways at Jake. "But if I told you how I did it I would have to kill you." He smiled. Connor didn't miss the exchange of looks between Peter and Jake.

"Well, I wouldn't want you to kill me," Connor responded, "because if you did I wouldn't be able to kill Jake for doing the dirty work for you." It sounded menacing but Connor was smiling proudly at Jake when he said it. "Some day," he continued while looking at Jake, "you're going to have to tell me how you did this."

"Some day I will, boss. Some day I will," he said.

During the entire process, the unknown passenger hung by Tommy's side, looking out of place and shy. Dylan was about to inquire about him when Brent spoke.

"I hate to spoil a good party, but I have an important appointment to keep." He was making for the door when Dylan spoke.

"Oh yeah, what's her name – this appointment?" he asked.

"Hmm," Brent responded with a furrowed brow, "I guess I better ask her that. Thanks for reminding me."

"Very funny. We'll catch you later?" he asked.

"Count on it. Where will you be?"

Dylan looked around the room hoping to get some non verbal confirmation from the others. One by one they nodded their heads. All except Grant, who seemed to notice a conspiracy of some sort forming up, but had no idea what it might be.

"The Outlaw," Dylan confirmed.

Jake whooped, and Brent said, "Good choice."

"Wasn't so tough," Dylan conceded.

Later, at The Outlaw, the talk had grown more lively and the re-telling more embellished, thanks to a couple of pitchers of locally brewed pale ale.

Grant appeared to have successfully and happily adapted to the circumstances. In fact, when he reflected on it many weeks later, he considered it one of the best vacations he had ever had.

When Brent walked in with his stewardess in tow they all cheered and made a couple of spaces at the table for them.

"Hey, Brent, come on over and sit down," Jake hollered. He seemed to have adopted The Outlaw as his home page.

Brent ambled over and introduced his girl.

"Everyone this is Isabel. Isabel this is everyone. Don't worry, you'll get to know their names sooner than is good for you."

"Don't listen to him, Isabel, we don't. Do we everyone?" They all yelled 'no' in unison.

"I'm Dylan; this is Joan, my fiancée. We're glad to meet you."

His use of the word fiancée instigated the loudest cheers so far and Jake ordered more pitchers of pale ale in celebration of the engagement. Unfortunately Joan was not as happy about the surprising, and somewhat indirect, proposal. It wasn't exactly her idea of romantic.

"Dylan O'Connor," she reprimanded, "what kind of proposal is that?" Hell was forming in back of her scorned mood, and Dylan was inspired to act quickly by a sudden interest in his continued survival.

One of the things that Dylan's mother had bequeathed him was a diamond ring that she had especially prized. Because it was considered so valued by his mother he had carried it with him in his pocket since her death. He hastily reached into his pocket and pulled it out. When he got down on his knee the entire establishment became hushed. James recognized the ring as the one he had given Jesse [Brenda] when he proposed to her, but he withheld comment about it so as not to spoil the proud moment for his son.

While on his knee Dylan said, "Joan, you are the only woman in my life. The only woman I will ever need or want in the remainder of my life. I can think of no other than you. Will you please make my life complete and marry me?" Then he placed the ring on her finger, amazed that it fit perfectly.

In his own mind his proposal was legendary and he was certain that it had impressed Joan as much as it did him. To his disappointment he was wrong.

"And a short life it just may be, Dylan O'Connor," she responded. "Of all the cowardly and rude things to do, and if you think a pretty little speech like that...." The remainder of her expression of indignation was cut short by Dylan's placement of his lips over hers. It was a long and passionate kiss and when it was over, Joan was too busy catching her breath to speak.

When she could finally talk she said, "Well, now that you put it that way; yes I will marry you, Dylan O'Connor." She was beaming as she hugged her new groom.

More cheers arose and it was decreed that another pitcher would be in order. As pints were being filled, Dylan noticed the mysterious passenger next to Tommy.

"Who's your friend?" he asked.

"This is Willy. He saved my bacon at the Bass Pro Shop in Vegas. I owed him for it, and I always pay my debts. He likes to fish, and said it has always been his dream to fish in Montana. So I flew him in." Willy grinned shyly and a new cheer roared up, inciting an order of another pitcher of ale.

A few hours went by in a few minutes and finally Anna, Helen and Joan rose from the table and announced that it was time for them to leave.

"Why?" Charlie wanted to know.

"We have wedding plans to make."

"Now? The party is just getting started," Tommy replied.

"Yes, now. It takes a long time to plan three weddings. We want to get started." All three women held up their hands to display their rings. All three grooms looked around the table and shrugged sheepishly. Isabel looked longingly at Brent.

"Don't look at me like that," Brent said worriedly. Isabel laughed at her own joke and the rest of the table guffawed as well. Brent sighed with relief, but secretly, Isabel was starting to wonder how she could snare Brent for her husband.

Dylan leaned over to James and said, "Hey, dad, will you be our best man?"

Dad; shit, he called me dad, James told himself proudly. Today the world was OK.

THAT'S A WRAP!

READ ON FOR A PREVIEW OF *TOUGHER CHOICES*. THE SECOND BOOK IN THE DYLAN OCONNOR MYSTERY SERIES COMING SOON ON AMAZON. WATCH FOR RELEASE ANNOUNCEMENTS ON CLIFF BONNER'S PAGE.

facebook.com/CBonnerauthor

TOUGHER CHOICES

CHAPTER ONE

"I will not marry someone without a job!" she shouted, "I will not!" Bang! There go the door hinges, Dylan thought.

"What the hell does a job have to do with being married?" he asked through the door. To his way of thinking there was no logic to it.

"You are impossible, Dylan McDermott," she shouted back through the door.

Me impossible, he wondered. I'm not the one locking myself behind a door. Of course he knew better than to mention that out loud. He was no idiot.

"Why can't you love an unemployed person?" he asked. "Is there some law against that or something? Is it a sin? Or did you just read that in a woman's magazine?" The last question slipped out before he could stop it. Oops, hell's coming.

"Arrrghhh!" She arrrghhhed. "Go away. I don't want to talk to you."

Always willing to do as ordered, in order to please her, he walked away from the door and into the kitchen. He opened the fridge and pulled out a cold beer. He looked outside and noticed snow falling. He shrugged and opened the beer. No law against drinking a cold beer on a cold day either, he thought.

He sat on the sofa watching the snow out the window. There was no wind and the large flakes floated straight down, creating a white veil that was difficult for the eye to penetrate. It was one of those story book scenes, like in a glass snow thingy. He couldn't remember what they were called, but he knew you had to shake it up first and then watch the snow fall down inside it.

Watching the snow outside had the dubious effect of carrying a person away in thought, like a fire in the fireplace does. He was well and far away when the phone rang. It startled him out of his reverie and he dropped the beer bottle on the floor.

"Shit," he said. He stood up trying to avoid putting his stocking feet in the beer puddle, but failed. "Shit," he said again. He barely made it to the phone in time to keep the answering machine from taking over.

"What?" he almost shouted into the phone.

"Nice to hear from you too," the voice on the other end of the line said.

"Oh, hi, Brent," Dylan said more politely. "Sorry."

"Sounds like you are having a bad day," Brent said.

"Yeah, no shit," he replied.

"Joan again?" Brent asked.

"Yeah. The job thing again," Dylan admitted.

"I told you, man," he lectured, again. "Its a big thing with women." If Dylan could see him, through the phone lines, stifling a laugh, he might have thrown a fit.

"Yeah, so you've said," Dylan told him. "I've been trying, but the jobs just aren't out there. She just doesn't get it, and she won't marry me until I'm working. And I just don't get that."

"You sound pathetic," Brent said. Any other person would not get away with a statement like that. But Brent was Dylan's best friend. His childhood friend. Therefore they insulted each other routinely. It was how they knew they still loved each other.

"Fuck you too," Dylan said. And if Brent could have seen him through the phone lines he would have seen him smiling. "So why did you call? Just to give me shit? If so, I get enough already thanks."

"No," Brent said. "I got good news for you. Maybe. Maybe bad. I'll let you decide."

"Ok, what is it?" Dylan asked.

"I've got a job for you."

CHAPTER TWO

"You can come out now," Dylan shouted through the door. "I got a job." He listened for a response but heard nothing for several minutes. Maybe hours. OK it was five seconds.

"You're lying," she finally muttered back.

"No, I'm not," he replied, "Brent just called. He's got a job for me. In Vegas." More waiting. Maybe hours. OK, several seconds. Then the door flew open.

"If you are lying to me I'll kill you," Joan said in the even, unmistakable tone that said she could be either mad or happy. Dylan put his money on mad. Less to lose that way.

"I'm not lying," he told her. "Brent said it was a sure thing. And it pays well," he added.

There was something in the way he said how well it paid that made Joan suspicious. It wasn't something she could point out as a definite clue, but it was something she had come to know in Dylan. A certain way he spoke, combined with the way he gazed at her. As if to dare her to challenge the truth of whatever he had said.

"What's the catch?" she challenged.

"There's no catch," he alleged. Bang! There go the door hinges again.

"Ok, but it's not a catch, exactly," he admitted. Days went by without a response from beyond the door. Could have been weeks. Was probably ten seconds. He thought about walking back to the fridge to get a fresh beer and do some more snow watching, but it took him longer than ten seconds to think about it. The door flew open again.

"I hate you!" Bang! The door didn't come off its hinges, but it should have.

Dylan didn't think, he got a fresh beer and went back to the sofa to watch the snow. The flakes were smaller now but they were coming down harder and visibly was waning. He looked closer at the snow and noticed that it was not coming straight down any more. It was slanted toward the south, which meant the wind was coming out of the north. A blizzard was coming.

Thirty minutes later the house was dark. The power had failed, no doubt due to the strong winds of the blizzard. Joan sat on the couch next to Dylan, holding him tight. Together they watched the storm out the window.

Joan had come out of her bedroom the moment the power went out. She stood in front of Dylan, who was still on the sofa, and looked at him. She didn't utter a word. Dylan nodded once and she sat down, wrapping her arm around him. The silent exchange was all that was needed to put the previous disagreement completely behind them, as if it never happened.

They sat on the sofa watching the blizzard, without speaking, until it was too dark to see outside. Dylan picked up the remote and clicked it at the TV. It remained dark and silent. Like Dylan. He enjoyed the quiet solitude and tight proximity of Joan, but he was preoccupied with something and Joan took notice of the fact.

In spite of her burning curiosity to know what he was fretting about, she knew better than to ask him. He would tell her in his own good time, and not before then. It was a trait in Dylan that she had become familiar with, and it maddened her. But it also endeared him to her.

CHAPTER THREE

Dylan watched the first half of the news with only half interest, still preoccupied with what Brent had told him. Halfway into the news program, he sat up on the sofa and stared intently at the screen. He picked up the remote and turned up the volume.

Joan had been sleeping with her head in Dylan's lap and his motion woke her. She followed Dylan's gaze to the TV.

"When did the power come back on?" she asked in a sleepy voice. Dylan didn't answer, his attention monopolized by the television.

Joan looked at the screen again, wondering what had gotten Dylan's rapt attention. The news anchor was talking about a notable murder in Las Vegas. They were showing footage of crime scenes surrounded by yellow crime scene tape, a white sheet draped over a shape that looked a lot like a body. The broadcast captured her attention now. She sat up and leaned toward the screen.

"Holy shit," she said in a near whisper. Dylan did not respond until the news broadcast was over. He turned off the set and looked at Joan. His eyes told her more than his words could have.

"So there was a catch," she said to him.

"There was a catch," he agreed. Her dread overcame her anger, and therefore no door hinges were damaged.

"We're going to Vegas," she said. She's getting way too good at the connection thing, Dylan thought.

"We're going to Vegas," he confirmed. Joan recalled a saying that bull riders used; it's not if you get hurt, it's how bad.

"How bad is it?" she asked. Here's the catch, Dylan thought.

"The pay is fantastic," he replied. There go the hinges again.

OOOO

"Open the door, Joan," Dylan pleaded. "I'm sorry. But the pay really is good. I thought you would like that."

"Fuck you," came through the door. OK, maybe she didn't like it. Maybe the rewards really don't outweigh the risks after all. At least not in the mind of an irrational woman. Oops. That was NOT a politically correct thought to be having at this particular moment. Everyone knows that the rewards should never outweigh the risks. There, that's better. Unless you are a broke pissant. Wanting to get rich and get married. Like Dylan.

"Ok, never mind. I am still unemployed," he informed Joan. "Maybe we can get married next year. If I get lucky and get a really good paying job. With no risks." No response from beyond the door, which was truly frightening to Dylan.

"Just tell me what I wanted to know," Dylan finally heard through the, now, out of plumb door. "How fucking bad is it?" And Dylan thought Irish women knew how to swear. They should take note of English women.

"Ok, I will. Just come out of there. I hate talking through a door," he pleaded.

A crack appeared in the door.

"Don't fuck me," Joan said through the crack, with a dark storm looming behind her eyes. Yikes. What sort of choice does that leave a man. Thank god he knew she didn't intend the phrase to be taken literally.

"I promise," he said. "I will tell you what I know. Everything Brent told me. Just come out."

CHAPTER FOUR

"Brent took a leave of absence from the Flatrock police," Dylan explained to Joan. "He's going to Vegas too. Him and Tommy. Tommy is the one who came up with the job. Brent didn't tell me much else on the phone, but then when I saw the news report, I connected a few dots. I think the job has something to do with Bennett Alivio." He'd concluded this when the newscast revealed that the identity of the corpse under the tarp was indeed, Bennett Alivio.

Nothing in the newscast, of course, told him that the job Brent had offered him had anything to do with Bennett, and neither did Brent's phone call. None of that mattered to Dylan, who was ever certain of his 'hunches'.

"Oh, God, Dylan," Joan lamented. "He's the drug lord in Vegas. The one your mom helped to get convicted."

"Yes, exactly." She turned scorned so quickly Dylan nearly missed it. By the time he caught it, it was too late.

"So why, for fuck's sake, would you ever want to have anything to do with him?" There was a time in their early history that he thought her manner of speech was mannered. Something had influenced a change in her in that regard, and he prayed it was not him. Not that the swearing bothered him, he just didn't want to bear the blame for it.

"I'm not sure that I do," he said. "But I do know that Tommy does. And that Brent does. And that they asked me to help them." Joan responded to that the way Dylan hoped she would. The same way he had.

"Oh," she half whispered.

"You want to go with me," he asked. "Or do want to stay here?"

"I better go with you," she said, not as mad now. "No one else knows how to keep you out of trouble as well as I do." The statement ended with the same smile that always attracted Dylan to her like a powerful magnet would attract ferrous metal.

"You know I agree with you," he admitted. "But if you ever leak that bit of information to the general public, my macho rep may be permanently impaired."

"Didn't know you had a rep with the general public," she told him.

"You know what I mean."

"Sure I do. But I'm still looking out for you." Dylan was not about to disagree. What male in their right mind would?

"Ok, I'll call Brent," he informed Joan.

OOOO

Brent had agreed to meet Dylan at the Flatrock Police Station as soon as the blizzard completed its mission in the fair sized Montana town. Dylan and Joan took advantage of the waiting period to begin packing and making arrangements to leave their sylvan Montana home for the concrete jungle of Las Vegas.

That night they discussed the possibilities of what the job in Vegas would involve. It was mostly guess work, but Dylan was pretty good at making accurate guesses sometimes. His late mother was mostly responsible for that. She'd been a gifted woman, and, alas, a marked one as well. Her fate came to an end barely six months prior when, in spite of being under the protection of the witness security and relocation program, a corrupt Las Vegas detective tracked her down in Montana and killed her. That event precipitated Dylan's first trip to Vegas, where he was privileged to watch the slaying of the cop that killed her. Bennett Alivio had been there that day as well.

"I get the chills when I think about what we are getting into," Joan confided to Dylan. "It is such an evil world that Bennett belonged to. And now he's been murdered. It would take someone truly dangerous to pull off a hit like that." For a refined woman, Dylan thought, she could be pretty damn worldly. He agreed with her assessment wholeheartedly.

"I know, babe. I don't get the greatest happiness out of the possibilities myself."

OOOO

Like Cliff's FB page to follow announcements for the release of TOUGHER CHOICES and to receive more previews.

facebook.com/CBonnerauthor